"Tom? Are you there? It's Kelly."

"Yes," he said. "I'm here. What's wrong?"

Tom understood that something must have happened. Something bad. Kelly hadn't called him in ten years, though at first he had deluded himself that she might.

"I don't know if you heard about Lillith Griggs. I mean, she became Lillith Griggs—you knew she and Jacob got married, didn't you?"

"Yes, I knew that." He and Jacob still kept in touch, still wrote now and then, though of course, Jacob didn't admit that to Lillith, who had, like Kelly, been one of Sophie's bridesmaids and therefore subscribed to the official position that Tom Beckham was scum. "What about Lillith?"

"She was killed in a car accident. Three days ago."

Tom hadn't known Lillith well, but she'd always seemed much more...alive than most people. She was a beauty, a brain and a class clown all in one. What kind of accident had been potent enough to extinguish all that?

"I'm sorry to hear that. How is Jacob?"

"He's a mess," Kelly said. "That's why I'm calling. The funeral is tomorrow and he hopes you can come. He needs a friend... and you seem to be the one he wants."

It was subtle but he could hear how inexplicable she found that fact to be. "Okay," he said.

"You'll come?" She must have been expecting an argument.

"Yes. Tell him I'll be there. What time is the funeral?"

"One. But Tom, if I tell him you're coming, and then you..."

"Kelly, I'm telling you I will be there. Have I ever lied to you?"

"No," she said slowly. "Not to me."

Dear Reader,

The editors at Harlequin and Silhouette are thrilled to be able to bring you a brand-new featured author program beginning in 2005! Signature Select aims to single out outstanding stories, contemporary themes and oft-requested classics by some of your favorite series authors and present them to you in a variety of formats bound by truly striking covers.

We plan to provide several different types of reading experiences in the new Signature Select program. The Spotlight books will offer a single "big read" by a talented series author, the Collections will present three novellas on a selected theme in one volume, the Sagas will contain sprawling, sometimes multigenerational family tales (often related to a favorite family first introduced in series) and the Miniseries will feature requested, previously published books, with two or, occasionally, three complete stories in one volume. The Signature Select program will offer one book in each of these categories per month, and fans of limited continuity series will also find these continuing stories under the Signature Select umbrella.

In addition, these volumes will bring you bonus features...different in every single book! You may learn more about the author in an extended interview, more about the setting or inspiration for the book, more about subjects related to the theme and, often, a bonus short read will be included.

Watch for new stories from Janelle Denison, Donna Kauffman, Leslie Kelly, Marie Ferrarella, Suzanne Forster, Stephanie Bond, Christine Rimmer and scores more of the brightest talents in romance fiction!

We have an exciting year ahead!

Warm wishes for happy reading,

Marsha Zinberg

Marsha Zinberg
Executive Editor
The Signature Select Program

Dear Reader,

Sometimes, true love makes an appearance at the worst possible moment. When you're too young, when you're living on another continent, when you're on opposite sides of a stormy issue. Or when you're about to marry her best friend.

For Tom Beckham, the hero of *Happily Never After*, falling in love with Kelly was the dumbest thing he could do. Well, maybe the second-dumbest. The first was getting engaged to beautiful but troubled heiress Sophie Mellon.

The three glamorous Mellon siblings have always been clouded in a miasma of rumors. Their neighbors hear things they can't quite understand—and don't dare to repeat. But Tom, a young, ambitious lawyer, didn't care. Sophie's good looks and impressive mansion could help his career, and that was all that mattered.

Until he fell in love with her bridesmaid. Until ugly rumors became hideous truth. Until he left Sophie at the church, dressed in antique lace, her beautiful face streaming with tears.

He spent ten years trying to forget Kelly—and the terrible truth about the woman he almost married. But now members of the wedding party are starting to die. He'll have to face all his old demons—including his love for Kelly—if he's going to survive.

I have a special fondness for the "reunion" romance. I adore the thought that, like water seeking an outlet, true love can trickle through the years, overcoming the most daunting barriers, navigating the most amazing bends and turns. And then, somehow, find its way safely home. I hope you enjoy watching Tom and Kelly earn their second chance.

My next Harlequin Signature Select book, *Quiet as the Grave*, will also feature a couple who must endure years of separation. Thanks to my Firefly Glen readers who wrote asking for Mike and Suzie's story, these two fascinating characters will finally find out whether puppy love has the strength to survive in the real—and very dangerous—adult world.

I love to hear from readers! Please visit my Web site at www.KathleenOBrien.net, or write me at P.O. Box 947633, Maitland, FL 32794.

Warmly,

Kathleen O'Brien

CHAPTER ONE

THE BEST VIEW of the tortured and beautiful Mellon house was from the top of the East River Bridge. In winter, when the elm trees had shivered themselves to skeletons, you could see everything, right down to the statue that had toppled over in the fern garden twenty years ago and had never been set right.

Mrs. Mellon must hate to see the sheltering leaves fall, Kelly Ralston thought as she turned right on Market and headed toward the bridge. The proud old woman would hate feeling so exposed. Coeur Volé had been built a hundred years ago, but even then it had been designed for privacy. And that was long before Sebastian's accident, Mr. Mellon's death or Sophie's…

Long before tragedy knocked on the door of Coeur Volé and apparently moved in to stay.

Even so, Kelly—and probably half the population of Cathedral Cove—never crossed the bridge without slowing down to stare. She did it now, though it was a foggy autumn midnight, not winter, and she couldn't realistically expect to see anything but shadows.

Lillith Griggs, whose restored Jaguar was right in front of Kelly's, wasn't slowing down, though. Lightning Lillith, as her husband teasingly called her, was infamous for collecting the most speeding tickets in Cathedral Cove. Of course, she was a lawyer, so she wiggled her way out of a lot of them.

Suddenly the cell phone tucked into Kelly's cup holder vibrated noisily.

"Hey, I meant to ask you," Lillith said without preamble. "Did you hear that Sophie's checked herself out again?"

"No. Really? Is she back at home?" Kelly maneuvered onto the bridge, keeping close to her friend's car. In an uncharacteristic display of caution, Lillith had asked Kelly to follow her home from the bar where they'd had a late dinner. Lillith was ordinarily the most self-confident person Kelly had ever met. But she'd been getting weird phone calls, she said. And for the past few days, she'd had the feeling someone was following her.

Kelly had a horrible thought. "God, Lily. Are you saying you think *Sophie's* been following you?"

"Well, no, probably not. Actually, I'm sorry I even mentioned that. I'm probably imagining it all." Lillith laughed, and for the first time tonight she sounded like herself. "It's probably just this spooky feeling of having another person living in my own body. Pregnancy is weird, if you really think about it."

Kelly laughed, but kept both hands on the wheel. The East River Bridge was steep, and they were reaching the peak. "No, it's not. It's perfectly normal and wonderful. I can't wait to hear what Jacob says when you tell him. Promise you'll call me immediately."

"I won't have to. You'll hear him all the way out to your studio, beating his breast and whooping like the darling dumb jock he is. He'll be insufferable. He'll act like his sperm has made a field goal from the fifty-yard line."

"In a way, it has." Kelly didn't pay much attention to Lillith's acerbic tone. The Griggses had been married six years, and they were silly in love. Kelly had always struggled with a little jealousy, not being very good at the marriage thing herself. And now that there was a Griggs baby on the way…

But just then Kelly caught her first glimpse of the strange, needlelike tower of Coeur Volé piercing the low-lying fog, and she remembered that she had a lot to be grateful for, after all. She might not be as happy as Lily Griggs, but at least she wasn't cursed.

Her car crested the top of the bridge, just feet behind Lillith's. Over the phone line she heard Lillith's sudden intake of breath. "What the hell?"

"What?" Kelly asked, but then she saw it. The stained glass in the highest tower window was glowing. "It's probably Sophie. She's always had trouble sleeping, even as a teenager. And now that she spends so much time in institutions—"

She heard a low curse from Lillith's end, and an ominous, repetitive thumping sound. *"Damn it,"* Lillith said harshly. "What's wrong with this damn thing?"

"What?" But suddenly Kelly realized that Lillith's gasp hadn't been a reaction to the tower light. She probably hadn't even seen it.

Something was wrong with Lillith's car. She was taking the down slope of the bridge much too fast, even for Lightning Lillith. Fog shot from beneath her tires like jet contrails. Her taillights were pulling away, stretching the distance between their two cars.

At the foot of the bridge, hidden at the moment in a blanket of damp silver fog, the road made a sharp right-hand curve to avoid the first of the riverfront mansions. If Lillith didn't slow down…

"Lily!" Kelly realized she was shouting into the cell phone. But Lillith's car was still gathering speed, sucked down by gravity, going twice as fast now as Kelly's. Kelly had to fight the instinct to hit the accelerator, to try to catch her. That would be madness. And yet, it was impossible to accept that there was nothing she could do.

"Lily, for God's sake, slow down!"

"Damn it." Lillith's voice was tight and husky, as if her throat were raw. The thumping sound continued. "What the hell is *wrong* with you?"

"What's happening?"

"The brakes." And then Lillith's voice seemed to come from a distance, and Kelly knew she'd dropped the cell phone. "Damn it, damn it. *Catch,* damn it. Why won't—"

"Lily! The hand brake! Pull the hand brake!"

Was that the right advice? Kelly's mind wasn't working, didn't have time to work. Maybe Lillith should turn the car in a circle, or try to use the median to interrupt the momentum—

The red sports car changed lanes, deliberately, Kelly thought. Then it clipped the guardrail of the bridge. Yellow and white sparks flew as the two metals kissed. It helped a little, but they were running out of time, running out of bridge. Kelly began to pray.

At the last minute, Lillith swerved, but it was too late. The car was still going much too fast. Though Kelly was now a hundred yards behind, she felt the shudder as Lillith's car lifted off the asphalt, bumped over the curb, shot across the smooth green grass of an elegant lawn, and finally rammed headfirst into the scarred trunk of an ancient, unyielding oak.

The car seemed for a horrible instant to be trying to climb the tree, but of course it couldn't be. The nose of the car collapsed like an accordion, and the air exploded with lightning bolts of broken glass.

And then everything was still.

Kelly slammed on her brakes and tumbled out of her car without even stopping to turn off the engine. She was trying to punch in 911 on her cell phone, but her fingers were like rubber, and she misdialed twice before she got through. She ran, but her legs were shaking so hard she twisted her ankle and had to hobble the last few yards.

"We need an ambulance. There's been a terrible accident."

"Where are you?"

She looked around. For a moment she couldn't think where they were. It was so dark. Everything was foggy and silent, except for the hiss of something coming out of Lillith's car.

"The bridge," she managed to say. She stumbled over the curb and dropped the telephone. Somehow she found it again, just in time to hear the voice on the other end asking her which bridge.

Which bridge? This bridge. This cruel, dangerous, deadly bridge. But what was it called? She needed to be more coherent. She had always hoped she was the kind of person who would be good in a crisis. But she felt as if her heart and mind had collapsed, just like the hood of Lillith's car.

"The foot of the East River Bridge," she said. "The south side, the Destiny Drive side. She hit a tree. Please. Send someone right away."

Her toe jammed a boulder half-hidden by the fog. Pain streaked up her shin, and once again she dropped the telephone. This time it clattered against other rocks and disappeared into the fog. Kelly felt the ground for it briefly, but then she heard a sound coming from the Jaguar. A low, moaning sound.

"I'm here," she called out. She scrambled over wet grass until she finally reached the car.

It was the saddest sight she'd ever seen.

Everything gaped unnaturally, pitifully exposed. The right front headlight had been knocked free and was dangling by wires. Both doors had been ripped open, and the trunk was open, too. Even the glove box had been knocked loose.

Lillith's personal things were scattered all over the ground—her purse, a pair of running shoes tied together by the laces, an old McDonald's cup with the straw still in it, her billfold with a picture of Jacob smiling, and a Boudoir Boutique sack full of smashed bath beads that filled the air with the scents of sandalwood and vanilla.

It was so wrong. Lillith was always so elegant and organized. Though Kelly knew it didn't really matter right now, she had to fight the urge to gather up the things, to protect the privacy that had been so heartlessly violated.

"I'm here," she said again, though she hadn't heard any more sounds. She rushed to the driver's side. Lillith was still sitting upright, the lap belt still connected. This old classic sports car didn't have an air bag, though Jacob was always bugging Lillith to install one.

Under the distorted hood, the hoses were steaming and hissing, as if they were mad with fury. The front tires no longer touched the ground, and when Kelly reached out to touch Lillith, the car wobbled.

"Lily," she said. "Lily, are you all right?"

Lillith turned her head slowly and tried to speak. Kelly

felt the air draining out of her lungs, the strength out of her muscles, but somehow she found the courage to keep from fainting.

It wasn't even Lillith anymore. Blood coated everything, but under the blood Lillith's face was crushed. One cheekbone had disappeared entirely, and her eye seemed to melt into the hollow below. Her nose was flat, and something white poked through the bloody mess of skin. And her mouth...

Everything was swollen, and broken and rearranged. Kelly saw a tooth lying in a gleaming pool of blood on Lillith's chin, and her stomach spasmed, sending a gag of half-digested spaghetti erupting toward her throat.

She fought it back.

"Hold on, Lily," she said, and suddenly her voice was strong again. "The ambulance is coming."

Lillith seemed to be trying to shake her head. She closed her eyes—though the one over the sunken cheek wouldn't shut properly.

"I've already called 911," Kelly said. Miraculously, one of Lillith's hands seemed untouched. Kelly took it into her own. It was cold. "They'll be here soon. They'll know what to do."

Lillith moved her lips again. Kelly tried to hear—she made out an *e,* but the consonants were all a bubbling mush of blood.

Maybe it was *Kelly.*

Or maybe *baby.*

Or perhaps it was simply *Help me.*

"Lily," she said again. In the movies, people always begged dying friends to keep talking. Was there some magic in that? But how could she ask those mangled lips to try to form words?

God, she was useless. The truth was, she had no idea what to do.

"Lily, I love you," Kelly said, because there was nothing else to say, and because it seemed important. She was aware that tears were flooding down her face.

Lillith nodded a fraction of an inch. Or maybe Kelly just wanted to believe she did. And then Lillith seemed to try to speak again. Kelly leaned forward.

It was as wet and half-formed as before.

But this time it sounded like *Sophie*.

It was the last word Lillith Griggs ever spoke. She was dead before the ambulance arrived.

CHAPTER TWO

TOM BECKHAM HAD A SIXTH SENSE about parties. He could predict to within about ten minutes when they were going to go bad or get ugly.

As a rule, that instinct was quite useful. He always slipped out the door just before the champagne or the conversation fell flat. He said his goodbyes five minutes before the fight broke out on the patio or the junior partner puked in the pool.

But fat lot of good that sixth sense could do him today, at this party, which was being held on a boat, about three hundred yards off the Georgia coast. Though his instincts were definitely telling him to get the hell out of here, he couldn't really do anything about it.

He glanced over the side of the seventy-five-foot yacht, where the Atlantic was sparkling under the cold September sun like a million sequin-tipped knifepoints. Swimming was out of the question, he supposed.

But if things kept deteriorating—and the ratio of guests to alcohol indicated it would—he just might consider it.

"Tom!" A hand grabbed Tom's forearm so hard he spilled his drink, which, now that the ice had melted, was filled to overflowing. Watered-down scotch mapped cool trails down his hand. "You're not thinking of jumping overboard, are you? The Smythe case couldn't have bothered you that much. Everybody loses now and then."

Shaking scotch from his hand, Tom turned with a smile. Bailey Ormonde, senior partner and head estate-planning attorney in Tom's law firm, always talked too loudly and shook hands too firmly as a way of compensating for being about five-three. But he wasn't at heart a bad guy.

"If I jump, it won't be because of Smythe," Tom said. "I didn't lose that case—justice won. The guy had a second set of financial records hidden in his underwear drawer, for God's sake. It took them about five minutes to find it."

"What a moron." Bailey snorted. "Still, this is the second time you've mentioned Justice, capital *J,* in the past week. Not a good thing in our favorite civil litigator. I'm starting to worry about you, pal. What's the matter?"

Trust Bailey to home in on the real issue. Lawyers in the elite firm of Ormonde, White and Murray weren't supposed to value Justice over Victory. Justice was a malleable concept. It was whatever you wanted it to be. Victory, on the other hand, was absolute. In the lofty heavens of their penthouse world, the Client was God, and the Blind Lady was either supposed to join the choir or get out of the way.

Tom had understood that when he'd joined the firm ten years ago. He understood it still. So what *was* the matter with him? Midlife crisis? A little early for that, at only thirty-five. Professional burnout? Ditto on that.

Too soon to grow a conscience, as well—his portfolio wasn't anywhere nearly big enough yet.

Nope, too early for any of that. So why, in some deep, unspoken place, did he sometimes have the feeling it might be a great deal too late?

But this wasn't the time for soul-searching, and Bailey was no Freud anyhow. So instead of answering, Tom sipped at his drink and squinted at the cluster of guests near the starboard railing. Such beautiful people, bronzed by expensive machines, and then gilded by the sunlight until they looked like golden statues from the lobby of some fin de siècle opera house.

Bailey was too smart to push it. He knew that, in his way, he'd put Tom on notice, and he trusted Tom to read between the lines.

"So where is your gorgeous lady friend?" Bailey raised one eyebrow. "I hope you haven't let Coach O'Toole get his hands on her."

Tom scanned the crowd. Darlene was undoubtedly in there somewhere, though she had arrived on her own, as she'd been running late this morning.

Yep, there she was. Bailey wasn't exaggerating. She was gorgeous. She stood in a nimbus of sunlight, one hand at her breast and the other lightly curved just at the apex of her thighs, looking for all the world like a Botticelli Venus—not a coincidence, Tom felt sure. Her dress was virginal white, but so filmy and formfitting she looked as if she'd been dipped in milk and set out to be licked clean.

Tom waited for the appreciative twitch to register in his groin, but it didn't come. Poor Darlene. Not even a twitch, where once there had been earthquakes.

She had no idea, but their clock had just struck midnight. Her magic had run out.

Frankly, he hadn't even wanted her to come today. She'd begun vigorously working the crowd at these events, smiling her heart out while she talked him up. It annoyed him. It looked like an audition for the role of trophy wife.

"You're a lucky devil, Beckham," Bailey said, shaking his head and making a noise that, if he hadn't been the senior partner, would have been smacking his lips. "When does her lease expire? You always trade 'em in after a year, right? Any chance she thinks short guys are hot?"

Tom wondered if his thoughts about Darlene had registered on his face. He rearranged his features. "Women don't care if you're small as long as you've got a great big—" he grinned "—credit limit. In that department, you've got everyone on this boat whipped. Even Coach O'Toole, in spite of that ridiculous bonus the alums have just added to his paycheck."

Bailey eyed Mick O'Toole, the head coach for the Midwest Georgia University football team, who stood talking to his host, the most arrogant MGU alum of them all, Trent Saroyan. Saroyan owned the boat, and it might be successfully argued that he owned O'Toole, too.

He'd thrown the party today to celebrate a strong 2–0 start for O'Toole's second season as MGU head coach. The Spitfires had had a 15–2 season last year, almost making it to the National Championship game. The party, the yacht and the bonus were just the alum's polite way of saying that this year it had better be the gold ring.

"You think he knows he's going to get shitcanned if he loses even one game this season?" Bailey's shrewd eyes held a hint of pity. But just a hint. Their firm represented Trent Saroyan, the yachtsman and check-writer, not the coach.

"Nope," Tom said. "Look at him. He's still naive enough to think he can get loud with the boosters."

Oh, hell. That must be what had activated his sixth sense. Mick O'Toole and Trent Saroyan were standing too close together, and their voices were rising, developing sharp edges. They were arguing about O'Toole's choice of starting quarterback.

"Crap," Bailey said. "I'd better try to do something about that." He dropped his cocktail glass on the mahogany bar and departed.

Not a moment too soon, either. Saroyan held a shot glass in his right hand, but his index finger was extended, and he'd begun to jab it toward O'Toole's left shoulder, which was a very bad sign.

And here came another one. Apparently noticing that Tom was alone, Darlene began murmuring and air-kissing her way out of her crowd and gliding back over toward him. Her smile didn't look right. *Shit.* What had he done now? Had he violated the twenty-minute rule? That was about how long she could take being ignored without getting snitty.

Tom glanced at the water again and wondered how many degrees it was. If only he weren't wearing his most comfortable old cords, he might actually do it. Between Darlene and O'Toole, this party was going down.

"Hey," Darlene said, making the word two warm syllables with honey on top. Darlene's body might be Botticelli, but her voice was pure *Gone with the Wind.* Still, her smile didn't look right.

"Hey, there," he responded carefully. He wondered if it was possible she'd heard Bailey's comment about her lease expiring. Like all good old boys, Bailey did tend to boom a bit.

But would that be so terrible? Tom was going to have to end it soon anyhow. He didn't want a trophy wife. He didn't want a wife period.

Ten years ago, after the…fiasco…he'd decided his life needed some strict ground rules. He had no intentions of living as a monk, all hair shirts and no sex, but he did try to keep all his relationships clean and sweet and mutually satisfying. He'd been pretty successful, so far. That sixth sense about parties applied to love affairs, too, ordinarily.

"I stopped by the apartment on my way over here," she said.

He tried not to react to her word choice. *The* apartment, she said these days. Not *your* apartment. It was just one step short of *our* apartment, and it was a big mistake, though she obviously didn't know it.

"I got Otis to let me in," she added casually.

He wasn't sure why that shocked him so much. Otis was the seventy-year-old doorman, and he was drooling in love with Darlene. Otis would probably agree to let her into any apartment in the building, even if she were carrying a metal detector and a large black sack.

Tom supposed he was shocked that Darlene would take advantage of the nice old guy like that. Whatever the reason, his smile felt tight.

"And why did you do that?"

"I'd left my driver's license next to the sofa," she said, and he had to admit she told the lie beautifully. "Anyhow, I also picked up the mail for you. I knew you'd been waiting for that transcript."

"Really. Was it there?"

"No." She lifted her gold clutch and opened it deftly. "But this was."

She held out a small pink envelope. Immediately he caught the cloying scent of gardenias.

Damn it to hell. He had hoped he'd never see another

one of these. But even if he had to, he wasn't supposed to get it yet. Not for another week.

Could it possibly be a coincidence?

But he knew it wasn't.

He knew it was Sophie.

As always, he felt his lungs tightening, as if they wanted to reject the sickeningly sweet smell. Or was he just trying to reject the idea that Sophie had sent him another "anniversary" card? Every year he told himself that surely this would be the last. She'd forget, she'd lose interest, her therapists would finally convince her that it did no good, especially since he never responded.

It had been ten years now. Ten years since he'd walked out of a church filled with these poisonously sweet white flowers. Ten years since he'd walked out on Sophie.

But she'd never forgotten. And she clearly intended to make sure that he didn't, either. Which was fairly ironic, actually.

Darlene pushed the card forward a fraction of an inch, and he realized he needed to do something. He held out his hand calmly and took it. He flipped it over, glanced at the return address just to be sure the gardenia smell hadn't tricked him, then flipped it back to see whether Sophie had addressed his name the usual way, with a small heart where the *O* in Tom should be.

She had.

No wonder Darlene's smile looked so tight and thin.

"Well?" She snapped her little gold clutch shut sharply.

"Well, what?" He slipped the envelope into his windbreaker pocket, patted it to be sure it was secure, then zipped up his jacket against the fresh, high wind that hinted at a squall before sunset.

Darlene paused, her mouth half-open. She obviously knew the next few moments were dangerous and was looking for the right words.

"It's really too cold for a boat party, don't you think?" He hunched his shoulders. "But I guess Saroyan couldn't wait till spring to show off his new baby."

In his head Tom begged Darlene to be very careful, to take the conversational fire exit he was offering. He didn't like being cornered, and she'd gone too far when she'd pawed through his mail. And he damn sure didn't want to talk to her about Sophie.

If she forced him to do this now, he might say things he'd regret.

She wasn't great at reading his thoughts, though, and he knew his face revealed only a tilted smile and a slightly sarcastic arch to one brow. It was an expression he'd perfected over the last decade.

The arched brow probably tipped her over the edge. Darlene had odd moments of self-respect, and though she might let a man cheat on her, she wouldn't stand for being mocked.

"Who *exactly*," she demanded, "is this Sophie Mellon?"

What a stupid question. What did it matter? When a love affair was over, did it make any difference exactly what, or who, had killed it?

When he didn't answer, Darlene's jaw tightened. "So far I know this much. She writes your name like a lovesick adolescent, and she soaks her cards in cheap perfume. Things haven't been right between us lately, Tom. Is this why? Is she someone I should worry about? Or is she just a—"

A what? Darlene seemed to understand she'd gone too far, but the echo of the unspoken thought seemed to hang in the air between them. What word had she been going to say?

And what was the right word, anyhow? What was Sophie? Slut? Stalker? Psycho? Maybe all those labels applied. And many more, as well.

Maybe the best word was *cursed.* Poor beautiful, tormented Sophie was cursed, and still she signed his name with a heart.

Suddenly Tom realized he was furious. If Darlene insisted on doing this right here, right now, he was ready. He felt his smile tilt another inch. It probably looked like a smirk by now. He didn't give a damn about that, either.

"Sophie Mellon is the woman I almost married."

"What?" Darlene's eyebrows knitted hard. "Married? When?"

"Ten years ago."

She shook her head, looking confused and slightly annoyed. She looked, he thought, like an infant rejecting an unappetizing spoonful of strained peas. "But surely…" She took a breath. "If that's true, why—why didn't you ever tell me about it?"

"It wasn't important."

Her chin went up. "Wasn't *important?*"

He shrugged. "Not to you."

That was rough. Two circles of hot pink broke out on her skin. But her chin didn't waver. She was a strong woman, and a distant part of Tom admired her. Maybe she was strong enough that, someday soon, she'd thank him for setting her free.

"When you say you *almost* married her… What does *almost* mean? How close did you come?"

"Close enough to hear the wedding bells at my back as I drove out of town."

"My God. You mean you left her waiting at the altar?"

"No," he said, still smiling. "Technically, that's what jilted grooms do. I believe the bride waits in an anteroom off to the side until her husband-to-be shows up and takes his place."

She hesitated. "But you didn't. Show up, I mean."

"No."

The pink cheeks had faded, leaving behind an ivory pall of shock. It was finally sinking in. Her gaze scoured his face, as if she wondered where her charming Tom had gone.

He wouldn't be receiving cards from this one for the next decade, that was sure. *Good.* One tearstained ghost, annually rattling the rusty chains of his ruined conscience, was enough for any man.

She swallowed. "But why? Why didn't you go through with it?"

For the first time, he hesitated, too.

"Let's just say…I decided I'd make a rotten husband."

Amazingly, she balked at that. She wasn't ready to let go of all her illusions—or her plans.

"Oh, Tom," she said, reaching out with gentling fingers. "Honey. Don't say—"

He backed up a quarter of an inch and restored his tilted, insulting smile. "Why not? It's true—I'm *not* good husband material. I think I knew that the night I almost screwed her bridesmaid."

A gasp. And then, as if by instinct, she reared back and slapped him.

It would have caused quite a stir, except that, at the

exact same moment, Trent Saroyan shoved Coach O'Toole over the yacht's elegant teak railing and into the Atlantic Ocean and, as Tom had predicted, all hell broke loose at the party.

THOUGH IT WAS ONLY about eleven-thirty, the darkness out here in the rural Georgia woods was cool, deep and damp, the kind of night that predicted pea-soup fog in the morning.

Kelly stood at her worktable, so absorbed in cutting a very expensive sheet of purple drapery glass that she listened to the muffled twig-cracking sound several seconds before she realized it was the wrong sound at the wrong time. Most of the little animals that shared these woods with her went to bed early—and few of them were capable of producing such big noises anyhow.

Carefully she put down the glass cutter and listened. The sounds continued, quite close now.

It was probably nothing. Maybe something bigger than usual, like a deer, had wandered into her yard.

Still, a shiver of fear shimmied through her.

She stared at the studio window. She couldn't see anything, of course. Nothing but her own reflection. The old, warped glass distorted a lot, but she still saw a skinny, scruffy redhead with a sad, wide-eyed face.

A sudden heavy, muffled thud came from just beyond the back door.

What was wrong with her? She couldn't just stand here, frozen. When she'd bought this old place for her stained-glass studio three months ago, her ex-husband Brian had warned that she'd be a nervous wreck way out here with no neighbors. She hadn't been, though. She'd done fine until two nights ago, when Lily had…

When Lily had died.

In the long, painful forty-eight hours since then, Kelly had been reduced to a mass of singing nerves and emotional confusion. Tears were never more than one thought away. And fear, too. Not active terror, but a shadowy sense that the world was not benign, or even neutral, but was instead somehow malignant, just waiting for you to make a mistake it could exploit.

Like Lily, who'd rushed through life and had never wanted to stop for boring maintenance chores, like putting brake fluid in an aging car.

Or like Kelly, working alone late at night in a falling-down studio with no locks on the doors.

The doctor who'd seen Kelly that night had assured her this reaction would be quite normal. He had prescribed sleeping pills, which she didn't take, because they seemed to open the floodgate to dreams. She turned to her work instead. She had several commissions to complete in the next weeks, and besides, the precision and focus required calmed her. The careful piecing together of small, seemingly random shapes, which came together to create a coherent whole, comforted her. Stained glass, she realized, was a pretty good analogy for life.

It had only been two days, she reminded herself. The funeral wasn't even scheduled until the day after tomorrow. Eventually, she'd find her equilibrium again. For now, she just had to force herself to pretend a courage she didn't really possess.

Though she'd been cutting without her work gloves on—one of her habitual sins—she quietly reached over, opened her drawer and slid her right hand into the soft, protective leather.

Then she picked up the freshly bisected sheet of glass, which came to a lethal point at the tip, and walked to the back of the studio.

She adjusted her grip on the glass. Her heart was beating so hard she could feel her pulse in her fingertips. Slowly, she opened the door....

And found herself looking into the shining black-marble eyes of a raccoon, who had somehow managed to climb to the very top of her three-tiered plant stand and was trying to reach the bird feeder that hung from the soffit.

The poor thing looked mortified, just as frozen into his awkward position as she had been moments earlier. He was huge, with a fat, sprawling belly that suggested this wasn't his first late-night raid. The long gray streamer of moss that dangled from his ear proved he had tried other approaches first.

One of the branches of the nearest oak came within six feet of the bird feeder. That must have been the thud she'd heard. The little scavenger had jumped and missed.

His stricken gaze seemed to be asking her to pretend she didn't see him. Smiling a little, she turned her head away. She wasn't even sure raccoons ate seeds, but if he wanted them that badly, he could have them. She could refill the feeder for the birds in the morning.

It was time to go to bed. She put her hand on the doorknob.

Someone touched her shoulder.

Electric currents of panic shot, primal and unwilled, through every vein. Her right arm came up.

"Kelly?"

"Jacob?" The sudden withdrawal of adrenaline left her

limbs weak. With a loud exhale, she slumped against the door, just under the bare bulb that served as an entry light.

"God, Jacob," she breathed.

Thankfully she'd recognized the voice before she'd had time to slash out with the glass. As it was, she had already raised it to breast level.

Jacob Griggs, Lillith's husband, looked down at her makeshift weapon, but it didn't seem to frighten him. He seemed beyond caring that he'd come within six inches of being impaled on a dagger of cut glass.

"I scared you," he said heavily. He looked up at her. "I'm sorry."

He looked horrible. His face was gray, but his eyes were small and red-rimmed inside puffy circles of grief. His hair, normally so thick and shiny Lillith had rarely been able to keep her fingers out of it, seemed to have dulled and thinned almost overnight.

"It's okay," Kelly said. She took his arm, and realized it was shaking. Two days ago, Jacob had been a thirty-five-year-old lawyer who jogged and played racquetball and danced and gave great parties, and generally made every woman in Cathedral Cove jealous of Lillith. In forty-eight hours, he had turned into an old man.

But what was he doing here at nearly midnight? She looked into those eyes again and wondered if he even knew where he was.

"Jacob, do you want to come in?"

He just stared at her.

She squeezed his hand. "Did you need to talk?"

To her horror, he began to cry. His face twisted with the agony of trying to hold it back. "I don't know," he said. "I don't know."

"It's okay," she said. She put her arm around his waist, though he was a full five inches taller. She wasn't sure he wouldn't collapse.

He was still repeating the same broken words. "I don't know, I don't know," he moaned.

"What is it? What don't you know, Jacob?"

He shook his head, back and forth, back and forth.

"I don't know anything," he said. His lips were dripping with tears. Finally he groaned and bent over double, his hands on his knees, like a runner pushed beyond endurance. "I don't know how to live without her."

CHAPTER THREE

IMOGENE MELLON HAD LONG AGO stopped believing in justice.

Maybe, she thought as she slowly descended Coeur Volé's wide, twining staircase in the predawn hours, that had happened on her wedding night. The longest night of her life.

The night she'd discovered her handsome, socially prominent husband wasn't normal.

Well, maybe she should choose another phrase. In Imogene's youth "not normal" had been a euphemism for *homosexual,* and lots of young women had no doubt found themselves married to men who were merely looking for camouflage. Imogene believed she could have lived with that. At least then, maybe she and Adler might have learned to be friends.

Instead she had discovered that Adler liked women just fine. He specifically liked to hurt them. Nothing too dramatic. Nothing that left marks or required care. He'd called it "spicing things up." He'd implied that if you peeked into any bedroom in town you'd find a few of these "toys."

It made him extremely potent. By the end of her first week of marriage, Imogene was pregnant with Sebastian. A year later, Sophie was conceived. After that, Imogene took birth-control pills secretly for several years. When Adler found out, he broke her wrist, and two months later she was pregnant again, with Samantha.

Her beautiful babies, almost all of them conceived in undignified tableaux of sadism and pain. Still, the children should have been her consolation, her reward for enduring without complaint. And they were, for a while. Then, gradually, she'd begun to understand that they weren't normal, either.

So much for justice.

She reached the wide staircase landing now, and, as she did almost every morning, she paused to appreciate the way the rising sun lit the huge stained-glass window. She liked to watch the figures come to life. It made her feel less alone in this haunted mansion.

Jean Laurent, the French artist Adler had hired, had done a magnificent job. The twenty-by-twelve window of St. George slaying the dragon had bold colors and great drama.

The dying dragon dominated the bottom third of the window, his sinuous body curled around the feet of the knight, his scales shining like peacock feathers. Up from the dragon, St. George rose like a human tower, tall and triumphant. He lifted his sword into the air, and on the tip of the sword he had impaled the dragon's glowing red heart.

It was not any failing of Jean Laurent's talent that caused Imogene to identify more with the dragon than with the resplendent knight. After all, from ground level, the dragon was mostly what one saw. And, naturally, Imogene couldn't help comparing the handsome St. George to the handsome Adler Mellon. St. George seemed to be enjoying his kill a little too much.

Imogene sometimes wondered whether Jean Laurent might have liked the dragon best, as well. The artist had spent so much time and empathetic energy on the dragon's face. Its eyes were almost human—green, gray, silver and blue pools of inarticulate misery.

It took about twenty minutes for the sun to climb high enough to illuminate the entire window, but Imogene always waited patiently for the transformation to complete itself. The heart, naturally, was the last to burst into brilliance. The red, jewel-like heart, so real it seemed to be still throbbing.

Imogene had asked Jean Laurent if the window had a name, like any other work of art. He had smiled and turned to Adler with a bow. *Coeur Volé,* Jean had said. *Of course.*

Another reason to think perhaps Jean had sympathized with the dragon.

Coeur Volé was French for *Stolen Heart.*

"Mom?" Samantha was standing about ten steps above her. She still wore her nightgown. "Are you all right?"

"I'm fine," Imogene said. What a ridiculous question. Of course she wasn't all right. She was dying. They had told her she had maybe a month or two, no longer. "I'm fine. Go back to bed."

"Do you want some breakfast?"

"No."

Still Samantha hesitated, her hand on the banister. "Do you want anything?"

I want to live.

And I want justice. For my own tormented body, and for the poisoned lives of my children.

She let her gaze leave the agonized eyes of the doomed dragon. She let it slide up the shining armor, through the muscular thighs and powerful shoulders, and into the lusty, inflamed eyes of St. George.

Yes, she thought, feeling something stir in her own loins, finally. This, here at the very end, was what she wanted.

I want, for once in my life, to be the one holding the sword.

TOM HAD A BAD TASTE in his mouth, and it wasn't from the salmon salad, which he ordered every time he came to this restaurant and which had been as delicious as ever.

The taste came instead from the conversation, especially his part of it. His words had a sticky, artificial aftertaste. The hard-to-digest flavor of manipulative half-truths and sugarcoated threats.

From the minute Coach Mick O'Toole had been fished out of the ocean, red-faced and spluttering and flailing his arms wildly, splashing everyone on the boat with salt water, Bailey Ormonde had made it clear that it would be Tom's job to make sure the man didn't sue.

Thus, this hastily arranged lunch with O'Toole, who hadn't even had the sense to bring his own lawyer.

Tom knew the drill. There wasn't much O'Toole could really do to hurt Saroyan, even if he did decide to sue. People like Saroyan paid big bucks to Ormonde, White and Murray to do what they euphemistically called "asset-protection planning." That was Murray's specialty, and he was good at it. Saroyan could pretty much get drunk and run down a convent full of nuns with his SUV, and, though he might do time in the slammer, he'd emerge as rich as ever.

One soggy football coach claiming whiplash didn't

have a chance. But he could annoy and embarrass Saroyan, who had a very thin skin. Saroyan didn't want a nuisance lawsuit that would keep this unfortunate anecdote alive at every party for the next year. As he'd said during their meeting yesterday, "Goddamn it, boy, just make it go away."

Considering that Saroyan was only about ten years older than Tom, and had earned every penny of his fortune buying up slums in Atlanta and then painting over the rotten buildings and raising the rents, that "boy" comment had annoyed the hell out of Tom.

Still…this was his job. Bailey always said lawyers were actually diplomats. More like gymnasts, was how Tom saw it. He'd just spent the past hour kissing O'Toole's dumb ass while twisting his arms back and tying his hands.

He ordered coffee to help with the foul taste in his mouth.

"You know, I'm used to tempers," O'Toole was saying. He adjusted his neck brace, which did look damn uncomfortable. "Try coaching a bunch of college kids, and you'll learn about tempers, that's for sure. The real problem with Saroyan is that he doesn't understand football. And if he thinks he's going to call the plays on the field, he's got another think coming."

Tom considered giving O'Toole a little friendly advice, but then he looked at that thick neck and those beady eyes, and he decided to have another sip of coffee instead.

"Saroyan didn't even play football when he was at MGU. He was a math major." O'Toole said *math* as if it were something ridiculous, like majoring in tiddlywinks. He didn't seem to see the connection between Saroyan's studies and his ability to buy and sell O'Toole ten times a day.

Tom drained his coffee and tilted his watch under the table. Fifteen more minutes of this, at least, before he could check his watch openly, gasp and imply that he'd been enjoying himself so much he'd lost track of the time.

Diplomat? Gymnast? Babysitter might be more accurate. Ego babysitter. He tried to tune out the little voice that said this was nothing a grown man should be doing for a living.

Suddenly, his cell phone began to vibrate. Apparently there was a God.

Giving O'Toole a "gosh, isn't this annoying, just when we were having such a good time?" smile, Tom unclipped his phone and answered without even bothering to look at the caller ID. Ordinarily he screened, having just enough old girlfriends to be cautious, but right now he'd welcome a call from any one of them.

"This is Tom Beckham," he said formally, already folding his napkin and crooking a finger to let the waiter know it was time for the check. Whoever really was on the other end of this telephone, as far as O'Toole was concerned, it was urgent firm business.

At first there was just silence. And then he heard a soft female voice.

"Tom?"

For about six tenths of a second he honestly didn't recognize the voice. And then it hit him. Hit him hard.

It was Kelly.

An image rushed toward him, leapfrogging the years. An image of the two of them in a dark corner, laughing at first, and then touching, and then she was crying, and he was up against her, and she was kissing him and whispering his name, but crying, crying the whole time.

Her red-gold hair falling loose against the green satin of her dress, the fresh-apple smell of her, the salt of her tears on his lips, the insanity inside him.

"Tom? Are you there? It's Kelly. Kelly Ralston...I mean Kelly Carpenter."

"Yes," he said. "I'm here. What's wrong?"

Now that his mind was working again, he understood that something must have happened. Something bad. She hadn't called him in ten years, though at first he had deluded himself that she might. No one from the wedding party had ever called him, except Mr. Mellon, who had actually come out to Atlanta ready to beat Tom, he'd said, until he no longer knew his own name and had to be fed with a straw.

"I—I don't know if you heard," she said, her voice still somber and husky. He wondered if she'd been crying again. Who made her cry these days?

"Heard what?"

"About Lillith. Lillith Griggs. I mean, she became Lillith Griggs, you knew she and Jacob got married, didn't you?"

"Yes, I knew that." He and Jacob had been good friends back in law school. Jacob still kept in touch, still wrote now and then, though of course he didn't admit that to Lillith, who had, like Kelly, been one of Sophie's bridesmaids and therefore subscribed to the official position that Tom Beckham was scum. "What about Lillith?"

"She was in a car accident. Three days ago."

"Is she all right?"

"No." A wretched pause. "She was killed."

The waiter came over then and held a check for Tom to sign. He scrawled something, almost glad of the distraction. He needed time to absorb the news.

He hadn't known Lillith well, but she'd always seemed much more...alive than most people. She was always the one laughing, playing practical jokes like wearing stiletto heels to the rehearsal so that the lineup by height suddenly seemed all wrong. She was a beauty and a brain and a class clown all in one. What kind of automobile accident had been savage enough to extinguish all that?

"I'm sorry to hear it," he said carefully, glancing over at O'Toole, who was tonguing around in his empty drink, trying to hook a piece of ice and suck any lingering vodka from its surface. O'Toole met Tom's gaze over the glass and frowned, pointing at the telephone.

Tom covered the mouthpiece with his palm.

"We're done here, O'Toole," he said, though he knew that those four words might well undo all the goodwill he'd spent the past hour building.

O'Toole put his glass down slowly, giving Tom an incredulous look. "Damn right we are," he said. He tossed his napkin on the table, scraped his chair back loudly and walked away.

"Tom, are you still there?"

Tom took his hand off the telephone. "Yes. Sorry. How is Jacob?"

"He's a mess," Kelly said. "That's why I'm calling. The funeral is tomorrow, and he asked me to let you know. He hopes you can come. I do, too. He needs a friend...and you seem to be the one he wants."

It was subtle, but he could hear how inexplicable she found that fact to be.

"Okay," he said.

There was another pause. "You'll come?" She must have been expecting an argument.

"Yes," he said. "Tell him I'll be there. What time is the funeral?"

"One. We're all meeting at the house and riding together. His house." She took an audible breath. "But Tom…if I tell him you're coming, if I get his hopes up, and then you—"

"I'll be there." He heard the doubt quivering in her silence. He couldn't blame her. She couldn't know that, since he'd left Cathedral Cove, he had never made a promise he didn't keep. Of course, he made damn few promises.

"Kelly, I'm telling you I will be there. Have I ever lied to you?"

"No," she said slowly. "Not to me."

"Then trust me," he said, and in spite of himself a wry note crept in. He could feel his tilted smile nudging at his lips. But come on. Had anyone on this earth ever spoken a more ironic sentence? "I'll be there."

KELLY KNEW BETTER than to trust Tom Beckham, so she couldn't understand why she was so upset when he didn't show up at the funeral home, or at the graveside service.

She was just mad at herself, that was all. She should never have told Jacob that Tom was coming. He had kept glancing over his shoulder at the service, and now that they were back at home, every time the door opened he looked up expectantly.

She stood in the kitchen, carefully pulling the plastic wrap off plates of deviled eggs and pans of meat loaf, and trying not to feel a little angry with Jacob, too.

But darn it. He had friends, lots of them. People who really cared about him, people who filled his house and his refrigerator, people who called and stopped by, who prayed at his side and cried at his side and loved Lily almost as much as he did.

Why weren't they enough? Why did he need Tom Beckham, too?

Why did *anyone* need Tom Beckham?

The door opened, and to Kelly's surprise a lovely blonde walked in, dressed in the most elegant little black funeral dress she'd ever seen. It was Samantha Mellon, Sophie's little sister.

"Hi, Kelly," Samantha said softly, brushing her long, silky hair back behind her shoulder and smiling. "They told me you were in here. I thought maybe I could help?"

Kelly stuffed the plastic into the trash can, wiped her hands on a towel, and reached out to give Samantha a hello hug. It was very sweet of her to come—and probably somewhat risky. Over the years, her mother and brother had developed an intractably hostile attitude toward every one of the young men and women who had been in Sophie's wedding party.

As best Kelly could understand, Mrs. Mellon and Sebastian felt that the bridesmaids and groomsmen had all abandoned Sophie after she'd been jilted. True friends would have stuck by her, defended her. If they had, Sophie might never have ended up in an institution.

Was that true? Kelly's memory of that time was clouded with misery and guilt. It was true that the friendships had ended when the wedding fell apart, but whose choice had that been? Had Sophie avoided them because they reminded her of a day so horrible she couldn't bear to relive it? Or had they avoided her, the way you might instinctively avoid someone whose luck seemed to have turned spectacularly bad?

Some of them had tried to make contact in the weeks after Tom disappeared, Kelly was sure of that. But Sophie hadn't been willing. Or maybe she just hadn't been ready.

Maybe they should have tried harder.

Kelly hadn't been able to try at all. A huge wall stood between them. She always wondered if Sophie knew about the night that Kelly and Tom had...

Just as she'd always wondered whether that night had played a part in the tragedy that came next.

But there was no one to ask. Tom was gone, and, soon after, Sophie was lost to them, too.

Kelly and Samantha hadn't seen much of each other through the years—things would always be too awkward for that. But Kelly was still fond of her.

Suddenly she remembered what Lillith had been saying right before the accident. That Sophie had been let out again.

"Sam, Sophie didn't come with you, did she?"

Samantha's gray-blue eyes widened. "Of course not. Sophie is—" She hesitated. "She's still in North Carolina."

In North Carolina. Is that where the newest mental-health facility was? Over the past decade, if the grapevine could be trusted, Sophie had been in and out of five or six different resident institutions.

So did that mean Lillith had been wrong? Did that mean the light in the tower window hadn't been Sophie after all?

"She hasn't come home? I heard that she had."

"No, she's not up to being on her own right now. The doctor said, with the anniversary coming up so soon..." Samantha looked perplexed. "Who told you she was?"

"I think Lillith had heard it somewhere."

Samantha shook her head sadly. "The gossips must be

at it again. I think the anniversary always stirs things up, don't you? But frankly, this terrible accident would be so hard for her. Just this once, I'm glad she's not here."

Kelly reached out and touched Samantha's hand. Poor Sam. Now that Sebastian had married and moved to Raleigh, Sam was living alone at Coeur Volé with their mother, who had never been a picnic but who had become even more eccentric through the years.

Sam looked amazingly like Sophie these days. All the Mellon siblings looked similar—the lush blond hair, the deep-set eyes, the sex appeal and the elegance. Sebastian and Sophie had often been mistaken for twins. They were only a year apart and they had an intimacy that seemed almost preternatural, the kind you sometimes do see in twins.

Samantha was five years younger, and it wasn't until she grew up that the striking Mellon looks displayed themselves. Now the only real difference was in the eyes. Sophie's and Sebastian's were a dramatic peacock blue, and they sparkled with an essence of danger, a flash of the untamable. Sam's eyes were light, and her gaze was gentle, almost humble.

It made Kelly's heart ache to look at her. This was what Sophie should have been.

"Well, anyway, I'd love some help," Kelly said. "So many people have brought food. He'll never eat it all, so we might as well use it up today."

Samantha nodded and began efficiently stacking small sandwiches on a large silver plate. "He seems very weak," she said. "It's so terrible. It's obviously broken his heart."

"Yes." Kelly blinked back moisture. This wasn't her tragedy. This wasn't her day to cry. But it was hard. A week ago she'd been in this kitchen drinking coffee with Lily from these same cups. "I suppose time will help. It's still so new."

"When I talked to him just now, he told me he was waiting for Tom Beckham." Sam looked over at Kelly somberly. "Is that true, or is it just wishful thinking? I didn't think we'd ever see Tom in Cathedral Cove again."

Kelly sighed and slid the rest of the potato salad into the refrigerator. "I honestly don't know," she said. "He asked me to call Tom, and I did. Tom promised he'd be here, but—"

Samantha smiled ruefully. "But historically Tom's promises haven't really been worth much."

"Right. You wouldn't believe how distant he sounded on the phone when I told him about Lillith."

She didn't mention that it had taken her two hours to get up the nerve to dial the number, and when he'd answered she'd found that she needed to sit down, because her legs wouldn't hold her.

"Ten years," she said. "We hadn't exchanged a single word in ten years. And yet, throughout the call his voice was completely bland and impersonal. He might as well have been talking to his secretary."

Samantha lifted one graceful shoulder philosophically, as if to say *what did you expect?*

Good question. It made Kelly feel ridiculous to admit that she *had* expected more. In the private photo album of her heart, Tom Beckham had been the most-often-relived memory, in spite of the ache it always brought. She had about a dozen pictures that never seemed to fade: Tom in the gardens of Coeur Volé, with roses behind him and the river at his feet; Tom dancing with Sophie, tall and handsome in his tuxedo, with Sophie's silver dress flashing rainbows as she twirled under the chandelier; Tom turning to Kelly in the darkness, fierce and full of hunger...

She was a fool. While she'd been wistfully fingering those images, she'd assumed that he, too, took them out now and then and remembered. But apparently he'd long since thrown them away. As she should have.

"I heard that you were behind her when it happened," Samantha said suddenly. "I heard you were with her when she died."

Kelly looked up. "Yes."

"That must have been awful. I'm so sorry. But at least— at least she wasn't alone at the end."

"Yes." Kelly had thought of that, but she wondered how much comfort she had really been. Lillith had seemed dazed, already moving away from the blood and the fog and the hissing car. Her cold hand had not responded to Kelly's touch. Kelly had been just inches away, but in every way that mattered, Lillith had died alone anyhow. Perhaps everyone did.

"Was she still conscious? Did she say anything?"

Kelly closed her eyes. "I'm sorry, Sam, but if I keep talking about this, I'm going to fall apart, and Jacob doesn't need that today." She picked up the plate of deviled eggs and handed it to the other woman. "Let's get the food out there, okay?"

"Of course. I'm sorry. I wasn't thinking." Samantha was embarrassed, her fair skin tinged with pink.

Kelly remembered how easy it used to be for Sophie to hurt Sam's feelings. "Scram, brat," Sophie would say, and Sam's blue eyes would fill with tears. She had idolized her older siblings, and Sophie and Bastian had exploited that shamelessly.

"It's okay," Kelly said, giving Sam a warm smile. "Do you think you can grab that plate, too? Jacob doesn't like meat loaf, so if it doesn't get eaten today it'll go to waste."

"No problem." Sam balanced both trays like a waitress, and Kelly took a deep breath and opened the kitchen door. She looked around, trying to locate Jacob in the crowd, which had swelled considerably while she was in the kitchen.

And then she saw him. He was at the door, shaking hands with a tall, dark, handsome stranger who wasn't a stranger at all.

It was Tom Beckham.

CHAPTER FOUR

THE LIVING ROOM of the Griggs' house was huge and airy, the perfect room for two energetic lawyers with a healthy combined income and a zest for entertaining.

One whole wall was ceiling-to-floor windows that overlooked a sunny bricked garden, and the ceiling was at least thirteen feet high.

Upstairs, there were three bedrooms, three luxurious bathrooms and a billiard room—which would soon have become a nursery. And of course the kitchen was terrific, but most of the square footage of the house was found in this one gracious room.

At the moment, though, it didn't seem big enough. The minute Kelly recognized Tom at the door, she felt short of breath, as if the room didn't hold enough air for the both of them.

Samantha seemed a little taken aback, too. She paused just in front of Kelly. "He did come," she breathed. "I can't believe it."

But then something strange happened.

Nothing happened.

No one gasped, no one froze with shock, no one jumped from his seat and pointed at Tom, screaming, "There he is! He's the one!"

A couple of women glanced over toward the door—and then surreptitiously ran hands over their hair or adjusted their skirts more flatteringly around their knees. But, for the most part, Tom Beckham's return to Cathedral Cove was a nonevent.

Though Sophie Mellon's jilting and the emotional breakdown that followed were legendary in the Cove, Kelly realized that very few people in the room had ever met Tom Beckham or knew what he looked like. In their minds, he probably looked like a movie pirate, or a highwayman—someone bigger than life and as cold as the last stroke of midnight.

The kind of mythical man who could destroy a woman simply by not wanting her.

Looking at him now, Kelly realized that, in her mind, too, the same thing had happened. Tom Beckham had become an idea, not a human being.

She had forgotten real-life details, the little things that made him Tom, and not just the infamous runaway groom. Things like how long-waisted he was, which always made it look as if he were wearing his slacks low on his narrow hips. Like how the right side of his smile lifted slightly higher than the left. Or how he tried to keep his dark brown hair off his broad forehead, but never quite could.

"Kelly," Samantha said quietly. "I think I'm just going to slip out the back, if you don't mind. It's awkward. I mean, I didn't think he—"

"I understand," Kelly said. Of course Samantha wasn't eager to come face-to-face with Tom Beckham again. "I'll tell Jacob goodbye for you."

"Thanks," Samantha said. "I'll—I'll talk to you soon."

They both knew it wasn't true. They had seen each

other maybe half a dozen times in the past ten years. But it eased the moment, and Kelly appreciated it. She nodded, and watched as Sam set her plates down on a table, then retreated to the kitchen and, from there, presumably out the back door.

Kelly began to circulate with her platter of deviled eggs. Watching Jacob and Tom from the corner of her eye, she tried to subtly wind her way over toward the piano, the spot farthest from the front door.

But she wasn't much of a strategist. When the room was this crowded, the large grand piano and the semicircular mauve silk sofa created a beautifully decorated dead end. She turned around and found herself staring at Tom, with no escape route in sight.

Damn him for being even more attractive than ever.

"Hi, Kelly." His smile wasn't big enough to be inappropriate at a funeral, but it still had that lopsided effect that always made him seem to be secretly laughing at everyone. "It's been a long time. You look great."

Like hell she did. She had been crying for four days, and she wasn't wearing any makeup, in case she started crying again. Besides, she was thirty-two now, not twenty-two, and women didn't just keep on getting better the way men did.

She was glad the half-empty deviled egg platter kept her from having to decide whether to shake his hand.

"Hello, Tom," she said. "I'm glad you could finally make it."

He obviously heard the implied criticism. He dropped the smile. "I'm sorry I didn't get here for the funeral. I did try. But I was at the mercy of a very inconsiderate jury."

"It doesn't matter," she said briskly. "I'm sure Jacob understands."

Tom glanced back toward the center of the room, where Jacob was sitting on the edge of an armchair, talking to Lillith's parents. Lillith's mother had her purse in one hand and a mangled tissue in the other. They had to fly back to Ohio, and they must be saying goodbye to Jacob. All three of them looked exhausted.

"He's much worse than I expected," Tom said. "I thought— He was always so tough."

Kelly gave Tom a look. Hadn't he learned anything in the past ten years? Hadn't he found anyone he could truly care about?

"He's still tough," she said flatly. "But he loved Lillith. A lot. They had one of the happiest marriages I've ever seen."

Tom's smile returned, just for a flash. "Ahh," he said. "But is that really saying very much?"

She chose not to respond to that. She wasn't really shocked—he'd always had a cynical side. And life had a tendency to deepen cynicism, not eliminate it, especially when you weren't even trying to fight back.

No, she wasn't shocked, but she was sorry. She didn't remember many of the things they'd said to each other back then—most of it had been silly and inconsequential, all the deeper meanings and growing awareness lurking between the lines. On their last night, though, he'd spoken one line she would never forget.

When he had finally accepted that they could never be lovers, not even once, he had looked at her with the bleakest face she'd ever seen, and he'd said, "I would have liked to know how it felt to make love to you—I might have built a soul out of a memory like that."

Through the years, she had sometimes felt generous

enough to hope that some other woman would bring him a memory like that. One untainted with the guilt and shame theirs would have carried.

"Have I offended you, belittling wedded bliss?" He arched an eyebrow. "Are you still such an idealist, Kelly? I heard you tried marriage out for a little while yourself. Was it all silver bells and scented bowers?"

"No," she said. "I'm sure you know that Brian and I divorced two years ago."

"Yes. Jacob mentioned it. I'm sorry."

"Don't be. It was amicable. Brian and I are still friends."

"Good for you," he said. "Very civilized."

She didn't answer that, either. She couldn't tell if he was making fun of her, or if that slightly snide tone was natural to him now. But there really wasn't anything to say about getting into or out of a marriage that didn't take them down a dangerous conversational road.

She shifted the platter, which was starting to feel heavy. "I guess I'd better offer these around," she said. "But it's good to see you. I'm glad you could make it. I know Jacob would have been disappointed if you—"

The murmur of subdued voices that had been softly pulsing through the room was broken suddenly by the jarring sound of musical notes. Four of them, played on the piano.

Kelly and Tom both looked quickly. Jacob sat on the piano bench, his head lowered onto his arm, which was draped across the edge. With one finger, he stabbed at the piano keys. Four notes. Over and over.

Kelly knew that tune. It was the refrain of "Alexander's Ragtime Band." Lillith had loved its jazzy, upbeat charm.

Kelly could almost see her now, dancing out of the kitchen with a platter of perfectly roasted Cornish hen, which she'd just whipped up for the dinner party, singing, "Come on and hear, Come on and hear…"

Jacob kept playing. Everyone in the room was watching.

Kelly dropped the deviled-egg plate onto the coffee table and hurried over to Jacob. She knelt beside the piano. Though she couldn't see his face, she could tell by the movement of his shoulders that he was crying. The four notes grew louder, more strident.

"Jacob." She put her hand on his arm, which was as hard as rock. "Jacob, don't."

His fingers paused, and as the seconds ticked away she felt the tension drain from his muscles. He lifted his head, and his face was running with tears.

"I haven't slept, Kelly," he said, as if they were alone in the room. "I can't. I wake up, and she's not there."

"I know," she said. Had he really not slept in four days? No wonder he couldn't cope. "You miss her. But you need to sleep, Jacob. She wouldn't want you to make yourself sick."

"I don't *care* what she wants," he said, his voice harsh, though new tears kept coursing down his flooded cheeks. "She left me. She didn't care what *I* needed."

"Oh, Jacob. You know that's not true."

He buried his face in his arm again, unwilling to listen. Kelly scanned the room, checking all the shocked and pitying faces. Was Jacob's doctor here? His minister? This was grief more profound, more complex, than she had any idea how to handle.

She felt a hand on her shoulder. She looked up.

Tom was standing behind her. He tilted his head slightly, asking her to move away and let him in. Reluctantly, she did so. At the very least, it would free her to call the doctor.

"Jacob, listen to me," Tom said with a voice that was amazingly gentle. "Let's go upstairs. You're falling apart, pal. You've got to get some sleep."

Jacob frowned, but to Kelly's surprise he seemed to be listening. "How?" he asked, sounding like a child who would like to obey but doesn't understand what's required. "How?"

"Simple." Tom held out his hand. Dangling from two fingers was a big gold-labeled bottle of scotch. He must have grabbed it from the liquor cabinet beside the sofa. "We'll get wasted. We'll drink till we drop, just like the old days."

Jacob blinked. Tom reached out, hooked one hand under his friend's elbow and urged him to his feet. Jacob nodded wearily. He rubbed his hand over his face, wiping away the tears just as if he had a handkerchief, though his palm was bare.

He put his other hand on Tom's shoulder. He already looked a little drunk, though Kelly knew it was simple exhaustion.

"Did I tell you?" Jacob frowned hard, staring with glazed eyes at Tom. "Did I tell you Lily was going to have a baby?"

In the back of the room someone sobbed softly.

"No," Tom said, never relinquishing eye contact with Jacob. "You didn't tell me. Come on upstairs, and let's talk about it."

When they were gone, and the voices in the room began

to murmur again, Kelly turned and shoved through the swinging door into the kitchen. She put the heels of her hands on the blue granite counter and tried to take deep breaths. *Help him, Lily,* she prayed silently. *Help him to go to sleep.*

"You should stay away from that one."

Kelly's head jerked up. She had come stumbling in here, half-blinded by emotion. She hadn't considered the possibility that the kitchen was already occupied.

What awful luck. It was Trig Boccardi, who lived next door to the Mellons. He had gone to high school with Sophie and Kelly, where he'd been the wrestling team's star. His friends called him Trig, short for Trigonometry, the same way they might call a fat boy "Slim."

He'd always been slow, but Kelly always wondered if he might have found himself in one headlock too many, because by the time he had gotten out of high school he was downright weird.

And he'd carried a torch for Sophie for about fifteen years now, although she'd never given him a single ounce of encouragement. The day Sophie's wedding fell through, Trig had been so angry with Tom that they'd had to call a doctor to sedate him.

She'd never been comfortable around him, but she tried to compose her features. "What do you mean, Trig? Stay away from what one?"

"It's not safe to be with *any* of them now," he said, and the flat warning in his voice made her skin crawl. He frequently didn't quite make sense. Was this just another of those times?

He still wore his sandy-brown hair in the buzz cut the wrestling coach had required and his muscles were still cut sharp and powerful, as if he thought he might be called on to throw down a few opponents on the mat at any moment.

"People have to pay for their sins," he said. "And you'd better stay away from him. He's dangerous when he's angry. He'll make you pay."

Usually she tried to be pleasant to Trig when she encountered him, but today she'd had enough. Today she had nothing left.

"Who?" Her voice was sharp. "Who is dangerous? Who will make me pay?"

Trig rolled his eyes upward.

"Someone upstairs? Who? Do you mean Jacob? Do you mean Tom?"

Trig shook his head slowly. "I mean God."

WHEN JACOB WAS SUFFICIENTLY talked out and liquored up, which took about three hours, he collapsed into a deep, noisy sleep. And then, wishing he could do the same, Tom went back downstairs.

Everyone was long gone, the house straightened up to perfection. All that remained was a refrigerator full of plastic-covered food and a note from Kelly that read simply "Jacob's friend Joe will be coming over at nine. I'd appreciate it if you can stay till then. If you can't, please call me." And then her telephone number.

It was eight o'clock already. And he didn't have anywhere to go—just an empty hotel room that he hadn't even checked into yet. So why not stay?

He started to throw away the note, but he changed his mind and pocketed it instead. He didn't delude himself. He liked knowing he had her number, even though he'd be a damn fool if he ever called it.

Fresh air. That's what he needed. Jacob's pain had filled that bedroom like a poisonous gas, and Tom had been breathing it for hours now. He didn't know how Jacob had survived the past four days, with nothing but agony for air.

Just one more reason never to get married. Tom had been keeping a list for a decade—and he was up in the hundreds now.

The backyard garden of the Griggs' house was beautiful, but right now Tom needed open spaces with no walls. He made himself a cup of coffee and went out front to drink it.

He plopped down on the stoop, undoubtedly verboten in a swank neighborhood like this, but so what? He put the coffee on the step below him, between his feet, and stared out into the cool, clear evening.

He liked autumn in Georgia. He liked the crisp little silver stars, swimming in the black sky like minnows. He liked the breeze in the Chinese elm, which hadn't lost its leaves yet. He liked the smell of wood fires burning in nearby houses.

He shut his eyes. Several streets over, someone's dog was barking. The sound echoed on the sides of hills three miles away, and the dog must have enjoyed that, because he kept barking. Maybe he imagined he was a wolf.

After ten minutes or so, when the coffee was drained, Tom felt better. His head had cleared enough that he could think.

And the first thing he thought of was Kelly.

On the surface, she hadn't changed much at all. Still skinny and unaffected, still not quite sure how to control her long, curly hair. Still an honest look in those wide blue eyes, and a vulnerable bow at the top of those full, pink lips. Still about ten times sexier than she had any idea she was.

But on the inside, things had definitely changed.

For one thing, she didn't love him anymore.

He heard footsteps coming down the sidewalk, not uncommon at eight-thirty in a safe, comfortable neighborhood. He wondered if Kelly was coming back to check on him, to see if he'd stayed as she'd asked.

But it was Samantha Mellon, Sophie's little sister. He felt his muscles brace. He'd seen Sam scurrying out of Jacob's house today the minute she'd laid eyes on Tom. He assumed that meant she didn't trust herself to be polite.

So if she was coming back now, it must mean she'd decided it was time for a little therapeutic rudeness. He climbed down the stairs, down the front walk, hoping he could meet her on the sidewalk. She might get noisy—she had every right to. The important thing was not to wake Jacob.

To his surprise, when she saw him her steps quickened. She reached him with hands outstretched. "Tom!"

He allowed her to take his hands into hers. This wasn't what he'd expected, but he certainly wasn't going to complain if she'd decided not to claw his eyes out.

"Hey, Sam," he said, smiling. "I hardly recognized you, kiddo. You've really grown up."

Her pretty smile faded. "Yes. I look like Sophie now. Everyone tells me so. Does it—does it make you uncomfortable?"

He laughed. This was really strange. But kind of refreshing. Was it possible she was willing to discuss Sophie openly? He wouldn't do it, of course, but it was a novel feeling to think he could.

"Of course not," he said. "Sophie was beautiful. And so are you."

"Thank you." She squeezed his hands. "I'm so sorry, Tom. I shouldn't have avoided you earlier. It's been so long, and I wanted so much to talk to you. I just didn't know how to begin."

"Well, you're off to a good start. What did you want to talk about?"

She didn't answer right away. In the moonlight it was difficult to tell, but he thought maybe she was flushing.

"I—I think I just wanted you to know that, in spite of what Mother and Sebastian may have said, not everyone in our family hates you."

He smiled. "I think that just leaves you, doesn't it? But I appreciate it, Sam. It's generous of you."

She shook her head. "It's not. It's merely the truth. I don't know why you didn't marry Sophie, but I do know that we're—" She bit her lower lip, as if she couldn't think of the perfect word. "Mellons aren't easy people. And look at Sophie—she can't even live on her own. She's not stable, and she never was, not really. So how could you have brought yourself to marry her? I wanted you to know I don't blame you."

Now he was the one who didn't know what to say. He felt as if he'd just received a papal blessing—a blessing he hadn't asked for and didn't deserve. "Sam, I'm sorry. I appreciate what you're saying, but this really isn't something I'm comfortable talking about."

She tilted her head to get a better look at him. "Not even to me?"

"Not even to you."

"I see." She dropped his hands slowly. "Of course, I understand. I probably shouldn't have come all the way out here, bothering you when obviously you're tired."

"It's all right, Sam. I'm glad you came. It was good to see you again."

She still looked slightly crestfallen. He wondered what kind of reception she'd been expecting. Had she thought he would go down on his knees and thank her for the absolution? She must know that the only one who had the right to "forgive" him was Sophie herself. And that wasn't likely to happen.

She must also know that, in the past ten years, he'd found a way to stop tormenting himself about all of this. He was quite contented now to carry on unforgiven.

But instead she seemed to feel oddly rejected.

"Well, I should go home, anyway," she said. "Mother will be wondering where I am. I'm the only one she has left now, you know. She gets possessive. It's…it's pretty hard."

"Sam—"

She laughed, a little too loudly. He instinctively glanced toward Jacob's window, hoping he wouldn't hear.

"I didn't mean to whine," Samantha said. "It's not that bad, and I remember how you hate melodrama. Sophie told me about that—she said she would have to learn to control herself because emotion irritated you."

Had he said that? Probably he had. Sophie's broad, unpredictable and, to his view, overindulged emotions had annoyed the hell out of him. She'd cried for hours, and he hadn't felt a thing. But perversely, when Kelly had wept in his arms, every tear had been a little drop of fire.

What a bastard he'd been.

Correction. What a bastard he still was.

Just ask Darlene, who had been crying on the telephone this morning. Knowing she could go on for hours, he'd set the phone on the bed and continued packing. When he came back, she'd been gone.

"Sam, look—"

"No, it's all right, really. I still don't blame you." She seemed to be trying to find some middle ground between the eager welcome she'd started with and the uptight formality she'd briefly switched to. It obviously wasn't easy for her to find the right note. In the end, they didn't actually know each other very well, in spite of the fact that they'd come within twelve hours of being in-laws.

"I just want to ask you one thing, Tom, and then I'll go. It's important. Have you seen Sophie lately? Do you know where she is?"

"Where she is?" Tom frowned. "I thought she was either…in residence somewhere, or at home. Isn't that the case?"

"Usually. But—" She ran her fingers through her hair. "We don't know where she is right now. Mother called the clinic in Raleigh, but Sophie is just a voluntary patient, and apparently she checked herself out. She said she was coming home."

"But she didn't?"

"No. At least—"

A leaf skittered past. Samantha glanced behind her, as if she expected to see Sophie walking toward them. For some strange reason, the gesture made the hair on the back of his neck stand up.

"No, she didn't come home. We're not making this public, but Mother and I haven't heard from her in weeks. And we need to find her. Mother is… She's…" She reached up and began playing nervously with the buttons on her shirt. "Oh, you don't care about all this."

"Yes, I do. What about your mother?"

She looked at him with huge eyes, her fingers still picking at the top button. "She just found out she's dying. It's a brain tumor. Inoperable. Funny, I always thought that word was just too cliché. But it really means something. It means there's no hope."

"Oh, my God. Sam, I'm sorry."

"No, you aren't. She was terrible to you. She's terrible to everyone. I'm the only one left now, though, and so I get it all."

For a minute he thought Samantha might cry, too. She deserved to cry, with everything she'd been through—and all the heartbreak that undoubtedly lay ahead, as she nursed a dying mother.

But why bring her tears to him? Did she have no friends, no lover, no intimate of any kind? Surely she hadn't kept her emotions bottled up for ten full years, waiting for him to materialize and listen?

Or maybe she'd done exactly that. God, these irrationally emotional Mellons! He was sorry for her. No wonder she was on such an emotional seesaw. But frankly, he just didn't know if he could take it right now. Being with Jacob had sapped him of any strength he had possessed when he'd arrived.

"Sam, I'm sorry, but it's been a long day, and I think I'd better—"

"I know. You're tired. I shouldn't have come. But there's something else I have to tell you. I hope—hope you're not staying long in Cathedral Cove."

"Why?"

"That sounded rude, didn't it? I didn't mean it to be. It's just that Mother is— She's not herself. There's no telling what she might say if she ran into you. And Sebastian is here, too, did you know that?"

"No, I didn't. But so what?"

She tried to smile, but she was opening and shutting that top button repetitively, as if she couldn't convince herself she had properly fixed it. The overall effect was extremely odd.

"Well," she said finally, "it's just that…if you think Mother hates you, you should hear the names Sebastian calls you."

Tom stifled a yawn. Sebastian Mellon didn't frighten him in the least. In fact, it might feel wonderful just to take the gloves off and have it out with that effete snob once and for all.

"I'd love to," he said. "Send him over."

CHAPTER FIVE

"BRIAN, STOP. I'd like to drive by Jacob's house one more time, just to be sure he didn't end up all alone."

Kelly's ex-husband, who was giving her a lift home from the dealership, where she'd just deposited her car for service—no one who knew Lillith was likely to postpone routine maintenance anymore—made an annoyed sound.

Even so, he obediently slowed the car and signaled for a right-hand turn.

"What's the problem?" He glanced over at her. "I thought you said Beckham was keeping an eye on Jacob."

"I think he is, but I just want to be sure. Tom is—" She was silent a moment, watching the commercial buildings give way to masonry cottages, and then to elegant brick houses with wide, well-manicured lawns. Jacob and Lillith had been able to buy in one of the best Cathedral Cove neighborhoods. Not the truly elite old-money enclave by the river, where the Mellons still reigned, but close enough.

"Tom is *what?*" Brian sounded grumpy. He had moved to Cathedral Cove and opened up his sporting-goods store only about six years ago, and, like many newcomers, he seemed to think the story of Sophie's wedding was about seventy-five percent trashy fiction.

And even if it was true, his sympathies naturally lay

with Tom Beckham—one, because Tom was just a regular guy, comparatively speaking, and two, because everyone knew those Mellons were a bunch of inbred freaks.

Kelly sighed. "Well, after what he did to Soph—"

"It was ten years ago, for God's sake," Brian broke in. "You don't know *what* the guy is anymore."

"Exactly," she agreed, not in the mood to fight. Besides, Brian's down-to-earth practicality had always been his most appealing quality. She had felt very comfortable, very safe, in the two years of their marriage. "He's an unknown quantity. That's why I want to check."

"Fine. We'll check."

But when they got to Jacob's street, she could immediately see Tom's expensive silver sedan in the driveway. She knew it was his because it had been the only car remaining on the street when she had left Jacob's house after doing the dishes. Also, it had Atlanta license plates, and it just screamed overpaid big-city lawyer.

Tom must have pulled it into the driveway sometime after she'd gone. That had a settled-in feeling, and she relaxed a little. Jacob was probably fine for tonight.

"I guess Tom did stay," she said softly. "Good for him."

"Of course he did," Brian said. "Guys don't walk out on their buddies."

She glanced at him with a wry smile. "Just on their women? Well, you should know."

"That's right," he responded archly, and she could see the white of his teeth as he grinned in the darkness. "Especially if their women are cold-hearted bitches."

She chuckled. This was an old joke with them, as comfortable now as a well-worn sweater. After two years of a pleasant but fire-free marriage, Brian had confessed that he'd fallen in love with Marie Eller, his lovely, loyal accountant. Kelly had been sad but not quite heartbroken. She knew Brian deserved a passion she simply didn't feel—and apparently Marie could give him that.

What she'd told Tom today was true. She and Brian had divorced without acrimony, and they'd never stopped being friends.

In fact, right now Marie was the one who was giving Brian a hard time. Last month, she had asked him to move out, telling him she needed "space" and time to think. He was pretty upset, but handling it in his usual sensible way, working hard and hoping for the best.

"Okay, boss-lady, now where? Shall we do the official Sophie's Wedding World Tour? We've checked on the runaway groom. Shall we go by the House of Usher and see how the rest of the weirdos are doing?"

Kelly had heard people call Coeur Volé "the House of Usher" before. She supposed it was inevitable. The Mellons were reclusive, the structure was Gothic and Sophie's story offered such great fodder for the imagination. But it always seemed a bit cruel to her. It made a joke of things that she knew weren't funny.

But she decided to ignore it. He didn't mean anything, really. The working class always bashed the snobbish old guard. She'd done it herself, before Sophie had picked her for a friend.

"No, thanks," she said. "I've had enough drama for one day. Did I tell you Samantha came by to see Jacob? She wasn't at the service, but she stopped in at the house afterward."

"Yeah? Did she bring her crazy brother?"

Kelly settled onto the truck's sensible cloth seats and

shut her eyes. Brian had owned this pickup ever since she first met him, and the familiar smell and rhythmic rocking were relaxing.

"You mean Sebastian?" She shook her head sleepily. "No, Sebastian lives somewhere in North Carolina. He's not even in town."

"Yes, he is."

She opened her eyes. "What are you talking about? Sebastian is back in Cathedral Cove? How do you know that?"

"I saw him. Today, in the store. I sold him a hunting knife and a pair of sneakers. Too bad he didn't want to buy a gun. I would have loved to do a background check on that one. I'll bet we'd find that he's been in more loony bins than his sister."

She sat up straight. "Sebastian is back?"

"That's what I said, like three times now." He cut a quick glance her way. "What's wrong with that? He's weird, but no weirder than the rest of them."

"But…" She felt a tightness in the pit of her stomach. What a coincidence that Sebastian should come home right now, just when Lillith died, just when Tom showed up for the first time in ten years.

And Lillith had told Kelly that Sophie was back, too. If all of it was true, this would be the first time the whole Mellon family—and Tom Beckham—had been in Cathedral Cove together since the wedding.

She braided her fingers in her lap. It just didn't feel right. It felt downright unnatural, as disturbing as if she had looked up and seen the stars crawling out of their prescribed places, sliding slowly into some new, mysterious configuration.

Could this be what Trig had meant when he'd said, "He's dangerous when he's angry"? Could he have meant Sebastian? Kelly had seen Sebastian angry only a few times during their teenage years, but it had been a sight to remember. Trig, living next door, might have seen even more.

Was it possible that, in his foggy, incoherent way, Trig had been trying to tell her something important?

"Talk to me, Kel. What's the big deal about Sebastian being home?"

She tried to focus, to articulate her vague anxieties. "It's just that…if Sebastian's here, and Tom's here…" She paused. "I wonder if he *knows* Tom's here?"

"So what if he does? You think Sebastian will hunt down Tom Beckham and kick his ass for what he did to sister Sophie ten years ago? Cripes, will you people ever let that damn story *go?* It's over, for God's sake. Get a grip."

She told herself that Brian probably was right. Even lava-hot emotions could do a lot of cooling down in a decade. At the time of the jilting, Sebastian had been very defensive for Sophie. But though Sebastian and Sophie had been inseparable as young people, they must have grown apart through these past few years.

Sophie had spent so much time in institutions. And Sebastian, Kelly had heard, had married out in Raleigh. He had children and a career, stockbroker or something. Obviously, at least to some degree, he had moved on.

They were nearing the Mellon house now. She could see the tower from here. It was completely dark tonight. But that didn't mean it was empty, only that the lights were out. She shivered, thinking of someone standing up there, in the shadows, looking down.

How much could you see from there?

Could you see the foot of the East River Bridge?

"Brian," she said suddenly. "Will you sleep at my place tonight? I've put a bed in the guest room, so you wouldn't have to take the sofa."

He tilted his head, smiling. "Spooky old dump finally starting to give you the creeps?"

"No," she said quickly. "It's just that—"

She thought of the waiting, silent trees around her studio. She thought of Lillith's face covered in blood, and Trig standing in Jacob's kitchen, talking cryptically about God and danger.

To heck with saving face. Tomorrow she'd be strong. Tonight she needed a friend. "Yes."

Brian drummed his fingers on the steering wheel and clicked his tongue against his teeth. "Well….Marie won't like it."

"Oh." She tried to control her disappointment. But the idea of being out there alone tonight, with no car… "Never mind, then. I wouldn't want to cause trouble between you two. If you think you shouldn't—"

"I never said that. I just said Marie wouldn't like it. Maybe that's a good thing." He waggled his eyebrows. "A little jealousy might be exactly what the doctor ordered."

"Thanks," she said, almost ashamed of the relief that coursed through her. She definitely had to get back to being tough tomorrow. "I appreciate it, Brian. I really do."

She turned her head and stared out the window. They were approaching the spot where Lillith had hit the tree. In a minute they would have to cross the East River Bridge, over to the area unofficially known as the "Left Bank." Over there, the houses were smaller, funkier, just starting to come back from a long economic down-slide.

Tight zoning was a luxury the Left Bank couldn't afford. Artsy yuppie condos were haphazardly mixed in with coffee shops, antiques mini-marts and New Age candle boutiques. Beyond the Left Bank lay the rural fringes, where your neighbors were mostly trees, or people who owned guns and horses and dogs named Zeke.

It was out there that Kelly had bought her new place, a surprisingly charming run-down cottage with a detached garage that made the perfect studio. So though she definitely lived, in Cathedral Cove parlance, far, far on "the wrong side of the bridge," she loved it. Most of the time.

Just not tonight.

"Look," Brian said. "Someone has already put up a marker for Lillith."

Kelly saw it at the same time. On the side of the road, just a couple of feet from the tree, a waist-high circular sign stood, announcing to all passersby that tragedy had visited this spot.

Through the years, she'd seen a hundred roadside markers just like this one. But they had always seemed comfortably impersonal, just small, circular plaques that said Drive Carefully, sometimes decorated with crosses, sometimes with flowers, depending on how recent the accident had been. She had always driven by without much more than a generic whisper of sympathy.

But this one was different. She wondered who had put it there. It hadn't been there this morning.

Jacob hadn't been in any shape to think of such a gesture. Someone had, though. At least four arrangements of flowers clustered on and around it—and an elaborate floral wreath had been hooked over the top of the sign, like a crown or a halo.

And there was something else. Was it a ribbon? There was very little wind tonight, and yet the thing—was it fabric?—was fluttering oddly, so light it seemed to defy gravity.

She squinted. What *was* that, draped over the left side of the wreath, undulating, as if it were alive and trying to get her attention?

It looked almost like a streamer of fog, or moss…or…

Something cold gathered around her heart. No, it couldn't be that.

The breeze was playing with it.

"Brian, stop," she cried.

He sighed even as he put on the brakes.

"*Now what?* Come on, Kel, I'm tired. Whatever it is, can't it wait until—"

But she had already opened the car door and climbed out. She couldn't hear the end of his sentence.

She walked over to the marker and took the soft, fluttering, weightless scrap into her numb hands. She turned it over. She traced its familiar, exquisite pattern with disbelieving fingers.

It wasn't fog or moss. It was exactly what she had thought it was.

It was a piece of lace from Sophie Mellon's wedding dress.

MARY JO'S CAFÉ AND SWEET SHOP was charming from the street side, all hanging baskets of red geraniums, green awnings and shiny black wrought-iron tables and chairs.

But from the alley out back, it looked like any other

strip retail business, just a no-frills utility door, an over-filled Dumpster, a teetering stack of wet wooden palettes and an empty plastic bag bumping up against the wall, shoved around by the wind.

Kelly pulled into the dead-end alley, did an automatic three-point turn to leave her minivan facing out and then cut the engine. Here under the trees, it was cool and damp and dirty. The twilight was a mournful blue.

She suddenly wished she'd put this chore first on her list today, not last.

But she had to stop this foolishness. She wasn't by nature a coward, though she certainly had been acting like one ever since Lillith's death.

Like last night. Asking Brian to stay had been ridiculous. He had sacked out in the guest room, exhausted from his own long day, the minute they got to Kelly's place. She'd spent another several hours in the studio, working, essentially alone anyhow.

Still, it had been nice to know another human being was nearby.

He'd taken her to get her van as soon as the dealership had called, and then, as pleasantly as ever, they'd gone their separate ways. They'd both had a million things to do.

Now she was tired. But Kelly had promised Mary Jo she'd return all the café trays they'd used for the funeral food, so, in spite of the eerie blue shadows in the alley, she had to do it.

The café was still open—it would be serving dinner till ten—but most of the other stores on the street were already closed. The only two cars in the alley were Mary Jo's Honda and Kelly's minivan, which wasn't glamorous but was convenient for transporting the big sheets of stained glass she needed for special projects.

Kelly had called ahead, so Mary Jo was waiting for her at the utility door. They unloaded the trays efficiently without much chatter and stacked them in the café's kitchen.

"Thanks for bringing the stuff back," Mary Jo said as she walked Kelly to the van. "I can use it tonight. You know what weekends are like."

Kelly nodded. And they walked the rest of the way in silence. Apparently Mary Jo didn't feel like making small talk any more than she did.

Maybe Mary Jo realized, just as Kelly had, that handling the funeral food had been the last little chore they'd ever do for Lillith.

After the accident, the first day or two had brought a mercifully numb shock. After that, the details of the funeral had been hectic and distracting.

But now it was over. Life went on. And they had to face that it went on without Lillith.

When they got to the van, Mary Jo hugged her. "Did you get that starter looked at?"

Kelly smiled. "Yeah. Transmission needed work, too. Two thousand dollars altogether. But at least it starts right up."

"Ouch." Mary Jo grimaced. "Well. Take care."

"I will." Kelly watched as Mary Jo turned and walked slowly back to the store. She didn't look as if she had enough energy to get to the door, much less shepherd her café through the dinner rush. Tragedy had so many repercussions, big and small.

"Oh—wait—" Kelly said suddenly. "I meant to ask you. Have you heard anything about Sophie being back in town?"

Mary Jo turned. She shook her head. "No. Dale over at the Texaco came in for lunch today, and he said he'd seen Sebastian, which surprised me. It's been a couple of years since the Mellon heir graced us with his presence, hasn't it? But Sophie? No. As far as I know she's still an inpatient."

Kelly thought about mentioning what Lily had said, but decided against it. And there wasn't any point asking Mary Jo about the scrap of lace. Mary Jo hadn't been a member of the wedding party, so she would never have seen Sophie's dress anyhow.

So Kelly just said goodbye again and watched Mary Jo go back inside. Then she opened the door of her van, eager to get out of this alley now that she was alone. Something was rummaging behind the Dumpster, but Kelly couldn't see what. The limp blue twilight had lost its struggle with darkness. Only small patches of light lay between long, black stretches of shadow.

Definitely time to go. Besides, if she went straight home now, she could put in a good four hours on the wine-shop project, which was falling seriously behind.

But darn it. Down at the front end of the alley, a large refrigeration truck had pulled in, blocking the exit. Behind her, the alley came to a dead end, so she'd have to wait.

Maybe the driver would make his delivery quickly. In the meantime, she could at least check on the glass in the back. With her keys still in her hand, she circled the van and opened the hatch doors.

She'd had special slots installed in the cargo area so that she could transport sheets of glass safely. Today, all the slots were filled.

The wine-shop project was the most challenging commission she'd ever landed—a tunnellike entryway for the upscale establishment, with lush stained-glass grapevines winding on both sides, and even on the ceiling.

This afternoon she'd picked out half a dozen sheets of the most beautiful green full-antique glass. It had cost a fortune, virtually eliminating any hope that this project would turn a profit. But the glass had such extraordinary linear striations, which would produce grape leaves so textured and real no customer would walk through that entryway without reaching out to touch them.

She hadn't been able to resist. Anyhow, if this project turned out to look as spectacular as she hoped, it would be worth its weight in permanent advertising.

She adjusted a couple of boxes so that everything was wedged in snugly, and then, hearing an odd noise behind her, she turned.

Trig Boccardi was standing only about four feet behind the truck, a glower on his heavy face, erasing what little good looks he had left from his high-school glory.

Unnerved, Kelly glanced around. Mary Jo's café was the last store at the dead end. Unless he had climbed over the alley fence, or come out of the café kitchen, he had pretty much materialized out of thin air.

"Hi, Trig," she said neutrally. She whisked shut the van's cargo doors. She didn't like to have those pricy sheets of glass exposed to anyone as unpredictable as Trig. "Where'd you come from? You startled me."

"You took it." Trig's brows hung low over his eyes. "Didn't you?"

She didn't like his tone, which was strangely aggressive. And, as usual, he wasn't making sense. "I don't know what you mean. Took what?"

"The lace. You took the lace from the wreath. Don't pretend you didn't. I saw you do it."

Kelly's stomach tightened. He had *seen* her? He had been watching her? From where? No wonder she'd had such a creepy feeling about spending the night alone.

How often did he do that?

"Yes," she said. "I took it."

"You shouldn't have. It's not yours."

She glanced toward the front of the alley. The refrigeration truck was still there. But that wasn't all bad. It meant that somewhere nearby was a truck driver, too. Just in case.

And Mary Jo was just inside the café. She'd come out if she had any idea something was wrong. Kelly began to move around the van a little, toward the driver's side. Toward the horn.

"You shouldn't have taken it," he repeated. He had followed her all the way around, still staring intently.

"Why not?" She paused by the door, wishing she'd left the window open so she could just reach in and touch the horn. She tried to read his expression, unsure whether he was very sad, or very angry—or maybe even a little frightened himself. "Did you put the lace there, Trig?"

He recoiled. "Of course not. *She* put it there."

"She? Who?"

He blinked several times, always a sign that he was agitated. "You know who. It's hers." He advanced a step. "She'll be mad that you took it."

Behind her back, she began to rearrange her keys in the palm of her hand, so that the metal points stuck out between her fingers. Trig was big and muscular, but his thinking was slow, and she hoped his reflexes were, too.

"Maybe you're right," she said. "Maybe I shouldn't

have. I was just surprised when I saw it, and I wasn't thinking. Maybe I should put it back."

He thrust out his hand. "I'll put it back. You shouldn't have taken it."

Did he think she carried it with her everywhere she went? "I don't have it with me," she said. "Don't worry about it, Trig. I'll take care of it later."

"No," he said. He took another step, his head ducked low, like an animal who was considering an attack. She'd never appreciated how much like a bull he actually looked, with that bulky body and that triangular head.

The groan and grind of gears just ahead told her the truck was leaving. Taking advantage of the distraction, she pulled open the door and climbed quickly into the driver's seat. Shutting herself in, she rolled down the window and looked sternly at Trig.

"I want you to go home now, Trig. And I want you to leave me alone."

He put his hand on the door. "No," he said harshly.

"Yes," she said, putting her keys in the ignition and turning over the engine, which, thankfully, started right up. Suddenly the two thousand dollars she'd paid the dealership seemed like a bargain.

"You have to go home now. And listen to me, Trig. I don't know why you were watching me the other night, but I want you to stop it. You can get in a lot of trouble for things like that."

He frowned, backing away a couple of inches, as if her stern tone startled him. He shook his head, a jerky and un-coordinated denial.

"I wasn't watching you," he said thinly. He blinked several times. "I was watching *her*."

CHAPTER SIX

THE NEXT MORNING Kelly sat at her studio's semicircular work desk, heart-shaped pieces of glimmering green glass littering the countertops. It looked as if, sometime during the night, the ceiling had rained enchanted leaves.

But she wasn't paying any attention to the freshly cut pieces, which were ready to be burnished with foil. Instead, she was listening to the ringing telephone crooked between her ear and her shoulder, and staring at a photograph she held awkwardly in her newly bandaged fingers.

She hardly noticed the bandages. She always sliced or burned herself while she was cutting and grinding small pieces. If nothing required stitches, she considered it a good day's work.

Besides, the picture held all her attention. She hadn't looked at it in years. It had been tucked carefully away in the pages of an old scrapbook. It was a picture of Sophie's wedding party, taken the night of the rehearsal dinner.

No wonder she'd been reluctant to keep it where she could see it. It was as potent as an uncorked vial of magic smoke. Kelly found that she could remember every moment of that night, as if it had been yesterday.

Such vivid memories... The scratchy seams of her green dress, which had been a little too tight. The way they'd all laughed because the cello player was out of tune. The time Lillith had sprayed champagne through her nose when Kent Snyder told a vulgar joke.

She remembered it all, every emotion, right down to the deep, scraping ache in the hollow of her heart.

While the others had been laughing and drinking and playing silly games, Kelly had been counting the hours until Tom officially belonged to Sophie. *Twenty-four, twenty-three, twenty-two...*

By the time the wedding party corralled a waiter and asked him to take this picture with Kelly's disposable camera, it was one in the morning. Only seventeen hours until the wedding.

Looking down at those faces now, with all the bitter knowledge of hindsight, Kelly thought maybe she could detect the turmoil seething under the surface smiles.

Against her ear, the phone was still ringing. She hung up and dialed a second time, in case she'd made a mistake. As it began to ring again, she tilted the picture, to better catch the light.

Nine young people. It should have been ten, but Samantha, the maid of honor, had been only seventeen, too young to drink and dance and giggle the night away with the others. She'd been sent home with her parents hours before the picture was taken.

Which left just nine. Sophie and Tom, the bride and the groom. Sebastian, who was the best man. Three ushers— Kent Snyder, Bill Gaskins and Alex VanCamp. Three bridesmaids—Dolly, whose last name was now Tammaro, Lillith, and Kelly herself.

All young. All smiling. But how many of them, Kelly wondered, had been hiding something that night?

Kelly's own sick guilt was fairly obvious, she thought. Her eyes looked shadowed, and she had her hands clasped in front of her, white-knuckled, almost as if the camera were a harsh deity from which she begged forgiveness.

Sebastian's head was turned away from the camera, but his jaw was set at a stiff angle, and his shoulders were oddly braced. It was impossible to tell whether he was staring at Sophie or Tom.

Sophie looked gorgeous, of course, in her ice-blue party dress. But her smile was too bright, too fake, as if she were dramatically intoxicated, though Kelly remembered that Sophie had hardly touched her wine that night.

Dark-haired Lillith was making a kissy face, just as energetic and full of spunk then as she had been until the night she died.

Kelly shut her eyes briefly, unable to look at Lillith very long.

They were standing just as they had planned to stand the next day, lined up by height. Dolly, the shortest of the bridesmaids, was on the very end, holding up her dress, because she'd just caught her hem in her high heel and torn it. She was glaring over at Kent Snyder, who, Kelly remembered, had just made a rude joke about Dolly, the clumsy cow.

Kent had been very drunk. The photographer had caught him sticking his tongue out and holding up two fingers to make devil horns behind Bill Gaskins's head.

Alex VanCamp looked bored. None of them had known Alex very well. He'd been a special friend of Sebastian's from college, and he'd seemed as if he could have been interestingly dangerous, if he'd found them worth the trouble of leading astray. Dolly had flirted with him, to no avail.

Kelly remembered thinking how peculiar it was that no one in the wedding party seemed to be connected to Tom, not even his groomsmen. Should that have tipped them off? He had seemed like a stranger at his own wedding.

Which brought her, finally, to Tom's handsome face.

This was the one face that should tell the whole story, and yet, even now, it didn't. Gorgeous in his tux, he was smiling that familiar lopsided smile, and one of his eyebrows was arched, as if he found the whole thing entertaining, but unimportant.

He seemed unaware of Kelly, of course, though just thirty minutes before she'd been with him in a corner, crying, touching his face one last time. But then, in a weird way he seemed unaware of all of them, as if he were alone in the picture.

Sophie clung to his arm, her whole body yearning toward him. But his body wasn't responding. Not a single muscle bent in her direction even a fraction of an inch.

Still, though any stranger could look at this picture and see that the bride was more in love than the groom, Kelly didn't think anyone would guess that, less than seventeen hours later, the groom would disappear.

"Hello?"

Kelly dropped the photo, shocked to realize that someone had answered the telephone. It was a woman.

"Hi. My name is Kelly Ralston. I'm trying to locate Kent Snyder. Do you know if I have the right number?"

A pause stretched oddly. "Yes," the woman said finally. "This is the right number."

Kelly couldn't believe her luck. She'd been trying all morning to reach any of the other members of the wedding party. She wasn't sure why—just a vague sense that one of them might know something about the wedding lace she'd found on the roadside marker, whether it really was a match for Sophie's gown.

But they'd all moved away. Only she and Lily had stayed in touch. Tracking even one of the others down had proved more difficult than Kelly had imagined.

Kelly wouldn't have chosen to start her inquiries with the hard-drinking, slightly vulgar Kent Snyder. But she'd take what she could get. Though she'd left messages several places, this was her first breakthrough.

"Oh, good. I'm sorry to bother you, but Kent and I—" What could she say? They hadn't been friends, exactly. She'd spent a lot of time with him for the week of wedding festivities, and then she'd never seen him again.

"Some years ago we were in a wedding together. I needed to get some information, and I thought perhaps he could help me. Is he there?"

"No," the woman said. "Look, what did you say your name was?"

"Kelly Ralston." Kelly thought the woman sounded edgy. Darn it. Kelly hoped she hadn't stumbled into some kind of divorce tangle. "I was Kelly Carpenter at the time. We were both in Sophie Mellon's wedding, ten years ago, in Cathedral Cove."

"Well, I'm sorry to have to be the one to tell you, Kelly, but Kent is dead."

Kelly was so surprised she couldn't speak for a moment. Her glance fell on Kent's picture. He had been a good-looking young man, in a thick-neck, not-very-bright sort of way. He'd been putting on weight even in his early twenties. His shirt was too tight, the buttons threatening to burst. And his face was already too red, flushed by alcohol.

"Kelly?" The woman on the telephone softened her voice, though she still sounded edgy. "I'm sorry. I know it's a shock. It was to us, too. It was an accident. Two weeks ago."

Kelly's voice felt rusty, as if she'd been mute for hours, not seconds. "He had an accident? A *car* accident?"

"No, although God knows it's a miracle he never did, the damn fool." The woman cleared her throat. "It was a hunting accident. He must have stumbled. His gun went off."

"I'm so sorry." Kelly shut her eyes. "But are you sure? I mean, are you sure it was an accident?"

"I guess you didn't know him all that well. I lived with him for eight years. I knew him inside and out. He was a good man, but he drank too much, no reason to sugarcoat it. He had no business handling a gun, the condition he was in, but there was no stopping him when he had his mind made up."

Somehow Kelly got through the rest of the call, offering condolences and apologies for calling at such a terrible time. When she put the telephone down, her hands felt cold.

Strangely numb, she picked up one of her rich green-glass leaves and held it to the light. The striations really were lovely. She hoped she'd got all the veins "growing" in the right direction.

She remembered what her first stained-glass teacher had told her, all those years ago in the basement of the Mellon house. A gorgeous young French artist, Jean Laurent, had been hired to create a two-story St. George and the Dragon window to hang at the top of the Coeur Volé staircase.

Kelly and Sophie had both instantly fallen in love. But while Sophie lusted after the Frenchman's black hair and bulging shoulders, Kelly had fallen in love with the glass. The shining green of the dragon's scales, and the rich, glowing red of his bleeding heart, the twining vines and billowing clouds behind St. George's triumphant sword.

Probably Jean had become Sophie's lover. Kelly remembered odd absences, lingering glances. But he had also recognized Kelly's passion and he had given her hours of his time.

When you cut your leaves, he showed her, or created your clouds, you couldn't just pick the prettiest spot on your sheet of glass. You had to pick the one that followed the correct lines and rhythms of life.

Hair curled, leaves grew, shadows fell, and even dragons died, according to natural laws. Violate them in the glass, and the entire piece would always be vaguely unsatisfactory.

She picked up a second leaf, twirling it slowly in her bandaged fingers.

Natural laws.

She picked up the picture in her other hand. Two of those smiling people were dead now. Did that follow the laws of nature? Two of ten was twenty percent. If you took any random group of ten relatively intelligent, well-to-do twenty-somethings… Would twenty percent of them be dead within ten years?

The phone rang again.

She dropped the picture but held on to the two leaves. She clicked the talk button.

"Hello."

"Is this Kelly Ralston?"

"Yes. Who is this?"

"This is Phil Tammaro."

At first Kelly didn't recognize the name. Tammaro? Did she know anyone named Tammaro?

"I'm Dolly's husband."

Oh, of course. She'd left a message there, after she'd finally tracked Dolly down through three completely different marriages, names and addresses.

"Yes," she said, eager to make up for not remembering. "Yes, Phil, thank you for calling me back."

"I just came in. I heard your message. I thought I'd better tell you—"

His voice broke, and at the sound Kelly's heart stopped.

"—tell you about Dolly. You see, Dolly was in an accident. She—she's dead."

TOM HAD BEEN LOOKING for Jacob more than an hour before it occurred to him to check the cemetery.

It was a beautiful Saturday morning, still warm but with a crisp hint of fall. After the funeral, Jacob had asked Tom to stay in Cathedral Cove a few days. Jacob didn't need to be alone right now, and since Tom wasn't eager to get back to the whole stupid Coach O'Toole mess—not to mention the phone messages that would be waiting from an injured Darlene—he'd said yes.

He'd let his office know he was taking a week of vacation time, which hadn't gone down well with Bailey, but so what? Every vacation Tom had taken for the past five years had been a working trip, schmoozing some potential client or attending some business conference. They owed him.

Besides, there wasn't really any such thing as "getting away" if you had a cell phone and a laptop.

Yesterday, Jacob had slept late, so Tom had spent all morning answering e-mails, issuing instructions to his paralegal and hand-holding a couple of clients who wanted to know why you had to notify everyone on the planet before you set a court date for a hearing.

He assumed today would be the same. This morning, though, by the time he got off the phone, Jacob was gone. And he'd left his cell phone behind, which seemed to hint that he'd like to be alone.

It had been a sticky moment. Tom didn't want to crowd Jacob, who was free to go wherever he wanted. Tom wasn't exactly the prison warden. But still…though Jacob seemed to be pulling himself together a little, it had been only a week since his wife had died. He was still fragile enough that Tom would rather keep an eye on him.

Finally, just when Tom was starting to admit he was worried, he spotted Jacob's car. It was pulled off the road, near the entrance to Edgewater Memorial Gardens.

Great. Just perfect. Tom felt for Jacob, really he did. Losing Lillith had put the man through sheer hell. But to tell the truth, Tom had endured all the hair-tearing and teeth-gnashing he could take for a while.

This definitely wasn't how he handled his own challenges. His personal recipe for emotional recovery was a fourteen-hour workday followed by a run of maybe ten miles, or fifteen, or whatever it took to wear out every muscle and brain cell he had.

Cemeteries were for wallowing, and he didn't wallow. His own parents, who had died when he was in college, had been cremated and scattered at sea. Clean and sensible. No desolate angels clinging to crosses, no granite effigies, no gut-wrenching epitaphs. No tilted, weed-covered tombstones and withered flowers to remind you that, in the end, even love gets tired of grief and forgets to mourn.

But what could he do? He couldn't exactly call Jacob's friend Joe and say, *Hey, could you go get him? He's in the cemetery, and I don't do cemeteries.*

So, indulging himself in one heavy sigh, he parked his car and began walking around, looking for Jacob.

This particular cemetery was a pleasant surprise. It was restrained, with no marble explosions of showy grief. Just neat rows of well-tended headstones, and comfortable benches under apple trees and spreading oaks.

For a cemetery, it seemed strangely full of life. The trees were restless with chattering squirrels and noisy birds, and ahead of him on the path a young couple walked slowly hand in hand, as if this were just another pretty park.

Off to his right, toward the river, a funeral service was in progress. A soft blue tent held a dozen mourners and a priest. The priest smiled at him as he passed. Smiling back seemed strange, so Tom merely nodded and walked on.

To his left, where the cemetery blended comfortably into a neighborhood of old, charming, well-kept houses, Tom saw three little girls, maybe ten or eleven years old, playing among the trees. One girl had a sword made of an apple branch, and the other two wore crowns of tinfoil and Shasta daisies.

Jacob sat on a bench very near the children, though he faced the other direction. Tom braced himself, took another deep breath, sat on the bench beside him.

"Hey, buddy," he said. "You had me a little worried there."

Jacob looked over at him. Just as Tom had feared, Jacob

had been crying. But for the moment, at least, his red eyes were dry.

"Sorry," Jacob said. "I just felt like I had to come see her."

Tom glanced over at the lawn. Though he could tell where the freshly dug grave was, he saw no headstone. Of course not, he thought. It wasn't ready yet.

"I haven't even decided what it should say." Jacob had followed Tom's glance. "We never talked about it. You don't think of things like that, not at our age."

"No," Tom said. "Of course you don't."

"We had wills, of course," Jacob went on. "We were lawyers. We took care of that. We thought of everything. But we didn't for a minute think we'd ever *need* them."

"No," Tom said. For an uncomfortable moment, he imagined his own neatly typed will, duly notarized and filed. Everything went to charity. *Everything,* right down to the pictures on his walls and the ties on his rack. It was the will of a completely unencumbered man.

But here, next to Jacob's aching grief, in the presence of all these dearly departed, Tom realized how pathetic his will would sound when it was read. Like the antiseptic record of a thoroughly unlived life.

Maybe, he thought impulsively, he'd go back and change it. Maybe he'd leave a few things to Jacob, who was the closest thing to a real friend he'd had since elementary school. Tom also had a painting of a red-haired girl standing on a hillside. It was worth a great deal of money, but he knew he'd bought it only because it reminded him of Kelly. Maybe he'd go back and write in a clause leaving it to her. She'd be pretty shocked, wouldn't she?

"I wish I had fixed the damn brakes myself," Jacob said suddenly.

Tom looked over at him. "What?"

"Lillith's brakes. She needed to have the whole system fixed. Everything was leaking. She had to put brake fluid in every few days. I was always carping at her, telling her to just bite the bullet and get it taken care of."

"But she didn't?"

Jacob shook his head. "She hated stuff like that. Boring stuff. I knew she hated it. All that time I spent, bitching about how she was letting it go. Why didn't I just *do* it?"

Tom didn't answer. He knew Jacob didn't expect him to. There *was* no answer. Jacob hadn't fixed Lillith's brakes, and he was just going to have to live with that.

The fact that Lillith would undoubtedly be happy to forgive him didn't make much difference. Jacob had to learn to forgive himself. If he could.

Sometimes, Tom knew, you couldn't. Sometimes life's lemons just couldn't be turned into lemonade, no matter how hard you tried to squeeze the facts.

Oh, yeah. Tom knew all about that.

The sound of the girls squealing and laughing was closer now. Apparently they were in the middle of a war, with pinecones for cannonballs. One of them had just ricocheted off the branch above Tom's head, and suddenly another came sailing over and caught Jacob in the shoulder.

"Oh," the young, high voices said, still giggling, "oh, shit!"

Two of the children disappeared behind tree trunks, but the girl who had thrown the pinecone came over, dragging her sword behind her. "I'm sorry," she said. "I am Sir Lancelot, and I'm trying to rescue Guinevere. I'm not very accurate."

Jacob smiled. "That's okay. You throw good and hard. When you fix your aim, you'll be lethal."

She smiled at him, retrieved her pinecone, and ran back down the hill toward her buddies. Their daisy crowns could just be seen peeking around the edges of the massive trees.

Jacob looked at Tom. He almost smiled. Then he looked down at his hands.

"I would have liked to have children," he said.

"I know." Tom wondered if he should add the conventional statements, like *you would make a terrific father,* or *you will someday.* But all those things sounded hollow. Jacob had lost so much. Tom's instincts told him not to try to minimize that loss.

"What about you?" Jacob glanced up at Tom briefly, then went back to staring at his hands.

"Me? What about me?"

"Don't you ever want to get married? Don't you want to have kids?"

Tom shifted on the bench. "Oh, I don't know," he said. "Sometimes it seems that ship has sailed, you know? There's not a lot of time, and I haven't really met anyone I—"

"Is it because of Sophie?"

Tom gave Jacob a hard look. "What do you mean?"

"I mean—" He took a deep breath. "Darn it, I know this subject is supposed to be off-limits. Always has been. I can feel it every time I get even close. But I've just learned a lot about how short life can be, you know?"

Tom didn't answer.

"Well, it is," Jacob went on doggedly. "And so it's stupid to avoid talking about things that matter. If I had Lillith back, you know what I'd do? I'd spend every minute just talking to her. Just telling her how I feel, and finding out what matters to her. I'd never go to an office again."

Tom tried to chuckle. "That might be a little hard on the budget."

"Screw the budget." Jacob shook his head. "We've got enough money. Why did we think there should always be more?"

Tom was silent a moment. The priest's voice drifted sonorously over the gentle air, reaching them as pure feeling, no content. The feeling was peace. Comfort. Forgiveness.

For that one moment, Tom could almost believe such things existed, even for people like him. After all, it must be for people like him that the concept had been invented. If you'd never done anything bad, you wouldn't need forgiveness, would you?

"I guess it is partly Sophie," Tom said. "I came so close to making a terrible mistake. I loathe the idea of making another one."

Jacob nodded. "I can see that." He paused, and Tom could tell he was trying to decide how far to push. "Did you—did you ever love her in the first place?"

"Jacob," Tom said. "I'm not going to do this."

"I guess that's my answer." Jacob sighed. "Have you ever been in love with *anybody?*"

Tom tapped his foot, a small movement that barely disturbed the yellow leaves that had fallen into the mulch around the bench. Though the cemetery was wide and open, the breezes fresh, he had begun to feel claustrophobic.

Had he ever been in love? What kind of question was that? For a few days, ten years ago, he'd been obsessed with Kelly Carpenter. He had hungered for her like an animal. When he'd looked at her, he'd felt as if someone had tied his intestines into knots and beaten his chest with a mallet.

And when he looked at his future, he felt blind and bewildered, as if the torch he'd been carrying to light the way had just flickered and gone out.

But had he been in love?

"You know," he said, crossing his arms over his chest, "I'm afraid I'm not even sure what love is. I don't think I've ever found a definition that can pass the bullshit test."

"A definition of love? That's easy." Jacob closed his eyes, and he smiled, just a little. "It's when someone is so important to you that you can't be happy unless they are."

Tom thought of Kelly's tears, which she had tried so hard to hold back. He had wanted her to cry. He had wanted her to admit, even in that small way, that she cared, that she hurt. That he wasn't the only one.

"Oh, well," he said, shrugging. "If that's the definition, I can safely say no. I have never been in love."

CHAPTER SEVEN

AFTER PHIL TAMMARO'S CALL, Kelly didn't even attempt to go on working. She couldn't think clearly, and if she tried to use sharp knives and grinding machines in this state, she'd probably lose a finger.

So she decided instead to do one last thing for Lillith. She decided to go check out the brakes on her Jaguar.

She knew where it was—at Dave and Sons Towing and Salvage. She'd been there a couple of days ago to retrieve Lillith's things from the car, which really didn't even look much like a car anymore. She'd combed through the wreckage, ignoring stray dimes and half-empty lipstick tubes while she hunted for anything important.

It had been hard, but she'd steadied herself by repeating, *At least Jacob will never have to see this.*

Dave and Sons was even farther out of town than her own studio, and the roads were so bumpy she was glad she wasn't carrying any glass. Signs of civilization were far apart, first a sagging Bar and Lounge, then two miles of scrappy fields before she saw a couple of rusty trailers, with a huge, incongruous satellite dish squatting between them.

Out here, the ground cover was spotty, mostly weeds, and the Georgia clay was more conspicuous than in town.

By the time she reached the salvage yard, her minivan was two-toned, white on top, the bottom third coated with an orange-red dust.

They had moved Lillith's car to the large, fenced-in back lot, she saw, which meant that the police and the insurance adjuster must have finished with it, and it was now ready to be picked over, its body parts sold piecemeal.

She knew better than to try to enter the lot alone. Dave had two very large rottweilers who, when strangers arrived, would throw themselves at the chain-link fence, growling and drooling, until Dave gave them the okay signal. "Back off, boys," he'd say, yawning, and they'd subside immediately, though they continued to drool, as if they hadn't forgotten what a good lunch a person would make.

Ignoring their noisy chaos, she headed straight for the large, square cinder-block building that served as Dave's office. Opening the door, she steeled herself to greet the balloon-like breasts of Miss September, whose picture topped the wall calendar behind Dave's counter.

"Hi." The young man behind the counter stood up politely from his stool, smiled and set down his submarine sandwich. "What can I do for you?"

Kelly smiled, too, but she was disappointed. This wasn't Dave, the rough but sensible middle-aged man with whom she'd managed to build a pretty good understanding last time. This guy was only about eighteen. He must be one of the "and Sons."

"Hi," she said. "I'm sorry to interrupt your lunch, but I was wondering if you'd let me take a look at one of the cars you have out back."

He wiped his hands on a Subway napkin, not that it did

much good. The grime under his fingernails had been there for months, and it wasn't going anywhere.

"Sure," he said, but his gaze raked doubtfully over her, as if he didn't think it was a very good idea.

She wasn't sure which part of her didn't pass muster. Surely she didn't look too citified to prowl through old wreckers. She never spent a whole lot of time on her clothes—and today she was just wearing a white polo shirt and a cutoff pair of blue jeans. She wasn't big on makeup, either, and her hair was pretty much always a mess.

"Which car?" He looked down at her legs. "Is it your own car? You were in an accident?"

What? But then she remembered that, as usual, she had quite a few Band-Aids on her hands and legs. She never thought much about it. Nicks and cuts were just an occupational hazard for stained-glass designers—and these were no big deal.

Now that one under her knee—that had been a doozy. She had stupidly left a sheet of glass standing out next to her stool. That cut had required twelve stitches, and that scar was a permanent part of her physical inventory.

Her mother, who had always thought the only good thing to do with a redheaded daughter who grew to a lanky five-eight was turn her into a runway model, had been horrified. Never mind that Kelly had been twenty-nine when it had happened, and ten years too old for modeling anyway.

"No," she said. "The car belonged to a friend of mine. The Jaguar. It was brought in a week ago."

"Oh, the Jaguar." The boy's face grew very somber. "I'm sorry about that. But they cleaned that car out already.

Did they forget something?" He pointed behind his back. He seemed to be pointing to Miss September, but probably he meant to indicate a cautionary notice hanging next to her. "We don't accept responsibility for personal items left in the vehicles."

"We didn't forget anything. It's not that."

She had been rehearsing this in her head all the way over. She didn't want to sound like a nut, but she really couldn't think of any way to get the answers without just coming out with the truth. Once again, she lamented that it wasn't Daddy Dave, who had a phlegmatic streak and wasn't easily rattled. Plus, he'd seemed to know a lot about cars.

"Actually, I was hoping I could get one of you to look at something for me. The police said the accident was caused by brake failure. I was just wondering if anyone could look at the brake system and tell what really went wrong."

The boy ran his teeth over his lips, top and bottom, several times. Either he was checking for stray mayonnaise, or he needed time to think.

He narrowed his eyes. "You planning to sue somebody?"

"No," she assured him. "I just wondered if there's any way to tell why all the brake fluid drained out."

He shrugged. "Bad hoses, probably. You gotta really stay on top of those old cars. They haven't got redundant systems, not like the new ones."

Now he was beginning to sound like his daddy. Her spirits perked up a little. Maybe he knew his stuff after all.

"But is there a way to look at the hoses and tell if they really were bad? I mean, does it look different if they're just old and leaking…or if, say, maybe they'd been cut?"

"Cut?" He frowned. "What do you mean, cut? You mean like deliberately?"

She hesitated. And then she simply nodded.

He stared at her, still frowning. "That's crazy."

She nodded again. "Yes, probably," she said. "In fact, I hope it is. I just want to be sure. Would you be willing to look at it for me?"

"Don't need to," he said. "I already looked at that car. I was wondering if there might be some way—I mean, it's a pretty hot machine. And I'm good at fixing stuff. Just because the insurance dude totals it doesn't mean it's a goner, you know?"

"You were thinking about restoring it? For yourself?"

He fiddled with his shirt awkwardly, trying to tuck it more neatly into his pants. "I was gonna pay for it. Dad doesn't let us just take anything he had to pay good money for. But it's just too far gone. Nobody's bringing that baby back from the dead."

He caught himself. He grimaced. "Oh, darn. I'm sorry. I didn't mean to disrespect your friend—"

"That's all right," she said. "I'm really just interested in the brakes. Did you look at them carefully? You didn't see anything—suspicious?"

"No," he said. "Your friend had a hot car, but she didn't take very good care of it, you know? Those hoses should have been switched out a long time ago. Main gasket, too. Whole thing was brittle, dried out, probably leaking like Swiss cheese."

He seemed very sure. And she knew herself that Lillith begrudged the time it took to do any maintenance. She even fussed when she had to stop and buy gas.

Damn it, Lily, Kelly thought. *Why didn't you take better care of yourself—for Jacob's sake, if nothing else?*

The young man apparently took her silence for doubt.

"Well, if you don't believe me, you might as well know the police are always looking for hinky things when there's an accident. The insurance dudes, too. If there had been anything shady, they would have seen it."

She nodded. She had known that was true. The police weren't fools. It was just so—

"So that's a good thing, right?" The boy looked worried, as if he didn't know what to say to make her leave. "Well, I don't mean a *good* thing, but an accident's bad enough without having to go round thinking it might have been murder."

She nodded, hoisting her purse up over her shoulder and giving him as much smile as she could manage. "Yes," she said. "It's a good thing."

Now if only she could make herself believe it.

If KELLY HAD REMEMBERED that she had a blind date that night, she would have canceled it.

But she'd forgotten entirely.

So at five-thirty she found herself, still in cutoff blue jeans, opening her studio door to a very nice-looking surgeon from Atlanta who was in town to visit his sister Jeannie, one of Kelly's friends. And at six, she found herself sitting next to him, across the booth from Jeannie and her husband Greg, at Rick's Riverside Ramble, still apologizing for forgetting.

"It's okay," the surgeon, whose name was Lawton, said. "I should have called first. Jeannie told me everything you've been through this week. It's no wonder you weren't thinking about dinner."

She appreciated his understanding. And he really was attractive, which was kind of a shock, considering what most of her blind dates were like. Ever since her divorce, her friends had been united in their determination to find her a new man, in spite of her emphatic assurances that she didn't want one. The ridiculous parade of dull, self-centered, needy and nerdy men they'd offered up for her consideration had only made the single life more appealing.

This one, though, seemed like a real human being. She felt a little guilty for being unable to focus on their conversation. But her mind just kept drifting to that picture of the wedding party, and thinking...*three of us.*

Three out of the ten are already dead.

Then she'd jerk herself back to reality, and try to say something scintillating, which sometimes seemed to be a bit off topic. She saw him exchange a quizzical glance with Jeannie.

Poor guy. He'd probably go home and tell people about how his sister had set him up with the most moody and boring woman in Cathedral Cove.

At least she knew he was getting a good dinner. Rick's was one of the best restaurants in town. To her disappointment, because of the mild, clear weather, the outside tables were full. Everyone loved to eat by the river, to the music of the water tumbling over a small but picturesque rocky fall. Still, the interior was elegant, and a guitar player was already warming up in the corner.

She didn't plan to mention that most of the stained-glass windows in here were her own work, and she hoped Jeannie and Greg wouldn't say anything, either. She already looked self-absorbed enough, and she wouldn't want Lawton to think she'd chosen this spot just so that she could show off.

Unfortunately, Rick noticed her, and he came over to take their order himself. Once he'd recommended the trout and the asparagus, he began telling her about how one of the western windows, the one of the speckled fish, seemed to be wiggling a little.

"I'll take a look at it later," she said, casting an apologetic glance at Lawton. "Maybe after we eat."

Rick shook his head. "Do it now," he said. "While there's still enough light. I'll tell the cook to hold your order a few minutes. The rest of you can have another round on the house."

Kelly laughed. Rick was a perfectionist, which was why his restaurant was so great. You couldn't really wish him any other way.

"I guess I'd better go take a look," she said, smiling at the others as she dropped her napkin on the tabletop and slid out of the booth. "Rick's got a one-track mind. He won't feed us until I do."

As soon as she got outside, she wished she'd brought her sweater. The temperature was dropping along with the sun, which was already low enough to cast a pink sizzle on the river. Rick had been right, of course. After dinner it would be far too dark to evaluate the problem.

Excusing herself and squeezing in among the tables, she approached the window. First she ran her fingers along the soldering lines, checking to see if the individual pieces were holding firm. They were. That was good. She packed all outside windows with cement, aware that they would face the elements, and she was pleased to see that the connections were still airtight.

The problem appeared to be with the placement in the window opening, which was a simpler matter. Some of the cement along the edges was breaking away. It wasn't in imminent danger, but if she didn't reinforce it soon, the whole thing might topple over the next time Rick had one of his jitterbug weekends.

She could come back in the morning. It was all outside work, so the Ramble didn't even have to be open.

She began making her way back through the tables when she noticed that one of the diners was Jacob Griggs. She started to go over to say hello, but then she realized that he was deep in conversation with Reverend Banks, the minister who had officiated at Lillith's funeral.

She glanced around, wondering if Tom were somewhere nearby. She knew that he'd decided to stay with Jacob a few days. The two men had eaten lunch twice in Mary Jo's Café, and of course Mary Jo had called Kelly right away to fill her in.

Kelly scanned the other tables. No Tom. Then she remembered the overlook, a small, rounded boardwalk that jutted over the river for sightseeing. Rick had installed pellet dispensers so that children could enjoy feeding the fish below.

About half a dozen people were out there now, appreciating the sunset on the water. Tom was one of them. He bent over the railing, a little separate from the others. Something in his posture told Kelly he wasn't particularly fascinated by the fish or the river. He was probably just giving Jacob some private time with the preacher.

It was the chance she'd been waiting for.

She cast a guilty glance toward the interior of the restaurant. Lawton, Jeannie and her husband seemed to be enjoying themselves—maybe even more than they had when

Kelly was with them. They wouldn't miss her if she stayed away a few more minutes.

She walked out onto the overlook.

"Hi, Tom."

He turned slowly.

"Hi, there," he said with that tilted smile. "What a coincidence. I was just thinking about you."

That stopped her in her tracks. "You were?" She wondered if he was teasing her. "What were you thinking?"

"I was thinking how well you captured the mood of this river in your stained glass."

In spite of herself, she looked back toward the restaurant. Now that the light was shifting, and it was brighter inside the dining room than out here on the patio, the stained-glass windows were clearly visible.

She knew which one he meant. In one three-foot arched window, she had designed an abstract version of the river at sunset. She had combined some extraordinary green and pink ripples and exquisite blue mottles for the water, and pink and blue opals for the sky. She'd found the finished product extremely satisfactory, although Rick's patrons always seemed to prefer the more representational windows, like the speckled fish or the bridge between the trees.

"Thanks," she said. "It's easy to create when you're inspired by something this beautiful."

"I can imagine," he said.

And then he seemed to wait, as if he were aware she must have something specific to say. He had always been good at reading her mind, she remembered. For instance, he had seemed to know the very second she fell in love with him.

"Something has happened," she said. "Something strange. I don't know what it means. Or if it even means anything. I wanted—I wanted to know what you thought."

He leaned against the railing and kept his gaze on her. "All right," he said. "Tell me."

She glanced one more time toward the restaurant. They still didn't seem to be missing her. She'd steal these minutes, and then, when she returned, she'd make it up to poor Lawton by being completely focused on him.

She wished she'd brought her purse out with her. The piece of lace was in it. Ever since Trig Boccardi's strange confrontation in the alleyway, she hadn't felt quite safe leaving it lying around.

"Have you seen the roadside marker that someone put up in the spot where Lillith died?"

Tom nodded. "Jacob saw it. He's still pretty emotional, of course, and it doesn't take much to set him off. But he seemed pleased to know that someone cared enough to do it."

"Did he have any idea who had put it there?"

"Not really. He said maybe Lillith's parents had arranged it, but when he talked to them, they said no. Then he thought maybe you had. I take it you didn't?"

"No. I have no idea who did. But the other night, when I first saw it, there was a piece of lace draped over the wreath of flowers. Not part of the arrangement, just stuck there, almost as if it had fallen across it by accident."

He cocked his head. "So?"

"So it was an unusual piece of lace. Unique, actually. Handmade, very beautiful, with an intricate pattern of skylarks and cherry blossoms."

She waited to see if he registered any awareness.

He didn't. He frowned a little, as if he wondered where this was going. "And?"

"And I've seen that pattern, that lace, before. Haven't you?"

"I don't think so. Where would I have seen it?"

"On Sophie's wedding dress."

"Oh." He made a low sound. "I see."

"I brought it with me tonight, in my purse. I wish I could show it to you. You know Sophie's dress was one of a kind. Her mother had worn it, and her grandmother before her. If I could show you, you could tell me if you recognize—"

"No, I'm sorry." He stopped her by holding up one hand. "I couldn't. Sophie's mother was very old-school. Believed it was bad luck for the groom to see the bride in her wedding dress." He paused, and the tilted smile was back. "Rather ironic, when you consider how things turned out."

She didn't respond. Perhaps he made himself feel better by wryly mocking the whole situation, but she wasn't going to join him.

"Anyhow," he went on, "what difference does it make?" The shadows were lengthening, and she could no longer make out all his features clearly. "Maybe it is a piece of her dress. Maybe she put it there, or asked her mother to put it there, as a way of saying goodbye to Lillith. Is that so terrible? She was fond of all of us, once."

"Yes, but why, after all this time? No one has been in touch with Sophie in years. Some people went to see her, in the early days, but she wouldn't ever let them in. There may be more bitterness there than you realize."

"Perhaps, but just toward me," he said. "They never found out about—"

"About me? Are you so sure? She wouldn't see me, either. The word is that Sebastian and Mrs. Mellon, and maybe Samantha, too, held us all responsible. The whole wedding party. They feel that we gave up on Sophie too soon. They hold us responsible for her breakdown."

"Samantha doesn't," he said with a curious certainty. "And the others don't really believe that, either. If they say it, it's just because it's easier than the truth."

She looked at him, the question pushing at her throat. She had wanted to ask him this for ten years. But it had taken this disturbing week to give her the courage to speak the words.

"What *is* the truth, Tom?"

He met her gaze for a long minute, and then, finally, he turned and stared out over the blackening river. "The truth," he said without inflection, "is complicated."

It felt a little like being slapped. All these years she'd wondered, struggling with a suffocating guilt. Had he run away because of her? Had her foolish, star-crossed adoration led to her friend's emotional disintegration? He owed her an explanation. But then, he had owed one to Sophie, too, and to Kelly's knowledge he'd never given her one, either.

She stiffened her back.

"All right," she said. "Keep your secrets if you want to. After ten years, they aren't important to anyone but you. But there's something else. Something even more disturbing than a piece of old lace. Did you know that Kent Snyder and Dolly Dauten are dead, too?"

He turned, then, and she took a petty pleasure in seeing that this time she had shocked him. "You can't be serious."

"Yes, I am. I just found out this morning."

"What happened?"

"Kent was in a hunting accident two weeks ago, according to his girlfriend. He never stopped drinking, apparently. They think he was drunk and mishandled his gun."

"What about Dolly?"

"Apparently she had an accident, too. Six weeks ago. I talked to her husband this morning. He says she was standing on a crowded curb, waiting for the light to change, and she lost her balance. Remember how klutzy she was? She fell into the path of an oncoming truck."

"How horrible." He ran his hand through his hair. "I can't believe it."

"I couldn't either, at first. But it's true. And do you see what that means, Tom? That's three. Three out of ten in the past six weeks."

He frowned for a moment, and then he shook his head. "Don't think of it like that—it's misleading. It's not three out of ten, it's three out of three million. We weren't a family, or any statistically cohesive group. They are just three people who had tragic accidents. It doesn't *mean* anything—"

"Are you so sure of that? The night she died, Lillith told me—" She hesitated. She had meant only to ask him if he could identify the lace, and to see what his reaction was to the news of Kent's and Dolly's deaths.

This might be the one sentence that truly went too far.

"Lillith told you what?"

"She told me she'd heard that Sophie is out again."

He went very still. His eyes glimmered in the fast-fading light. When he spoke, his voice was low. "For God's sake, Kelly. What are you saying?"

She gripped the railing hard, just for the comfort of feeling something solid. For days now, she'd been grappling with formless nightmares, and she'd told herself that the courageous thing to do was to tear off the veil and call them by their name.

But what if their name was a name she had once loved?

"I don't know," she said. "I honestly don't know."

CHAPTER EIGHT

SEBASTIAN MELLON was not in a good mood.

First, the news about his mother's health was grim. He'd skipped a week of work to go to Coeur Volé, and it was a week he could scarcely afford to miss.

While he was there, they had discussed Sophie, of course. He'd had to lie to his mother, just to calm her down. He'd told her that Sophie was fine, that he knew exactly where she was.

But he didn't. And that, perhaps was at the heart of his foul humor.

He knew Sophie was getting his e-mails. Why the hell wasn't she answering him?

He stood in front of the full-length mirror in his bedroom, buttoning his collar and straightening his tie. He could see Gwen in the background, hovering over by the door, trying to get up the courage to speak.

Perversely, that whipped-puppy look annoyed him, too, although he knew he'd been harsh earlier. He crooked his finger. "Come here," he said. "I'm not going to eat you, for God's sake."

Gwen smiled, just a touch tremulously, and her reflection began walking toward him in the mirror. She put her hand on his shoulder. "You look great," she said. "That suit is super."

He tugged one more time on his tie and scanned the overall effect with a critical eye. She always said that, particularly when she was trying to placate him, so her compliments meant very little. But this time she was right. The tailor had done a good job.

"I'm sorry about earlier," she said. "You know your scars don't bother me, Sebastian. I never even notice them."

He bit back a curt response. If she didn't notice the scars, why was she always talking about them? She was forever mentioning something she'd seen on TV or read in the papers, some miracle lotion or massage, some breakthrough in cosmetic surgery.

He knew his scars were hideous. He should—he had lived with them since he was fifteen years old. He could draw a map of every purple-red, crosshatched welt—or *pigmented keloid,* as the doctor preferred to say, because it sounded less disgusting.

More to the point, Sebastian had had the scars when he'd met Gwen, when she'd agreed to marry him. He'd shown them to her. And she had sworn she didn't care. She'd even smothered them in kisses, to prove how much she loved every inch of him.

Pure theater, of course. He'd always known they turned her off. She made love with her eyes shut from the very first night. But he didn't care. He always shut his eyes, too. Like her, he would rather let his imagination build a more perfect picture.

Still, they'd managed to produce two very special children. Tessa was four and Seamus was three.

"Isn't Tessa going to be late for preschool?

Gwen glanced at her watch. "We've got another four minutes. She's putting her shoes on."

Sebastian picked up his briefcase. "I'll go in and kiss her goodbye."

Gwen stood where she, too, could get a goodbye peck, but he didn't offer one. If she couldn't be sensitive to his feelings, he couldn't see why he should be sensitive to hers.

Tessa was different. He stood in the doorway for a minute, just admiring the determination with which his daughter was attacking the problem of shoelaces. She was going to be a beauty, with her perfectly shaped blond head, her spunky blue eyes and flower-bud pink lips. She was going to be sexy and smart and brave, and no one was ever going to hurt her.

"Daddy!" She sensed his presence and jumped up, leaving one sneaker untied. She wrapped her arms around his waist and buried her face in his stomach.

He took her head in his hands and ruffled her silky hair. "What are you going to do at school today, Tessie?"

She lifted her face and grinned up at him. "I'm going to learn a million things and be the smartest girl in the world."

This was their daily ritual. And every night, when he tucked her into bed, he asked her what she was going to dream. "I'm going to dream about you, Daddy," she'd say. They'd link pinkies, and he'd say, "Okay, then. See you in dreamland."

He couldn't help being proud of her. He had done this, created this perfectly confident and joyous creature. He had defied his Mellon heritage, his role models, his own rotten childhood. He had, for four long years, managed to control whatever beasts lay buried in his genes.

He had never, ever laid a hand on this little girl. He'd never even raised his voice to her, and when she was in the house he was careful to speak softly to Gwen, too, however harsh the words themselves might be.

He didn't believe in God, but still he said a prayer to whatever Fates controlled these things. *Please,* he said. *I must not fail. When she gets older, and even more beautiful...*

I won't become my father.

Tessa hugged him again, rubbing her face against his belly. "I love you, Daddy," she said.

He picked up his briefcase, and he noticed that the palm of his hand was sweaty. God. Not already.

He *must* find Sophie. He couldn't do this alone, but if he had her to help him, he might be all right.

It was ironic, really. Sophie, the most dysfunctional, the most damaged of all the Mellons, still had the power to save him.

And by God, she'd better do it.

"BRIAN, BRING ME THE SCISSORS, would you, please?" Kelly reached her hand out from under the paper-covered frame of the half-finished winery entrance. "And stop looking at naughtycollegegirls.com on my computer. You're going to get me on every pervert spam list in cyberspace."

Brian made an indignant sound. She heard the scrape of his stool, and then he peeked under the sheet that covered the frame. He held out the scissors.

"I'll have you know I'm not looking at porn," he said. "For your information, I'm browsing the autumn sale site at cheapweddingrings.com."

She shook her head, accepted the scissors, and then returned to her work. "Born romantic, aren't you?" She blew a strand of hair out of her eyes. "No wonder Marie kicked you out."

"That's not why." His sneakers shuffled back toward the computer. "Marie kicked me out for the same reason you kicked me out. Because I leave the OJ out and the toilet seat up. And I belch my beer."

"Good for her. Power to the sisters."

Brian chuckled softly and began tapping the computer keys. After a couple of moments of comfortable silence, Kelly heard someone knocking at the door.

"Hey," she called out. "Get that for me, would you?"

"But of course." The stool scraped back again. "I live to serve."

Brian opened the door. She heard murmuring, but she couldn't identify the voices. After a couple of seconds, curiosity got the better of her, and she crawled out of the winery tunnel to see what was happening.

The man standing at the door, wearing an expensive suit and tie, was a total stranger. He was holding some kind of portfolio under his arm. He looked like a salesman, except that his face was long and sad, without an ounce of that perky boy-cheerleader style she'd come to associate with door-to-door types.

Still, he must be a salesman. She wondered why Brian, who knew she didn't have any money to spend on new gizmos right now, hadn't dispatched him right away.

"Someone to see you," Brian said, shrugging and giving her a *How should I know, it's your door* look.

The dark-haired, well-groomed stranger stared at her intently, as if she wasn't at all what he expected. She reached up and pulled a dust bunny from her hair, wondering how scruffy she looked.

"Are you Kelly Ralston?"

She came forward and set down the scissors. "Yes," she said. "And you are—?"

"Phil Tammaro. I'm Dolly's husband. We spoke on the telephone a couple of days ago." He hesitated. "Do you remember?"

"Of course." Kelly couldn't have been more surprised. When they'd talked, Phil had offered nothing but negatives. No, he hadn't ever heard about Sophie Mellon. No, Dolly hadn't mentioned getting any weird phone calls shortly before she died. No, the police didn't think there was anything suspicious about the accident. No, he hadn't seen any scraps of unusual lace lying around that might have come from a wedding gown.

Actually, by the time they'd hung up, Kelly had the impression Phil Tammaro thought she might be just this side of certifiable.

"Please, come in, Phil," she said, whisking the unsorted mail from the only real chair in the room. "It's just that I—I wasn't expecting to see you. Did you drive here all the way from Atlanta?"

He nodded. "It's only a couple of hours. And I—" He looked around the room with a lost-puppy look in his large brown eyes. "I am taking some time off from work anyhow, right now. I have plenty of time."

He looked as if he hadn't had much sleep in weeks. Though the two men were physically very different, right now he looked a lot like Jacob Griggs.

"I'm glad you did," she said. "It's good to meet you in person. I'm so sorry about Dolly."

He nodded. "Thanks."

Finally she remembered her manners. "Phil, this is my ex-husband, Brian."

Brian handled it well. She'd told him all about Kent Snyder and Dolly Tammaro. He didn't find the coincidence as alarming as she did, but he hadn't completely dismissed it, either. Not like Tom Beckham. In fact, that was probably why Brian was hanging around the studio so much these days. He might think, in his gut, that it was all a tempest in a teapot, but he still had that sweet protective instinct.

"Hi, Phil," Brian said. "I'm so sorry to hear about your wife. It must be a really rough time."

"Yes." Phil sat down on the chair Kelly had cleared for him. He was holding the portfolio in his lap carefully. Kelly got the impression he was by nature an extremely careful man. What a strange match for clumsy, impulsive Dolly.

"I'm sorry to just show up like this," he said. "Ordinarily I wouldn't, but I found something while I was going through Dolly's studio. I thought about calling, but it seemed better just to let you see it."

Kelly's stomach knotted. "What did you find?"

He was frowning, tapping his fingers lightly on the leather portfolio.

"I don't know. Maybe it's nothing. But—" He broke off. "Dolly was a fashion designer, did you know that? She wasn't exactly haute couture, but she was making a name for herself in Atlanta. She always got offered more work than she could accept."

"No, I didn't know that," Kelly said. "I— We hadn't been in touch in a long time. Not since the wedding."

"I know. That's why I'm explaining. For the past year, she'd been doing mostly uniforms, you know, for major hotels and restaurants in town who wanted their staff to have a special look. It's a bigger market than you'd realize, though of course it wasn't exactly her dream job."

Kelly tried not to show any impatience, though she was dying to know what was in that portfolio. Luckily, Phil seemed to recognize without prompting that he was wandering off topic.

"I only mention what she'd been designing lately, because, well, it helps you to understand why I was so surprised by what I found. And after your call, after what you described, well, I just didn't know what it meant."

He still sat there, staring up at them, his hands limp on the portfolio, as if he couldn't think what to do next.

Brian, ever practical, jumped in. "Maybe you should just show us," he said with an encouraging smile. "You know, a picture's worth a thousand words, and all that."

Phil nodded. He untied the leather strip that held the portfolio together and held it out to Kelly. "Yes, look for yourselves. You'll see what I mean."

Kelly slid the large portfolio onto her cutting table, where the light was good. Brian came over to get a better look, but Phil just sat in the chair, as if he might be slightly catatonic with depression.

She opened the leather binding and looked at the first page. And then the second. Nothing unusual. Just a haphazard smattering of sketches of smartly tailored uniforms. Some aprons, some shirts and skirts. Even a logo or two for name badges.

Dolly had a flair for style. Kelly's artistic eye recognized real talent. Interesting that Dolly's personal awkwardness had not extended to her designs.

But this all seemed to match what Phil had said her commissions were. What had shocked him so much he had loaded this portfolio into his car and driven two hours to show it to her?

She kept turning. More pages, more uniforms. Blue slacks with yellow polo shirts. Pink pinafores that vaguely resembled hospital candy stripers, except with a subtle elegance. White shirtwaist dresses, next to which Dolly had printed, in bold letters, IMPRACTICAL.

Kelly turned another sheet. And then she saw it.

Sophie Mellon's wedding dress.

Over and over, obsessively, Dolly had sketched the unique and glamorous gown that Sophie Mellon would have been married in. Sometimes she drew the entire dress, sometimes just a detail of the lace, complete with cherry blossoms and skylarks.

The first few full-length sketches weren't quite right, and some of them she'd scratched through, as if annoyed with herself for forgetting how the princess neckline had been rimmed in white fur, or how the bodice had been gathered between the breasts. With each sketch, Dolly had come closer, until finally she had it exactly right.

She never seemed to guess about the lace itself. The sketches of the lace were always perfect, down to the smallest detail.

Brian touched her arm, and she realized she'd barely been breathing. "Is this it?" he asked.

She nodded.

"Are you sure?"

She nodded again. She went over to her purse and

pulled out the long swatch of lace she'd found on the road-side marker. She unfolded it carefully, then lay it on the sketchbook, next to the life-size detail that Dolly had drawn.

They were identical.

"But—" Phil Tammaro had finally risen from his seat. "What can this possibly mean?"

Kelly started to say something, anything. But Brian beat her to it.

"It means somebody better check to make sure Sophie Mellon is still in that loony bin where she belongs. That's what it means."

SOPHIE MELLON ENTERED her apartment with a lurch and locked the door behind her. Then she sat on the edge of the bed and tried to catch her breath.

The key in her hand felt hot. She must have been squeezing it very hard. She scanned the room, which was neat and clean, though not lovely. If only there were some place to temporarily hide the key from herself. Just until the worst of the anxiety passed.

This was the hardest part about being out of the clinic. The knowledge that no one was in charge. The awareness that, if she felt the urge to do something bad, the only person who could stop her was the person she trusted least of all.

Herself.

She went into the bathroom and dropped the key into a bottle of shampoo. There. At least now she'd have to fish it out and wash the suds away before she could use it. Sometimes, just five minutes was enough to make a difference.

But going into the bathroom had been a mistake, too. Because suddenly she saw the razor.

She yanked the shower curtain shut, hiding the piece of cheap green plastic with its shining silver head. She mustn't even think about it. She mustn't imagine the thin line of blood beading on her skin, the small opening that released so much pressure and finally allowed her to breathe.

If she pictured it too clearly, she'd have to do it.

And cutting was wrong. Everyone had said so, all her life. The wrong way to handle things, Sophie. The wrong way to deal with stress.

Only problem was, she didn't know what the right way was. None of their pills or self-help mantras or group therapies did any good, not when she was so swollen with tension and fear that she thought she might explode.

So what was she supposed to do when the feelings built up like this? How was she supposed to give herself any relief? One stupid doctor had said she had "suicidal ideation," which was crap. Cutting wasn't about dying. It was about feeling better.

She never cut very deep. Just a little blood, a little pain. Surely that wasn't as destructive as the other things she'd thought of doing.

The other things she *had* done.

And would undoubtedly do again, if she couldn't get relief any other way.

She reached behind the shower curtain and picked up the razor. She'd rather have the old fashioned kind, with real, double-edged blades you could take out and hold in your hand. But the therapists had told her it wasn't wise to keep temptation so close. They had advised her to use an electric system, but she didn't like that. It left stubble on her legs.

And besides, it made her feel safe to know the razor was here. Just in case of an emergency.

Like today.

She wasn't sure how to get the blade out of the handle. She bent and pulled until the tips of her fingers were nicked and sore. The frustration was making things worse. If she didn't get it open soon, she'd just have to use it like this, although it wouldn't be as precise.

And she liked the control. Needed it. The control was part of the relief.

Finally, as she grew more frantic, she put the head of the razor between her teeth and bit down until the green plastic cracked. She felt the blade give, and then she was able to wiggle it out easily.

She felt calmer right away, just holding it, just knowing its power was hers. The urgency died down a little, and she was able to take off her clothes slowly, folding them on the foot of the bed.

Then she lay on the bed, too, face up, and shut her eyes, allowing faces and feelings to float in front of her. Her father. Her mother. Sebastian. Tom.

She lifted her hand and let the cool blade touch her skin. The faces came faster as her lungs tightened, and her legs stiffened in anticipation. Bill, Sam, Alex, Lillith, Kent, Kelly, Sebastian, Dolly, Tom, Kelly, Tom, Daddy, Tom…

She could tell by the slicing pain that she'd gone deeper than she'd meant to. But maybe she'd needed more this time, because it had been so long.

It felt good. She could feel terrible things rushing out of her.

She opened her eyes and rose up on her elbows, eager to see. A red line, two inches below her belly button, ran from hipbone to hipbone. The blood spurted a little as she leaned forward, exerting pressure.

She fell back against the pillow, soothed by the wet tickle of the blood seeping across her skin. It kept coming, until its warmth ran down into the fine, blond hair between her legs.

She closed her eyes. Sleep would follow quickly, and this time there would be no dreams.

CHAPTER NINE

WITH A PHOTOCOPY of Dolly's sketches tucked under her arm, and the swatch of lace folded in her purse, Kelly rang the bell beside Jacob Griggs's front door.

She had been relieved to see Tom's sports car was still in the driveway. This wasn't going to be easy, but Jacob seemed to draw strength from Tom's friendship, so she was glad they'd be together when they discussed these troubling new developments.

Plus, it seemed only fair that Tom should be warned, as well.

She checked herself. *Warned* might be too strong a word. She didn't want to come across as paranoid, which would just make them discount everything she said. Still, though she didn't know what was really going on here, whatever it was clearly focused on Sophie's wedding party.

And Tom was, without doubt, the most important member of the wedding party.

It took a couple of minutes, but finally the door opened. It was Tom.

"Kelly," he said. "Hi."

It amazed her how composed he always managed to appear, even when she knew he must be surprised to see her.

She didn't have that skill. The sight of him had always roused too many contradictory emotions. Attraction, guilt, anxiety…it was instant psychic chaos. Her heart began to jig around awkwardly in her chest, and she knew he knew it, and there wasn't a damn thing she could do about it.

Except ignore it, the way she might ignore heartburn, and get on with the business at hand.

"I hope this isn't a bad time." She spoke more formally than she had intended, like a Realtor showing up to do an appraisal or something. But she had to overcome that foolish instinct to flutter. "I need to talk to you and Jacob."

His face tightened slightly. His gaze flicked to the papers she had under her arm. "About what?"

The question wasn't just a perfunctory conversational bridge. He wanted to know, and he didn't intend to move away from the door until she told him.

He tilted his head, as if her hesitation made him suspicious. "About what, Kelly?"

Maybe the stress of the past week and a half had left her edgy. But suddenly she found his arrogance annoying as hell.

Who did he think he was, passing judgment on her right to enter? Kelly had been a welcome guest in this home a thousand times. She'd helped Lily pick out the living-room wallpaper. That Chinese vase on the mantel had been her housewarming gift.

She even had her own emergency copy of the front door key.

So how dare this man, who hadn't set foot in this town for ten years, appoint himself keeper of the gate? She'd forgotten more about Jacob and Lillith Griggs than Tom Beckham would ever know.

She glared at him for a long second, and then she simply pushed past him. He didn't resist very hard. When her shoulder hit his chest, he gave way easily.

Once she was inside, she looked around the great room, which was empty. Profoundly empty, as if Lillith's absence had changed everything.

Kelly turned back to Tom. "Where is he?"

"Asleep." Tom seemed to have accepted his defeat gracefully. He shut the door without a sound and stood there watching her. "He went through some of Lillith's clothes today, and it did him in. He's still pretty weak, you know."

"Of course I know," she said. "But I wouldn't be here if it weren't important."

"I'm sorry. He's sleeping."

She lifted her chin. "Wake him up."

"No." Tom shook his head. "If you'd seen him this morning, Kelly, you wouldn't ask me to. He almost never sleeps. He's making himself sick."

He crossed the foyer and put his hand on her shoulder. "Look, we're on the same side here. We both want to help him. You said you wanted to talk to both of us. Why don't you start with me?"

She felt her feathers go down a little. He was right. They both wanted the best for Jacob. And, if her fears about these three deaths had any truth to them, they might have another goal in common, too.

Staying safe.

"Okay," she said. She shifted the sketches to her other hand. "I know you didn't believe there was anything unusual about the fact that three members of Sophie's wedding party have had fatal accidents—"

"I didn't say it wasn't unusual," he corrected her. "I just didn't think three accidents in three different places over the course of ten years inevitably led to the kind of conspiracy theory you were building. Life's messy, Kelly. Bad things happen."

"But what about the piece of wedding dress I found on the marker?"

He raised his shoulders. "I don't know. My best guess would be that one of the Mellons could have put it there, as a way of saying goodbye to Lillith."

"Yes, I know you suggested that before," she said. "And I considered it. But why do that? Why not just send flowers? Tearing a strip of lace from an heirloom, one-of-a-kind wedding dress, and then anonymously hanging it on a roadside marker is a very strange way of saying goodbye, don't you think?"

He smiled. "The Mellons are strange people. But maybe it's not even the same lace. Maybe you saw lace, your subconscious jumped to conclusions, and—"

He must have seen the rejection in her eyes, because he stopped himself midsentence.

"Okay, so maybe you really can remember every detail of a wedding dress you saw a couple of times, more than ten years ago. If Sophie's family put it there, even if they meant it as an accusation of some sort, it's just pathetic, not sinister. There was no weird lace-offering associated with the other two deaths, was there?"

"I didn't think so." She walked into the dining room and lay the sketches on the glossy mahogany table, where several days ago funeral casseroles had spread from end to end. "Until today."

He followed her slowly. She watched him cross the

foyer, rolling up the sleeves of his white oxford-cloth shirt, which he wore untucked over a pair of jeans. He wasn't looking at her. He was eyeing the papers she'd just set down.

He reached out and flipped two or three of the pages over. "What is this?"

"It's Sophie's wedding dress. Dolly's husband brought these sketches to me this morning. It seems Dolly drew them just days before she died."

Tom paused at the page that showed the full-length dress in the clearest detail. It occurred to Kelly that this was his first-ever view of the gown Sophie would have been wearing while she waited for him to show up at the church.

Kelly wondered if he had any idea how completely magical Sophie had looked in it. Its fragile white beauty against her ivory skin and blond hair had been perfect— she'd seemed to be carved out of sparkling snow. When she'd begun to cry, her tears had sparkled, too, and she had only looked more beautiful.

"Why?" He looked over at Kelly. "Why was Dolly drawing this dress?"

"I wish I knew," she said. "That's the question, isn't it? But it can't have been a coincidence. It wasn't as if Dolly was obsessed with Sophie or the wedding. She'd never even mentioned it to her husband."

"She's talented," he said thoughtfully, turning the pages back and forth. "Is she an artist?"

"A freelance fashion designer."

"Well, then, that must be it. She was designing a wedding gown, and this one had impressed her. So she dug it out of her memory, and—"

"Except she wasn't designing a wedding gown. She was working on a set of uniforms for a chain of five-star steak houses."

He didn't have an answer to that one. She watched him wrestle with the logic, trying to find a way to interpret these signs any other way.

He obviously couldn't.

Finally he looked up at her. "Do you still have the lace you found on the roadside marker?"

She nodded, opening her purse. She extracted the lace and handed it to him.

At first, he seemed reluctant to touch it. Finally, with a hint of determination, he slid two fingers under it and scooped it up. He stared at it for a long minute, dangling there from his hand.

Two small tears spoiled the pattern, and the edges were sooty from the time spent hanging on the side of the road. But even so it was exquisite, like spiderwebs from fairyland. Even a man would recognize the hours of blinding, delicate work that had gone into every yard of such remarkable fabric.

Slowly he spread it out on the table, lining it up carefully next to Dolly's sketch. He took in a hard breath, just as Kelly, Brian and Phil had done when, in her studio, they had first recognized the perfect match.

She wrapped her arms across her chest, feeling a sudden chill. She had dreamed about this lace many times through the years. Sometimes she was wearing it, but hiding in shadowy corners, ashamed that she had stolen Sophie's dress. Sometimes she dreamed that Sophie wore it, but she could never see Sophie's face. The lace swaddled her like mummy wrappings. Like a shroud.

"I see why you were so sure," Tom said quietly. "It is… unforgettable."

Yes. Unforgettable. That was the perfect word for the whole incredible experience. None of them had ever been able to forget.

Taking a deep breath, he stood up straight. "I know what you're thinking, Kelly. And I agree that there are plenty of serious questions that need to be answered here. But let's don't jump to wild conclusions. There is probably still a logical explanation."

"What is it, then?" She shook her head. "If you have one, please, tell me. Prove that I'm paranoid, crazy, delusional, the victim of an overactive guilty conscience, I don't care what. I just don't want to be right."

His hands were on his hips. His dark eyes were narrow, his mental focus all directed inward.

Then he glanced toward the staircase. "I don't want you to mention this to Jacob, not yet. Can you do that, Kelly? Can you give me a day or two to ask some questions, see if I can sort this out?"

Instinctively, she lowered her voice. "Don't you think he has a right to know? I mean, if Lillith's accident wasn't—"

"There will be time enough to tell him, if it turns out there really is anything to be worried about." He gave her a small smile. "Probably it's nothing, you know that, don't you? Don't let your nerves get away with you. The old adage is true. The simplest explanation is usually the correct one."

Her throat felt strangely dry, but she didn't take her eyes off his. "And what is the simplest explanation?"

"That's what we have to find out."

"How?"

He caught the dirty lace up in his hand and closed his fingers over it firmly, making a fist.

"We'll have to start by finding out where the rest of this dress is. We'll have to start at Coeur Volé."

As Tom drove up the curving entrance to Coeur Volé, he tried to remember exactly how this place had looked to him ten years ago.

He'd been only twenty-five then, and not particularly sophisticated about what it took to succeed in the professional world. He had assumed that, just because Coeur Volé was old and huge, it would have been an asset to any ambitious young lawyer.

He had pictured himself practicing law in Atlanta, of course, with Sophie, his sexy blond heiress wife, at his side. But occasionally they'd invite important clients back here for a dose of social shock and awe. *Why don't we spend the weekend at Coeur Volé,* he had imagined himself tossing off casually. *Do a little fishing, take a breather from the city.*

That pompous-ass attitude might have worked if his clients had all been dukes and marquesses out of nineteenth-century British novels instead of rock stars, slumlords, computer-software geniuses just out of high school and guys with thick glasses and no social skills who had become millionaires by inventing the world's most comfortable jockstrap.

And it might have worked if Coeur Volé hadn't been so damn creepy. Why hadn't he seen that? He certainly saw it now, as he drew closer and the house slid into view.

The architecture was a mess, part Victorian wedding

cake, part Gothic cathedral. The windows were hooded and secretive, like half-shut eyes, its doors heavy and unwelcoming, like a mouth taped shut.

And that thrusting tower—it was so clearly phallic it was almost like a visual dirty joke.

The landscaping was the worst, though. Who would have thought that nature possessed so many purple, garnet, black-green and chocolate plants? Would it have killed the groundskeepers to plant a nice pink periwinkle or something?

With the exception of the elms, which had been planted strictly for privacy, the trees were all Gothic and strange— cedars that had white, wind-tortured bodies, and weeping willows that drooped suicidally over the black-mirror surface of the ornamental pond.

He parked his car by the front door and got out, listening to the autumn wind playing the willows like mournful green harps. No, Coeur Volé wouldn't have been an asset—it would have been an albatross. *Beckham's wife is a weird one,* people would have said behind his back. And other people would have answered, *Hell, yes, she is. And have you seen that spooky old crypt she grew up in?*

On the other hand, if he had married Sophie, if he had taken her away from all this, maybe she would gradually have stopped being so weird.

Maybe.

But he hadn't married her. And it was too late to go around beating himself up over it now. Self-flagellation might make him feel virtuous and purified, but it wouldn't do Sophie a damn bit of good.

He rang the bell, hoping that Samantha would answer. Mrs. Mellon had never liked him much, even before he'd ditched her daughter. Samantha, at least, had made an effort to be polite, the night he arrived, the night of Lillith's funeral.

He got lucky. Sam opened the door almost immediately, and the sight of her was like a ray of sunshine making its way into a dungeon. She wore a pretty pink dress, the exact pastel that he'd felt was missing from the landscaping. Her shining hair was tied back loosely at the nape of her neck, and her surprised but welcoming smile made her look sixteen again.

"Tom!" She put out her hand. "How great to see you! Come in!"

He smiled back, but resisted her tugging. "I'm not sure that's a good idea, Sam. I don't think your mother would want me in her house."

Samantha raised her eyebrows. "It's my house, too," she said softly. But she stopped tugging. Obviously she knew he was right.

"Let's not risk stirring her up," he said. "Especially since she's sick. I just wanted to talk to you for a few minutes. Can we maybe sit out here?"

"Well…" She glanced back toward the staircase, a little nervously. With the door open like this, Tom could just barely make out the lower third of the St. George window, one of Coeur Volé's truly beautiful works of art.

"Let's go out back, okay?" Samantha smiled again. "There's more privacy there."

Tom disagreed with that, but he didn't say so. He hated the back gardens, and had never felt truly alone out there. It was all those disturbing statues.

There were so damn many of them.

Angels with bony, bat-like wings. Naked nymphs, their

arms up in front of their faces, warding off some invisible terror. Sly gargoyles and hooded *pleurants.* Marble snakes, always coming toward you. Bronze fawns, always startled…

And of course the infamous fallen woman, a female figure knocked over by God only knew what force of nature, and inexplicably left there to sink into the earth, swallowed up by the hungry ferns. Ten years ago, only her hand and her white, resigned face had been visible. By now she was probably only a memory, and a troubling lump under the grass.

"Sure," he said, trying to sound enthusiastic. "That would be fine."

She led him past the gardener's shed, out to the sunniest spot in the garden, a nook off in the western corner, one of the few places not overlooked by any of the mansion's windows. You could hear the river here and the hum of traffic from the bridge.

He liked it, until, after a minute or so, the hair on the back of his neck began to crawl. Was someone watching them? He turned, scanned the bushes, and finally found a pair of eyes. A frozen, cast-iron child stared blankly at him from behind a bank of dark red climbing roses.

Samantha followed his gaze, laughed a little and patted the statue on the head. "They do get on the nerves a little, don't they? But mother loves them. And eventually you just get used to them."

She plucked a weed from the rose bed, and then sat beside him, twirling it between her thumb and index finger. "So, what did you want to talk about, Tom? It must be something important, to get you back here after all these years."

"I'm not sure how important it is," he said, "because I'm not really sure what's going on. It's awkward, Sam, but I was hoping you could help me figure it out."

"Okay. I'll try, but—" She hesitated. "What's it about? Is it Sophie?"

At first he wondered why she zeroed in on Sophie, but then he realized it made sense. Sophie was the only point of intersection between Tom and the Mellon family. And for much of Samantha's adult life, her troubled sister had probably been the subject of most "awkward" discussions at Coeur Volé.

"In a way, yes. Actually, it's about her wedding dress."

She frowned. "Her *wedding* dress?"

He watched her carefully. If he'd had to place a bet, he would have guessed that her shock was genuine. This was not what she'd thought he was going to say.

But, he reminded himself, he didn't know her very well anymore. The past ten years might have turned her into quite an actress.

"Yes. Some odd things have been happening, Sam. A strip of lace that looks an awful lot like Sophie's wedding dress turned up on the roadside marker where Lillith Griggs had her accident."

She was still frowning. "Really? How weird."

"It gets even weirder. There's reason to believe that another of Sophie's bridesmaids, Dolly Dauten—do you remember her?—had seen a piece of that wedding dress recently, too."

"Wait, I'm lost. Are you saying you think Dolly somehow got hold of a piece of Sophie's dress and put it on Lillith's roadside marker?"

If only the answer could be that simple.

"No," he said, choosing his words carefully, glancing over his shoulder. He wished he could lose the edgy feeling they were being watched. Maybe he should knock that creepy little girl statue over, too, and let her join the fallen woman. Maybe he should knock them all over.

Samantha leaned forward. "Why not? Couldn't that have been what happened?"

"No," he said again. "Dolly couldn't have done it, because Dolly is dead, too. She died six weeks ago."

"Oh, my God. How?"

"She was in an accident, too. Not a car accident. Just one of those crazy, terrible things that happen sometimes."

Samantha looked away for a minute, staring out toward the low rush of the river, although you couldn't see much water from here, just a sliver of silver ripples between the trees. Her hands, folded in her lap with the plucked clover between her fingers, were clamped very tightly together.

Finally she looked back at him, and he saw that she'd started putting the pieces together and didn't like the picture that was developing.

"What exactly are you saying, Tom? Before we go any further, I think you'd better be very clear about what you're implying."

"Sam, I'm sorry. I'm honestly not sure. All I know is, three members of Sophie's wedding party are dead—"

She narrowed her eyes. *"Three?"*

"Yes. Kent Snyder is dead, too. A hunting accident. But there's no reason yet to believe that any lace showed up in connection with his death. Anyhow, I don't know what it means, but the lace is there, Sam, and it needs to be explained. Your shock pretty much tells me you didn't have anything to do with it. So who might have?"

Samantha leaned over to pull another small clover from the rose bed. And then another, as if she couldn't bear them to remain there another minute. And then another.

It was a strange reaction. For the first time, he wondered if she was crazy, too. Was the Mellon gene pool so poisoned they couldn't produce a single normal offspring?

Or maybe she just needed time to think.

Finally she'd pulled all the ones she could reach from the bench. She straightened up, a bouquet of clover in her hand, and looked at him again.

"I'm not sure I should talk to you about this," she said finally. "Obviously you're saying that Sophie is somehow connected to those two deaths, and—"

"Not Sophie, Sam. Just her dress. I don't even know who has it now. Surely Sophie hasn't carted it around with her to one clinic after another for the past ten years, right?"

She bowed her head. "Of course not."

"So who has it? Who might have been able to get access to it?"

A shadow fell over their little sunny corner. Tom looked up, for one crazy minute entertaining the hair-raising thought that one of the statues had walked silently over to them. He noticed that Samantha jerked her head up, too.

But it wasn't a statue, though the woman standing there was as pale and gray as marble.

It was Mrs. Mellon.

"*I* have the dress," she said.

Samantha put out a hand. "Mother—"

Mrs. Mellon ignored her daughter. "Yes, I have it. It's here, at Coeur Volé. Hanging in Sophie's closet, where it has been ever since the day she took it off. The day you deserted and destroyed her."

Samantha stood up. "Mother, that's not—"

But Mrs. Mellon had eyes only for Tom. Fiery, over-bright eyes burning out of that ashen face. "You destroyed her, and you know it. You broke her trusting heart and her brave spirit and her poor, fragile mind. And now you dare to come here and accuse her of…of what? Of murdering her friends?"

He stood and faced the woman. How many years had she waited to say these things? Adler Mellon had spewed his fury right away, tracking Tom down after the wedding disaster, but Imogene Mellon had never had a chance to confront him. He waited, but she seemed to have run out of energy, for the moment.

If she thought he was going to defend himself by sud-denly, after ten years, blurting out his reasons for jilting Sophie, she was badly mistaken.

"I have no accusations, Mrs. Mellon. Only questions. Questions about the dress. I assume you heard what we've found."

"We? You mean you and that trashy Kelly Carpenter? Oh, yes, I know about her. I know that it took her a month to find the spine to visit Sophie, and that when she finally did Sophie refused to speak to her. I even know why."

He didn't answer that. He wasn't going to discuss Kelly with the Mellons.

"And how would you even know what Sophie's wed-ding dress looked like, Tom? You never saw it. I wouldn't let you see it. I knew from the start that there was some-thing wrong with you, that you'd hurt her in the end."

He didn't bother to refute that, either. He simply reached into his jacket pocket and pulled out the lace from the roadside marker. He shook out the folds and let it fall like water across the palm of his hand.

Samantha made a small, shocked sound. But Mrs. Mellon just stared at it for a long moment, her face hardening into lines of fury.

"I don't know what you're up to, you son of a bitch," she said. "But I want you to come with me. I have something I want to show you."

CHAPTER TEN

SHE TOOK HIM to Sophie's bedroom, which was on the third floor. Samantha followed them into the house, up the stairs, past St. George and the dragon, and all the way to Sophie's door. But there Mrs. Mellon, who had gone from gray to pure white from the exertion, turned and held up her palm.

"No, Samantha," she said. "Tom and I will go in alone."

The room was blue, of course. That didn't surprise him. Sophie's eyes were a striking turquoise, and she loved to echo that color everywhere, so that no one would neglect to notice.

What did surprise him was how like a little girl's room it was. In here, the color was bright and simple, like the blue you find in rock candy or bubble gum. The bed looked as if it came from an illustration for the book *A Little Princess*. Lacy white pillows were piled high on a shining blue satin comforter, and the whole confection was topped with a white canopy patterned with forget-me-nots. Against the pillows, stiff-legged and unnatural, a china doll dressed in forget-me-not ruffles simpered at him with an obscenely pink mouth and fixed, glassy blue eyes, like a catatonic nymphomaniac.

He stared back, strangely disgusted. It was just a doll,

and probably an expensive, collectible one. Still, he looked away quickly and told himself he was glad he'd never tried to make love to Sophie in here. He would have been as impotent as a twist of wet paper.

As Mrs. Mellon moved through the room, adjusting pillows, twitching the blue-flowered silky drapes, repositioning cushions, the scent of gardenias insinuated itself into his nostrils. He felt his stomach spasm, as usual, and he looked around the room for the source.

There it was, on the pristine white dresser—a low, wide bowl with at least two dozen blooms floating on the surface. He glanced at Mrs. Mellon curiously. He knew how fragile gardenias were. They didn't last long. If you so much as touched the velvety surface, it would turn brown under your fingers. Did she put fresh ones in here every day?

And where did she get them? They didn't bloom naturally in Georgia in the fall.

But there was no time to ask. She was already at the other end of the room, where an entire wall was nothing but doors. Closet doors. His stomach tightened even further. Behind those doors would hang a long line of sky-blue dresses, lilac sweaters, sapphire silk shirts…

And also, of course, a white lace wedding dress.

Mrs. Mellon didn't even look at him. She just slid open one of the noiseless doors. No fumbling, no false starts. She knew which one she wanted.

And there it was.

She took it out and, with her face set in grim lines, she hung it on a hook set into the wall for just such a purpose.

"Come," she ordered him. "You started this. Inspect it for yourself."

Tom was rarely at a complete loss, but this time he was. He was paralyzed, fascinated and repelled to the exact point of immobility, by the gown.

It glowed under the small crystal chandelier with an eerie light. Its hourglass, female form was brilliantly designed into the cut, so that it almost seemed the ghost of Sophie floated inside it.

He took in the details. Nearly transparent, fitted sleeves of the incredible lace. A regal rim of white fur around the low-cut, princess neckline. The fur so fine that it moved with every harsh breath Imogene Mellon took.

He, on the other hand, couldn't breathe at all.

He would never have guessed, from the one sad swatch of dingy lace Kelly had brought him, how magnificent the whole could be. The fabric gathered to a graceful knot between the breasts, and twinkling silver things, like tiny diamonds, were scattered everywhere. He could almost see Sophie gliding toward him, toward the altar. She would have looked like a walking moonbeam shot through with fairy stars.

"Can't you even bring yourself to touch it?" Mrs. Mellon grabbed the full, ethereal skirt and held it out. With a soft moan, she brought it to her cheek, which was almost as pale as the lace.

"No, of course you can't," she said. "You know this dress is made of my little girl's lost dreams. And my dreams, too, and her grandmother's. Three generations of Mellons have worn this dress, and you're afraid of us, aren't you?"

He shook his head. Ridiculous. And yet he didn't move.

"Oh, yes, you are." Her voice grew strident and her eyes blazed at him. "You're a coward, Tom. You always were.

You couldn't even face her when you changed your mind. You left her there, with all those people, all those flowers, all that shame."

She began to cry, an ugly, unpretentious noise. She balled the lace up in her fist and pressed it against her eyes. "You just *left* her there."

Damn it, he needed fresh air. He couldn't breathe.

"Mrs. Mellon, I wish things had been different. I wish I had been different. It doesn't help to say I'm sorry, but I am."

He was getting out of here. There was no need to prolong this ordeal, for either of them. He'd found out all he needed to know here. The material was the same, but it hadn't come from this dress. This dress was perfectly, hauntingly intact.

He wasn't sure she even heard him. He put his hand on the door. But then, all of a sudden, she seemed to realize that he was leaving. Dropping the dress with an anguished cry, she crossed the room and took hold of his sleeve.

"Wait," she said with an intensity that made him wince. "Tom, you know Sophie didn't do those terrible things. She's in a clinic, she's being taken care of—"

"I heard she was out," he said flatly. It was cruel, but this wasn't just another of the Mellon melodramas. Three people were dead. "I heard you don't know where she is."

"Yes, but she's back in now. She wasn't out when Lillith Griggs died." Mrs. Mellon fisted her hand on his sleeve and leaned closer. He could see the wet tracks of tears on her cheeks, and he could smell the desperation in her breath.

"Tom, please, be honest with yourself. You know what's wrong with Sophie. You must know better than anyone.

You know as well as I do that the only person on this earth she's ever hurt is herself."

IT TOOK TWO HOURS for Samantha to get her mother settled down after Tom left. Two hours to stop the tears and vitriol from pouring out of the newly opened crack in her heart.

It hadn't been easy, listening to her mother excoriate Tom with limitless fury. Samantha had bitten back all the natural responses that had been pushing at her throat. Responses like, well, if Sophie weren't so emotionally unbalanced, maybe people wouldn't think she was capable of dreadful things.

Responses like, has it ever occurred to you that some of us don't hate him? That some of us actually *care* about him?

She was proud that she had, in the end, been able to hold it all in. She'd learned, through the years, to articulate very little of what she was thinking.

But now that she was alone in the kitchen, she could ask herself the question that had been eating at her ever since she'd sat with Tom in the garden.

How deep did her feelings for him go?

All these years, she'd tried to tell herself her infatuation had been just that. A crush. A cliché, even. A seventeen-year-old girl, still in the ugly-duckling phase, meets the handsome prince who has come to woo her fabulous older sister. The prince is kind; the ugly duckling responds with fervent gratitude. She nurses the secret thrill of guilty love. But of course it isn't love, not really. Ugly duckling becomes a swan of her own, and remembers the kind prince fondly, but with self-effacing good humor.

That's how the story should have gone. But she should have known it wouldn't be that simple. The stories of the Mellon family never followed any "normal" script.

The truth was, she was still attracted to him. And more than that. She was drawn to his confidence, his intelligence…and something sad she thought she glimpsed behind his eyes.

God, more clichés. What was more ridiculous than holding on to an unrequited passion for ten years? Tom hadn't ever given her a thought as anything but Sophie's kid sister. He wouldn't have thought about her once since he'd been gone.

But she'd thought about him. A lot.

That one-way yearning wasn't just pitiful, though it was definitely that. There was something compulsive about it.

Something out of touch with reality. The kind of thing Sophie would do.

No, no, it wasn't.

She put her head down into her fists, though she refused to allow tears to form. Years ago, she'd decided there was way too much crying in this house, and she, for one, was going to show some restraint.

At least she *could* show restraint. Didn't that prove she wasn't as unstable as the others? So why was she tormenting herself?

She lifted her head. There was nothing strange about being attracted to Tom Beckham. She'd met him at a very vulnerable time in her life. When he had run off in the night, he'd become the stuff legends were made of.

She'd bet there were lots of women who would carry torches for him their entire lives. Sophie, for one.

Kelly Ralston, for another.

Samantha had to recognize that, while it was an intense attraction, which was normal, it was not love, which wouldn't be normal at all. She was just lonely. She had too much responsibility, too much pressure, as the only emotionally stable Mellon left at Coeur Volé.

She was not crazy.

She was not like Sophie.

She refused to be.

She realized she was fiddling with her top button, a clear sign of stress. She folded her hands tightly in her lap, trying to make herself relax.

But then, with her hands locked, it was as if the anxiety needed somewhere else to go, and she began worry about other, equally pointless, things.

Had she locked the back door? She stood up. She'd better check.

After that, she checked the front door. It was double bolted, but that made her wonder if she'd thrown the second bolt on the back.

No. She forced herself to sit down again, in the first front parlor chair. She was doing it again. She needed to stop. All the doors were locked and double locked. Everything was fine.

But the longer she sat there, the worse she felt. The huge grandfather clock that stood at the foot of the staircase, in the shadows of the first winding spiral, was ticking so loudly it almost hurt her ears.

She knew what it was telling her, with those slow, measured, inexorable swings of the golden pendulum. Into the shadow, then into the light. Black, then gold, black, then gold...

It was telling her that she would never escape the curse of the Mellons. It was telling her that time was running out.

TOM HAD AGREED TO JOIN Kelly at Mary Jo's Café for dinner. Jacob's poker club met tonight, and, after much urging, he had finally agreed that it might do him good to go.

Tom was glad to have a chance to talk all this over quietly. And he might as well admit it—he was also glad to have a chance to see Kelly alone.

She was already there when he arrived, sitting on a bar stool talking to the woman behind the counter. He paused for a minute in the doorway, appreciating the way she looked, leaning forward, with her long legs hooked behind the silver pillar of the stool, feet locked for balance. When he'd first met her, when she was only about fifteen, she'd been more like a gawky puppy. Those legs had been more than she could handle, and she'd been infamous for tripping over her own shadow.

At the time, the precocious Sophie had been far sexier. It wasn't until he came back to Cathedral Cove for the wedding that he'd seen the grown-up Kelly.

And realized his mistake.

"Kelly?"

She turned around. Her auburn curls caught the last of the sunset, and shimmered around her shoulders like gold smoke. "Hi," she said. She unwound her legs and stood. "Okay if we just take a booth, Mary Jo?"

The woman behind the counter nodded, giving Tom a smile and, he noticed, a very careful once-over. "Sure."

Kelly led the way, and as soon as they were ensconced in the booth at the back, she got right to the point.

"So what did you find at Coeur Volé? Did they let you in?"

"Yes. And they showed me the wedding dress." He had decided to keep it simple. "It is a perfect match, just as you said. But it's intact. Nothing has been cut out of it."

She leaned back against the bench seat, which was covered in a flowery fabric. The whole café was pretty frilly, hanging flower baskets and gewgaws everywhere. Luckily, the food was great, which made up for it.

"Did you tell them why you wanted to see it?" She wrinkled her nose. "I guess you had to. Otherwise, it would have looked pretty peculiar, showing up after all these years and asking to see the dress."

He smiled. "It looked pretty peculiar anyhow."

"How did they react?"

"Just as you'd expect. Samantha was shocked, and a little hurt, I think, that we'd imply…" He let it trail off. He wasn't ready to say what they were implying just yet. "Mrs. Mellon was more hostile. Although it probably was just a mother's natural defensive reaction."

A girl who looked to be still in high school came over and took their order. Kelly got vegetable soup and an ice-cream float. He had to laugh. It was the same crazy thing she had ordered at fifteen. For old time's sake, he chose a hamburger and fries, which had been his order back then, too.

She gave him a funny look. "Some things never change, huh?"

He just smiled. He didn't tell her that he hadn't eaten a hamburger in about twelve years. Fries, either, for that matter. Ambitious young lawyers hardly ate at all. When they did they stuck to power lunches, black coffee and then, when they finally needed to sleep, hard, amber-colored liquor on the rocks.

Neither did he did tell her about the approximately five million other things that had changed, as well.

He didn't want her to know how very different he really was.

"So what now?" She brushed her hair over her shoulder, out of the way, as the waitress deposited their drinks. "I'm glad the dress hasn't been ripped into pieces. That mental picture was disturbing, and I'm relieved to be able to erase it. But if the lace didn't come from Sophie's dress, where did it come from?"

He had thought about this a lot in the hours since he'd left Coeur Volé. "I'm not sure we'll ever know. There may have been extra fabric that remained when the dress was finished, and the family may have kept it, though Imogene isn't admitting that. Or, though the lace is clearly unusual, it may not have been unique after all. Someone else may have some."

"But that's—"

He knew what she was going to say. "I know. That's not even the real question, is it? Because wherever it came from, it ended up here, on Lillith's marker. The real question is who put it there? And why?"

She hesitated. "At first, I wondered if it might have been Trig Boccardi. Do you remember him—the odd guy who lives in the house next door to Coeur Volé?"

"Yeah. Poor goof. He had a few brain cells misfiring, didn't he? I remember he always had a thing for Sophie, and she loved it. Jerked him around like a puppet."

But then he shook his head. "I can definitely see Trig doing something creepy like that, and thinking it was normal. But that doesn't explain Dolly's sketches. I can't see him sending some of the lace to her. I can't see him having enough linear concentration to find her in the first place."

"I know. It was hard enough for me to find her. She's had three husbands, three last names."

Tom smiled. "Maybe that's the explanation. Maybe she was ready to go for number four, and she was making sketches of the ideal wedding dress."

They were quiet while the food was set in front of them. Kelly picked up her spoon and stirred her soup, which was steaming and clearly too hot to eat. She seemed to be mulling over his suggestion.

Finally she looked up and gave him a half smile.

"Maybe," she said. "I guess we should just forget it for now. I mean, as long as nothing else happens… Maybe you were right all along, and it's nothing sinister."

"I don't think it is, Kelly," he said. "At least not as sinister as you feared. After I left Coeur Volé, I stopped by the police station. I asked them about Lillith's car. They assured me they've checked it out thoroughly. Apparently they had already considered the possibility that it wasn't a simple accident. But they found nothing."

She nodded, as if that information didn't surprise her. "Okay. So…I guess we're going to operate on the theory that I've been imagining things. Maybe I have. Maybe, in the end, it was just the stress of seeing Lillith die."

"That must have been beyond terrible," he said. "It could easily have left you…fragile."

"Yes." She seemed unwilling to dwell on that. "So let's say someone, maybe Trig or Sophie or one of the other Mellons, put the lace on Lillith's marker. And the thing with Dolly—maybe, as you say, it was just a coincidence."

"Maybe," he agreed. "Probably, in fact."

She frowned, and then she sighed. "So why does it feel so wrong? Why does it feel like such a stretch?"

"I don't think it's as big a stretch as believing some psycho killer is, ten years after the fact, targeting members of Sophie's wedding party."

"No." She stirred her soup some more. "I guess not."

"Think about it, Kelly. The only thing that really went wrong with that wedding was that I didn't show up. So if there's some pathological amount of negative energy floating around out there, it's going to be directed at me. Not at Dolly, or Kent, or Lillith, who were all just innocent bystanders."

She looked up at him. Her blue eyes were shadowed, and her mouth was soft and anxious. He had to fight the urge to lean over and kiss her until she relaxed. He settled for putting his hand over hers.

But that was enough. In an instant, electricity coursed from her fingers straight to his gut. Her hand twitched, as if she felt it, but she didn't pull it away.

"*I* wasn't an innocent bystander," she said. She was staring at their hands.

"No." He tightened his clasp. "But you're not having any mysterious accidents, either. And besides, you weren't the reason I didn't show up, Kelly. Even if people guessed that we—felt something…"

Her hand twitched again.

"What we felt we couldn't help," he said firmly. "The only thing we could control was what we *did*. And we didn't do anything wrong."

"I did," she said. "I fell in love with my best friend's fiancé. And I let you see it. I could have hidden it, if I'd tried harder. But I let you know how I felt—"

"And you also let me know I could never have you, whether I married Sophie or not. I accepted that, Kelly. I believed you meant it."

"Yes," she said. "I did. But what does Sophie believe?"

There. One of them had finally said it.

Sophie.

It was such a soft name, a name made of bubbles and whispers. But he knew that, for both of them, it had become a dark, poisoned word. It was the name that, these days, always hung heavy in the air, stuck at the back of their throats, caught on the jagged edges of their hearts.

Sophie was the one they suspected. Not "some psycho killer" not "some negative energy floating around out there." Not even "the Mellons." All those things were just euphemisms, substitutes for the unpalatable truth.

"I don't know, Kelly," he said. "I'm not sure I've ever known what Sophie was really thinking."

SOPHIE WAS SO ANGRY that when she tried to swallow a bite of her lobster, she couldn't. It was as if she'd lost control of the muscles in her throat. She raised the soft white napkin to her lips and discreetly, she hoped, spit it out.

This was a bad sign, not being able to eat. The doctors told her it was another form of self-mutilation, and maybe they were right. But what difference did that make? *Idiots,* with their childlike confidence that simply naming a condition cured it.

Every patient in the institution knew that was a load of crap. Sophie knew it best of all.

For instance, she knew that her suicidal ideation had recently morphed into a homicidal ideation. But knowing that didn't make it go away.

She picked up the metal lobster cracker and slipped three of her fingers into it absently, all lined up in a row so that when she squeezed the bones rubbed together. She pressed harder and the lump in her throat dissolved a little.

The man at the next table, who was also eating alone, had begun to stare at her. She pulled her fingers free, then lifted the fattest lobster claw and wedged it inside the cracker and pressed down. The pink-ivory shell shattered into delicate triangles, revealing the soft flesh inside.

The man frowned, then quickly looked around for a waiter and asked for his check. Good decision, she thought, watching him openly, a small smile on her lips. Maybe he sensed that, for the first time in her life, just hurting *herself* wasn't going to be enough.

The misery, anger and confusion in her head were out of control now, and it was going to take something huge to stop it.

Something huge…that was just a euphemism. She felt her shoulders tighten. Why should she use a euphemism in her own head? No one could see into her brain.

She looked around the elegant restaurant, with its candles at every table. The candlelight made the faces of the diners look strange, as if they had watery skin and dark hollows for eyes. But she knew that, if someone flicked on the overhead lights, they'd just be people. There was nothing to be afraid of.

She had to be braver than this. She had to keep things honest and straight, at least in her own head. Now that she wasn't taking the pills anymore, it was important that she be vigilant about monitoring the strength of her connection to reality.

So no more euphemisms. The *something huge* that had to happen was this: someone was going to have to die.

And soon.

She looked down at her hands, which really were too thin. She must have pressed harder with the lobster cracker than she realized. Her fingers were sore, and she knew they'd be bruised tomorrow.

Still, they didn't look like hands that could bring death to a person, even if that person had betrayed her.

But there was no other way. She had a horror inside her, a poisonous fog that she couldn't banish with little tortures anymore. This horror could only be ended by the death of people she loved. Or had loved.

Even as she said that, she knew it wasn't true. There was another way to end it.

The person she killed didn't have to be someone she cared about. It could be someone she despised, someone who had always, always disappointed and betrayed her.

It could be Sophie herself.

She began to cry. She lifted the napkin to catch the tears, and the blob of lobster fell out into her lap. Humiliated, she grabbed it and tried to hide it on the plate. She was such a screwed-up mess. Her life had been pointless, even wicked. Why should the idea of ending it break her heart?

The tears kept rolling. The instinct to survive wasn't logical. It didn't add up like a math problem. Maybe she couldn't justify her life, but still, oh God, she didn't want to die. Not before she'd found a way to live in peace. Real peace.

But she didn't want to kill anyone else, either.

It began to feel confusing. How long had it been now since she'd had any of her medication? A month? Six weeks?

She drank a little water and tried to think. Maybe she was overreacting. Maybe there was still time to wait, and pray, and hope it would just all go away. Time to think of another answer.

Maybe the little things she'd always done to survive would still help.

She wiggled her fingers, activating the sore spots. Then she took her long lobster fork and dug out a strip of meat to use as a test.

This one went down easily.

Good. Clearly the pain still gave her that little bit of control she needed. Maybe, if she tried something new, something that ratcheted the pain up a notch or two, it would buy her some time.

She slipped the lobster cracker into her purse.

CHAPTER ELEVEN

THE MORNING AFTER TOM'S VISIT to Coeur Volé dawned a deep, strong blue, the exact color of Sophie's eyes, and Mrs. Mellon decided it was a sign.

She dressed warmly, knowing that clear blue dawns often meant a chill. As soon as she watched the window come to life, she headed carefully—and quietly—down the rest of the stairs to the front foyer.

As she was unwinding her scarf from the hall tree, she heard a noise in the adjacent parlor. Her hands froze. Adler had often sat in the Gainesborough armchair, whose upholstered back was high and broad enough to hide him from her view, and waited for her to come in at night.

Like a snake under a rock, she'd sometimes thought.

But it wasn't Adler, she reminded herself. She mustn't get foggy-minded, mustn't let this tumor take hold of her just yet. Adler was dead, lying in Edgewater Memorial Gardens, in a rectangle of land that had never grown grass properly, much to the dismay of the groundskeeper.

Imogene could have told him why.

"Mom?" Samantha's sleepy voice came from Adler's favorite chair. Her head followed and Imogene saw that her daughter's pale blue eyes were swollen and unfocused.

"Mom, what are you doing up so early?"

"I'm going out," Imogene said. "God, Samantha, you look terrible. Have you slept in that chair all night?"

Samantha got out of the chair, still clumsy with sleep. She smiled sheepishly and brushed at her crumpled dress, the same pink dress she'd worn yesterday. "I guess I did. I didn't mean to. I must have dozed off."

"Well, go upstairs and get some proper sleep. You don't want to make yourself sick."

Samantha was awake enough now to bristle at Imogene's tone. Imogene understood. Samantha was twenty-seven, and a very sensible young woman. She wasn't Sophie. She didn't need her mother to issue orders about everyday, common-sense things.

Besides, they both knew that, of the two of them, Imogene was by far the more physically frail, and the one who was more likely to make herself sick. Imogene wanted to apologize, but she couldn't think how to begin. Sometimes maneuvering the emotional waters of her treacherous family was just too much for anyone.

She realized she was very tired of it. Maybe, she thought, her death sentence wasn't such a tragedy, after all. Maybe it was just an early release, time off for good behavior.

"Mom, where are you going so early? It's barely dawn."

Imogene looked down at her scarf. "I'm going to see your father."

Samantha frowned. "Mom—"

"Don't worry, I haven't lost my mind yet. I know he's dead. I mean I'm going to the cemetery. I have some things I want to tell him."

Samantha's frown just deepened.

Oh, the young! They didn't know very much about any

of the big things in life. They didn't know that love and hate could grow so closely together that they entwined, like poorly planted trees, and eventually couldn't be safely separated. They didn't know that, sometimes, death didn't mean the communication was severed. That sometimes people lived in your heads, and you heard them more clearly than you heard the world around you.

They didn't realize that sometimes you had to talk back, in whatever way you could.

At least *Samantha* didn't know these things. Sebastian probably did. And poor, unhappy Sophie…

"Samantha," Imogene said. "What do you remember about your father's death?"

Samantha's eyes widened. "What do you mean? It was only eight years ago. I was home at the time. I remember everything."

"I don't mean the basic facts. I mean…do you remember that, right before his heart attack, he and I had been arguing?"

Samantha nodded. "Yes," she said. Her gaze softened. "I know that must have been very difficult, having him die so suddenly before you had a chance to make up."

Imogene just looked at her. Was there any chance Samantha was acting? Was it possible that any nineteen-year-old child could have been so naive? But of course she could have. Her innocence had been guaranteed, bought and paid for by the rest of the family.

And it had come at a very high price.

Especially for Sophie.

"I remember coming into the room," Samantha went on. "I remember seeing you on your knees beside him. You were crying. I think you were praying, too."

That was true, in a way. Imogene had definitely been

talking to God. She'd been thanking him for finally noticing that she needed some help. Thanking God for killing
Adler so that she wouldn't have to.

"Yes, well, I just want to go talk to him now," Imogene
said. "I have things to say, and I don't want to wait until
the tumor…until I…"

Samantha had begun to worry at the button on her dress.
Imogene had seen her do that a lot lately, ever since the
diagnosis. Samantha knew she'd end up being the primary
caretaker, which wasn't going to be easy. And, of course,
she knew that, after Imogene died, she'd end up here alone.

The burden was clearly too heavy for her, and the small
quirks she had, like a slight tendency toward perfection-
ism, were starting to intensify.

Imogene didn't pray anymore, but she sometimes did
tell God things she thought He needed to know. Right now
she told Him that it wasn't fair to Samantha if He let Imogene's illness go on too long. Samantha was the only Mellon left who had a chance in hell of living a normal, happy
life.

Imogene told God that it would be wicked to do anything to jeopardize that.

She tied her scarf around her neck, and then she went
into the parlor to hug her daughter. She gently pulled Samantha's hand down from the button, and then she kissed
her on the cheek.

"Samantha, look at me."

She took her child's sad little face in both her hands and
tried to smile.

"I want you to remember that, no matter what happens
to Sophie, or to me, none of it is your fault." She shook
her head, hushing Samantha's confused murmur. "Just

remember. You didn't start the troubles this family has endured, and you can't do anything to stop them. All you can do is try to save yourself."

"GO HOME, BRIAN," Kelly said, yawning. It was only 9:00 a.m., and she wasn't ready to wake up yet. She'd spent a long night working on the winery glass and she needed at least another hour's sleep.

Besides, it was raining out. It was gray and getting cold, and she'd kicked her socks off in the night, as she always did. Standing here with the door open, her toes were going numb.

"Selfish witch," Brian said, scowling. "I just want ten minutes of your time. I've got four diamond rings in my back pocket, and I want you to tell me which one Marie will like."

Kelly yawned again. "The big one," she said. "Now good night."

She blew him a kiss, and then she shut the door.

"You're not getting out of this," he called over the drumming of rain on the porch's aluminum roof. "I'm coming back later."

"Do that," she mumbled to herself, yawning and smiling at the same time. "*Much* later."

As she moved away, she heard something crinkle under her feet. Looking down, she saw that the mail had already been delivered and slipped through the slot in her front door. It was early, but the postman probably had been trying to beat the storm.

She glanced out the window. It was one of those days that warned you winter wasn't far away. The sky was the color of steel, and so heavy the earth seemed in danger of being smothered. In weather like this, her woodsy cottage setting looked like something out of a horror movie. The air smelled of decayed leaves and fresh mud. The trees sagged and dripped, and they seemed unnaturally empty, as if every living thing had fled for somewhere less dismal.

She heard Brian's car start up and roll off, and for a minute she regretted sending him away. His level-headed good humor would have been the perfect antidote for such a day.

But then she remembered how comfortable her little bed was, with its thermal blanket, its down comforter and the six pillows that she didn't have to share with anyone. Brian had always hogged the covers shamelessly. On the list of unforgivable sins, it had been right up there with the belching.

Besides, if Brian were here, he'd want her to fix him things to eat and agonize over diamonds and listen to his woes about Marie. *Nope.* Maybe she'd just stay in bed all day long, reading and napping. Pure hedonism—one of the many joys of being single. She might get up long enough to make hot tea, and then again, she might not. The decision was entirely, deliciously, *hers.*

It crossed her mind that she wouldn't be so keen to spend the day alone in bed if it had been Tom at the door. If it had been his body hogging the covers…

But she didn't let the thought linger. She had ten years of experience ignoring stray thoughts about Tom. She wasn't going to let the fact that he was back in town undo all those years of training.

Anyhow, right now it was too damn cold to stand around thinking about any man. She bent down and picked up the mail, then scurried into her bedroom and crawled under the covers, shivering.

She felt around with her feet until she found her socks.

She put them on, and then, for about ten or fifteen minutes, she tried to go back to sleep.

But it was too late. She was awake, and the rain was making too much noise. A branch was swishing against her window, and it sounded unpleasantly like someone whispering. Every now and then something large would thud onto her roof. A pinecone, probably, but every time it happened her heart thumped a little and she woke up even more.

Finally, grumbling under her breath about the things she'd like to do to Brian, she propped the pillows behind her and sat up. She dug the remote out of the clutter on the nightstand, then turned on the television, if only for something to drown out the alien sounds produced by the storm.

It took a while, but she finally found a sitcom that didn't seem too stupid, and then she lay back to open the mail.

Bills, bills, junk and bills. What had happened to the fine art of correspondence? All her fun messages were probably waiting for her on e-mail. But the computer was in the workshop, and she'd have to run through the rain to get there. The fine art of correspondence could wait.

Then she noticed there was one piece of mail that looked personal. It was a large, rectangular white envelope, and it looked vaguely familiar, as if she might know the sender.

She turned it over, but there was no return address. The paper of the envelope was high quality, almost too nice. And it was addressed in a neat, old-fashioned hand, the kind of penmanship found only in convent schools and in computer typefaces designed to look like real handwriting.

Which might mean it was junk mail after all.

She almost didn't open it. But boredom won the day,

and she slipped her finger under the heavy, satin edge of the envelope and tore it open.

She pulled the card out halfway and read the first few words without really understanding them.

"Mr. and Mrs. Adler Mellon request the honor of your presence at the wedding of their daughter, Sophie Elaine Mellon…"

But in half a second, they had sunk in. She stopped breathing, and then she read them again.

"Mr. and Mrs. Adler Mellon request the honor…"

No wonder she had thought the envelope looked familiar. One of these had come to her in the mail before.

Ten years ago.

She read the rest of the invitation, her heart thumping uncomfortably. It was exactly the same. Even the date was the same. Today's date, September 19.

September 19, ten years ago.

Who would do this? She pulled the card all the way out of its envelope, knowing that no one would sign such a thing, and yet foolishly hoping that perhaps someone had. A name. A note. A clue. Anything.

And they had.

At the very bottom, just below the "regrets only" line, someone had scrawled four short words in what looked to be fingerpaint. This was not the elegant, restrained handwriting of the envelope. This was printed in blotchy block letters that somehow managed to look both childish and very, very angry.

The message was simple, and somehow terrible in that simplicity.

"Stay away from him," it said.

She was so shocked by the message that it took her several seconds to notice the flaky, rusty quality of the paint, and the slight metallic scent.

A few seconds more to realize it wasn't paint at all.

It was blood.

"BAILEY, RELAX." Tom held the telephone away from his ear, but he could still hear the other man yelling. "You're going to give yourself a heart attack. I didn't say I was quitting. I just said I'm going on hiatus."

"What the hell is a hiatus?"

Tom moved the phone to his other ear. "It's a gap, a missing space. In this context, it's time off."

Bailey made a furious bubbling noise, like a sink that is trying to drain but can't. "I know what a hiatus is, damn you. I mean what does hiatus mean to *you?* How big is this so-called *gap?* A week? A month? A year? Damn it, Tom, you can't really be planning to be gone a *year!*"

"I didn't say that. You did. I don't know exactly how long, but probably no more than a few weeks. You'll survive."

Jacob came into the kitchen, wearing a sweatsuit and running shoes. Tom smiled, then pointed at the window. Hadn't Jacob noticed it was pouring? The dense sheets of rain had taken over the world. The wavy, gray shadows had even saturated this bright room, undulating on the walls, the countertops, even the floors.

Jacob just shrugged and looked at his watch, as if he believed it might stop in time for him to take his usual morning run.

Bailey was still sputtering. "What about O'Toole? You screwed up on that one big time, you know. He's going to want an apology."

"He's not going to get one."

"Oh, yes he is," Bailey bellowed. Tom could imagine how red his face must be by now.

"Oh, yeah? Come to think of it, Bailey, I might need a year after all."

Bailey took a moment to collect himself, which he obviously needed. When he spoke again, he sounded grim.

"Take a year, and you won't have a job when you get back. You're good, Tom, but frankly you're slipping. Six months ago you wouldn't have blown off O'Toole like that."

"Probably not." Now that Bailey had come to earth, Tom dropped the joking tone. "Maybe that's why I need a hiatus. Maybe I'm burned out on the O'Tooles of the world for the moment."

Bailey made a low, harrumphing sound. But he liked Tom, both personally and professionally, so he kept his tone mellow, too.

"Okay, I'll buy that. But don't push it, Beckham. You're not the only litigator in Atlanta, you know."

Tom did know. And he also knew that, no matter how much Bailey liked him, the senior partner would make good on that threat if he had to. The firm wouldn't wait forever.

"Sounds as if you may have ticked some people off," Jacob observed as Tom hung up the phone.

He pulled out a chair and took a seat beside Tom. He had a large glass of orange juice in one hand and a piece of toast in the other. Tom was glad to see that Jacob had decided, without any prompting, to have breakfast. It might be baby steps, but he did seem to be recovering.

Tom dropped the phone onto the table. "Nothing serious. Bailey is about ninety percent noise."

Jacob took a bite of toast. "And the other ten percent?"

Tom smiled. "No one is sure. We think maybe human, but we could be wrong."

Jacob smiled, too, but his didn't last long. Still, Tom counted even a two-second grin as a victory.

"Seriously, though," Jacob said, setting his glass down. "I hope you're not doing this just to babysit me. I'm okay, you know. Or I will be. I've decided Lily would want me to pull through, so I'm going to."

"I know that," Tom said. "And believe me, I'm not doing this just for you. If I don't get a break from those people I'm going to lose my mind."

"What if you lose your job instead?"

"I won't. But even if I did, I'm not sure I'd give a damn."

He realized as he said it that the statement was actually true.

How strange. As far back as he could remember, he'd always wanted to be a lawyer. His grandfather had been a well-respected criminal attorney, and Tom had admired him more than anyone else in his life. Certainly more than his own parents, who had never worked, living on their inheritance and spending it down to the last dime, so that when they'd died in a train crash in Europe, they'd left a twenty-year-old Tom without enough money to pay for law school, much less enough money to sustain the cushy life he was used to.

Right then, this job had become his dream. He'd taken out loans, and he'd done without sleep for two full years trying to get credentials impressive enough to land a job with Ormonde, White and Murray.

Of course, that was before he realized the job was just

ten, twenty, thirty more years of no sleep, no vacations, no personal life and no way to avoid kissing the ass of every sleazy bigwig who had a bank account large enough to interest the firm.

"Okay," Jacob said, obviously accepting that Tom was a big boy and could make his own decisions. "In that case, let me admit I'm really glad you're not leaving."

He stood and took his glass to the sink. He stayed there a minute, staring out into the rainy gloom. The storm had just grown worse. It was whipping the trees around, hurling raindrops against the window so hard they sounded like hail.

Jacob turned. "You're right. Even I can't run in this." He raised his eyebrows. "So what should we do? How are you planning to celebrate your newfound freedom?"

Tom smiled. "I hadn't thought that far."

"Well, let's see…" Jacob's eyes widened. "I know! What's Kelly doing today?"

"I have no idea. And get that look out of your eye, Jacob. There's nothing going on between Kelly and me."

Tom hoped Jacob would believe that. Jacob hadn't been at the wedding, having been called home to be with his seriously ill father, so he hadn't see Tom and Kelly together.

"But there used to be something going on, right? Lillith said there were some heavy sparks flying between you two, at some of the pre-wedding events. In fact, she said that was probably why—" He stopped. "Well, you know. Why you decided you couldn't go through with it."

Tom had to work to keep his frustration in check. This wasn't the time to get rough with Jacob about anything, but damn it. How many times did he have to explain that he wasn't going to discuss this?

"It was ten years ago," he said. "Believe me, any sparks would be pure ashes by now."

"So it's true?" Jacob rubbed his hands together glee-fully. "There were sparks?"

Tom growled. He was all for distracting Jacob, but this was above and beyond. "Who cares? It was ten years ago. Read my lips, Jacob. *Ten years.*"

"Ten years," Jacob said with a glint in his eye that made Tom seriously consider breaking his vow of tolerance, "is nothing."

He picked up the phone and held it out. "It's not ashes, I guarantee you. Call her."

"Damn it, Jacob—"

But at that moment the telephone rang. Even Jacob seemed surprised and he glanced down at it with amaze-ment.

"Hello? Hey, Kelly. Yeah, I'm doing okay. Tom? Yeah, he's right here. Yeah, sure. Hold on."

Then he extended the telephone one more time.

"It's for you," he said. And then he added, with a grin, *"Ashes, my ass."*

AS TOM EXPECTED, the Cathedral Cove police station was located on the "wrong" side of the bridge. The old money on Destiny Drive liked to believe that only the upstart en-trepreneurs, unpredictable Bohemians and trailer-dwelling riffraff from the Left Bank westward actually committed crimes.

The Cathedral Cove police knew better. The only dif-ference was that the East End crimes tended to be prose-cuted by agencies with sanitized initial names, like the SEC or the FBI or the IRS. Or they weren't prosecuted at all, like the bastard whose wife swore she got her bruises moving her patio furniture, or the cocky kid whose DUI just suddenly "went away."

As a lawyer, Tom knew better, too. It was the same in any city.

Which was why Detective Vince Kopple, who had been assigned to look into the bizarre wedding invitation Kelly had received today, seemed to be reluctant to call Coeur Volé and ask Imogene Mellon to join them at the station.

"She's a tyrant, that one," Kopple said. "No respect for the police. Thinks that house out there is its own little world, with its own little laws."

"It's tricky," Tom agreed. He knew how to make nice with the police—it was basic survival strategy when you were a litigator—and he'd already established himself as Kopple's buddy.

But the truth was, he'd been alone with Kopple in this puke-green room for an hour and he was starting to get impatient.

"You know, my dad was on the force back when they investigated the boating accident," Kopple continued, his tone infuriatingly conversational, as if they had all the time in the world. "You know, the one about eighteen years ago? Mr. Mellon was okay, but it messed up Sebastian pretty bad—he was burned so bad they weren't sure he was going to make it. Sebastian is the son, you know. The only boy."

He stopped abruptly and grinned. "Oh, yeah, of course. You probably know more about them than I do, don't you? Anyhow, Dad said that when they went out to the house to ask questions, like who'd been driving the boat, had anybody been drinking, stuff like that, Mrs. Mellon told them if they didn't get off her property she was going to shoot them for trespassing."

"I hear you." Tom smiled again. What did that ancient history have to do with what had happened today? "But still, you know you can't investigate this properly without talking to the Mellons."

"It's not really a crime, you know, sending nutty letters to people. There wasn't even a threat in it. Not straight out. And we haven't even established that it's really blood."

Tom's smile felt as if it were made of iron. "Come on, Kopple. What about the lace, and the other deaths? You know there's something weird going on, and obviously the Mellons are at the heart of it."

"Maybe." Kopple, who had a big brown mustache to try to camouflage the fact that he was only about twenty-nine, grinned. "But even so, which Mellon? You've got so many bats in that belfry, there's no telling."

"Guess that's what interrogations are for," Tom said, shrugging philosophically, though he'd had just about enough of the buddy act. He wanted someone to *do* something.

Kopple chewed on his lower lip a minute, then, cussing softly, reached over to pick up his phone.

"Get the Mellons down here," he said. "Huh? Hell, I don't know who all is living there these days. Just throw a net around the old mausoleum and see what you get."

He punched Off, then turned back to Tom. "So…just gut instinct here. Who do you really think sent it? Sophie? Her mom? Her little sister, who probably thinks you're hot? How about the brother, who, according to my sources, thinks you're the devil incarnate? Or how about this? How about if the redhead sent it to herself, to get your attention?"

"Well, Sophie is the obvious choice, of course."

"I'm not asking about the obvious choice." Kopple pulled on his mustache, a tic he exhibited whenever he was thinking hard. "I know what that is. I'm asking what your gut is telling you."

Tom sat up a little straighter, relieved that they were finally getting to the heart of the matter. The first twenty minutes, Kopple had probably just been keeping Tom busy while they ran a background check in the other room. The second twenty had probably been to make sure his story matched the one they'd heard from Kelly. But for the past twenty minutes, they'd just been wasting time.

He decided to be candid. That was the quickest way to the truth.

"My gut reaction?" He held out his hands, palms up. "I think it was Sophie. Problem is, my gut is compromised on this one. It's hard for me to be objective."

Kopple's brown eyes narrowed and looked amazingly a lot shrewder.

"So which one of them messed with your gut, Beckham? The bride? Or the bridesmaid?"

Tom met the detective's gaze. "Both of them," he said honestly. "The whole episode just plain sucked, Vince. Start to finish."

Kopple looked at him a minute, and then he smiled.

"I bet it did," he said, and his voice sounded sincere, gruff with a blunt, man-to-man sympathy. "I've heard the stories, of course. Frankly, I'm surprised you came out in one piece."

"Me, too."

"And I'm even more surprised that, if one of the Mellons has decided to start offing the wedding party, they didn't begin with you. Actually, the very fact that they didn't makes me wonder whether there's any offing going on at all. Plus, three different police investigations have already ruled these deaths accidents."

"I know," Tom said. "I hope they're right."

"I wouldn't bet anything I needed on three police departments being wrong at once," the detective said. Then he smiled. "But, if I were you, I wouldn't go walking on any cliff edges at night, either. Not for a while, anyhow."

"Thanks for the advice," Tom said. "I'll keep it in mind. So…are we done here? I'd like to talk to Kelly."

Kopple stood. "Yeah, we're done. But Kelly's gone. She went home with her ex-husband about half an hour ago. We didn't see any reason to keep her, not until we finish analyzing the blood, anyhow." He grinned. "We don't really think she mailed it to herself, you know."

She was already gone? *Damn it.*

Tom scooped up his jacket and walked out into the front room, a much more attractive area, which clearly had been decorated knowing the public would see it. The designer of the interrogation rooms had obviously believed that anyone in them was a criminal and didn't deserve any better.

Late afternoons in Cathedral Cove were quiet, apparently. The large front office held only two detectives, who sat at facing desks and were both studiously typing on computer keyboards. On the surface created by their back-to-back monitors, they'd placed a large pizza that smelled fantastic.

Tom realized he hadn't had anything to eat since yesterday.

And he probably wasn't going to eat for a while longer. He wanted to get to Kelly's house ASAP. The ex-husband was an annoyance, but not an impediment.

He said goodbye, mindful to maintain the camaraderie, and then, as soon as he got outside the door he began to move quickly. He had loped down the station steps, his keys in his hand, and was ready to jog to his car when a blue-and-white CCPD car pulled up and parked right in front of the stairs.

Though it was still gray and raining, Tom paused, curious to see whether the poor cop who had been given this suicide mission had, in fact, been able to drag Mrs. Mellon out of her fortress.

He had. Though the young, uniformed patrolman looked decidedly harried, red-faced and damp with rain, he opened the back door with dignity and allowed Mrs. Mellon and Samantha to climb out.

Both women saw Tom immediately. He scanned their faces, hoping they would show something…either guilt or innocence. Anything that would give him another piece of this puzzle.

What he saw surprised him. Imogene Mellon looked thin and limp and shockingly pale, even paler than the last time he'd seen her, which was saying something. She hardly registered Tom's presence, apparently interested only in reaching the shelter of the front portico overhang.

She couldn't possibly be responsible for the officer's agitation.

Samantha, on the other hand, was ramrod straight, and as flushed as the cop. She stood there, frozen in place, as though she wanted to refuse to enter the station at all.

And when she looked at Tom, her eyes were filled with an unmistakable emotion.

The emotion was hatred.

CHAPTER TWELVE

KELLY WAS WORKING, bent over her table, carefully scoring a piece of mottled blue glass. Pattern piece number ninety-four. If she could ever get it right, it would become an abstract oval of perfect blue sky peeking out from behind her lush purple grapevines.

But that was a big *if.* She'd cut the same shape three times already because she'd cracked the glass each time. Scoring too hard. Scoring too lightly. Using the wrong pliers, the wrong angle…

She looked down at the remaining half sheet of blue that she'd propped beside her. Half-gone already? She should stop. This glass was damn expensive.

She looked around the studio, which was well lit—she needed perfect lighting to judge the glass—but still felt underwater, thanks to the unrelenting downpour. No alternatives for working off this nervous energy presented themselves.

Brian, who had heard about the bloody wedding invitation—he always got news first, there at his sporting-goods store—had shown up at the police station within an hour of her own arrival and had insisted on following her home.

Now he was sitting on the workshop stool, leafing

through pattern booklets, pretending a fascination with stained-glass designs that she knew for a fact he didn't feel.

Glancing up at him, she smiled. Too bad he hadn't been this thoughtful when they were married.

He had his cell phone out where he could see it while pretending to read. Marie was due back tonight after a trip to see her family in Florida. Brian was like a little kid, surreptitiously checking the phone every few minutes to be sure he hadn't missed a call, then hurrying back to the stained-glass books so that Kelly wouldn't realize what he was up to.

Poor guy. He'd suffered enough, and Kelly hoped Marie would call soon, even though she knew that meant Brian would be eager to rush home.

And Kelly would be left alone.

She redoubled her focus on the glass, although she could tell she was scoring too hard again.

Alone.

Well, so what? That wasn't a dirty word. Living alone was her choice. This was just a temporary bump in the road. Sooner or later, they'd find out what was going on, and everything would go back to normal.

In the meantime, she could handle it. If the crazy Mellons thought they could terrorize her with a few scraps of lace and some ten-year-old paper, they were dead wrong.

"I'm going to spoil this whole sheet if I don't settle down and get this right," she said. Not that Brian gave a damn, but she wanted to sound as normal as possible. If she just kept standing here in total silence, he'd know what a nervous wreck she was inside.

And then he wouldn't leave, not even for Marie. He had

that stupid, gallant kind of loyalty. He still treated Kelly like family, like a sister. It probably drove Marie crazy.

It would have driven Kelly crazy, if she'd been in Marie's shoes. Kelly had always thought that women who leaned on their exes were wimps. Selfish wimps, at that. They didn't want a real relationship, which would involve giving, sharing, tolerating, trusting. They just wanted to be able to pick at the leftovers, choosing the bits they still needed and discarding the rest.

"Why don't you give it up for now?" Brian looked at her over the stained-glass book. "Maybe it's like any problem. If you come to it fresh tomorrow, you'll see the answer."

"I know. I just want to get this one piece right, and then I'll quit."

The scoring was complete, so she began pinching away the extra glass. Once again she felt the pliers go wrong. It was subtle, but she knew instantly, the way Brian, who loved golf, knew even before he looked that a ball was going to slice on him.

A hairline crack sped into the piece of glass, just a pale white line, like summer lightning streaking through a blue sky.

"Damn it," she said dropping the piece, pliers and all. "What's the *matter* with me?"

Brian sighed. "You're stressed, Kel. Stop pretending you're not. Nobody's falling for it anyhow. And why shouldn't you be nervous? Heck, I'm creeped out, and I didn't even see the damn thing."

She took a deep breath, trying to relax her shoulders. It made her feel a tiny bit better.

"I'm not nervous," she said, finally realizing the truth.

She'd been breaking those pieces of glass because she was repressing not fear—but fury. "I'm not scared. I'm mad."

He tilted his head. "Mad?"

"Yes. I didn't focus on it until just now, but I'm mad as hell. There may not really be a murderer out there, but, at the very least, there is some anonymous person who's determined to terrorize me. Wouldn't that make you mad?"

Brian nodded slowly. "Yeah. I think it would."

"I know the police didn't take the note seriously," she said. That was an understatement. They figured it was some kind of catfight over Tom. "Their evidence guy said he doubted it was even real blood. Well, I don't care if it's food coloring, or pig's blood, or red Magic Marker. The person who wrote those words knew I would *think* it was blood, and they hoped it would scare the hell out of me. But I refuse to live in fear of some anonymous coward. And that coward is damn sure not going to tell me what I can do, and who I can see."

Brian smiled. "You go, girl."

She smiled back. She knew he was only teasing, but it did feel better to be angry. The whole room seemed a little lighter, suddenly.

"You know," he said, "I wonder if all this could just be a diabolical plan to punish you guys. Maybe no one has really killed anyone. Maybe whoever is behind this is just exploiting random accidents."

"What do you mean? You think the Mellons are playing mind games with us?"

"Yeah, why not? If Sophie really resents the wedding party, maybe it's all about messing with your heads. I mean, all those problems already existed in the lives of their victims, right? The Snyder guy, you said he drank and hunted. I mean, that was an accident waiting to happen, right? And the artist. You said she was always clumsy."

He seemed to be warming to the idea. "And, hell, we all know about Lillith and her car."

Kelly stared out the window, trying to hang onto her anger. Trying not to see Lillith's face, streaming blood. If she thought about Lillith too much, the starch would go out of her, and she couldn't afford that now.

It was getting darker. She couldn't see the trees anymore. She could see nothing but jagged silver rivers moving down the pane.

It was sweet of Brian to come up with such a comforting theory, but unfortunately, in the end, it just didn't ring true. As a mind game, it was too chancy. No one would even have known about the first two wedding-party deaths, if Kelly hadn't asked so many questions. The lace had been a subtle touch. No evil mastermind could have been certain anyone would notice it before the wind and rain mangled it beyond recognition.

"It's an interesting theory," she said. "But I can't cling to it just because it's comforting. I also have to consider the possibility that Sophie—that this person really is dangerous. I have to try to find a way to stop whoever it is. I'm not going to sit here passively and wait for my own accident to happen."

"Your own accident? God, Kelly. See what I mean? Maybe that's what they want you to do, get all paranoid and—"

She shook her head. What good would a false sense of security do her? She had to face the truth, whatever it was.

"If there *is* a list, Brian, I'm on it. I can't hide my head in the sand. I have to ask myself—where is the danger already lurking? What am I already doing that they could use against me?"

She could tell that the answer occurred to them at exactly the same moment. Both of them stared down at the sharp, gleaming blue pieces of broken sky that littered her worktable.

The glass.

For her, the danger lay in the glass.

"Damn it," she said, her voice low and hard. Her anger spiked to a dangerous level. Nobody, *nobody* was going to sneak an invisible hand into her life and destroy the joy she got from her work.

By God, she was going to find out who was behind all this, whether it was manipulative sadism or psychotic murder. And she was going to bring the bastard down.

Even if it was Sophie.

Suddenly lights flashed against the runny window, briefly turning the water as creamy as spilled milk. A car was pulling into her driveway. She could hear its tires skimming through puddles that stood two inches deep on the muddy ground.

"Someone's coming," she said unnecessarily. Brian was already at the window, looking out into the wet gray shadows.

After a second, he turned. She could see the relief on his face. "It looks like Beckham's car," he said. "Little silver job? Costs more than my house?"

She nodded. "Yes," she said. "That's Tom's car."

Clearly they had only another few seconds alone. Brian turned to her with a hint of urgency.

"Look. Let's cut to the chase here. I know there's stuff

simmering between you two. If he wants to stay, what do you want me to do? I can tell him to go to hell, or I can just get in my car and go home. Your call, but you'd better tell me now."

"I'm not sure why he's here," she said. "When I left the police station, he was still being questioned. Maybe he just wants to know what the police said to me."

Brian's practicality again cut through the baloney.

"Maybe, but that's not all he wants, and you know it. He either wants to hatch a plan to unmask the bad guy, or to have sex with you, or both. The only question remaining is, what do *you* want?"

She shook her head, though the thought of having sex with Tom sliced through her like the blade of a sword. "It's not about sex, Brian. Tom's not interested in that, and even if he were, he knows it's not an option."

Brian grinned. "Hey, you're allowed to have sex if you want. I intend to, if Marie ever gives me another chance."

She chuckled, but she kept her eyes on the front drive. Tom had turned off his lights, but he hadn't opened his car door yet. She wondered what he was waiting for.

Brian watched, too, silent for a few seconds. When he spoke again, his voice had sobered a little.

"Don't forget, Kelly, this is the guy the note warned you to stay away from. Do you think it might be smarter to avoid him, just for a little while?"

She shook her head, absolutely certain what she was going to do. "And let the anonymous coward win? What if the next note tells me to stop making stained glass, or to wear green lipstick every Thursday, or to send a million dollars to a numbered account in the Cayman Islands? Do you expect me to just do whatever the notes tell me to, until my life isn't my own anymore?"

Brian looked at her a minute, and then he chuckled.

"Hell, no," he said. "I expect you to catch this pervert, whoever he or she is, and kick their ass. And if Tom Beckham can help you do that, I say let's open this door and get started."

TOM LIKED BRIAN RALSTON, though he hadn't expected to.

When Tom had heard that Kelly had married a jock who owned a sporting-goods store, he'd built an unflattering picture of a no-neck Neanderthal who thought in sports clichés, when he thought at all, and made love like a running back falling on a fumbled ball.

Tom had imagined Kelly's creativity stifled, her beauty underappreciated, her intelligence trapped behind the cash register, ringing up endless pedometers and Little League uniforms. He imagined her enduring the nightly tackles, dreaming of the one man who had touched her the way a woman should be touched.

Talk about clichés. And yet, bastard that he was, the picture had pleased him. He'd far preferred to imagine Kelly languishing in a miserable marriage than accept that she could be happy without him.

The real Brian Ralston didn't fit the picture at all. He wasn't conventionally handsome, but he had smart eyes and an open smile. And he clearly respected the hell out of Kelly.

Tom should have sent him a mental apology, but he didn't. He still didn't like the idea that Kelly had ever been happy with this guy, and yet she must have been. There was a residual devotion between them as they sat together, side by side on matching stools, that made Tom's shoulders bunch up with the primitive urge to shove Brian Ralston out of the way.

They spent the first few minutes talking about the wedding invitation, which Kelly had left with the police. They shared notes, and they all agreed that, unless it turned out to be human blood, the police probably wouldn't give this whole thing a very high priority.

And then Brian's cell phone rang. While Tom watched, Brian and Kelly exchanged glances, volumes of wordless communication passing in an instant. The phone kept ringing.

Finally Kelly smiled and touched Brian's shoulder, breaking his trance. "Answer it, you goof. You don't want her to hang up, do you?"

"No." Brian gave Tom an apologetic glance. "Sorry. I've been waiting for this call." He grinned. "It's Marie."

"No problem," Tom said. He liked that grin. He liked the way Brian said *Marie,* as if it were synonymous with *heaven.* A man couldn't feel like that about a Marie if he were still in love with a Kelly.

And he most definitely liked the way, after a short, sugary exchange of meaningless phrases murmured into the cell phone, Brian announced that he would have to go home now.

Tom and Kelly walked him to the door. Just before he opened it, Brian turned to Tom with a straightforward gaze.

"Listen, Tom," he said. "I don't know how to put this delicately. The bottom line is, I don't want her to be alone tonight."

"Brian—" Kelly began.

But Tom broke in bluntly. "Neither do I."

Kelly put one hand on each of their chests. "Hey. Anybody give a damn what *I* want?"

"Not really," Brian said. He turned back to Tom, holding out one of his business cards. "But here's the thing. You guys have had ten years to work this out, and you haven't been able to. So all I'm saying is, if she gives you the boot tonight, I want you to call me. I do *not* want her to be alone. You understand?"

Tom nodded. Man, did he like this guy.

"I understand," he said.

"Brian," Kelly said softly. "One of these days I'm going to kill you."

He leaned over and kissed her cheek. "I know. But not today. Today you know I'm right."

He reached out to shake Tom's hand. And then he ran through the rain like the jock he used to be, and folded his lanky body into his pickup truck.

Kelly shut the door slowly. When she turned to Tom, her face was edgy and closed-in. He could tell she was uncomfortable.

"Look, we may as well get this out of the way right now," he said. "I do want to stay. But just to be sure everything is okay. If you've got a couch, I'll be happy to sleep there."

She nodded. "All right. I'm not a fool. I appreciate the offer, even though I hope it's unnecessary. I hope we're overreacting."

"Me, too." But ever since he'd seen that wedding invitation, he'd had a hard spot in the pit of his stomach that just wouldn't go away. It wasn't like a scrap of lace, that might have meant nothing at all, or a remote report of a hunting accident. This wedding invitation, with its nasty message, was personal. It was focused, direct and immediate.

Kopple had shown him the invitation, safe in its clear plastic bag. Those dark red, splotchy letters had looked spiteful, full of hatred. Someone was very angry with Kelly. Could it possibly be Sophie, after all these years? Hadn't she moved on emotionally at all?

Maybe not. And why was that so difficult to believe? After all, ten years hadn't changed his feelings one bit. Here he was, still looking at Kelly Carpenter as if he were dying of thirst and she were the only water left in the world.

She scanned the studio, as if making sure everything was settled. She walked over and typed in a few strokes on her computer keyboard, shutting the programs down. Then she went around and turned off all the lights but one.

She didn't look at him directly a single time.

"We'll get wet, going over to the house." She picked up her raincoat from the hook by the door. "I haven't been able to afford to enclose the walkway yet."

He took his raincoat, which was still dripping. "Lead the way," he said.

She opened the door and carefully twisted the silly doorknob lock, which of course wouldn't deter a child. But until the past few days, she apparently had felt no need to add security.

The two of them huddled for a moment under the metal roof, close enough for him to smell her perfume, and then she dashed off into the rain, her coat held over her head.

He followed. It wasn't far, but, as she'd predicted, by the time they reached the cottage door they were drenched. She fumbled with the key, her wet fingers slipping. It fell with a plop into a puddle of rain.

"Damn it," she said softly. She bent and felt around in the mud, then straightened and tried the key again. It opened this time, and, shaking her drenched coat to get rid of the worst of the water, she made her way inside.

The room was small, but beautiful. An arched window covered one wall—he suspected that, in the daylight, he'd discover that it was one of her own works. A sofa faced the fireplace, and on the table beside it a stained-glass Tiffany-style lamp cast a rosy glow over everything. A couple of upholstered chairs stood by a bookcase on the west end of the room, and a vase of yellow flowers filled a small architectural niche just beside the door.

That was all, and yet he thought it was one of the most welcoming spaces he'd ever seen.

"I like it," he said. "It's very—"

But she stopped him by placing one cold, wet hand over his mouth.

"Don't," she said. "Don't say things just because you're supposed to. There's no use pretending everything is normal."

He waited, wondering what she would prefer he said.

The light was so dim he couldn't see her features very clearly. But her hair was soaked, sculpted to her head, and her eyes were very dark in the shadows.

She hung her coat on the hook by the door, arranging it carefully. She ran her fingers through her wet hair. And then, finally, she turned back to him.

"There are two things I want to ask you," she said. She wrapped her arms across her chest, hugging herself, as if she were very cold. "Two favors, actually. And I hope you will say yes to both of them."

"All right. What's the first one?"

"I want you to help me find out what's really going on here. I don't think the police are going to work very hard at solving this mystery, and I need to know who sent me that note. I need to know what happened to Lily. I don't think I can get on with my life until I do. And you understand the Mellons better than anyone else I know. Will you help me find out what the truth really is?"

He didn't even have to think that one over. He'd come here today with exactly the same thought.

"Yes," he said. "If I can. We're in this together anyhow. We'll help each other."

"Even if the answer is Sophie? It almost has to be, you know. Who else would have sent me that invitation?"

"I know that," he said. "But yes. Even if it's Sophie. She has no right to terrorize you, or any of us. And she certainly has no right to try to keep you from seeing anyone you want. She has no claim on me anymore. If you and I sinned in the past, we've paid for it, don't you think?"

"Yes," she said. "I do." She took a deep breath. "And now the second thing."

He waited.

"You used to say you wanted me. Sexually. Do you still?"

He would have smiled, the question was so absurd, except for the shining intensity he glimpsed in her eyes.

He settled for simplicity. "Yes."

"Good." She tightened her arms. "Because I want you, too."

He felt his body respond to the words as if they'd been a hot touch on naked skin. But his body operated on mindless reflex, heard only the words themselves. His brain registered the melancholy in her voice and the incongruous body language of those crossed arms. His brain understood that something wasn't right.

What kind of passion was so totally devoid of joy?

He spoke carefully. "Are you sure, Kelly? You—you look exhausted. Maybe you just need someone to be with you while you sleep. I can do that."

"No," she said, and the expression in her eyes was hotter now, a distant kin to passion…but closer, he thought, to desperation. "I decided today that I'm not going to wait passively for things to happen. I'm going to go after what I want. I want to find out why Sophie sent me that invitation. If she's been—hurting people—I want to see to it that she's stopped."

"Yes," he said. "Of course. But—"

She lifted her chin. "And I want you to make love to me."

He glanced down at her tightly folded arms. She was so thin her elbows were white from the pressure. "Kelly, have you thought this through?"

"I've thought of everything. But there's just one thing I want you to do first. I want you to promise that in the morning we can pretend it never happened. No complications. No repeats. Can you promise that?"

He hesitated, trying to make sense of her words.

"No," he heard himself saying. "I'm not sure I can."

She smiled tensely. "Why not? Isn't this every man's dream proposition?" Her voice was strained. "Just sex. No strings, no long discussions in the morning about what it meant. I want it to mean *nothing*."

He wanted to reach out and lift that wet strand of hair from her forehead. But he couldn't. If he touched her at all, he'd be lost.

He settled for stepping a foot closer. "No, you don't, Kelly. That isn't you."

She raised her chin. "How do you know? You don't know anything about me. And you don't need to. All you need to know is that you've come at the perfect moment. I'm cold, and I'm lonely, and I'm tired of thinking about blood and death. I want someone's arms around me."

The numb distance in her tone stung him. "*Someone's* arms? Would anyone's arms do? Because I got the impression your ex-husband would be happy to oblige."

"If he thought I really needed him, yes, he probably would. But he's in love with Marie, and I don't want to cause trouble between them. And besides—"

She bit her lower lip. "Don't play games, Tom. You're not really jealous of Brian. You know it's your arms I want. You've always known that."

Yes, he had. When she'd first confessed her love, all those years ago, he had never understood it, but he had never doubted it. It had radiated out from her like music from a wind chime. He had never possessed her fully, but sometimes, when the memories in his mind blew a certain way, he could hear a far-off note or two.

He heard it now. It made him twenty-five again, and his body ached, remembering how hopeless he had felt back then, caught between what he had vowed too early and what he had discovered too late.

"Then why do I have to make such ridiculous promises? We've waited a long time for this, Kelly. Why just one night? Why shouldn't we have more? Why shouldn't we have as much as we want?"

"Because we won't want the same things. You'll want a couple of great days, a few fun weeks. But I don't want that. I want either the rest of your life, or one unforgettable night. And the only one of those you can give me is the night."

She must have seen him jerk forward, instinctively, stupidly, ready to protest, because she shook her head and held up a hand.

"Don't bother to deny it, Tom. It doesn't matter, really. We both know what kind of man you are."

He felt an irrational anger surge through him, though she spoke nothing but the truth. He was not the kind of man who could promise a woman forever. He'd done that once, and, like a meteor crashing into an ocean, it was still sending out ripples. Pain and fear, definitely. Maybe even madness and death.

"What makes you so sure you know what kind of man I am? Maybe," he said stubbornly, "you know as little about me as I know about you."

"That's quite possible," she said, her voice falling back into an exhausted listlessness. "So let's be strangers, Tom. People with no past, no future. We'll know nothing. We'll ask nothing. Nothing except one night of…" She shut her eyes. "One night of peace."

"Kelly." He touched her neck and she shivered. "Kelly, please—"

"I need your promise first." She was so tense he could feel the muscles in her neck thrumming. "Can you accept me on those terms?"

His whole body ached.

But how could he take advantage of the condition she was in? Chivalry wasn't something he ordinarily put on his résumé, but this was different.

The woman standing in front of him truly believed Sophie might be planning to kill her. She wanted comfort. And, he knew, she didn't want to die without having spent at least one night in his arms.

He felt the same. They had dreamed of each other too long to let anything, even Sophie, even death, snatch it away now.

The only difference was, he didn't believe she was going to die. He simply wouldn't allow it to happen.

They'd find Sophie, and they'd see to it that she got put away, not as a voluntary outpatient trying to mend a broken heart, but as the dangerously unstable woman she really was.

Together, they would make the terror go away. And when it was over, when it was possible to make sane decisions again, he'd take her and make love to her until the sky shook and the stars rained down like salt.

He might not be able to give her forever, but that night she wanted...he would make it magic.

If, when it was over, she still wanted him to.

She continued to stare at him.

"Well? Tom? Can you?"

"I'm sorry," he said, closing his eyes so that he wouldn't have to watch the disappointment douse the brilliance in hers. "I don't think I can."

CHAPTER THIRTEEN

STANDING IN THE SHOWER with his head flung back and his palms flat against the tiles, Sebastian let the hot water pound against his chest for several long minutes. He stood there until his scars began to burn.

But he knew he couldn't stay forever. Gwen needed to take a shower, too. They were going to the opera, and though Gwen couldn't tell Mozart from Metallica, she always welcomed a chance to preen before the cultured elite.

So he turned off the water and opened the shower door. To his shock, Tessa was sitting on the closed toilet, her blue-flowered dress twisted and her little legs dangling several inches above the floor. Her face was red, as if she'd been crying.

For his daughter's sake, Sebastian controlled his fury. His robe was hanging by the stall, as always, so he reached out calmly and put it on. But Gwen would pay for this. She was supposed to make sure Tessa and Seamus were safely in their rooms when Daddy took his shower.

Sometimes Sebastian wondered whether Gwen let the children wander around on purpose, just hoping he'd have to face the humiliation of having his scars exposed.

He belted his robe and went over to where Tessa sat,

sniffling into her hand, apparently oblivious to the fact that her father had just stepped naked from the shower. He picked her up, sat down on the cold lid of the commode himself and swung her around so that she straddled his thigh.

He ducked his head to look into her pretty blue eyes, now wet and red, the lashes matted together with tears.

"Hey, there," he said softly. "What's made my little girl cry?"

Tessa looked at him, a frown between her brows. "Seamus did," she said angrily. "I wouldn't give him Mr. Bear. And then he tore Mr. Bear's arm off."

"Poor Mr. Bear," Sebastian said. He brushed tears from Tessa's hot cheeks. "But I'll bet Mommy will sew his arm back on."

"She is right now. But I still hate Seamus."

Sebastian smiled. "Maybe Mommy can fix that, too."

Tessa scrunched up her little pink mouth. "How?"

He put his finger on the blue flowers of her dress, just above her heart. "Maybe Mommy can sew the love back on, right here, just like with Mr. Bear."

As he had hoped she would, Tessa laughed. "You can't sew love on somebody, Daddy. Love isn't a thing all full of stuffing, like an arm."

"No?" He pretended to be shocked. "Well, what is it, then?"

She fell forward, throwing her arms around his torso. "It's a way you *feel*. It feels like this—" she squeezed him tightly and made a grunting bear-hug sound "—when you love somebody."

He put his arms around her, too, and bear-hugged back. Snuggling happily against him, she pulled one arm free and stuck her thumb in her mouth. She rested her head against his chest, and then she wriggled a little, rubbing herself against his leg. She didn't even think about it, of course. She just knew that it felt good to hug Daddy, and it felt even better if she wiggled her bottom a little.

After a minute, he heard her thumb pop free of her pink lips, and then he felt her hand making its way inside the collar of his robe. She pressed against one of his welts with a tiny fingertip, testing. She did it again, on another spot.

"Daddy," she said in a muffled voice, her face still against the terry cloth. "Where did you get so many boo-boos?"

He tried to think which words he should use for the four-year-old version, but he was distracted by the rhythmic pressing of her fingertips.

"I was in an accident," he said.

"In a car accident?"

"Like a car accident, only with a boat. It was a long time ago."

She nodded. "We don't have a boat," she said. And he knew she was glad about that. She was afraid she might get scars someday, too, if they had a boat.

She was still exploring, pressing and lifting. He knew the scars flattened and turned white under her finger, then filled up again with pink blood when she let go. He could imagine how fascinating that seemed to a child.

She tilted a look up at him, as if to see whether he minded. "Do they hurt?"

"No," he said. He wished she would stop, but he didn't make her take her hand away. "Not very much."

"Will it help if I kiss it better?" She ducked her head, nuzzling between the two lapels of his robe.

"No," he said, inhaling sharply.

God, no!

He lifted her and set her down on the floor. "Better go see if Mommy's finished with Mr. Bear," he said. "You wouldn't want Seamus to get hold of him again."

She smiled, all sunshine and blue flowers, completely unaware of his agony.

"Okay," she said. "I will." And then she scampered out of the room. He sat there several minutes, breathing as evenly and steadily as he could.

No, no, no.

Why had this curse been put on him? He loved his daughter. Just like any father. He would die for her. This other thing—it wasn't him.

The bathroom door cracked and Gwen poked her head in.

"Are you almost done? I need to clean up, too, you know," she said in that high-pitched voice that didn't quite reach a whine but grated on his nerves nonetheless.

"I would have been out of here ten minutes ago," he said harshly, standing up and retying his robe with stiff fingers, "if you hadn't let Tessa come in."

She blanched and came into the room. "Oh, no, did she? I'm sorry, Sebastian. There was a dustup over Mr. Bear, and I was trying to calm things down. Seamus was crying—"

Sebastian walked up very close to his wife. He was much taller than she was, so simply getting in her face like this was as intimidating as raising his hand or his voice. It helped to let off steam.

"Seamus was crying? And that was too much for you? Maybe we shouldn't have had two children, Gwen, if you can't handle both of them."

She must have been more frazzled than he realized, because she seemed prepared to fight back. Ordinarily she knew better.

She tried to glare at him, but it was difficult, given how she had to look up to find his eyes.

"We wouldn't have had two if you hadn't insisted," she said. "At least not this close together. I wanted to wait. I told you so. Maybe if you'd been willing to control yourself, but no, whenever we fight, whenever I say no, it just turns you on more and—"

"For God's sake, Gwen. Stop it."

"No, I won't. You have a problem, Sebastian." She glanced down, her movements jerky and furious. "Look at you. Even now, you need it, don't you? It's because Tessa came in here. You like being angry—"

He slapped her.

At least, he meant it to be a slap. But somehow she ended up stumbling back. She would have hit the wall if she hadn't caught herself on a towel hanging from the rack behind her. She grabbed the cloth and, as it slid from the porcelain bar, she drifted slowly to the floor.

And lay there crying.

"Goddamn it, Gwen, don't carry on like that. Get up. You're not hurt."

He started to bend over and pull her to her feet, but as he glanced at the bathroom door he saw Seamus standing there. The boy looked frozen, staring wide-eyed at his mother.

"Seamus. Son—"

The rest of the words Sebastian had wanted to say simply died in his throat. In his head, he saw another doorway, another little boy paralyzed with fear. He saw himself, staring at his own mother, who lay on her bedroom floor, crying. He saw his father standing over her, his pants open, revealing an erection that terrified the child.

"Son—"

Seamus turned his horrified blue eyes toward his father for just a fraction of a second. And then he turned and fled down the hall.

Seamus. My baby.

Gwen found the strength, then, to get to her feet and follow her son. The look she gave Sebastian as she exited the room was beyond description. Beyond contempt.

He felt his legs go limp. He lowered himself to the vanity chair and dropped his head, which suddenly seemed too heavy to hold up.

He had tried—God himself could give witness. For so many years he had tried to prevent this. He had, for the sake of his family, kept a beast locked in his breast, allowed it to gnaw at his own bones rather than let it out where it would hurt the people he loved.

And yet, in the blink of an eye, without any warning, the beast had simply burst free.

Sebastian began to cry noiselessly into his hands.

Sophie, I've failed.

Seamus...

And so the terrible cycle began again.

WILLOW HILL REHABILITATION Center looked more like a country club than a mental-health institution. Set on twenty-five acres in North Carolina, its redbrick main building had white pillars and Palladian porticoes. From the parking lot, Tom and Kelly could also see a long blue swimming pool, at least four smaller cottages and a tennis court, on which two sleek teenagers were playing a very competitive game.

Though Tom and Kelly had left early, right after sunup, the trip had taken more than three hours, so it was now almost eleven. It had been a quiet drive, with little chitchat, but considering how tense their conversation had been last night, Tom wasn't particularly surprised.

All things considered, she'd been quite civilized about it. Once he had declined her offer of a one-night stand, she had let the subject drop. She'd found him an extra set of pillows and blankets to make the sofa comfortable, offered him a nightcap, which he'd also rejected politely, and finally withdrawn to her own room.

He didn't know if she'd slept, but he certainly hadn't. He'd still been awake when, just before dawn, the rain had stopped. He had walked barefoot to the window and watched as the last of the clouds blew away, revealing a crescent moon and about a million stars.

He would have liked to think the clearing was symbolic, that all their problems were going to blow away, too, and bring them a fresh start. But he was a lawyer, not a poet. He knew that, however beautiful the stars might be, they didn't *mean* anything. They didn't grant wishes or pour down blessings. They didn't glitter to provide a beacon to the lost or to inspire the weary to try again. They glittered because they had to. They were just stars.

"It's an amazing clinic," Kelly said. She'd been taking in the whole of Willow Hill with wide eyes. "I'm glad Sophie has been staying in a place like this. The first one, the one I visited, was—" She broke off.

"Pretty grim," he finished for her. "I saw it, too."

She looked for a minute as though she'd like to ask about his visits, but she stopped herself and looked away.

"She wouldn't see me, either," he volunteered. "The doctor came out and told me he thought it would be better if I didn't come back."

"That's what they told me, too. I went back once, a couple of months later, and got the same answer. I should have ignored them, I guess. But I never did go again after that. Did you?"

He shook his head. "It was a miracle I went at all. I didn't want to. I took the doctor's dismissal as my get-out-of-jail-free card. I just put it in my pocket and headed for the border."

He was overstating it, but he knew it was better to nip in the bud any illusions that might still be hiding in her subconscious. He had been so angry, so caught up in his own problems. He hadn't really cared whether Sophie had rotted behind those clinic doors forever.

Kelly looked out the window again. "All right. So what exactly happens now? You're going to talk to the doctor—"

"Who of course won't tell me much. But I might be able to scare up how long she's been gone, at least."

"Right. And while you're with him, I'm going to wander around and see if I can find anyone who knows Sophie."

"I've done some research on this place," he said. "It doesn't have any extraordinary levels of security. It's got a lot of outpatient therapies, and some transitional treatment programs, kind of a halfway-house idea. Very few of their patients actually live full-time on the premises. They have only twenty beds. So you should be able to move around freely."

She nodded. "Okay, then," she said, as if to herself. She

smoothed her jeans with the palms of her hands. "I'm not much of a detective, but I'll do my best."

"You'll do fine," he said. "Remember, we're not expecting anything major. It's just the first step. And, if the doctor isn't too uptight about the privacy laws, maybe I will be able to read between the lines. I might be able to deduce just how disturbed he thinks she is."

She turned her shadowed eyes toward him. No, he thought, she hadn't slept last night, either. "You're sure she's *not* here?"

"I'm not a hundred percent sure of anything. But, before she knew there was any reason to hide the truth, Samantha told me they hadn't been able to find Sophie for several weeks. Imogene said Sophie was back in care, but that was later, after we'd told her about the lace."

"She told the police that, too," Kelly said. They had talked to Vince Kopple before they'd left this morning, and he had filled them in on the basics of Imogene Mellon's testimony. Samantha, apparently, had refused to tell the cops anything. "Would Mrs. Mellon lie to the police?"

"If she thought she had to, if she thought it would protect Sophie, I think she might." Tom touched Kelly's shoulder lightly. "Sophie's not here, Kelly. But if she were, that would be a good thing. When she's here, she undoubtedly takes her medication regularly. She would be less dangerous here than anywhere."

She tried to smile. "Yes," she said. "I know."

He left his hand on her shoulder and she didn't pull away. They sat there another couple of minutes, watching the people come and go on the grounds. Some wore white uniforms and walked briskly. Others went more slowly, sometimes staring at the ground.

None of them was Sophie.

"I guess we'd better get started," Kelly said. "It's not going to get any easier."

She wasn't a coward, that much was certain. She was nervous, of course, but she wasn't about to admit it.

"Kelly," he said, tightening his hand on her shoulder.

She turned. "What?"

He didn't say anything. He just leaned over and kissed her softly on her open mouth. She tasted like toothpaste and smelled of yellow flowers.

She didn't protest, but she didn't exactly melt, either.

And she didn't ask him why he'd done it.

Which was a good thing, because he didn't have an answer.

KELLY FOUND HERSELF on a garden path, where wooden picnic tables had been placed artistically among the overhanging, autumn-colored trees.

It felt good to be out of the car. Locked in that bubble with Tom, watching the highway speed by outside, had tested her control. Though neither of them referred to last night, she knew the memory of it rode with them every mile.

Still, she wasn't sorry she'd asked him to make love to her. She was finished letting regrets—or fear—rule her life. She had wanted him, and she had told him so. There was no shame in that. She wasn't sure why he'd turned her down. Maybe he had some mistaken notion of honor that prevented him from taking advantage of the strange circumstances. Or maybe he just hadn't liked having ground rules laid down in advance.

It didn't really matter why. He had said no, and she had

coped with that the best she could. That, too, was part of the new Kelly. She could face whatever she had to.

She turned her attention back to the task at hand. Several patients were out here having lunch, some of them with guests, she deduced. Funny how you could sort of tell who was just visiting and who had begun to call this place their home.

In a strange way, the visitors all looked the same—they all had a determined cheer, a falsity, in their faces. The patients were a more mixed bag. Some looked angry, some heartbroken, some frightened. Some just wore a drugged and lethargic blankness. But there was nothing fraudulent about them. The emotions they struggled with were painfully real.

She walked slowly, wondering where to begin. She smiled at a few people, and they smiled back. But beginning a conversation seemed impossible.

Every time she saw a blond head, she felt her steps falter. If she did run into Sophie, she wondered what she would do. And what would Sophie do? What emotion was stamped on Sophie's beautiful face, after all these years?

She wound along the path, increasing the distance from the main facility. The tables were farther apart out here and most of them were empty.

As she reached the last table, the one where the path ended under the shady branches of a stately, fire-red maple, she noticed that the one woman sitting there was looking at her. The thirty-something blonde was smoking a cigarette, and something in her posture, the sleek cut of her hair and the perfection of her makeup, reminded Kelly of Sophie.

If Sophie and this woman had ever been at Willow Hill

together, Kelly thought, they could have been friends. No one in this expensive clinic was poor, but this woman seemed to exude that mysterious elegance, that slight tip toward decadence, that characterized the Mellons.

It was a place to start, at least. Even in a psychiatric ward, people of extraordinary wealth and privilege probably tended to bond. Perhaps especially in a psychiatric ward, where their sense of superiority and importance was threatened by communal living and the leveling power of mental illness.

The woman was still looking at Kelly, still smiling.

Kelly smiled back. "I guess I've reached the end of the road," she said, gesturing toward the rounded tip of the path, which looked a little like the end of a thermometer. Beyond that, there were only trees and shadows.

"I guess you have," the other woman said. She chuckled and waved her cigarette, which Kelly now saw wasn't lit. "In more ways than one."

Kelly sighed heavily, as if the long walk from the building had tired her, and then sank onto the picnic bench opposite the other woman. "I was looking for a friend of mine, a patient here. But I must have missed her. I didn't see her anywhere."

The blonde tilted her head. The silken hair shifted. It was as beautifully tended as Sophie's had been, but cut shorter, in a lazy, swinging bob. "You're a visitor? I took you for one of us."

Kelly tried not to show how startled she was. "You did?"

The blonde laughed softly. "Yeah," she said. "Not because you look crazy. We're not all crazy here, anyhow. You just look super tired. That's what we really have in common. We're all exhausted from wrestling with our demons."

That was so close to what Kelly had been thinking. The woman seemed to have read her mind.

"I'm Tina. And this little guy is my demon," the woman said, waving her cigarette around in the air. "Well, not him specifically. Addiction generally. All kinds. Alcohol is my personal favorite."

She ran the cigarette deftly through her fingers, like a cardsharp showing off his skills. "Anyhow, who were you looking for? I might know him."

"Her," Kelly corrected. "I'm looking for Sophie. Sophie Mellon."

The blonde grinned. "No kidding? Is Sophie back? I knew she would be. That girl has her addictions, too. Except hers aren't anywhere near as much fun as mine."

Kelly wondered exactly what Tina meant. She thought about asking, but where was the line? When did it stop being legitimate investigation into possible crimes and start being prurient snooping into Sophie's private hell?

"Actually," Kelly confessed, "I'm not sure whether Sophie has checked herself back in or not. I haven't seen her in a while. Last time we talked, though, she was here."

"That must have been a couple of months ago," Tina said.

"Has it been that long?"

Tina languidly lifted her leg, planting her foot onto the bench beside her. She wore red satin pants with Chinese dragons writhing down the sides. She rubbed her palm across her kneecap, as if she enjoyed the feel of the satin.

"Yeah, Sophie's been gone at least a month, I'd say. I know, because it's not the same when she's not here. Lots of these people have trouble remembering not to drink out of the toilet, you know? But Sophie's like me. She knows what day it is. It's just that sometimes—" Tina stared at her cigarette with a dreamy look "—sometimes she just can't help being a bad little girl. And then she has to punish herself."

Kelly swallowed. "You mean—"

She searched her memories and found one. Seventeen-year-old Sophie at a party, holding her finger over a candle until Kelly had smelled burning flesh. She'd pushed Sophie's finger away from the flame, and Sophie had laughed, so proud, so strangely euphoric, though her fingertip was red and blistered.

And Kelly remembered the other girls' faces, both awed and disgusted, and the way they had looked at each other, as if they knew it wasn't just a parlor trick.

She decided to risk it. "You mean the way she hurts herself?"

Tina laughed. "Oh, honey, we all hurt ourselves, that's why we're here. If we hurt other people, we'd be in prison instead. But yeah, she's a cutter. God only knows why she does it. Daddy didn't love her. Daddy loved her too much. Mommy was a bitch." She smiled at Kelly. "Those are the usual explanations, anyhow. It's pretty much one size fits all when it comes to psychoanalysis, you know. Just ask Freud."

"Why do *you* think she does it?"

Tina shrugged. "I think she does it because she feels like shit and cutting makes her feel better. Why do *you* think she does it?"

"I've never been sure," Kelly answered honestly. She could suddenly remember a half a dozen times when Sophie had done equally horrifying things. Kelly had always assumed Sophie was trying to look cool, tougher than the rest of them. Now she saw how fatally she had misread it. "I wish I knew more about it. I wish I understood it better."

For once, Tina's smile faded and fell away. "No, you don't, honey," she said, her voice throaty. "No, indeed you don't."

Suddenly Kelly knew she had crossed the line. This was the quick and terrible glimpse into hell. But when, she wondered, had Sophie's urge to hurt herself transformed into the need to hurt other people? Had it been that day at the church, when she'd cried diamond tears and finally crumpled into her brother's arms? When she'd stood up again, was she a different Sophie entirely?

Kelly didn't speak for a long minute, trying to get her emotions under control. Luckily, Tina showed no signs of leaving. She just stilt-walked her cigarette across the planks of the picnic table, humming to herself in an off-key contralto.

When Kelly felt she could speak calmly, she cleared her throat.

"Do you know where she went, Tina? Do you know where Sophie planned to go when she left here?"

Tina looked up, her fingers paused midmotion. "Not really. Maybe home, although I'm not sure about that. She was pretty ambivalent about home. Most of us are."

"Where, then? Was there anywhere she *wasn't* ambivalent about?"

Tina put the cigarette in her mouth and pretended to drag on it. Then she squinted, as if she felt invisible smoke curling around her face.

"Maybe her brother," she said. "She was pretty screwed up about him, too, but she sure talked about him a lot."

"Sebastian," Kelly said.

"Yeah. Him. She was always carrying on about all the things he'd done for her, all the sacrifices he'd made. Hell, I saw him, you know. He looked like a damn cold fish to me. But she might have thought he could help her."

"Yes," Kelly said. "That's a good idea. I'll check with him. Thank you, and—" She hesitated. Was it patronizing to wish the other woman good luck?

Tina smiled coldly, as if she knew what Kelly was thinking. She rose and shook her silk pants into graceful folds.

"Or hey. She may have bled to death in a hotel room somewhere. Who knows? Cutters are weird. Give me a nice, predictable alcoholic any day."

CHAPTER FOURTEEN

SEBASTIAN'S HOUSE was so ordinary Kelly found herself double-checking the address. How could this middle-class, split-level bungalow, the kind of family home featured on commercials for diapers and life insurance, belong to the heir of Coeur Volé?

They'd been driving for hours, and Kelly noticed that, as they neared Raleigh, Tom's mood grew increasingly grim. He had agreed that Sebastian was the obvious next stop, but she'd sensed that he disliked the prospect intensely.

She wondered why. It was awkward, of course, but no more so than going to Coeur Volé to look at the wedding dress. Less, actually. Sebastian and Tom had never been great friends, but they had seemed to get along all right, before the wedding. And Sebastian had never come stampeding into Atlanta, ready to draw and quarter Tom, as rumor said Mr. Mellon had.

Tom parked the car in front of the cute redbrick house and killed the engine. He didn't seem eager to get out. Instead he surveyed the property, as if he thought he might see Sophie hiding behind the bushes.

But surely not. This place didn't look as if any Mellon had ever set foot in it. Not Sophie, and, Kelly had to admit, not Sebastian, either. Where was the melodrama? Where was the eccentricity? Where were the snobbery and decadence?

Not a whisper of any of that touched this discreetly prosperous home. The windows fluttered with crisp Irish lace. The neatly clipped lawn was bright green, rare in September, and was pleasantly littered with a scooter, a tricycle, a big blue foam baseball bat and a multicolored plastic ball.

In the driveway, just in front of an open garage door, sat a tan minivan and a shiny black vintage Corvette.

"The car is his," Tom said. "The rest of this is just window dressing."

Though Kelly had been surprised, too, by these stereotypical middle-class trappings, she wondered why Tom felt so sure it was purely an act.

"It's been a long time," she ventured. "Maybe he's changed."

"Maybe." But the look Tom shot her said *not this much, not in a million years.*

"Shall we go in?" She agreed that the Corvette must be Sebastian's. "It looks as if he's home."

Tom drummed his fingers on the steering wheel a second or two. Then he turned toward her, his face darkly serious. "I still think I should drop you off at the hotel. This isn't likely to be a lot of fun."

"I know," she said firmly. They'd had this discussion three times already. "But we are going to do it together. I have just as much at stake as you do."

He squeezed the steering wheel once, hard, and then he nodded.

"All right," he said. "Let's go, then."

They didn't have to ring the front bell more than once.

An extraordinarily sweet-looking brunette answered the door. She had an oven mitt on one hand and a spatula in the other.

"Hi," she said cautiously. She probably was afraid they were selling encyclopedias or religion. "May I help you?"

Tom smiled. "I'm Tom Beckham. This is Kelly Ralston. We're old friends of Sebastian's. Is he here?"

A little girl, maybe three or four, peeked around her mother's skirt. Kelly had to work to hold back a gasp. The little girl looked like a miniature Sophie, right down to the devilish sparkle in her beautiful blue eyes.

Tom must have noticed it, too. He bent down immediately and he smiled warmly at her.

"Hi," he said. "Is your daddy home?"

"Yes." The little girl eyed him as suspiciously as her mother had. "But he's busy. He's reading Seamus and me a story."

"Tessa," the woman said, removing the oven mitt and putting a warning hand on her daughter's head. "Would you please go tell Daddy someone is here to see him?"

"Tom Beckham," Tom said again, enunciating clearly. "Tell him Tom Beckham is here."

The little girl frowned, obviously not pleased that her time with her father was about to be interrupted. The frown was pure Sophie. Her mother's hand tightened and eased the little girl into an about-face.

"Okay," Tessa mumbled. "I'll go."

When the child left, the woman seemed uncomfortable, as though she were more accustomed to dealing with people indirectly, with her children as the filter.

"I'm Sebastian's wife," she said with a careful smile. "Gwen."

"Hi, Gwen," Kelly said. But there didn't seem to be anywhere to go from there. Gwen wasn't letting them in the house before Sebastian said it was okay.

Finally there was commotion in the hall, and Sebastian appeared behind his wife. At least Kelly assumed it must be Sebastian. Actually, it looked more like a watered-down copy of a copy of the man she'd once known.

The Sebastian she remembered had been bigger than life. More beautiful than other people. More exotic. More eccentric. He had dressed with flair, talked with flair, and even smiled with flair.

This man looked just like any other button-down businessman in this happy-valley neighborhood. Khakis, a hunter-green polo shirt, loafers and a conservative haircut. He even had a hint of a beer belly in the making.

"Kelly," he said with a moderate amount of warmth. "This is a surprise." And then he turned to Tom. "Beckham," he added, his warmth dying instantly. "I definitely didn't expect to see you here."

"Hi, Sebastian," Tom said without any particular intonation. "We've driven a long way. May we come in?"

Sebastian hesitated. Kelly could see that he wanted to say no, but his wife, his daughter and a sober-faced little boy of about two or three all stood behind him, waiting and listening.

"It's important," Tom said. "It's about Sophie."

Gwen seemed to know what that meant. She began herding Tessa and her little brother together, whispering something about leaving Daddy alone.

"I'm not sure I want to talk to you about Sophie, Beckham," Sebastian said. "I'm not sure you have that right."

Tom shrugged. "Okay. You can talk to the police instead."

Behind Sebastian, Gwen looked up, her face anxious, her body still hovering protectively over her children. "Sebastian?"

He ignored her. "What do you mean, the police? Has something happened to Sophie?"

"We're not sure. That's one of the things we need to talk to you about." Tom took a step forward, subtly assertive. "May we come in?"

Sebastian backed away from the door.

"Of course," he said. He turned to his wife. "Gwen, honey, do you mind finishing the story for the kids? We were at the part where the sailor dog builds a tent."

"No!" Tessa broke away from her mother and ran to wrap her arms around her father's leg. "I want you to read it, Daddy. You promised."

Sebastian bent down. Kelly watched him pinch his daughter's chin. She was amazed at how much gentle affection that one touch could demonstrate. She looked over at Tom, but his eyes were fixed on Sebastian, too.

"Tessie," Sebastian said softly. "Daddy has to talk grown-up talk right now."

The little girl folded her arms over her chest mulishly. But she had begun to lean in toward her father, already relenting. Obviously she adored him.

"I hate when you talk grown-up," she said.

"Me, too," Sebastian responded with a smile. "But sometimes I have to. Like when you have to eat your peas."

The little girl smiled back. "Sometimes I *don't* eat them," she said, holding up a chubby forefinger in a simply adorable way, indicating a big secret. "One time I put them down the potty."

"Tessie," her mother said, teasingly shocked. Tessa chuckled, aware that she'd amused the grown-ups.

Sebastian eyed Kelly and Tom with an attractive grin. "Well, these two grown-ups are really too big to put in the potty, don't you think?"

Tessa giggled.

"So maybe," Sebastian went on thoughtfully, "I should just talk to them for a little while, and then I'll finish your story."

He wiggled Tessa's chin. "Okay?"

She sighed, but she was still smiling. "Okay."

Sebastian straightened up and nodded at Gwen, who hustled the children down the hall.

"Let's talk in my study," Sebastian said to Tom. "It'll be quiet in there."

The study was just as conventionally suburban as the rest of the house. Sebastian had a laptop on his desk, a globe in the corner, and a lot of paperback thrillers in the bookshelves, mixed in with dozens of thick, impressive tomes on investing.

Kelly remembered that she'd heard Sebastian was an investment planner these days. A fairly successful one. Perhaps that would account for the atmosphere of restrained prosperity and good, common-sense middle-class values. Nobody wanted an investment planner who looked exaggerated and decadent, as if he might go off half-cocked at any moment.

Nobody wanted a financial planner who looked like a Mellon.

Once they were all seated, Sebastian leaned forward over his desk and offered them an apologetic smile.

"I'm sorry I was abrupt at the door," he said. "But you

have to understand, Beckham. Old habits are hard to break.
Your name has been mud in our family for a decade now.
In fact, I still don't quite understand why you're here."

Instead of answering, Tom picked up the framed photograph Sebastian had on the edge of his desk. He turned
it over and looked at it. It was Gwen and the two children,
smiling together. It was a lovely picture.

Sebastian clearly didn't like the way Tom was manhan-
dling his photo, but he seemed determined to keep things
polite. He didn't say anything.

That alone was worthy of note, Kelly thought. In the
old days, she and Sophie hadn't dared to touch any of
Sebastian's things. He'd been very possessive. He would
have been furious.

But everyone grew up sooner or later. Eventually, even
the most spoiled rich boy learned to play nice and share.
She had a feeling his children might have helped teach him
about all that.

"You have a delightful family," Tom said, setting down
the frame. "Congratulations."

Sebastian moved the picture an inch or two, back to its
original position. "Thanks," he said. "I'm a very lucky
man. But you didn't come all the way up here to get a look
at my family. Why did you come?"

"We want to know if you have any idea where Sophie is."

Sebastian opened his mouth, as if he were going to
speak, but nothing came out. He ran his fingers through
his fine hair. And then he stood, pushing his desk chair
back with a good bit of noise.

"No," he said finally. "No, I don't know where she is.
And to tell you the truth, Beckham, I'm worried. I have
been for some time."

"Why?"

"Because ordinarily, when she leaves the clinic, she keeps in close touch with me, or with Mother and Samantha. She knows we like to monitor her…her health. This time, she hasn't said a word to any of us. We don't know where she's staying, how she's feeling, whether she's taking her medication—"

He broke off abruptly. "You haven't heard from her, have you?"

Tom shook his head. "Of course not."

"No, I suppose she wouldn't call you." Sebastian turned to Kelly. "What about you?"

"No," she said. She and Tom had already discussed how much they planned to reveal, which was very little. They had decided this was purely a fact-gathering mission, not an information-sharing one. They just needed to know if Sophie was hiding here, or if Sebastian knew where to find her.

"What exactly are you worried about?" Tom kept his gaze on Sebastian, though the other man was restlessly prowling the room. "What's the problem? What do you think she might do?"

Sebastian shook his head. "I don't know. It's been a month." He looked over at Tom. "She's very ill. You know that, don't you? She's desperately unhappy, and confused, and though we all try to help her, sometimes—"

He sat back down abruptly. He seemed to be struggling for composure. "Sometimes we don't succeed. This doesn't come as news to either of you, I'm sure, but as a family, the Mellons are pretty screwed up. Sometimes it feels like the blind leading the blind."

Tom didn't say anything, but Kelly's heart twisted. The

handsome, arrogant Sebastian she had known ten years ago was hardly visible. Something had worn all that gloss away. Now all she saw was exhaustion and pain.

"I'm sorry, Sebastian," she said. "I know how much you love her."

Tom made an abrupt movement, quickly stifled, but Sebastian saw it.

"I know what you're thinking," he said roughly. "You think I should have loved her a little less. I should have demanded less of her. And you're right." He put his hand into his hair. "You're right, damn it. I've spent the past several years trying to make up for it, but—"

Tom raised his eyebrows. "But the damage was done?"

Kelly frowned. When Tom had said this wasn't going to be pretty, she had thought he meant that Sebastian would be accusatory and vengeful. She hadn't imagined that he meant he himself would be so bitter.

What exactly was going on between these two men? It was like watching a play in a foreign tongue. She could read expressions and body language, but the real significance of the words wasn't always clear.

Sebastian glanced at Kelly. "I'm sorry you have to hear this, but Tom and I…there are things we need to say. We have spent ten years avoiding it, but it's time to get things sorted out."

"It's all right," she said. "We were all left with a lot of emotions after the wedding. Maybe it is healthier to talk about them."

"Yes. But it's not easy. I couldn't have done it ten years ago. Not even five years ago." Sebastian took a deep breath. "But I think I can now. Say whatever you must, Tom. I know a lot of Sophie's problems are my fault."

Tom smiled. "Really? Well, stop the presses."

Sebastian flushed. "I even understand why you're bitter. I made things hard for you, back then, didn't I? I was so jealous. I was so afraid that, when Sophie married you, she wouldn't have any more time for me. I needed her, Tom. And I thought she needed me. We were so close. We were the same, fighting the same heredity, the same childhood baggage."

"Codependent, I think, is the polite term…one of them, at least," Tom said. "But pick your own."

"Codependent will do," Sebastian said quietly.

He looked too tired to be drawn into anger, no matter what Tom said. Kelly wondered whether Tom was trying to goad him into losing his temper, thinking Sebastian might reveal something. But Sebastian already looked stripped raw, humbled beyond imagination.

The suburban dream home might be an act, but this wasn't. This man was suffering. Kelly didn't doubt that for a minute.

"It wasn't anything—perverted," Sebastian said, looking at Kelly, as if he needed her, particularly, to understand. "It was just that I counted on her too much. When the boat crashed, I was only fifteen. I was still a kid in a lot of ways. But I was left with scars, deep, ugly scars, all over my chest and back."

Kelly was shocked. This was news to her. She knew there had been a bad boating accident, but no one had ever mentioned that Sebastian had been permanently disfigured. And because she'd never seen him shirtless, she'd had no idea. She had always assumed he was as beautiful all over as he was in the face.

"I didn't know," she said. "I'm so sorry."

He nodded acknowledgment.

"For many years it was very hard. I was sure no woman would ever be able to—stand me. But Sophie accepted me. She gave me courage, and comfort. And I needed those things so badly. I've come to terms with it now, mostly." He cast a quick glance at the photograph. "Thanks to Sophie, and to Gwen."

"Yes," Tom cut in. "Your lovely wife. How exactly did you get from that poor, wounded teenager…" He looked around the room. "To all this?"

"The hard way. Therapy, both physical and emotional. Years of it. Some of it was joint therapy, with Sophie. I had high hopes, for a while there, that both of us could find our way to something normal."

Tom raised one eyebrow. "But in the end you could only save yourself?"

Sebastian flushed. For the first time he seemed angry. "We're not at the *end* yet, Beckham. And I will never give up on the idea of saving her. Sophie is still young. She's still beautiful. She can still marry, and have a family of her own."

"Like yours."

"That's right. Like mine." Sebastian placed his thumb and forefinger on either side of his nose and pressed for a long moment. When he brought them away, Kelly could see a slight shining dampness at the corners of his eyes. "You've seen my daughter. Tessa is a miracle, a gift of joy I didn't deserve, and thought I'd never have. But, if Sophie doesn't come back to us, I might well lose it all."

Tom's face had lost a little of its cynical twist. "Why? What does Sophie have to do with your new family?"

"Everything! I don't deserve them. Gwen, the kids,

they're fantastic. But I'm no catch, I'll tell you. I'm a Mellon. I have my father's temper, and my mother's weakness. A terrible combination. But Sophie…" He shook his head. "Sophie steadies me. She keeps me from capsizing on the rocks."

Tom started to speak, but then he subsided. It seemed as if his desire to spar with Sebastian had died.

"That's why I absolutely have to find her." Sebastian put his face in his hands. "If anything happens to her—"

As if on cue, in the background they heard the high, happy sound of young laughter. Sebastian rose, went to the window and looked out into the backyard. Gwen was pushing both children on a swing set, one with each hand. All three of them were flushed and breathless with the silly fun of it.

"I know you're looking for Sophie, Tom," Sebastian said, never taking his eyes off the picture window that framed his laughing family. "My mother told me all about it. I know you think Sophie may have…done bad things. I think you're wrong, but—"

He paused. He still hadn't turned around. "If you find her before I do, will you tell her something for me?"

"What?" Tom had stood up, too.

"Please tell her I love her, no matter what she's done."

It was an innocent request. It didn't ask for promises Tom couldn't keep, like promises not to go to the police or to shield Sophie from the consequences of her actions.

It would have been the easiest thing in the world to say, "Sure, if I find her, I'll tell her."

But to Kelly's surprise, Tom didn't. He stared at Sebastian's back for a long second and then, without a word, he turned and walked out of the room.

CHAPTER FIFTEEN

THE BACK GARDENS of Coeur Volé were strange at night.

Sometimes, when a stiff wind moved branches and plants around, Trig found himself imagining that the statues were moving, too. A stony head would seem to tilt, as if its eyes followed Trig's progress through the garden. Or a finger would suddenly point a different way, as if to say, *Over there. Are you looking for secrets, Trig? You'll find one over there.*

But he already knew where the secrets were. He visited them, one by one, almost every night.

He always stood first at the foot of the garden and looked up at Mr. and Mrs. Mellon's bedroom. In his mind, that's where it had all begun, although he'd heard his parents say it had really begun long before that. *Don't fix your eye on either of those girls, Trig,* his father would say. *That blood went bad a hundred years ago.*

But Trig hadn't been around a hundred years ago, so for him it had begun in Mr. and Mrs. Mellon's bedroom. He'd heard muffled screams coming from there, as he crouched below in the darkness. He'd heard it so often that even now, all these years later, when he looked up he imagined that the window had taken on the shape and color of a scream.

Square, like a straining, gaping mouth. Silver. Sharp. As if the house itself were screaming.

After that, Trig would walk down to the river's edge and look at the place where the dock used to be. The Mellons used to have a boat, and once, when he was fifteen, Sebastian had even invited Trig to go skiing on the river.

But only once. For several weeks afterward, Trig had watched from the garden, wishing he could go out on the water again. He had been good at skiing. He was always good at physical things.

He had watched a lot. And so he had been watching the time Sebastian grabbed the wheel from Mr. Mellon, even though Mr. Mellon was yelling, and steered that boat right into the dock.

Trig had been so shocked that later he'd been confused about what he had seen. When people called it an accident, he didn't say any different.

He had stared at the fire, fire on the water, such a strange sight. He had been too scared to move. Later, when he'd heard his parents saying, *Oh, that poor family,* he'd felt bad that he hadn't worried about Sebastian and Mr. Mellon. But he couldn't help it. The truth was, his first thought had been *I guess I know why he didn't ask me again.*

Then he visited the fallen woman. He didn't care about the woman, he hadn't ever liked the way her face looked up at him, as if she were asking him to pull her out of the quicksand, which of course he would never do. He knew what was buried under her. Sophie's little white dog, with its stomach burst open and maggots eating all the parts inside.

At the end of his rounds, he visited less important places, places where he just thought he'd seen something happen, or where he'd noticed crushed flowers in the morning and sick smells that shouldn't be there. Places that felt sad, or frightened or mean.

He needed to visit them all, so that they'd know he was watching. It was better to be safe than sorry.

He was almost ready to go home when he saw Mrs. Mellon. She was sitting on a long, black iron bench, right next to the dark red climbing roses. She shouldn't sit there, he thought. It was one of the bad places. The roses used to be pink, but they had turned the color of Sophie's blood that day. They had climbed so high because they wanted to get away.

He tried to move past her without being spotted, hoping he would blend in with the wind and the darkness. But she saw him.

"Who's there?" She stood, her hands up against her heart. "Who is it?"

He didn't want to stop. He didn't like Mrs. Mellon. In his head, she was always screaming, even when her mouth was closed. Her mouth was square and wide and black, like a window.

But he stopped anyhow. "It's me, Mrs. Mellon," he said. "It's Trig."

She came out of the little nook, her hands still fisted on her chest, as if they had fused to the skin there.

"Trig, what are you doing here? This is private property. You are trespassing. Do you know what that is? It's something very bad, and you could get into a lot of trouble."

He didn't like the way she was talking to him. Did he know what trespassing was? Did she think he was stupid? Trespassing was when you were somewhere you didn't belong. But he belonged at Coeur Volé, just as much as she did. Sophie had asked him to take care of it for her while she was gone.

"Do you hear me, Trig? Trespassing is a very serious matter. A very bad thing."

He took several steps closer to her. He noticed that she backed up, which was good. "What about you, Mrs. Mellon? What about all the bad things you've done?"

She gasped softly, and her face turned the color of moonlight, as if he had shocked her. But she knew about the bad things. It was her family, after all. It was her window, her roses, her statues, her house.

Her hands fell to her sides, and when she spoke her voice was thin, not at all the mean voice she'd used at first.

"What are you talking about?"

"I'm talking about what I know." He nodded. "I'm talking about what I've seen."

"I see." She drew in a long, shaking breath. "Well, don't worry, Trig. For the bad things I've done, I'll answer to God," she said, and he had the feeling that, though she used his name, she was really talking to herself. "And very soon."

And then, abruptly, she made a strange sound. She bent over, her hands once again at her breast. She made a second sound, a gurgling syllable that might have been his name.

He looked at her. He wondered if God had heard her and decided that she should give Him her answers now.

But then the wind blew and the statues moved. They were all watching Mrs. Mellon. And Trig knew that God couldn't have heard her, because God had never, ever been in this garden.

He looked at her one more time. She was so still, bent over and barely breathing. Maybe, he thought, she was turning into another statue for the garden. Maybe she would like that.

He moved away without making a sound and found his way home in the dark.

THE HOTEL TOM FOUND just off the interstate in Raleigh wasn't anything thrilling, but he figured it would do. It was a business hotel, so the rooms were clean, fairly large and decorated with a certain amount of dignity, which meant the television was hidden in an armoire and the prints on the walls were nicely framed.

Tom booked two adjoining rooms, and after they ate dinner at a chain restaurant down the street, they were both tired enough to want to head right back and settle in.

That had been two hours ago. Since then, Tom had made a few calls and played with his office e-mail, though he couldn't really get enthusiastic about any of it right now. Nothing seemed real except the need to find Sophie.

And, of course, Kelly's soft, get-ready-for-bed sounds, which he heard through the walls.

He took out the picture Kelly had loaned him, the one of the wedding party at the rehearsal dinner. It was almost painful to look at—he remembered that moment so well. That whole night, Sophie had clung absurdly, leaning into him as if she couldn't stand up on her own. He hadn't realized how obvious his shrinking away had been. He'd imagined himself so subtle, so self-contained. But in the photograph he was tilting away from her as if she had a communicable disease.

He studied all the expressions, but he stared a long time

at Sophie, trying to see a murderer in that beautiful, needy face. But all he could think was…*I never really knew her at all.*

When his cell phone rang, he grabbed it and looked at the caller ID with his heart racing. He'd put one of his best investigators on the case this morning. Maybe the man had found something.

But it was just Bailey, and the instant Tom said "hello" the older man began to rant.

"Okay, Beckham. Enough is enough. You've got to come back. Trent Saroyan just got arrested for DUI. Apparently he hit some kid on a bike. At five-thirty in the afternoon, mind you. The man is an attorney's nightmare, but he's your nightmare. We tried to handle it, but he wants you, and only you, and he wants you now."

"Bailey—"

"And just so you know, Coach O'Toole is going to sue Saroyan after all. So you can handle them both when you get here. When exactly will that be? It's ten now, so you could be here by midnight if you step on it. I'll tell him one, just so he doesn't get antsy and—"

"Bailey, slow down. Let me get a word in. I can't come back tonight."

"The hell you can't. I don't give a damn about your burnout, son. If you want this job, you'd better get back here and do it."

Tom didn't answer.

There was that question again. *Did he want this job?*

He leaned back in the chair he'd pulled up to the room's small desk and stared at his computer screen. Two hundred and fifty-one unread e-mails. These past few days, he'd just let them pile up and he couldn't believe how freeing it had been. He'd fantasized about hitting a few keys, seeing the question "Delete all?" and simply keying in…*yes*.

All those overwritten documents alleging this and stipulating that. All those bored, bad-tempered rich people, suing one another for the sheer diversion of it.

He couldn't stand any of them, and he suddenly couldn't imagine himself going back at all.

"How is the kid?" he asked.

"What kid?" Then, remembering, Bailey made an impatient sound. "Shit, I don't know. Alive, I guess. They would have told me if they were enhancing the charge to manslaughter."

"You're joking." Tom was holding the phone too tightly. His knuckles ached. "You don't *know?*"

"No, I don't know," Bailey said defensively, "because, damn it, at the moment it isn't pertinent to our interests."

"God, Bailey. Do you hear yourself?"

Bailey was silent an ominous moment. "Do *you* hear *your*self? You sound like a friggin' Girl Scout. Don't get self-righteous on me, Beckham. I'll care about the kid tomorrow. Tonight Saroyan is my problem. No. Correct that. Tonight *you* are my problem. And Saroyan is yours."

Tom closed his eyes. In his head he could see his grandfather, Hadley Beckham, who had been born a millionaire, and hadn't needed to work a day in his life, but who had, for fifty years, spent sixteen hours a day helping people who couldn't afford lawyers of their own.

That work ethic certainly hadn't been passed genetically to his son, Tom's father. Hadley Beckham Jr. had received a law degree, passed the bar exam, and then had gone outside to play and hadn't come in again until the day he'd died.

Tom had often wondered which man he resembled. He worked hard, like his grandfather, but he did it purely for the money, which was more like his father. What would he have done if Hadley Jr. hadn't squandered the millions? Would he have worked at all?

Now he knew. It wasn't the law Tom had hated all these years. It was the kind of law he'd been practicing. He needed to be able to walk right up to Trent Saroyan and say, *Hell, no, I won't take your case, you drunken bastard. You hit a kid.*

"I'm sorry, Bailey," he said, "but I'm afraid you really do have a problem. Because I'm not coming back. Not tonight. Not ever."

KELLY'S BED WAS SO COMFORTABLE, the bedspread heavy and silky and warm. She was sure she'd finally be able to sleep. No one who wished her harm could possibly know that she was in room 411 at the Marquis Pointe Hotel, just off the highway in Raleigh, North Carolina. Tom had tucked her into this clean, attractive room the way he might have tucked a diamond ring into a vault.

But she didn't sleep. She dozed off and on for a while, but then she heard talking in the next room, and she lay there, listening to the murmur of Tom's voice.

The voices stopped, followed by a few minutes of silence. And then her cell phone, which she had put beside her on the bed, vibrated softly. She looked at the display. It was Tom.

She clicked on. "Hi," she said. She realized her voice sounded throaty, like someone who'd been lying down a long time.

"Were you asleep?"

"No," she said. "Why are you using the telephone? I left the door unlocked, you know."

"I know," he said. He made a small noise and she heard the sound of pillows shifting. She could imagine him propping himself up against them. "I thought maybe the phone would be…safer."

She was so dumb, for a minute she thought he was talking about safe from Sophie. But then she got it.

"Oh." She smiled, feeling the cool silver phone pressing against her cheek. "All right. The phone is fine. What's going on?"

"Nothing. I just felt like talking."

"Oh."

Well, that was scintillating. She rubbed her face, thinking maybe she needed to get some blood flowing. If she didn't offer better conversation than this, he'd be sorry he called.

"I thought I heard you on the phone a few minutes ago," she said. "Was it your investigator? Is there news?"

"No," he said. "It was my boss. I was just quitting my job."

She hesitated. Was he kidding? "You did? You actually just this minute quit your job?"

"Yeah." He yawned. "It was a terrible job."

"Want to talk about it?"

"God, no," he said. "It's boring as hell. That's why I quit it."

She smiled again. "Okay. What do you want to talk about?"

She heard a rustling sound. When he spoke again, his voice sounded raspy, as if he had propped the receiver against his jaw and his lips were a little too close to the telephone.

"I want to talk about how beautiful you look in this picture," he said.

She knew which picture he meant. The rehearsal dinner photograph. She'd given it to him at dinner.

She curled up on her side, nuzzling her head more comfortably against the pillows. "I was twenty-two," she said. "Everyone is beautiful at twenty-two."

"Not like you. But look how sad you are. Look at your eyes. I remember they were always swollen when you'd been crying."

He was silent a moment. "I'm sorry I made you cry, Kelly."

"I know," she said. She shut her eyes, making everything else go away but the sound of his breathing at the other end of the phone. "It wasn't your fault."

"Yes, it was," he said. "I met you first, remember? That day, when my grandfather brought me over to talk about your dad's case. Why didn't I see how much sweeter you were than Sophie?"

She had to laugh. "You were eighteen at the time. I don't think 'sweet' is at the top of the list for teenaged boys. I think 'hot' is. Sophie was always hot."

Kelly herself had definitely not been "hot." She'd been too tall, too skinny, too slow to develop the curvy spots that boys thought females should get as early and as abundantly as possible.

Tom's preference for Sophie had been inevitable, just a fact of teenage life. Kelly had been foolish to care so much.

His coming into her life had been a little miracle in the first place. Her father, a small-town pharmacist in South Carolina, had been sued by a patient who contended Mr.

Carpenter had given him the wrong medication. It wasn't true, but it had ruined Kelly's father's business and sent them to Cathedral Cove, Georgia, where they hoped the scandal wouldn't follow.

Then in walked Hadley Beckham, a big-time Atlanta lawyer who specialized in taking worthy cases involving people who otherwise couldn't afford him. He had driven out to Cathedral Cove to talk to her father, and he'd brought his eighteen-year-old grandson with him. Kelly had been only fifteen, but she'd thought Tom Beckham was to die for.

The meeting ended up going on for hours, and the adults had taken pity on the teenagers and sent them out to get lunch and have some fun. Tom had seemed irritated to be lumped as a "kid," and, desperate to think of anything that would intrigue him, Kelly had suggested they visit Coeur Volé.

She considered it the biggest mistake of her life. Tom had fallen for Sophie immediately, as all the boys did, and never looked at Kelly again the whole day.

He'd had to go home to Atlanta the next day, but six years later he and Sophie had run into each other at Emory, where Tom was studying law and Sophie was studying husband-hunting. They had become engaged within a year, on Valentine's Day, and set the wedding date for September 19.

"Yes, she was hot," he said. His voice was low and musing. "But look at you. It's not just that you're beautiful. You're…intelligent. And determined. Look at that mouth, that jaw—even with the swollen eyes it's clear you're not going to fall apart."

She heard the paper rustle again. Perhaps he was shifting it to get a better look. "And the sweetness is every-where. It's right there, in the way you've folded your hands, as if you're praying. And see how you've tucked your hair behind your ear like a little girl?"

"Tom," she said. "I can't actually see the picture, you know."

"Well, take my word for it. All the women in this pic-ture are good-looking, but you—"

He broke off.

"God," he said. "No. Wait. Do you think…"

He broke off again.

"What?" She lifted herself onto one elbow. "What is it?"

"How long ago did you say Dolly died?"

She frowned. The change of subject was unnervingly abrupt. "Maybe six weeks, now."

"And Kent Snyder?"

"In early September," she said carefully.

"God." More paper shuffling noise. "And Lillith died eleven days ago."

"Yes. So?" A chill swept through her. "What is it? What have you found? What are you thinking?"

Suddenly there was another, different noise, but this time it wasn't on the phone. Sitting up, her heart beating hard, she stared as Tom opened the door that linked the two shadowy rooms.

She could only see his silhouette. He was still holding the cell phone to his ear, though they were now no more than ten feet apart.

"There's a pattern," he said.

She held the phone to her ear, and still talked into it, weirdly afraid to confront whatever this was face-to-face. "What kind of pattern? What do you mean?"

He dropped his phone to his side, though she could hear that the line was still open. He was holding out the picture of the rehearsal dinner. In the semidarkness, she could just see a sliver of streetlight shining on glossy paper.

"There is a pattern to the killings. She's working her way systematically through the wedding party. She's taking us in order, according to where we were standing."

CHAPTER SIXTEEN

IF KELLY HAD BEEN CLUTCHING any last floating debris of hope that the deaths had been accidental, that hope was drowned now, too.

It was hard enough to believe that three members of the same wedding party had coincidentally died in bizarre accidents within six weeks of one another.

That the accidents would occur *in order*... That was impossible.

Tom had turned on the light in her room. She was still sitting cross-legged on the bed in her nightshirt. Tom, fully dressed, sat at the foot, talking to Detective Vince Kopple back in Cathedral Cove.

The photograph was lying on the sheets between them.

Even from just Tom's end of the conversation, Kelly could tell Kopple wasn't terrifically impressed with their breakthrough. When Tom hung up, he shook his head, confirming her suspicion.

"They think we're seeing bogeymen," he said. "It doesn't help that the writing on the wedding invitation turned out to be cow's blood, the kind you can get from draining the juice out of any steak in the grocery store."

Kelly fought back a shiver. Why did that make the police feel better? Didn't they see how twisted the psyche was that would do such a thing? She pictured Sophie standing in a kitchen somewhere, dipping her finger in the oozing blood, then drawing those hateful block letters on the paper.

Sophie's face was clear in her mental picture. But the kitchen was hazy. And, of course, that was the most important question of all. What kitchen had it been?

Where was she?

Kelly bent over, touching the figures on the photograph individually. Once Tom pointed it out, she wondered why they hadn't noticed the pattern sooner.

The sequence had started from the outside and was working in, alternating between the bride's side and the groom's.

Dolly, the outside bridesmaid, had died first. Then Kent, who'd stood at the outer end on the groom's side. Then back to the bride's side, to the next bridesmaid in line, poor smiling Lillith.

It they were right, and she knew in her heart they were, Sophie...no, they weren't a hundred percent sure it was Sophie. The *killer* would go next to the groom's side. The second in line there was Bill Gaskins, the one with the devil's horns behind his head, courtesy of rowdy Kent Snyder.

She studied Bill's picture. He'd been cute. Stocky, like a football player, with curly brown hair, a five o'clock shadow and sharp brown eyes. Taller than Kent, but significantly shorter than either Alex or Sebastian.

For a moment she wondered whether they could somehow be wrong after all. Was it really possible that whether a man lived or died depended entirely on how tall he was?

And whose wedding he had agreed to be part of?

"Are the police going to try to find and warn Bill?"

Tom lifted his shoulders. "Kopple said he'd mention our idea to Bill if he could find him. He didn't sound enthusiastic."

"Then we'll have to," she said.

Tom nodded silently. That seemed to go without saying.

But where would they find him? Except perhaps for Sebastian, none of them had known him all that well to start with. Kelly remembered Bill had a rougher edge than the others. He hadn't been rich, not like the rest of them. Compared to Bill, even Kelly's father's pharmacy had seemed like a big deal.

He'd had ideas, though. She remembered that Bill was always taking Sebastian into a corner and trying to sell him on some big new scheme that would make them both millions…as soon as Sebastian loaned him the money to get started.

She looked up at Tom. "Do you think Bill ever struck it rich?"

"I don't know, but somehow I doubt it," he said. "After I left Cathedral Cove, Bill was the only one—other than Sophie's father—to get in touch with me. He still wanted me to invest in one of his crazy ideas. I told him that, since I wasn't going to get my rich wife after all, I couldn't afford to bankroll him. It ticked him off big time. I never heard from him again."

Tom's "rich wife."

She dropped her gaze and plucked absently at the folds of the sheet. "You didn't really ask Sophie to marry you just for the money, did you?"

He didn't answer right away. When she peeked, she saw

that he was staring at the photograph, as if trying to refresh his memory about that time, about what his motives actually had been.

"Yes," he said finally, and their gazes met. His eyes were so bleak. "I think I did."

"But…" She frowned. "That couldn't have been your only reason. Sophie was very beautiful, after all, and—"

"Well, there was her position as a Mellon of Coeur Volé. I liked that. I was ambitious, and I knew an old name was as good as old money."

She sat very still, wondering why he was trying so hard to make himself sound as black as possible. Men always fell in love with Sophie. Why should he have been exempt from her charms? "Tom—"

"I'm not proud of it," he said. "But neither am I going to sugarcoat it. It is who I was, Kelly, whether you like it or not. My parents had recently died, leaving me with no money and an enormous burden of law-school loans. I had been brought up to believe I was very rich, and I didn't like the idea that it had been an illusion. Marrying money seemed easier than working for it, especially when the money came in such an attractive package."

"So you never loved her? Not even a little?"

He shook his head. "I was very hot for her, at first, but that's all I can honestly say. I didn't think that love mattered much, anyhow. I'd never been in love, so I had no idea how…powerful it could be. It wasn't until I met you again that I—"

He shrugged. "Of course, by then it was too late."

She felt herself flushing. She remembered so well the night she had said those words to him. "It's too late, Tom," she'd said in a voice choked with tears. "I love you, but I won't do this to Sophie. Even if you decided tonight not to marry her, we could never be together."

He gave her that sardonic grin. "Pretty unflattering story, huh? But it's the truth. I'm not going to lie to you."

"When you said you were hot for her *at first*—what do you really mean? What happened? Did you simply get tired of her?" She touched Tom's face in the picture. "I've always wondered why she was so unhinged by your defection. I mean, it was very hard, of course, but…"

She looked up. She might as well say it. "Is there any chance there was going to be a baby?"

"No. There was no chance there was going to be a baby."

"How can you be so sure?"

"Because we made love only once, a few days before the wedding. And I was careful." He gave her a shadow of that crooked smile. "I'm sorry. I know that's not the answer you want. It makes it worse, doesn't it? Particularly since I practically forced her to make love to me."

Kelly's recoil was instinctive and unstoppable. She stared at him, unable to react in words.

"No," he said quickly. "I didn't rape her." It was the first time he'd tried to defend himself in any way.

"Of course not," she said. He didn't have that kind of violence in him.

"But what I did wasn't exactly admirable. I pressured her. She wanted to wait until we were married. I couldn't even tempt her. She liked to be held. She loved to snuggle and hug, but anything else left her completely cold. I was going crazy. We'd been engaged seven months, and I had given up other women, of course."

Once again she admired his ability to control his emotions. He didn't move a muscle while he reconstructed these difficult days.

He took a breath. "Then, when I—when I saw you again, and my reaction to you was so intense, sexually intense, I decided it was Sophie's fault, that she'd kept me frustrated for too long."

Kelly remembered the meeting. From the moment she'd given him a hug to say hello and congratulations, she'd felt it, too. The tingle of sexual awareness, as distinctive, and as dangerous, as the shake of a rattlesnake's tail.

"So what did you do?"

"I went to her and told her what I needed. I told her that another 'no' was unacceptable. I made it clear I had no intention of finding myself married to a frigid woman. She gave in, of course. She could tell I was serious. Then we made love. Or rather I did. She just lay there and allowed it."

"Oh, Tom." She wanted to reach out and touch his hand, but somehow she stopped herself.

"She must have hated me. I hated myself. To my surprise, I discovered she hadn't just been toying with me. She had been a virgin. But the worst part was that it had all been for nothing. All I had done was confirm that I really was engaged to a frigid woman. I still wanted you so much I couldn't breathe."

Finally he moved. He ran his hand through his hair roughly. "And here's what an ambitious bastard I was. Even when I realized that I felt for you all the things I should have felt for Sophie... Even then I planned to go through with the wedding."

She waited. But he seemed to be finished. He didn't even seem aware that he'd ended on an illogical note.

He'd planned to go through with the wedding.

So what had happened to change his mind?

"But you didn't," she said gently. "You didn't go through with it."

He shook his head. "I swore to myself that I'd never tell a single soul why I left Cathedral Cove that day. But I'm going to tell you now."

She held her breath. "Why?"

To her surprise, for answer he held up the picture. "Because you have a right to know everything. No, not just a right. A need. You *need* to know everything."

She looked down and immediately she saw what he meant.

The pattern.

Bridesmaid, then groomsman. Outside, then in.

If they couldn't stop Sophie before she killed Bill Gaskins, the pattern would take them back to the next bridesmaid in line.

And that bridesmaid was Kelly.

For a split second, her muscles went strangely weak, but she closed her mouth, made a fist and tightened her jaw.

"All right," she said. "Tell me everything."

NATURALLY, THE MELLON-BECKHAM wedding was going to be the most spectacular event Cathedral Cove had ever seen. It had required bicoastal cooperation to pull it off.

The cake designer jetted in from New York City. The wedding planner came from Miami. Two different photographers, one videographer and a publicist had been imported from L.A.

The bridesmaids' blue satin gowns were designed and

fitted in Atlanta. The two hundred elegantly engraved wedding invitations were addressed by a calligrapher in Chicago.

Tom knew he was being perverse to find it all slightly ridiculous. After all, this was what he loved about Sophie. She was stinking rich, so rich she wouldn't have a clue what to do with her money if she couldn't squander it.

And squander it she did. Even Tom's own parents, who had somehow killed five million dollars in six years of touring Europe, would have been impressed.

At three that morning, with only fifteen hours to go until the wedding, Tom sat alone at a shadowy corner table in the commercial glasshouse the Mellons had bought and restored purely for the purpose of holding his wedding reception. He was watching the flamboyant designer do his thing.

For some reason Tom couldn't understand even when he was sober—which right now he definitely was not—Sophie had decided on a Japanese garden theme. She said it had something to do with her wedding dress, but he didn't know what, because he'd never seen it. The Dragon guarded it with her life.

He was sure this place would look just swell come six o'clock tomorrow, but right now it was messy, chaotic and loud. The designer, who purred like a kitten in the presence of the Mellons, was screaming like a banshee at his minions, not one of whom had thus far performed a single task to his satisfaction.

One team of his slaves was working on the "cherry trees," which, for some inexplicable reason, were being fabricated out of thousands of real white rose petals.

Tom almost spoke up and suggested that maybe they

could save themselves some trouble if they used actual cherry trees, which, if you thought about it, already looked like cherry trees. But the designer seemed to be teetering on the edge of a stroke, so Tom poured himself another shot of scotch out of the bottle he'd brought with him from the rehearsal dinner, and held his peace.

Besides, the skylarks were even weirder than the cherry trees. Hundreds of them, all made out of bright blue forget-me-nots, were flying around, hanging from the top of the glasshouse on invisible threads.

He leaned back and looked up at the ceiling.

Whoa. Big mistake. Looking at them, weaving and bobbing every which way, made him feel sick. Using the scotch bottle as a rifle, he pointed and shot down as many of them as he could. Unfortunately, Tom had never hunted in his life, so he wasn't even sure he had his trigger finger in the right spot on the bottle.

He'd better learn to hunt, he supposed. When they had time off from making money, the Good Old Boys in his law firm loved to kill things.

Bang, bang.

But then, in a freaky coincidence, just as he pulled off another round, one of the skylarks actually fell from its string and landed in a mangled blue heap two tables away. For a second, Tom thought he might cry.

Okaaaay. You've reached your limit, pal.

He put down the bottle of scotch. He had been looking for the happy state of *numb,* but it was possible he might have drunk himself right past that spot, on down to *maudlin.*

Another big mistake. Maudlin wasn't going to help him get through the night.

In fact, he wasn't sure what on this earth could do that. This must be what condemned prisoners felt as they waited for a dawn execution. What would he want for his last meal? He thought of his favorite foods and suddenly his stomach tightened. He made a choking sound.

The wedding designer, who was passing his table, stopped and glared ferociously. "If you're going to puke," the man said, "please get away from my skylarks."

Tom smiled, then squeezed his eyes shut, trying to hold the nausea back. Right. *No meals.* He'd never seen the point of a last meal, anyhow. Be realistic. If you were going to die in a few hours, would a cheeseburger and fries really ease the sting?

Now, some mind-blowing sex, that might help. If you were going to die in a few hours, and you'd never once, not once, had sex with the only woman you would ever love, then someone should deliver her to your cell, close the door and let you alone for a while.

Then maybe dying wouldn't be so rough.

The logic seemed unassailable, which perked him up considerably. If he explained it like that, even Kelly would understand why he needed her tonight. No one begrudged a dying man his last request.

He felt in his pockets for his cell phone. She'd only left the country club a couple of hours ago. She might still be awake. And even if she wasn't, he knew a little thing you could do to wake a woman up so that she didn't mind a bit.

But where was his damn cell phone? He kept patting himself down, sure he must have missed it. The wedding designer watched him carefully, as if he thought something disgusting was about to happen.

Shit. He must have left it at the country club. He stood, though his feet didn't seem to want to go in the same direction, and felt in his pocket for a hundred-dollar bill. Ah, there it was, his last one, in fact. Keeping up with the Mellons this week had been expensive. When this bill was gone, he'd have to hit the ATM and hope it didn't confiscate his card.

He dropped the money on the table for a tip. He couldn't remember what his bill had been, but he hoped a hundred was enough to cover it, plus a little something for the incident with the skylark. It wasn't until he saw the wedding designer go over and rip the bill into pieces that Tom remembered this wasn't a restaurant and that guy wasn't a waiter.

Oh, well, condemned men didn't really need money, either.

He just needed that cell phone.

It was a cold September night, and the crisp air slapped him in the face the minute he stepped outside. It sobered him up a little, helping him to decide against driving his own car.

Unfortunately, it also sobered him enough to make him remember he couldn't call Kelly.

Not now, at three in the morning.

Not ever.

It was dark out here and the gloom seemed to seep right into him. Now that he couldn't call Kelly, he didn't seem to have the energy to do anything. But he couldn't just slump to the ground. It was cold, and that guy inside would have an apoplectic fit if Tom was still here tomorrow when the guests began to arrive.

And he still needed his cell phone. At least that gave him a short-term goal. Luckily, there was a cab nearby. He raised his hand, climbed in, and, shutting his eyes, managed to say the name of the country club.

He might have dozed off. It seemed like only a second later they were already under the club's portico, and he was stone-cold sober. A horrible feeling. He'd better pick up another bottle while he was in here.

He asked the cabbie to wait for him.

The Mellons had rented the whole country club tonight, so the place pretty much belonged to them. He waved at a waitress who was running a carpet sweeper in the dining room. She seemed to be the only human being awake in the entire building.

He went first to the room where they'd been dancing. Several coats were still lying around on chairs, but his cell phone wasn't there.

He decided to look over by the pool, where he'd spent half an hour or so earlier tonight, when he'd needed to be alone. But it wasn't there, either.

Finally he decided to look at the other side of the pool, where the club had set up two or three small, private alcoves, no doors, no windows, just benches rimming the walls and a flat table in the center.

They were probably used for massages. To Tom, they suddenly looked like a good place to lie down and pass out.

But wouldn't you know it? As soon as he got within ten feet of the first one, he heard voices. Somebody was already using the darn things.

He thought maybe he recognized those voices. He cocked his head. *Yes.* One of them was definitely Sophie.

And wasn't that a man's voice, too? For one wonderful minute he thought maybe he'd caught her having an affair. *Oh, yeah.* That would let him off the hook, wouldn't it?

But the hope was short-lived. Tom moved closer, close enough to look right into the alcove. *Hell.* The man with Sophie was only Sebastian. Tom froze in place. He wasn't going to take another step forward. No way was he up to dealing with that pair anymore tonight.

Luckily, though he was now no more than six feet away, he was in the shadows. Plus, they seemed locked in their own drama and hadn't noticed him. Tom started to turn and steal away.

But something…he wasn't sure what…made him stop and listen some more. And then he realized that Sophie was crying.

"Stop," she said. "Please. Stop."

"I can't believe it." Sebastian's voice was a strangely shrill whisper. "I can't believe you've let him turn you into his whore."

What the hell?

Tom's head wasn't all that clear, but he knew that, as the fiancé, the knight in shining armor, he should do something right about now. He should bust in on them. He should punch Sebastian out cold, explaining that he had *No Right* to talk to Sophie like that.

But Tom didn't do any of that. He stayed where he was. Something in the scenario just felt…off. The two weren't touching, but Sophie's body language was submissive, almost supplicant, with her hands outstretched, palms up, pleading. Her hair was mussed, as if she'd been recently manhandled.

Sebastian, on the other hand, seemed oddly tense, his backbone erect. He looked so excited he was almost thrumming.

For a moment the voices dipped too low for Tom to hear

the words, although the tone was still the same. Sophie begging, cringing under the verbal lashing. Sebastian loving every second of it.

Suddenly Tom knew exactly what was wrong. There was a sexual component to this picture. Something unholy and intense.

Sexual.

It would explain so many things.

Or would it? What about the undeniable fact that, just three days ago, Sophie had been a virgin?

Tom waited. He listened. And he watched.

His gut insisted that this really was happening, even though his brain was mystified, in a kind of stupefied denial. It couldn't be what it seemed, he told himself. *He* had been her first lover. He must be misreading this.

"I'm sorry, Sebastian. I'm so sorry. But he said he'd leave me, he said he wouldn't go through with the wedding."

"Good." Sebastian's voice was louder, rougher. "I wish he had, the bastard."

"Please. *Please.* You know this is what we decided, Sebastian. It's the best way. But no one can ever really come between us, you know that. No one can spoil what we have."

Sebastian laughed, a cruel, whiplike sound.

"What *we* have?" He reached out, as if to grab Sophie by the hair, but, at the last minute, he dropped his hand. "What do we have, Sophie? I can't even touch you, while that fool Tom Beckham is going to spend the rest of his life screwing you whenever he pleases."

"Don't." Sophie put her hands over her mouth, as if by doing that she could stop the flow of words from his.

"Don't say things like that. You know we decided this was the only way. The only way we could be sure we wouldn't—"

"Did you like it, Sophie?" Sebastian's mouth twisted. "Did he do all the things I've always wanted to do? All the things I've only dreamed of?"

Sophie was shaking her head. "Don't torment yourself. It was nothing. I felt nothing."

Tom knew that to be true. He might as well have made love to a dead woman. He felt sick all over again. He swallowed hard, hoping the scotch wouldn't pick this moment to come back up.

"You know I have to marry someone," she said. "You'll have to marry, too, eventually. It's the only way. We've been strong so long, but how much longer can you—"

"Forever, if I have to." Sebastian stared down at her. "I was wrong. This isn't the answer. Don't leave me, Sophie. You don't know what I've suffered for you. I *need* you."

"I know, sweetheart," she said, her voice catching on a sob. "I know you need me."

And then, as if that had been the magic phrase, the long-practiced cue, she slowly lowered herself to her knees.

Tom's body had grown numb. No wonder they still hadn't noticed him. He barely existed. He was like a pair of eyes floating in a world of nightmares.

As Sophie knelt there, her face was just inches from Sebastian's groin, which was swollen, the fabric of his pants pushing forward obscenely. She had cried so many tears that, from where Tom stood, her face seemed made of water.

"I need you, too." Her voice was monotone now, like a

child saying well-rehearsed prayers. "I always will. When he touches me, I will always be thinking of you."

Slowly, still caught in the trance of ceremony, Sophie unbuckled her brother's belt, unbuttoned his pants and slid the zipper down.

She took his hand.

Though Sebastian resisted her at first, this, too, was no doubt a familiar ritual. He surrendered with a moan and allowed her to guide his fingers.

And then, while she knelt before him, never once touching him, but whispering a constant stream of love and reassurance, Sebastian closed his eyes and began to masturbate.

Tom felt himself choking.

He turned and walked out of the building. When he reached the lobby he knew he was going to lose the battle with the scotch. He got as far as the front steps and then he threw up in a planter.

When his stomach was empty, he began to run. He ran right past the cab. He ran without thinking, instinct instructing his feet. He knew only that he had to get away from a scene too sick to witness, from a future too hideous to comprehend.

And he'd kept on running for the next ten years.

CHAPTER SEVENTEEN

WHEN TOM WAS FINISHED, Kelly was cold all over. Her mind felt bruised, as if the story had been a series of physical blows. She could only imagine how he felt.

She had no idea what to say. No words existed that could undo the damage done to him that night. Pity was no good. And the only other thing she had to offer was the physical comfort of sex. With those images fresh in his mind, though, surely lovemaking would be profoundly unappealing. Maybe even impossible.

But he was obviously waiting for her to say something. And she remembered her vow to follow her heart, whatever the cost. She wasn't going to remain silent, just because she was afraid of saying the wrong thing.

"No wonder you hate Sebastian so much," she said. It seemed a safe place to start. "When I saw you with him today, I wondered why you were so bitter."

"I thought I did, but somehow I can't hate him anymore. Look at him. He's broken." Tom shook his head. "It was a cruel twist of fate, really, that made them brother and sister. He loved her far more than I ever did."

She thought of the anguish in Sebastian's eyes when he had talked about his fears for Sophie. And she knew that Tom was right. As sick as it seemed to an outsider, Sebastian had long been struggling with an incurable disease, and it was destroying him.

It had destroyed Sophie. Kelly thought of all the times Sophie had deliberately damaged herself and it made her wonder when the relationship with Sebastian had begun.

It had never been healthy. Perhaps, in the end, it had even twisted her into a murderer.

"I wonder sometimes whether I could have helped them." Tom was still sitting at the foot of her bed, still composed, even after the hell he'd just relived.

"How?"

"If I had told someone. Her father, maybe. Her minister. Her doctor. I don't know. But maybe, if they'd gotten help sooner—"

"Don't do that to yourself, Tom. You aren't a saint. You were twenty-five years old. You were in shock. You were hurt."

He shook his head again. "Shocked, yes, but was I really all that hurt? I think the biggest damage may have been to my pride. How selfish and immature is that? I was witnessing something so profoundly unhealthy, so destructive to both of them, but especially Sophie…and I was over there feeling sorry for myself, thinking, *Look how they were planning to make a fool of me!*"

How could she tell him that his reaction had been normal? That it was true? Sophie and Sebastian, driven to despair by the hopelessness of their situation, had used him shamefully. Sophie hadn't wanted him as a husband. They hadn't even seen him as a human being. They'd seen him only as a shield, a barrier against the sins they hoped they'd never commit.

How could she tell him that most men would have felt the same humiliated pride?

He didn't want to hear that. He didn't want to be like *most men*. He wanted to be better, even while he believed he was much worse. It was one of the things she loved best about him—as paradoxical as it sounded, this sardonic, cynical loner was actually a disappointed idealist.

From the beginning, he'd always been fighting a lonely war with himself.

She wanted very much to help him to put down the sword. If only for tonight.

Picking up the photograph that still lay, forgotten, on the bed, she stood. She took it over to the dresser, where she had put her purse and a few odds and ends from her pockets and set it there, facedown.

He had turned to watch her. She looked at him in the dresser mirror, the reflection of her eyes meeting the reflection of his.

"I don't know what to do right now," she said. "I want to make love to you, but I don't know if you're ready to think about anything like that."

The image in the mirror smiled a little. "I think about it all the time. Every day since I've come back. Every night."

She felt her muscles tensing, clenching and unclenching in a delicious, involuntary rhythm. Her body was getting ready. But her heart was still unsure.

"Do you think that you can really put all that out of your mind? If we make love, will those other pictures be playing in your head? If we make love, I want you to see me. Not Sophie."

He stood then, too, and came up behind her. She held his gaze in the mirror.

"It's the other way around," he said softly. "Even when it really was Sophie, I saw you."

She looked at his wonderful, tormented face. And then she nodded and shut her eyes slowly. They stood that way a long moment, though her muscles now were screaming for release. For all her brave vows of action and courage, now that the moment had come she wanted him to make the first move.

He put his hands on her shoulders, warm and strong. The relief was so sudden she bit her lip, holding back a moan.

"I want something from you, too," he said.

She didn't open her eyes. She just nodded again. *Anything.*

"I want you to promise that when we make love, it won't be sad. I don't want our first time to be a hiding, a crawling into each other's arms to escape the shadow of fear. I want it to be about happiness and passion. And life."

She opened her eyes. *Their first time.* Not their last time. Not their only time. Their first.

Whether they were true or not, the words filled her with something bright and hot.

"Yes," she said. "I promise."

It was the easiest promise she'd ever had to keep. When he turned her around and kissed her, when he put his hands in her hair and pulled her body up against his, the dam broke on ten years of hunger and need. And in the flood came fire and laughter, together, as if they were twins.

Every touch was heaven. They shed their clothes and found their way to the bed. She couldn't believe how perfectly joyous it was for him to take her breast into his mouth, how the tickling fire made her writhe and breathlessly laugh, and knead her fingers down his bare back in an ecstasy of possession.

They were like people who had discovered a vault of limitless treasure. They fell into it, into each other, rolling, twisting, glorying in the glow of the gold, the shimmer of the diamonds, the red throb of the small, hidden rubies. They wallowed in it, suddenly rich, and laughed because they couldn't hold all the happiness inside.

They left the lights on. There was so much to learn about each other and no need to hide anything anymore. He was perfect, male and strong and more ruggedly beautiful than any dream. He made her beautiful, too, with his mouth and his hands and his eyes always shining.

They teased and played. It was a frolic, a child's game, an easy, wonderful game that there was no way to lose.

But eventually something deepened, something changed, and suddenly they weren't children anymore. They were man and woman, and they needed this, they wanted this. They grew quiet. The movements of his hands became more focused, more deliberate. Even her breaths were smaller, shallower, trying to stay out of the way so that the ultimate goal could be reached.

The light in the room never changed, but she ceased to be aware of it. She was in a rapidly darkening spiral of pure need.

When he entered her, she cried out. For minutes…how many…an eternity…she knew nothing but him, nothing but flesh against flesh, need against need. It went on building, building, until finally, in one blinding moment, joy ceased to be something she felt, and became, instead, something she was.

When it was over, his fingers found the tears on her cheeks and touched them.

"I'm not crying," she whispered. That was all the breath she had left.

"Of course you're not." And when she looked up at him she saw that he was smiling. Not that tilted smile she knew so well, but a real smile, a smile that reached all the way to his damp, shining eyes. A smile that might, at any minute, break open into laughter and love.

"Neither," he said, "am I."

KELLY COULDN'T REMEMBER any day when she'd felt so strange. It was like being two people. One Kelly was still frightened, sickened by the possibility that a woman she'd once considered her best friend might be trying to kill her. The other Kelly was dazed and contented, barely aware of anything except the languid peace running through her veins.

When she woke up, Tom was already showered and dressed and back in his own room, clicking away on his laptop while he talked on his cell phone.

He'd left the adjoining doors wide open, so she drowsily wandered into his area, still rumpled, her hair uncombed, once again wearing the nightshirt she'd flung off in the night. He looked up from his desk, and the smile he gave her was so sexy it made her toes tingle.

"Hang on a minute, would you, Noreen?" He put the phone against his shoulder, crooked his finger to call Kelly closer, and, when she got there, he took her hand and tugged her down low enough to give her a kiss.

It was long and slow, and it made her shiver.

When he let go, he put the phone back. Though her legs were shaking, he seemed fully in control.

"No," he said into the phone, glancing down at his computer screen. "I want you to start just with any bankruptcy within a hundred-mile radius of Cathedral Cove. Yes, I know that includes Atlanta. But it's more likely to be a small-town address. This guy was definitely small-time. Pull out all the William Gaskins. Middle initial *I*, which is rare enough to help a little."

For a minute Kelly wondered how he knew that, but then she remembered that Sebastian and Alex VanCamp used to tease Bill about his odd middle name: Indiana.

"Come on, Indiana Jones, whip out your big whip for the ladies," Alex had quipped one night, typically obnoxious. Bill, who was not as glib as the others, had scowled and shot back, "Know what, VanCamp? You can take my whip and stick it up your—" He'd flushed bright red when Alex and Sebastian had exploded in laughter.

Poor Bill. For a minute, Kelly hoped against hope that he had really made it big and that it was snotty Alex Van-Camp who had ended up in bankruptcy court.

"I've already checked the business licenses and the patent applications," Tom was saying. "Nothing particularly promising. I'm moving on to civil suits."

She caught Tom's eye and mouthed the word *shower.* He wiggled his eyebrows, smiling, but then he turned back to his computer. "Tell you what. Let's also look at divorces, delinquent child support, stuff like that. He's probably—"

Kelly went back into her own room. It was too depressing, all the ways in which people could mess up their lives. She didn't want to think about it.

Maybe it was a bad thing to have discovered that oasis of happiness in Tom's arms last night. It had made her soft. She no longer really wanted to chase down evildoers out in the big, mean world. She wanted to stay in this hotel room forever, making love and pretending nothing bad could ever touch them.

She lingered in her shower, enjoying the sting of the water on her newly sensitized skin. She turned her face into the warm spray and let it fill her mouth. Even the soap was sexy, and as she washed herself she felt hungry for him all over again. Maybe he would hear the water and imagine her standing naked under it, and then he'd have to—

But he didn't come. Eventually she turned off the spigot and began to dry herself off. He was right, of course, and she was just being selfish. Bill Gaskins's life might well depend on what Tom could accomplish on that computer.

Her life might depend on it.

And Tom's.

When she returned to his room, her hair was still wet, but she was fully dressed, right down to her shoes. He was zipping his laptop into its case. He turned to her with a smile much smaller and more professional than the first one he'd given her this morning.

"I think we got lucky," he said. "I have an address."

"You found him? Already?"

"Maybe. There's a William Indiana Gaskins who operates a hot dog stand in Digger Beach."

"Digger Beach? That's only about ten miles from Cathedral Cove."

So close…and yet she'd never run into him.

It always surprised her how quickly that group of young people had split apart. Only she and Lillith had really been friends. The rest of them had been like vacationers thrown together on a cruise. It was a short period of intense intimacy, and then…nothing.

"Yes." Tom pulled his PDA out of his pocket. "Are you familiar with a small year-round carnival site there? Digger Beach Funland?"

She nodded. "I'm pretty sure I've been there. Mary Jo had her twins' birthday party at a carnival in Digger Beach two years ago. It's a little cheesy, but it's not too bad. Is that where Bill's hot-dog stand is?"

She wondered if Bill had seen her that day. The dozen or so little boys they'd had in their care had walked through the surprisingly scary haunted house, ridden about a dozen rides and spent an hour in the batting cages. She tried to remember if she'd bought any hot dogs, but she wasn't sure. If she had, she hadn't recognized Bill. And if he'd recognized her, he hadn't spoken up, either.

"His stand is at the Funland?" she asked again.

Tom seemed distracted. He was still tapping on his PDA, reading something she couldn't see. "Yeah," he said absently. "Apparently it's next to the haunted house and it's going to open in about three hours."

Finally he looked up. "Are you ready to go?"

"Yes." She threaded her fingers through her wet hair self-consciously. "I could fix myself up a little, I guess, but I figured we might be in a hurry. And—"

She sighed. What was the point in pretending? "I usually let my hair air-dry. It always does what it wants anyhow, so…well, I just don't fuss with it much."

She had his attention now. His eyes were dark and intense.

"I like your hair," he said. He put down his PDA. "Kelly, you know we shouldn't have made love last night."

She lifted her chin. She started to ask him not to say anything else. This was the kind of morning-after awkwardness she'd been dreading. But she hadn't extracted any promises from him last night, and if he wanted to get things straight, she could handle that, too. The new Kelly wasn't going to run away from either joy or trouble.

And she wasn't going to deny reality just to save face. If, of the two of them, she was the only one who didn't regret it, she didn't care. From now on, she was going to tell the truth as often as she could.

"I'm sorry you feel that way," she said. "I thought it was wonderful. It made me very happy."

"It was wonderful," he said. "That's why we shouldn't have done it. We have to stay focused on finding Bill right now, and yet, when I look at you, all I want to do is start all over again."

She smiled and put one hand on her stomach to quiet the butterfly wings. It was erotic to feel that gaze raking over her.

"I was thinking the same thing," she admitted. "Just now, in the shower, I wanted you to—"

"I got as far as the door. I was about to walk in fully dressed, shoes and all, before I came to my senses."

She laughed. "I wish you had."

"We'd still be there," he said. "And we can't. We have to get to Digger Beach." He took a deep breath. "But maybe it wasn't a mistake after all. Even if I can't think as clearly, maybe there is one thing I found out last night. One thing that may prove a hell of an advantage."

"What did you find out?"

He picked up his computer and his jacket, then turned to her with a dark-eyed smile.

"I found out how much I want to catch this killer. I found out how very much I want us both to live."

THE BRIDE STOOD IN FRONT of the mirror. There was no artificial light in the room, but moonbeams poured through the window. Her white lace dress glowed as if it had been bathed in something phosphorescent.

The veil hid her face.

She stood very still, never fidgeting with the gown, which fit perfectly. Her image might as well have been painted on the mirror, for all it moved.

Her long train glowed, also, as it trailed out behind her, finally ending in a thin tail of darkness.

A ghost would look like this, she thought.

The infamous ghost of the generic Dead Bride.

The universally feared Woman in White, who had been snuffed out in the high tide of passion, which now would never ebb. Frozen forever in the tragic, virginal moment of almost-love.

People feared the dead bride, because, on some subconscious level, they understood she carried in her red, pulsing heart the maddened fury of a woman unspeakably cheated, with nothing left to lose.

The bride raised her left hand slowly. No groom could be seen, but the hand trembled as an invisible ring of starlight slipped over the pale skin of the third finger. She lifted her hand higher, twisting it a fraction of an inch each way, so that the moonlight could catch on its perfect facets and give birth to tiny rainbows in the night.

The scent of rotting gardenias filled the air, but to the bride they were still sweet, because she smelled them only with her memory.

She was about to lift her face for that one, perfect kiss.

But she heard a soft creak, and she returned to perfect stillness.

Behind her, the door opened slowly.

She would have been afraid, except that there was very

little she cared about anymore. She looked at the other ghost approaching her in the mirror.

"Sophie," the woman's voice whispered. "Oh, my poor, darling Sophie."

The bride turned.

"I'm sorry, Mother," she said. "It's not Sophie."

The woman who had come into the room gasped. She put her hands against her heart. And then she reached out and, with shaking fingers, she slowly lifted the veil.

She stepped back. "Samantha?"

The bride nodded. Her naked face, which was running with tears, was cold as the night air swam over it.

"Yes," she said. "It's Samantha. I'm sorry."

"Shhh." Her mother put out her hands and gently rubbed at her wet cheeks, just as she had done long ago, when the bride was a little girl and noises had frightened her in the night. "There's nothing to be sorry about."

The bride didn't answer. That was so horribly untrue. The list of things to regret seemed to stretch out longer than this extraordinary train of lace.

She was such a fool to have put on the dress. It wasn't hers. It was Sophie's, and it always would be, no matter how insane she became. Even when Sophie was dead, it would still be her dress.

And then, with her mother's eyes on her, she felt suddenly as if she couldn't breathe, as if the gown were too small for her, just as it had been too small for Sophie.

She had to get it off. She might choke to death inside this dress. She couldn't look into the mirror, for fear she would see Sophie there, laughing to see that the two of them were finally dressed exactly alike.

And both of them alone. Both of them unloved.

She stretched her arms behind her, elbows jutting out and fingers grabbing desperately, trying to find and rip down the zipper.

But her mother caught her hands.

"It's all right, Samantha," her mother said. "I know, honey. I already know."

"Know what?"

"I know about Tom," she said. "I know how much you love him."

She shouldn't have said Tom's name. It made Samantha angry. That had been the one thing that belonged to her own heart. The one thing she didn't have to offer up, just to save this family.

In her anger, she wanted to hurt her mother.

And so she said the thing neither of them had dared to say, in all these days since Tom's visit to Coeur Volé.

"Where is it, Mother?"

Imogene let go of her daughter's hands, which suddenly felt as cold as a woman ten days dead. "Where is what?"

"Sophie gained weight before the wedding, didn't she? She was probably unhappy, because she knew, deep in her heart, that Tom didn't really love her. But what about the famous wedding dress, the three generations of women who had worn it? You couldn't stand to break tradition. You couldn't stand for the world to know that your beautiful daughter had gotten fat. And so, without telling anyone, you had another one made, didn't you?"

Imogene didn't speak.

"The problem is…you don't know where that second wedding dress is, do you, Mother? You don't know who might have been able to strip pieces of lace from it and give them to other women. Women who ended up dead."

Imogene's mouth opened, as if she were going to scream at her daughter. But no sound came out.

"No, of course you don't know." Samantha smiled. "But I do."

CHAPTER EIGHTEEN

THE ONLY THING THAT KEPT a small-town carnival from being either spooky or dismal—or both—was the presence of plenty of kids.

But Tom and Kelly had arrived at least an hour too early. By noon, she knew, the children would have come. And, as if their innocent faith in magic had power, the rides would light up. The cotton-candy machine would begin to whirl and throw off angel clouds of pink sugar. The air would fill with the scent of fried dough and hot dogs and onions. In the sawdust pits, the catatonic ponies would raise their heads and flick their tails in anticipation. At the front door of the haunted house, the derelict lounging on a metal folding chair would toss his cigarette into the dirt and tuck his shirt in, suddenly smiling.

But now, at only eleven o'clock, with rain gathering in the gray clouds overhead, things were very different.

To Kelly, the man at the haunted house looked dangerous. The endless repetition of the merry-go-round's music sounded slightly mad. The metal joints of the swing ride moaned and creaked, as if it were exhausted, but enslaved, forced to keep endlessly moving. The buckets of the slowly circling Ferris wheel were empty, but they swayed in the wind as if they were peopled by ghosts.

Or maybe it was just the mood she was in. Still, as if Tom sensed her discomfort, he took her hand and held it warmly. "You okay?"

"Yes." She smiled at him. "I'm fine."

It wasn't a lie. She was dejected, but not really frightened. Tom had already alerted the Digger Beach police, and though they hadn't taken them completely seriously, either, they had agreed to send an officer through the Funland at least once an hour for the next few days.

Just as Tom had been told, the hot-dog stand was right next to the haunted house. Though the stand had wheels at one end and a trailer hitch at the other, which indicated it expected to move along one day, it was not just an open-air cart. It was a fully enclosed workstation, in which the vendor could be protected from the elements.

It looked fairly new and rather sophisticated for a hot-dog stand. All silver, with Bill's Haunted Hot Dogs stenciled on the sides in bright red letters, it was probably twelve feet long, and it had a large double service window under a red-and-white striped awning.

From a distance, the interior was just a dark shadow. There was no way to tell if Bill was in there unless you went right up to the window and ordered something. Kelly scanned the menu, which was printed under the service window. It seemed to carry out the "haunted hot dog" theme.

Hot Dogs, Monster Hot Dogs and Ghost-Choker Hot Dogs, your choice of toppings, the ketchup and mustard and horseradish labeled "blood and guts and brains."

A menu only a kid could love.

Then regular and diet soft drinks. That was all. Apparently Bill liked to specialize.

As they approached the stand, the man in front of the haunted house sat up a little straighter and watched them. Kelly felt his eyes on her, but she kept her own gaze straight ahead.

The service windows were shut tight. No sounds or scents of hot dogs emanated from within. Kelly glanced at her watch. It was almost eleven-thirty. The carnival opened in thirty minutes. Shouldn't he be getting ready?

Tom rapped on the window with his knuckles, but nothing stirred inside. Kelly felt her shoulders tighten. She was trying not to dwell on worst-case scenarios, but…

What if they'd arrived too late?

Tom squeezed her hand. "I'll check the back door."

"I'll come with you."

He hesitated only a fraction of a second before nodding. He seemed to have abandoned his earlier desire to stash her somewhere safe while he did the legwork. Maybe he understood that she needed to be doing something.

The back of the stand had a large access door, which didn't seem to be locked. Tom knocked one more time, and then, letting go of Kelly's hand, he opened the door. Kelly stayed where she was, but Tom put his head in the open work area. "Bill?"

Bill should be there by now. The carnival was waking up. In front of her, Kelly saw a couple of children giving tickets to the guy at the Scrambler. Back at the haunted house, a taped track of ghostly moans and bloodcurdling screams began to play.

"No hot dogs till noon," a voice behind her said. "Anything else I can help you folks with?"

Kelly turned. It was the man from the folding chair in front of the haunted house. He looked stocky, slightly fat.

He had long, tangled curls and a thick beard that needed a trim. But now that he was closer, she saw that under his shaggy brows were a pair of sharp brown eyes.

It was Bill Gaskins.

Tom had heard him too, obviously. He backed out of the stand and shut the silver access door behind him.

"Hi, Bill," he said. "We were just looking for you."

Bill gazed at them coldly. "Yeah? Why is that?"

Kelly tried to smile. She was certain Bill knew who they were. Even if she had changed beyond recognition, Tom looked exactly the same.

"It's good to see you, Bill," she said. "It's been a long time."

He looked her up and down. And then he grinned, acting as if he'd just put the pieces together. "Well, well, well. If it's not the strumpet and the chump."

It was so gratuitously rude it knocked her smile right off.

"Yeah," Bill went on, still grinning. "That's what we called you, didn't you know? You guys were our favorite soap opera. Or did you think we hadn't noticed what was going on behind Miss Sophie's sexy back?"

"There wasn't *anything* going on," Tom said. "Which I'm sure you also know, if you were really paying as much attention as you say."

"Oh, sure, we knew nothing had happened. That's why we called you the chump." He gave Kelly a glance that might have been apologetic. "The strumpet was just because it rhymed."

Bill flicked his cigarette into the dust, without bothering to stomp it out. It just lay there smoldering. It was close enough to the hot-dog stand's propane tanks to make Kelly nervous. Was this Bill's fatal flaw? Would they hear, some-day soon, that he had burned up, trapped inside that metal box with the hot dogs?

Bill tilted his head and looked from one of them to the other. "How about now? Anything going on now?"

"Absolutely," Tom said with a cold smile of his own. "That's why we're here. We think there's something damn dangerous going on, and we wanted to give you a heads-up."

Bill brushed at his beard, as if he thought cigarette ash might still be lingering there. "Dangerous like what?"

"Like murder."

Bill snorted. "Give me a break."

Kelly found his attitude impossible. "We're trying to," she snapped. "Someone is killing off the members of So-phie's wedding party, and they're doing it in order. You're next."

Bill's mouth hung open. His beard was so unkempt that little curls of hair actually drooped over his lip and tickled his teeth.

"That's right," Tom said. "So could you maybe ditch the attitude and talk to us like a human being for a few min-utes? I promise you, pal, we come in peace. But that might not be true of the next old friend who shows up here un-expectedly."

Bill's eyes narrowed. Kelly could tell he was assessing the situation. He hadn't ever been stupid. Merely rough around the edges and trying to play out of his league.

He looked at Tom for confirmation. Tom nodded.

"Okay," Bill said. "Just let me get the grills going. In twenty minutes this place is going to be crawling with hun-gry kids."

He went inside, but he must have hurried, because he was back in less than three minutes. Behind him, things had begun to sizzle and kick off the scent of meat. Kelly, who never ate hot dogs, realized she must be starving, because they smelled heavenly.

Bill came out carrying a small caddie of mustard and ketchup. He motioned toward a picnic table a few feet away. He placed the condiments in the center of the table, then invited Tom and Kelly to sit down.

"Okay," he said. "Murder sounds crazy, but I'm listening. I don't remember ever thinking you were a head case."

Tom smiled. "Just a chump."

"Hey, we've all taken our turn in the chump chair, right?" Bill smiled, too, and it was clear that issue had just been settled, man to man. Kelly marveled at how quickly and nonverbally men could arrive at an understanding.

"So tell me." Bill stuck a toothpick in his mouth and chewed. "What's happening? You're serious about this, aren't you?"

Tom nodded. "Very serious. Though I have to admit there's little actual proof, so I can't say I'm a hundred percent certain."

And then, without any superfluous emotion, Kelly laid out the events of the past six weeks or so, from Kent's death to the bloody wedding invitation.

When she was finished, Bill asked a few pertinent questions. Kelly couldn't help noticing how different this interaction was from the one with Sebastian. Bill might be just a hot-dog vendor, but he was bright and direct and easy to deal with, now that he wasn't on the defensive.

Finally Bill leaned back and whistled. "I always knew those Mellons were sketchy, but this really blows a hole in the boat." He looked at Kelly. "You okay? They've put you through effing hell these past few weeks."

"I'm fine. It was hard, being with Lillith when she—" She took a breath. "But the invitation made me mad, which was much better."

Bill nodded approvingly. "I always knew you had guts inside that stringy little body. Hey, you managed to fend off Romeo here, which was fairly impressive."

She laughed and glanced at Tom, who took her hand across the table.

Bill leaned back, toying with the ketchup bottle and watching them. "Look, I'm not disagreeing about what's going on. I see what you're saying, and it looks pretty twisted to me. But here's my problem. What's the motive?"

Tom shook his head. "We don't know. That's the weak link, of course. It's probably why the police won't take us seriously. We just don't know."

"Of course, she is loony tunes, so maybe the question isn't really relevant. But still…" Bill shrugged. "I don't mean to sound cold here, but if she's gotta let off some steam about all this, aren't you the obvious target?"

Tom nodded. "Unquestionably."

"Okay, so maybe you're wrong about the deaths being murders, which would suit me just fine. My life may not seem that great to you, but I like it. A lot." Bill took out the toothpick and chewed instead on his upper lip, as if the beard were making it itch. "You said you're not a hundred percent sure. So what do you think the odds are?"

"I don't know," Tom said. "My instincts say ninety-nine percent. But the facts just aren't there yet, and we can't make a case out of instincts."

"I take it you're still a lawyer." Bill chuckled. "Okay, now how about the odds that it's actually Sophie herself? Is she the one I need to be scanning the crowds for? Not mom or little sister or big brother?"

Tom hesitated. "Seventy-five."

"That low?"

Kelly was surprised, too. She had been taking it for granted that Sophie was the problem. She hadn't realized that Tom wasn't yet completely convinced.

"As you pointed out, motive is still hazy." Tom flicked one hand, indicating uncertainty. "Without knowing *why,* it's pretty hard to know *who.* We think it's Sophie. But right now I wouldn't walk into a dark alley with any of them."

"Hell, I wouldn't have done that ten years ago!" Bill sniffed the air, which was now heavy with hot-dog odors. "I'd better get in there before I burn up the stock. Dogs aren't cheap. But I'd be glad to give each of you a Ghost-Choker on the house. As thanks for the heads-up."

He paused a moment, looked at the two of them, and laughed. "That's pretty funny, huh? With the past coming back to haunt us like this, a Ghost-Choker just might be exactly what we need."

THE DIGGER BEACH police station wasn't quite as quaint as the one in Cathedral Cove, Kelly thought as she sat in one of the back offices and ran through the story one more time for the detective. Its no-frills concrete structure reflected the blue-collar demographics of the smaller town.

The front room was busier, with one detective taking information from a crying woman holding ice to a black eye, and another grilling two teenagers in handcuffs. In comparison, Cathedral Cove seemed pretty tame.

Even the offices, where she and Tom were talking to their own detective, were cluttered and charmless.

She almost smiled. Who would have thought she'd become such an expert on police stations?

Though Tom helped with a detail now and then, she was doing most of the talking, just as she had with Bill. After all, she was the one who had been on scene for Lillith's accident, and she'd discovered the other deaths first, too.

Besides, Tom kept being interrupted by his cell phone. Every few minutes it would buzz, and then Tom would have to walk out into the hall to take the call. She overheard a word or two occasionally, and she deduced that someone—probably the investigator Tom had hired—was trying to track down Alex VanCamp.

To warn him, of course.

Bride's side, groom's side.

She tried not to think about the implications. But she knew as well as Tom did that, by the time Alex was in any real jeopardy, the killer would already have eliminated both Bill and Kelly.

When Tom returned, he took his chair, which was right beside hers, and reclaimed her hand.

"We can't be sure of anything, even the order," he said quietly, as if he'd read her mind. "Alex has a right to know."

She nodded. "Of course."

The detective, who had been looking at his computer, stood. "I'm going to call Vince Kopple and see what he has to say," he said. "I'll be back in a bit. Can I get you anything? A cup of coffee?"

They both declined. As the detective left the room, Kelly realized how glad she was just to be alone with Tom, even for a minute.

He leaned over and kissed her. She drank in the comfort of it and was sorry when he stopped.

"When we're finished here," he asked, "do you want to go back to Cathedral Cove?"

She would have loved to say no, let's go to Tahiti and make love on the sand for the rest of our lives, but that wasn't possible.

"I have to. I have commissions that are falling behind."

He frowned. "You have to go back to your studio right away? Today?"

"Of course," she said. "It's how I earn my living. But…"

She tried to decide whether she should invite him to stay with her. Jacob might still need him. Plus, she hated the possibility that she might seem clingy and insecure. She wasn't. She didn't want him around so that he could hold her hand at night and assure her everything would be fine. She wanted him there so that he could make love to her until she couldn't remember her name.

"Then I'm staying with you," he said.

Though she was relieved to hear it, she had to keep up appearances. She raised one eyebrow. "So speaks the caveman. What happened to asking my permission?"

He took her hand and raised it to his lips. He turned it over with a smile.

"Ms. Ralston," he said softly. "May I sleep with you tonight?"

She shivered as his lips moved against her palm. "Yes."

His phone buzzed again. He kept hold of her palm, using his other hand to slide the phone out of his pocket and flip open the keypad. He touched the talk button.

"This is Tom."

He listened a moment, and then, almost imperceptibly, she felt his fingers tighten against her hand. Her heartbeat sped up, though she had no idea what he was hearing.

"Okay. Be careful. Turn off all your equipment, if you can, and get out of the stand. I'll be right there, and I'll bring the police."

Then he hung up and turned to her.

"Sit tight," he said. "I'll be right back."

She didn't try to stop him. The expression on his face told her that would be hopeless.

Within a minute or two, he returned. He sat down on the edge of the chair, facing her. He took both her hands this time, and when he spoke his voice was very somber.

"I'm going to go caveman on you again here, Kelly. But this time I hope you won't argue."

She nodded, concentrating on breathing deeply.

"That was Bill. He says he's pretty sure he saw Sophie a few minutes ago."

"Oh, my God."

Her first thought was…they'd been right. It was Sophie, and she was following the lineup of the wedding party.

Her second thought was how much she had wanted to be wrong.

"He thinks she was in the crowd at the carnival, although she hasn't approached him yet. I've told the detective. He wasn't crazy about it, but he's just dispatched a patrolman to check it out. I need to go, too, and I want you to stay here."

She opened her mouth to protest, but he cut in before she could enunciate a single syllable.

"Kelly, listen to me. I need you to stay here. I don't want anyone to get hurt, not Bill or Alex, or even Sophie herself. But whatever is going to happen here today, it must not happen to you."

"Tom, I—"

"You're not listening," he said harshly. "It can't be you." His jaw was tight, his eyes narrowed and intense. "I couldn't handle that. Do you understand? *It can't be you.*"

Finally she heard him. Really heard him.

"All right," she said. "But do you have to go? Couldn't you just let the policeman—"

He shook his head. "I'll be all right. I promise."

She knew he couldn't promise any such thing. But she also knew he had to go. In his head, this was all his fault, and he had to try to set things right.

She clung to him then, to his hands, to his shoulders, to his lips, no longer caring whether she seemed needy. She did need. She needed him to come back to her safely.

"Be careful," she said. She kissed him and her heart was beating so fast she knew he could feel it. "Please be careful."

"I will," he said with a small smile. He touched her cheek. "Remember, I'm a man who very much wants to live."

TOM PRESSED DOWN HARDER on the gas, ignoring the rain that had just begun, turning the roads slick. He was also ignoring the low, in-town speed limit.

The patrolman had a five-minute head start on him, which Tom didn't like. But he hadn't been able to force himself to leave Kelly any faster. He knew how frightened she was, because that's how frightened he would have felt if she'd been the one getting in a car right now and heading for the carnival.

KATHLEEN O'BRIEN

269

"What the hell have you gotten yourself into, Beck-ham?" He looked at his eyes in the rearview mirror. "If you think you can screw this woman for a couple of fantastic weeks and then just say goodbye, you're crazier than you look."

But of course he was crazy. He adjusted the rearview mirror, disgusted. He was talking to himself, wasn't he?

After that, he flipped on his wipers and focused on the road. Digger Beach wasn't a big town, but the carnival was on the outskirts, and the police station was in the heart. It was going to take at least ten minutes more, especially now that the rain was snarling the traffic.

He wondered what Sophie had planned. The first three accidents had been almost brilliant. Carefully designed and seamlessly executed. Even the police hadn't been able to detect anything wrong.

Not for the first time, he wondered how Sophie Mellon, who had lived in mental-health clinics more over the past decade than she had lived in her own home, had managed to pull off such a feat.

"What the hell happened to you, Sophie?"

He took the last turn out of the downtown area and hit the gas again. Digger Beach didn't have much in the way of suburbs. It slid from downtown to residential to rural pretty quickly. But he wasn't there yet. He was still in a heavily populated commercial area with lots of strip malls and warehouses.

Damn the rain. It was taking too long. He thought of Bill Gaskins, who was actually a nice man, and cursed the five minutes that still lay between Tom and the carnival.

"Damn it, Sophie," he said out loud. "Don't do this. You don't really want to do this."

He heard a strange noise. The skin on the back of his neck prickled.

What the hell?

It sounded as if it came from the back seat.

He darted a glance into the rearview mirror.

And found himself looking into Sophie Mellon's eyes.

"Pull over," she said. "And do it slowly, so that you don't attract any attention. I have a knife, Tom, and I'll use it if I have to. I've fantasized about killing you for years."

CHAPTER NINETEEN

ALL HE COULD THINK WAS…thank God he hadn't let Kelly come with him.

After that, he wasn't as shocked as he would have imagined he'd be. It was almost as if he'd been expecting Sophie to rise up out of the pile of raincoats and umbrellas in the back seat of his car.

But of course, given everything that had happened lately, she'd been so much on his mind. The ten years apart seemed just a wisp of smoke, easily blown away.

He eased the car over to a strip-mall parking lot, wondering with an eerie calm why Sophie would pick such a public place to kill him? Maybe that meant she didn't intend to. At least not right away.

And yet… What else could she possibly want from him?

He glanced at her again. Though the rearview mirror showed him only odd, piecemeal rectangles, he could tell how much she had changed.

She'd lost at least twenty-five pounds. Right before the wedding, she'd put on a little weight, which had suited her. Now she was all sharp angles again, so jagged her nose looked like a beak, and her lips were thin and cracked.

Her skin, which ten years ago had been creamy soft,

looked dry and had turned a strange shade of gray. She seemed to have a rash on one of her cheeks. Her hair was dull, much thinner and less blond. He wondered how much of her earlier golden shine had come from chemicals she no longer bothered with.

But she still wore a dress of her trademark peacock blue, though it hung on her like a robe draped over a scarecrow.

When the car came to a stop, he kept his hands on the wheel but held her gaze in the mirror. "It's been a long time, Sophie. What do you want?"

"Right now I want you to pass me your cell phone," she said. "Very slowly. Keep one hand on the wheel."

He did as she asked. But when she got the telephone, she didn't even look at it. She just tossed it to the side. He heard it fall with a whisper against his jacket, which he'd left in the back seat earlier, right next to Kelly's coat.

Outside, people were rushing by, under umbrellas, or with hands or newspapers held over their heads. He'd parked between a bagel shop and a copy center, both of which had plenty of customers. He wondered if anyone would notice the odd drama playing out in the sedate sedan. But they were all focused on reaching their own cars without getting drenched. And besides, his windows were heavily tinted. So probably not.

He might honk, but what if she really had a knife, as she said she did? He might startle some poor people into dropping their take-out cups of coffee, but could anyone possibly intervene before she could use that knife…either on him, or, an even more horrible thought, on herself?

He decided to wait, to see what she had in mind.

In the rearview mirror, she was still staring at him. But he wasn't sure she really saw him. Her eyelids were heavy and her mouth moved strangely, her tongue darting back and forth against her teeth.

It was a pitiful sight. The Sophie he had almost married had been a vibrant beauty. In spite of her unhealthy relationship with Sebastian, she had been physically radiant. This Sophie looked like what everyone had said she was. A madwoman.

"Are you okay?" He tried to keep his tone neutral, tilting toward sympathetic without risking offending her pride. If she still had any, which her matted hair and musty, unwashed smell made him doubt. "You don't look well."

"I haven't taken my pills. They make me sleepy, and I can't afford to be sleepy right now."

"What pills?"

"All of them. I had to stop taking them. My brain is fuzzy if I take them." She sounded defensive, as if she thought his question had been an accusation. She tossed her head, throwing her hair over her shoulder. It was a gesture he remembered, but the difference was cruel.

"When I don't take them, though, I have such horrible thoughts." She shook her head and made noises with her tongue. "I try not to listen to them, but it's hard. And I have headaches."

He wished he could see the knife. Did she really have one? How big was it? How was she holding it? Did she know anything about how to use it? She didn't look strong. If he could just get a sense of the physical setup, he felt sure he could overpower her.

"What can I do, Sophie? Do you need a doctor?"

She laughed. "I have a million doctors. They can't help me. You're the only one who can help me. If you just will. If you just will."

"Of course I will." He felt the tension in his chest ease a little. She wasn't bent on murder, then. She wanted something from him. "I'll do anything I can. Tell me what you want."

"I want—" Her eyes suddenly filled with tears. "I want to tell you about Sebastian."

He swiveled his head a couple of inches, but she made a growling noise, so he turned back.

"I already know about Sebastian, Sophie. I know the two of you were—" He hesitated. What was the word? They hadn't been lovers, but—

"I know you were in love."

"Not that," she said. "I know you knew about that. You saw us, didn't you? The night before the wedding. I could feel you there, in the shadows, watching. I almost said, *Sebastian, Tom is here.* But he was in so much pain. He needed me." The tears began to fall. "He always needed me."

Tom swallowed hard. "Yes," he said. "I saw you that night."

"That's why you didn't show up for the wedding."

"Yes. That's why I ran away. I'm sorry, Sophie. I should have handled it better. I should have talked to you."

"I was very angry," she said. "For years, I hated you. But now I understand how disgusting it must have seemed. It was wrong, I know that now. But I was young, and he loved me, and I thought I loved him. I *owed* him. You don't know how much he had suffered for me."

Tom wondered if talking would do her good. He wondered if it would release some of the edgy tension that was making her body so restless and awkward. Or would it make her worse, make her dwell on things that tortured her?

"What do you mean, he suffered?"

She dashed tears away with the back of one hand. "You know about his body? About his burns?"

"Yes."

"He got those trying to protect me. He was only fifteen years old when it happened. I was fourteen. We didn't know what else to do."

"I thought it was a boating accident—"

She laughed, a fake, ugly laugh. "It was no accident. Sebastian took the wheel from my father, and he steered it into the dock. At full speed, right into the dock. He wanted my father to die, and he was willing to die, too, if he had to. It caught fire, all around him. But my father didn't die."

Tom winced, imagining the impact, the fire, the pain. "Why did he want to kill your father?"

"Because my father liked to hurt people. It excited him. He liked to hurt my mother. And then me. It would have been Sam next. We decided he had to be stopped, but Sebastian wouldn't let me do anything. He said he would take care of it."

She shook her head, her mouth slack, as if she still couldn't believe that fate had played such an evil trick. "But my father didn't die."

"Did he keep on hurting you?"

"No. He was afraid of Sebastian."

"Then how did you…I mean, why did you and Sebastian—"

She frowned. "Sebastian needed sex, too. All men do. They have to find release somewhere, and, because he was so damaged, he didn't have anywhere else."

She stared at him in the mirror, a sudden fierce clarity

in her eyes. "All men," she repeated ominously. "Even you needed it, didn't you, Tom?"

He shook his head, sickened by the memory. "It was different with us, Sophie. We were going to be married. We—we weren't brother and sister."

"Yes." Her eyes clouded, as if she looked at something inside herself. "I know that's how you saw it. And yet, for me, it was exactly the same. The only difference was that you didn't love me, and Sebastian did. He loved me enough to die for me, to let the fire burn away his beautiful body. How could I tell him no?"

"Sophie—"

"He loved me so much he didn't even let me—let me do anything. I would have, if he had asked me to. But he loved me too much. He only wanted me to be there. And to watch."

For a horrible moment Tom's mouth felt full of the foul, phantom taste of ten-year-old vomited scotch. His legs burned, as they had burned that night, desperate to run as far and as fast as he could.

"Even that was too much," he said. "He shouldn't have made you be a part of it in any way."

She frowned harder. She seemed to be struggling to keep her thoughts under her control. "I know that now," she said. "I even knew it then, but I just didn't have the courage to say no, not after all he'd done. And compared to what my father had wanted…"

She rocked a little, moaning. Then, as if she'd pulled herself together, she looked back into the mirror. "But now Sebastian has a wife. He doesn't need me. He doesn't have the right to keep making me—"

Tom's hands tightened on the steering wheel. "God, Sophie. It's still going on?"

"Not for almost two months," she said. She sounded proud. "I told him I couldn't stand it anymore. He has a wife. I said no. Don't I deserve to stop now, after all these years? He suffered for me, but I suffered for him, too. I wouldn't let him come to see me anymore. I left the clinic, and I didn't tell him where I was going. But I still get his e-mails, every single day, so I know how angry he is."

"How angry is he?"

"That's what I wanted to tell you. He's doing terrible things. He's trying to make me come back to him."

Tom's flesh began to creep, cold and slow across his bones. "What is he doing?"

She sighed. She shook her head, and her tongue was moving very fast, back and forth. "He's killing them. Don't you know that? He's killing them."

Tom turned around then. *To hell with the knife. There may not even be one.*

But when he faced her, he saw that the knife was real. It caught the watery reflection of the rain on its long, sharp blade.

And it was pressed against her too-thin rib cage, just under her overburdened heart.

He spoke softly. "Who is he killing, Sophie?"

"All of you. One by one, until I come back to him. He told me he would, when he saw that I wasn't going to do what he wanted. But I won't go back to him. I can't, not anymore. I'll never get better if I do."

Tom's muscles were tensed, a primitive need for action pumping through his veins. It was an act of great will to keep his voice calm.

"You're right, Sophie. You can't go back to him. But we need to stop him. We need to stop him *now*. Help me do that."

She was still shaking her head. "No one can stop him."

"Yes, we can, if only you'll—"

She began breathing heavily. "Everybody thinks I'm the crazy one, but he is. *He* is. The fire made him crazy. His burns made him crazy. Or maybe it's from my father. I don't know. I only know he'll never stop, not until he's dead. Or until I am."

His heart dragged, as if it were too heavy for his chest to hold it.

"Sophie, there's been enough death—"

"I know." She looked up at him. "Tell me what to do, Tom. I don't want to kill my brother. But how else will I stop him? The only other way is if I—" She began to sob. "But I don't want to die. I can't help it, I don't want to die."

"Sophie," Tom said gently. "Give me the knife. I'll help you."

"How?" She tightened her hold on the handle. Tom saw the flesh just under her breast give slightly as she exerted more pressure. "How will you help me?"

"We'll go to the police. We'll tell them about Sebastian, and they'll pick him up. They'll get him some help, Sophie. You know he needs help."

"No," she said. She'd begun to sweat. It beaded on her gray skin like dirty pearls. "They won't believe he did it. They'll think I did it. Sebastian said so. They can't stop him."

"Sophie," he said again. He reached out, hoping he could get the knife before she realized—

To his horror, the minute his hand came near, she dragged the blade of the knife hard against herself, cutting through the fabric, through her skin, just under her heart. A curving stain of red appeared and turned purple as it seeped into her blue dress.

He yanked the knife away. "Sophie!"

Suddenly she had her hand on the door. Before he could register the danger and flip the automatic locks, she flung it open and tumbled out of the car.

She began to scream. "Help me! He has a knife!"

Half a dozen people stopped to stare at him, forgetting the rain, paralyzed with horror. Sophie ran through them, and she kept running, disappearing almost instantly into a gap between the buildings.

He climbed out, too, even though he already knew it was too late. Three large men lunged toward him. One of them kicked the bloody knife, which he had forgotten he still held, out of his hand. It clattered on the wet sidewalk, where the raindrops began to wash away the blood. Several bystanders shrieked and jumped away.

The other two men each grabbed one of his arms. When Tom resisted, they yanked so hard they almost dislocated his shoulder.

"Call the police," one of the men yelled to the crowd. But he didn't need to. At least three cell phones were already open, fingers punching 911 as fast as they possibly could.

The Digger Beach police would be here soon.

But not soon enough.

Tom would have laughed if it hadn't been so tragic. Wasn't it the perfect final irony? He thought he was such a smart son of a bitch. And yet, in ten seconds flat, poor, crazy Sophie Mellon had completely outwitted him.

IT HAD BEGUN TO RAIN at the carnival, fat, cold drops that hit your skin hard and hurt. The late afternoon, already gray, turned suddenly to wet, shivering night. The few die-hard families who hadn't left were huddled under the concrete concession pavilions.

Sebastian watched as a couple of beleaguered parents dashed over to Bill's stand because their bratty kids insisted on having an extra hot dog to make up for leaving early.

It was like watching a silent movie. In the one bright light of the service window, Sebastian could see Bill shaking his head and waving his hands in emphatic negatives. The parents pushed hard—no surprise there, the brats had to hàve learned that whining from somewhere. But Bill wasn't budging. Finally the adults ran back through the rain empty-handed and hustled their complaining children out to the parking lot.

And then, though the colored lights still twinkled amid the raindrops, Sebastian and Bill were just about the only people left in the park. Sebastian waited until Bill had closed up and locked his stand, and then, keeping a careful distance, he followed him.

He had expected Bill to head straight for the parking lot, but to his surprise Bill loped up toward the haunted house instead.

Sebastian smiled. *Even better.*

He had noticed already that the haunted house was unattended, one of those walk-yourself-through jobs. In this weather, the place was empty, though the soundtrack continued to play. High-pitched screams and fake ghostly groans. Sebastian liked the idea. There was a sense of humor to doing it here.

Bill walked through the fake house's fake entry foyer, where, at the far doorway, a mannequin with a fake chainsaw leered at incoming guests. Bill, obviously very familiar with the layout, passed the mannequin without look-ing. He didn't even flinch when he stepped on the sensor that activated a pneumatic device, sending the mannequin lunging six inches toward him.

Sebastian stopped a second to lock the front door. He prided himself on his clear head and common sense. The storm had driven everyone away for now, but the rain wouldn't last forever, and the brats might eventually whine their way back.

As he traced Bill's footsteps, Sebastian was careful to avoid the pneumatic device. The chainsaw man probably had sent a thousand kids screaming in delicious terror, but Sebastian didn't want the telltale whoosh to alert Bill that he wasn't in the haunted house alone.

This time, Sebastian had decided he didn't have to be quite as careful. This one didn't need to look like an acci-dent. All he needed was to leave the lace, and the police would begin to hunt Sophie down like a dog.

If Sophie didn't care enough about these people to save them, perhaps she'd care enough about her own skin. She knew the rules. If she agreed to his terms, he'd provide an alibi. If she didn't…

If she didn't, she could rot in jail. It wouldn't be much different from rotting in that mental institution. Once, Se-bastian's life had been dedicated to protecting Sophie. Now it was Tessie. It was only fair that Sophie could ei-ther help him protect his little girl, or she could take what was coming to her.

He didn't close in on Bill yet, though he kept him in sight. The chubby little man was moving quickly, but not in any real panic. He was unaware that he was being fol-lowed. He walked through the second fake room, which had an empty chair eerily rocking beside a fake fire, and a bed with a sheet-covered figure that, Sebastian assumed, would periodically rise and make spooky noises.

Standing at the edge of the doorway, Sebastian stared at the bed. He liked that idea. Yes, it could buy him a little extra time to get out of town, even if the carnival opened up again after the rain.

He didn't need long, just long enough to get back to the hotel in Atlanta, where he was staying tonight. He had a perfectly legitimate appointment with clients first thing in the morning.

But then Bill reached out and opened a door that had been cleverly hidden in one of the walls. Sebastian, who had been about to enter the room, had to stop cold. The hidden door led to an undecorated area that was not part of the haunted house. It looked a little like a locker room or an employee break room.

When the door closed behind Bill, Sebastian went up to it and pressed his ear against the black-painted plywood. You could hear everything through these cheap walls.

Almost immediately, he heard the tinny notes of numbers being punched into a cell phone. *Stupid bastard.* Sebastian knew he couldn't wait any longer.

He had everything ready. He kept it ready, just in case he ran into Sophie.

So he pushed open the door, smiling. Bill sat on a metal folding chair, just like the one out front. He had his coat across one arm, and his cell phone in the other hand.

Sebastian didn't even wait for the shock on Bill's face to turn to recognition. He just moved across the room and took the cell phone out of the fat man's slack hand. It was really too easy.

He looked down at the display. Bill wasn't calling 911 and he wasn't calling the police. Sebastian looked at him. "Whose number is this?"

Bill looked nervous, but not terrified. Not yet.

He would be, soon, Sebastian was sure. Bill had a decent mind, actually, considering he'd had little formal education. Sebastian had considered investing in one or two of his schemes, but it had always been more profitable simply to take the ideas to someone else, someone who would be suitably grateful.

"It's my girlfriend." Bill's eyes were narrowed, as if he couldn't figure out what was happening. "I wanted her to know what was going on."

Sebastian still smiled. "And what is going on, Bill?"

Bill shook his head and stood slowly.

"I'm not sure," he said. "Maybe you can tell me. Maybe you can give me back my telephone."

"In a minute," Sebastian said pleasantly. "What did you want to tell your girlfriend about? Is it something about Sophie?"

Bill nodded. "Yeah. I've been hearing some messed up stuff about Sophie. And then, a while ago, I thought I saw her. But she looked different, so I'm not sure…"

His voice trailed off. He was starting to put the pieces together.

He backed up a few steps.

Sebastian wasn't surprised to hear that Sophie had come to the carnival. She knew the lineup of the wedding party as well as he did. Better. He was only surprised that she hadn't tried to warn Bill herself.

Sebastian had been afraid she might. He had tried to get here as early as he could, to circumvent that, but as usual

Gwen had made it difficult to get away without arousing suspicion.

"You saw Sophie? But you didn't talk to her?"

Bill shook his head. "No. I was told that she—" He stopped. "But you—are you with her? You two were always close."

"Yes," Sebastian said. "We were. But I've been looking for her, too. For weeks now. I can't find her, and I'm worried."

Bill's eyes were just horizontal squints and he was chewing at his upper lip. He clearly wanted to believe Sebastian, for obvious reasons.

But, equally clearly, he didn't, not quite.

He darted a glance at the hidden door, which was the only exit to this room. Sebastian stood squarely in front of it. Bill couldn't miss the possible implications of that.

"Well, I'd better get going," Bill said with a determined, matter-of-fact voice. "I've called the police, and they're going to be looking for me at my stand."

The police? Anger tightened Sebastian's chest and his scars began to throb. But he couldn't let it show. He was going to have to hurry this along, if this stupid sot had already called the cops.

"Okay," he said as pleasantly as he could. "But before you go, could you look at something for me and tell me if you know what it is? If it's what I think it is, I'm really concerned."

Every muscle in Bill's posture cried out his resistance. But he, too, was trying to hide the intensity of his secret emotions, so he just smiled weakly and said, "What is it?"

Sebastian reached his hand in his pocket and pulled out the plastic bag he put there every day, just in case. He began to open it, synchronizing his motions with his approach toward Bill.

"It's just this," he said. "It's a piece of lace, and I'm afraid it might be from Sophie's wedding dress."

Bill's body was tense, ready to spring now that Sebastian had moved a few feet away from the door. Sebastian could see his eyes darting from the door to the lace and back again. Thinking, thinking...

But in the end, of course, the poor slob made the wrong decision. He made the decision to play along. He bent his head to look at the lace Sebastian was holding out. When Sebastian jerked his hand upward, shoving the lace against Bill's nose and open mouth, there wasn't a thing Bill could do to stop him.

Sebastian, who was nearly a foot taller, held Bill's head with his other hand, making sure that every breath he took inhaled more of the chloroform. It took only about five seconds and the fat little fool slumped to the ground like a sack of flour.

Sebastian dragged him to the other room and tossed him on the bed with the fake corpse. He shoved aside the top sheet. He didn't want any visible blood, just in case someone else came in later tonight. He needed at least two hours to get back to Atlanta.

Then he sat on the edge of the bed, safely out of the line of blood spatter. He took out his knife and killed Bill quickly, just lifting that hideous beard and slitting the thick, meaty throat.

He started to get up and wash his hands in the employee break room, but an idea occurred to him. He had to use his time efficiently, but surely he had a couple of minutes to spare, just for a little poetic justice.

He couldn't do the chest, of course. That would point to him, which he couldn't risk. But there were other places, other ways.

"Hey, fatso." Sebastian smiled at Bill's expressionless face. "Remember that time you said my chest looked like a roadmap of hell? Got a lot of laughs with that one, didn't you?" He pulled out his knife. "So I'll tell you what. Maybe I'll return the favor."

CHAPTER TWENTY

THE RED TAPE INVOLVED with the police nearly drove Tom insane. As they tried to sort out the circus in front of the bagel store, he began to wonder how they ever solved any crimes at all.

The patrolman who had been sent to the Funland to check things out had returned, and he was now part of the melee outside the strip mall. Bill hadn't been there, he said, as if that solved everything. Tom almost choked him.

Luckily, there was one truly sharp cop on the Digger Beach police force, a guy named John Frank, who was nearing retirement and didn't seem to care if he cut a few corners.

Most importantly, he listened well. Tom was able to fill him in on everything with few interruptions, after which Frank went back to his patrol car, called the station and confirmed that everything Tom said was true. And then he set to work dealing with the most important items.

An alert should be sent out for Sophie immediately. And someone should ask the police in Raleigh to round up Sebastian for questioning. Frank and Tom needed to hurry the hell up and get over to the Funland to find Bill.

The rain had finally let up, and because they rode together in the patrol car, they covered the ten-minute drive in less than five.

The clouds might have stopped leaking for the time being, but they still hovered sourly overhead. It still looked like midnight. Looking at his watch, Tom was surprised to see that it was only about six o'clock.

The carnival was soaking wet, from the tip of the shining, dripping Ferris wheel to the muddy dirt paths underfoot. But even so, quite a few families milled about, determined to have fun or die trying.

It took Frank and Tom a minute or two to make their way back to Bill's hot-dog stand. Tom could tell from thirty yards away that the place was pitch dark. He tried not to let that discourage him. He had told Bill to turn all the machinery off and wait for him outside the stand. There was just something about that claustrophobic little tin box, with its grills and freezers and propane tanks, that had seemed uncomfortably vulnerable.

If Bill had done as Tom suggested, he'd be waiting nearby. Tom scanned the faces as they moved through the carnival, checking every man to see if he might be Bill—or Sebastian. But Tom didn't recognize anyone. They were all daddies or boyfriends. If Bill was still here, he was hiding himself pretty well.

When they reached the stand, Tom tried the door. It was locked. He had already filled in Officer Frank, so the older man simply nodded.

"He'll be waiting for you somewhere safe," Frank said. "Let's hold tight a minute or two. He may see us and come out of hiding."

One, two, three minutes went by. It seemed like an eternity.

Tom couldn't just stand there any longer. "Can you find out what kind of car he drives? I don't know him all that well, and I've never seen it. I don't know whether it's in the lot or not."

The officer nodded. "Already did that. It's a ninety-two Chevy. White. It's out there, but he's not in it. We parked right next to it."

Tom looked at Frank's face, which was well illuminated by the neon sign over the haunted house. The man was so well trained it was difficult to be sure whether he found the presence of Bill's car—and the absence of Bill—at all troubling.

Tom only knew that *he* didn't like it.

He tried again. "Does Bill have a cell phone registered?"

"That takes a little longer. But we're checking."

Tom wandered another couple of minutes, poking his head into nearby shooting galleries and cotton-candy stands. He asked several people whether they'd seen Bill, but no one had, not for the past hour, anyhow. Apparently Bill had closed up shop just as the rain got really bad and he hadn't returned. Tom got the idea that these other concessionaires thought such behavior was pretty unprofessional.

Tom thought it was damn unsettling.

Finally he went back to Officer Frank. "I don't like this," he said. "I think we need to get some more people out here and start searching in earnest."

"You feel that sure he's still here? You don't think he would have gone off in Mellon's car?"

Tom tried to think of any scenario in which Bill would have been dumb enough to do that. "No," he said. "I think he's still here."

Tom sensed movement to his left. He looked, hoping to see Bill's hairy face smiling at him. But it wasn't Bill. A family of five was coming toward them, like a parade of bright yellow ducks in their plastic ponchos. It would have been amusing at another time.

When they got close enough, Tom could see that the father, a huge man with red hair and a red face, looked upset.

Tom's shoulders tightened. Had these people perhaps seen something disturbing? Had they seen two men struggling?

Had they seen a body?

"Listen, we need to talk to the manager," the father said.

Officer Frank gave the man a mild look, ignoring his rude tone. "What seems to be the problem?"

"It's my son's birthday. First it rains, and then everything seems to be closing early. We came a long way to this park, and I don't think we should be shut out of the stuff he wants to do. He wants to do the haunted house."

Officer Frank turned around and looked at the big house-like facade, with its bright lights and the ghostly moans.

"That looks open," he said.

"Yeah, that's my point. It *looks* open, but it's not. I can see lights on in there. But the door is locked."

Officer Frank turned to Tom. The two men exchanged a hard gaze.

"I don't know," Tom said, just as if he'd been asked a question.

Frank blinked as he thought it through. Then he turned back to the man. "I'm sorry. Apparently the haunted house is closed, after all. Why don't you file a complaint with the manager?"

"Fine. Where the hell is the so-called mana—"

But Tom didn't hear the rest of the question. Though deep in his heart he feared it was too late, though he feared a few more seconds wouldn't make much difference, he and Officer Frank had already begun to run.

SIX HOURS LATER, just after midnight, Tom and Kelly checked into another hotel. It might have been the same one they'd slept in last night. It had the same minibar, the same television behind a honey-pine armoire. Tom thought he might even have been staring at the same nicely framed floral prints on the walls.

The big difference was that this hotel was in Cathedral Cove, just two miles from the police station.

And there was a somber-faced policeman parked on a chair just outside the door.

Neither Sophie nor Sebastian had been located yet. After Sophie had jumped out of Tom's car, she seemed to have disappeared into the rain. The Raleigh police had reported that Sebastian wasn't at home. According to his wife, he should be in Atlanta on a business trip, but so far he hadn't checked into his hotel, either. They had arranged for the Atlanta police to stake the place out.

And so that somber-faced policeman, or another just like him, would be occupying that chair in the hallway until both Mellon siblings were in custody.

However long it took.

Just one murder too late, the police were finally ready to take the whole thing seriously. They'd called in the state investigators and things had suddenly become deadly earnest.

Over the past hours, Tom and Kelly had talked themselves hoarse, going through everything one more time:

the three "accidents," the wedding-dress lace, the bloody invitation. The investigators had taken custody of Kelly's rehearsal-dinner picture, and they'd found a judge who'd stay late and give them a warrant to search Coeur Volé.

Once there, they had confiscated the wedding dress. Then they had begun combing the monstrous old vault for any other evidence.

They were still at the mansion, the last Tom had heard. He could only imagine Imogene standing at the head of the staircase, under the glowing St. George, stiff with autocratic outrage. But ultimately impotent. An august family name could get you kid-glove treatment for a while, but eventually even the nobility had to account for the blood all over their hands.

When she first entered the hotel room, Kelly had sat on the chair near the corner desk, and she was still there. Her auburn hair fell in loose tangles, obscuring the side of her face. Her purse was on her lap and she had threaded her fingers through the strap, as if she were afraid someone might try to take it from her.

She watched Tom as he accepted the room service that had just been delivered, clearing it through the policeman, of course. Once the door was shut and locked again, she spoke for the first time since they'd gotten here half an hour ago.

"The one person I pity in all this is Samantha," she said, seemingly at random. She had shed tears when she'd first heard about Bill, but neither of them had the will to discuss that fresh, gruesome tragedy in detail yet. The body had been unspeakably mutilated, his thighs carved up after death, which had served no purpose except perhaps to vent the killer's rage.

"Samantha?" Tom tried to focus on what Kelly was saying.

"Yes. She must feel very alone right now."

Tom nodded. "I thought of that, too. If she's somehow managed to escape the twisted Mellon genes so far, this could easily send her over the edge. And her mother won't be much help."

"Just imagine," Kelly said softly. "She lost Sophie years ago. Lost her to mental illness and the institutions. And now she's going to lose Sebastian, too. It's enough to break anyone's heart."

Finally Kelly let go of the purse strap. She put her hands over her face.

"It's too much," she said. She rubbed her eyes, smoothing out her brows as if her head ached. But he noticed she didn't give way to tears. "It's just too much."

Tom had ordered a bowl of vegetable soup. He lifted the silver cover and put a spoon in it. He could tell by her voice that she was probably numb with exhaustion, but she needed food. Neither of them had eaten for about eighteen hours.

He picked up the soup and brought it over to the small table. He shoved the telephone and guest directories out of the way and snapped on the wall lamp.

"Eat this," he said. "It'll help."

She looked down at the bowl. He wondered if she even recognized it as food. But then, taking a deep breath and squaring her shoulders, she picked up the spoon and began to eat.

Good girl, he thought. This woman had a lot of courage.

While she ate, he turned down the bedspread and

sheets. The police had offered them two rooms, but Kelly had shaken her head *no*. The woman at the registration desk had offered them two double beds, but again Kelly had indicated a firm *no*.

So now they had this beautiful king-size bed, and it would go to waste. He knew there would be no repeat of last night's lovemaking. He could see the bleakness in her eyes. She wanted his arms around her, but only for comfort and warmth. Not for passion.

Maybe it was different for a man. For him, sex would have helped. He would have welcomed a long, hardworking physical encounter, in which his mind would be focused only on her. The determination to bring her the peace of climax, the need to listen to every reaction of every muscle, no matter how small, would drown out all other thoughts.

It would be simple and satisfying. Energy and sweat followed by release and oblivion.

He might even, for a couple of hours, forget the sight of Bill Gaskins's body.

But sex wasn't what Kelly wanted. And though deep inside he was just a primitive, demanding man, tonight he'd try to be better. He'd make a stab at being whatever mythical creature—knight or hero or guardian angel—she wanted him to be.

He ran her a bath, and she thanked him politely. When she came out, her wet hair the color of dark wine, he took a quick shower, then pulled on sweatpants.

He got into bed beside her.

He took a deep breath, tried to think hero thoughts and reached out to take her in his arms.

To his surprise, her body was warm and naked under

the soft sheets. When he touched her, she turned with a low murmur and molded herself to him. She ran her hands up and down his back.

"Make love to me," she said.

The hero tried to make a stand, but the man, the real man, was hard and ready, and nothing on earth could have kept him from doing as she asked.

SHE DREAMED OF SOPHIE. They were teenagers again. Maybe fifteen. The age they'd been the year they first met Tom.

The two of them were in the back gardens, their favorite place to hang out when they were at Coeur Volé. Sophie had always liked to tell Kelly stories about the statues, stories so wondrous and strange that sometimes Kelly's spine tingled. She begged Sophie to stop, but secretly she was breathless, eager for the next installment.

Sometimes Kelly tried to invent a story, too, but hers were too saccharine, Sophie said. Still, she had to try. She couldn't always be the boring one.

In her dream, Kelly made up a little green fairy who lived under the rosebush, but Sophie took over the story and said that the fairy had been poisoned, that was why she was green, and that she was prisoner there, held in place by the thorns, and a caterpillar visited her each night and made love to her against her will.

Kelly covered her ears. There was no green fairy, she said angrily. There was no caterpillar. Sophie laughed and held out her hand. In the palm lay a bright green centipede.

"I had to kill it," Sophie said. "To save your little fairy."

Kelly heard a scream. Or was it a boat? Maybe a bell?

The irrational questions made her realize she must be dreaming. She shifted on the sheets, trying to wake up before Sophie could tell her a terrible story about the boat, or the bell or the screaming.

She came to consciousness like rising out of a fog. She lifted onto one elbow, gradually realizing where she was. *A hotel room.* She put her fingers against her stomach. *Naked.* She reached out and touched a man's bare skin, the feel of it sending warmth to unclench her muscles, which were still tightly humming with the fear in the dream.

Tom.

But as she lay back down and turned to nuzzle her head into his shoulder, she realized he was sitting up. He was talking softly on his cell phone.

Her stomach began to tighten again.

The buzz of his phone must have been what woke her. He didn't say much. He mostly listened. He hung up after only a second or two.

"Tom," she said. "What is it?"

He turned slowly, then gathered her into his arms.

"They've found Sebastian."

She held her breath. Somehow, maybe because the dream had prepared her, she knew what was coming.

"He's dead."

IT WAS JUST BEFORE NOON, a beautiful Saturday morning, the blue sky scrubbed clean by yesterday's downpours. It was a great day to be outside, Tom thought. He'd like to go sailing. He'd like to be about a million miles from civilization, with only Kelly by his side. He'd like to lie back and watch the clouds, imagining that they were lumpy white towers holding up the sky.

But instead he was in a bland, too-cold room inside the medical examiner's offices, with his arm around Samantha Mellon's shoulders. She was looking at a photograph the technician held out for her inspection.

It was definitely Sebastian. Though the facial muscles were slack, making the man appear older than thirty-three, and the signature bright blue eyes were shut, Tom recognized him instantly. He could tell by Sam's sudden intake of breath that she did, too.

The most disturbing thing was that, though he was dead, Sebastian looked fine. Tom had learned from the police that, sometime late last night, Sebastian had been shot once in the stomach. They were fairly certain he had died within thirty minutes or so, though he'd never found the strength to get out of his car, which was in a wooded parking lot at a bank at the edge of town. His cell phone had been found about twenty yards away, in the woods where, presumably, the killer had tossed it.

Horrible to imagine. But because this was only a photo of his head, his injuries weren't visible. He could easily have been napping.

Sam seemed frozen, so Tom nodded at the technician. "Yes, that's Sebastian. Thank you."

The other man didn't seem surprised. This wasn't even an officially requested identification. Because Sebastian had been found in his own car, with his driver's license in his back pocket, the police had been comfortable making a presumptive ID of him on their own.

The only reason Tom and Samantha were here was that Sam had needed to see for herself. Half an hour ago, to Tom's astonishment, she had called his cell, a number he hadn't even realized she possessed. She'd begged him to meet her at the medical examiner's office. She wanted to look at the body, but she wasn't sure she had the courage to do it alone.

It had been clear that the poor kid was trying to hold out one last, desperate hope that somehow a mistake had been made. Tom hadn't liked the idea of leaving Kelly while Sophie was still on the loose, not even under police guard. But Kelly, who definitely felt Samantha's pain, had urged him to say yes.

So here he was, in this anonymous-looking brown brick building, in a pleasant room decorated with two nice arm-chairs and a box of tissue on a table. A big window let in the crisp morning sunlight, and on the creamy walls, the shadow of a still-leafy oak branch fluttered, like someone casting playful hand shadows.

Tom had kept his arm around Samantha, so he knew the minute she began to cry. She bowed her head, and at first she seemed to be holding her breath. Then her shoulders began to tremble.

The technician looked at her glumly. He probably hated this part of his job.

"Sam," Tom said. "We should go."

"But why can't I see the body?" She looked up, her face streaming with tears. "A stomach wound isn't like the heart, or the head. Isn't there a possibility he's just uncon-scious?"

The technician shook his head. He fiddled with his white mask, which dangled around his neck.

"Absolutely not. Your brother's wounds were—"

Tom broke in. "They don't leave things like this to guesswork, Sam," he said. "Believe me, they're sure."

"But *I* need to be sure!" Her words were pushed

through a throat so constricted some syllables were hardly audible. She turned to the technician, grief distorting her face. "Why won't you let me see him?"

The technician held up his palms, as if he thought she might try to crash through the barricade of his body.

"Miss Mellon, no contact with the body is allowed. It's a very strict rule. Especially in a homicide."

She seemed to collapse when he said that word, and if Tom hadn't caught her she might have fallen to the cold, tile floor. Instead she fell against him. Tom held her and stroked her back while she cried.

The technician's gaze, catching Tom's over Sam's shoulder, asked a question. Tom nodded. He'd probably have better luck calming Sam if they were alone.

And they might do better outside, too. This room was thoughtfully appointed and the staff respectful, but the building had a subtle chemical odor that carried subliminal messages. He'd noticed a small landscaped area on the south side of the building. Probably the employees here needed fresh air occasionally, too.

When Sam's trembling finally subsided, he put his hands on her shoulders and moved her a couple of inches away.

"There's a little garden outside. Let's walk for a while."

She let him guide her, as passive as a sleepwalker. He realized he could have told her to do anything right now and she would have obeyed.

It was a nice park, the complete antithesis of anything at Cœur Volé. It was only medium-size, but clean, with straightforward brick paths through bitternut hickories. With every gust of the sharp breeze, a few yellow leaves drifted down and jeweled the grass on either side of the path. An occasional plain glossy-black bench offered a place to sit, but otherwise it was simple and uncluttered.

No statues, thank God. If he never saw another garden statue, that would suit him fine.

Eventually the fresh air did its work. After a few minutes, Sam lifted her head a little, put her tissue in her coat pocket. A few more and her stride became more confident, losing that slight shuffling drag.

"I can't thank you enough for agreeing to come," she said. "I know it was a lot to ask."

"I'm glad I could help."

He didn't give voice to any of the questions in his head. Questions like, why was *he* the one she wanted at her side at such a moment? Didn't she have friends? Didn't she have *anyone?*

"I know they're looking for Sophie," she said. "I know they think she—"

She stopped. He stopped, too, and looked down at her. The police had obviously told Sam and her mother everything, probably while they searched the nooks and crannies of Coeur Volé. He wondered what it had felt like to learn so many terrible things at once.

In this yellow-filtered light, she looked fair and golden, just as Sophie once had. She wore a pale blue dress that matched her gentle eyes exactly.

In his mind, he saw again the gray, nervous, disoriented woman Sophie had become, and he wished he could somehow throw up a bubble around Samantha, so that nothing could ever hurt her. So that nothing could ever take this innocence from her face.

And yet, in the shadows around her eyes and in the remnants of her tears, he could see how fatuous that wish was.

The grim realities of being a Mellon—her sister's troubles, her mother's illness and now her brother's death—had already begun to work on her.

It made him sad, and angry as hell, though he had no idea where to direct that anger.

"I don't know what to say," Samantha began. "I feel as if I should apologize, to you and to Kelly, for everything that's happened. If it's true that my brother—that Sophie and Sebastian—"

Tom shook his head. "Don't. You don't have anything to apologize for. It's complicated. It may be a long time before we're really sure what's happened. But whatever it is, it isn't your fault."

She didn't look convinced. "What about Kelly? I always liked her, you know, even at the beginning. Back then, the five years between us seemed like a lifetime. She and Sophie had no use for a pest like me, but I thought they were wonderful. I followed them everywhere."

She plucked a yellow leaf that had landed on her arm. "Do you think she hates me now? I wouldn't blame her for hating everyone with the name of Mellon."

"Kelly knows you had nothing to do with all this. She's been frightened, and she's heartbroken over Lillith. But she just said last night how worried she was for you. She knows you must feel overwhelmed right now, to say the least."

Sam twirled the leaf, seemingly mesmerized by its spinning gold point. "The two of you are very close, aren't you? The danger has brought you together."

He hesitated. "Yes," he said. "But I hope you understand that Kelly was not the reason I didn't marry Sophie. After what I heard, after what I saw… I couldn't have married her, Sam. I should have handled it better. But I couldn't have married her."

"I know," she said softly. "It wasn't Kelly then. But now…" She looked up at him. "It's Kelly now, isn't it?"

He nodded.

"Will you marry her?"

"I don't know. I had decided not to marry, not after Sophie. It's been ten years. I'm not sure I can change. But if I could for anyone, I think it would be for Kelly."

To his dismay, Sam began to cry again.

"Sam…"

"I'm sorry," she said, turning away. "I should go home. My mother will be wondering where I am. She's weak. Sometimes she doesn't even get out of bed."

He touched her shoulder. "Sam, I—"

"Look," she said, tears pooling on her lips. "I know I should wish you happiness. And I do. Really, I do. But it's just that—when you look at it beside what's happened to my family, your happiness seems almost obscene."

CHAPTER TWENTY-ONE

ONCE SEBASTIAN'S BODY was discovered, Kelly realized the idea of hiding out in a hotel under armed guard seemed excessive. Sophie hadn't been found yet, but no one really believed she had any intention of harming Tom or Kelly. Hadn't she killed her own brother to prevent any more deaths?

Besides, she'd had Tom at knifepoint less than twenty-four hours ago. And she had let him go.

As Tom pointed out, however, no one could be one hundred percent sure what was going on in a mind as damaged as Sophie's. He had suggested they should stay at the hotel, minus the cop on the folding chair, at least one more night.

Maybe by the next day Sophie would have been located.

Kelly agreed without argument. Another night in the lovely, if artificial, bubble of intimacy with Tom sounded perfect. Especially if they didn't have to share the room with the specter of fear.

They decided that Tom would go with Kelly to her workshop this afternoon, where she'd spend a few hours catching up on some of her stained-glass commissions. Two of them, the winery entrance tunnel and a restoration of a small window from the Episcopal church, were seriously behind schedule.

The minute they arrived, Tom insisted on double-checking every piece of equipment and machinery she used. She wondered if he thought Sebastian might have left some homicidal time bomb behind, like a frayed cord or a piece of jagged glass jutting out in an unlikely place.

Everything checked out fine. Kelly, knowing that coming here had been her idea, struggled for a while, cutting small pieces from inexpensive glass only, so that if she ruined them she wouldn't send herself to the poorhouse.

Six cutting mistakes and two small nicks in her fingers later, she gave up. She couldn't concentrate. She set down her knife, sucking on the index finger of her left hand, which was bleeding slightly.

"How could she have disappeared like that?" She looked over at Tom, who was working on the computer with the absorption she should have brought to her glass but couldn't. "Cathedral Cove isn't that big a town. And Sophie has the kind of looks people tend to notice."

Tom's fingers stilled on the keyboard. "Not anymore," he said. "She looks washed out and tired. She looks about fifty."

Kelly didn't know what to say. It seemed so unfair. Sophie had been the most beautiful woman Kelly had ever seen.

"Surely, when the police find her," she said, "they won't put her in prison. They'll just send her back to the clinic, don't you think?"

"They'll have to arrest her. And the state attorney will probably charge her. But I don't think she'll have any trouble proving that she's not competent to proceed to trial right away."

"But, if they charge her—what happens then?"

"She'll probably be sent to an institution until she can be brought back to competency. If she can, then they'd go forward with the trial. If she doesn't decide to plead out, her lawyer will undoubtedly use an NGRI defense."

Kelly shook her head. "Speak English. I'm not a lawyer."

"A not-guilty-by-reason-of-insanity defense."

Kelly nodded, but it all felt so academic, so impersonal. How could this be Sophie they were talking about?

"They will catch her, won't they?" She knew that sounded silly. "I mean…I know you don't have a crystal ball or anything, but they usually do, don't they? Catch people."

"Usually. There are exceptions."

"But those exceptions are the really clever people, the ones who know how to go underground, aren't they? Surely Sophie is not the type who—"

Tom joined her at the worktable. He took her hands in his and chafed them slightly, as if he found them chilled. When he saw the new nicks, he picked up the box she always left on the countertop and extracted a couple of Band-Aids.

"Don't let it get to you," he said, opening the paper packet and preparing the bandage for her finger. "They'll find her. Now that Sebastian is gone, she's going to need help. Maybe she'll even head back to Willow Hill. "

"And if she doesn't?" Kelly looked down as he folded the edges of the Band-Aid over. He was good, making it snug without being too tight.

"It's just that…" She looked back at him. "I don't want to be a wimp, but I'd rather not spend the rest of my life wondering if she's looking through my window at night."

He pulled her into his arms. "They'll find her," he said again. "And you are far from a wimp."

But she felt like one, especially when he held her like this. She could get dependent on this kind of man. She could learn to love this kind of warm, secure protection. With his arms around her, she felt she could face anything. But what about when he went home? What about when she was in this workshop alone again, with only the raccoons for company?

He leaned down and kissed her, a light one at first, but then, with a smile, he came back for more. She melted against him, instantly ready. She wondered if sex was just another opiate. Was this how she coped with the stress, where someone else would turn to liquor or drugs?

And how addictive would it prove to be?

He glanced over to the frame she'd built to help her position the pattern for the winery tunnel. Several metal arches lined up one after the other, with heavy paper draped over them, sketched and painted to recreate the stained glass that was still being cut.

Now, at almost twilight, the ruddy sunlight poured through the paper, making it glow like purple wine.

He looked back at her. "What about that tunnel?"

She smiled and nodded. The floor was hard under there, but it was worth it. It would be gorgeous and sexy as hell.

Chuckling, he scooped her up with a swashbuckling grace and carried her over to the tunnel. Though it was tall enough to stand, she crawled in, breathless with excitement. Her heart was beating fast, anticipating what would come next.

He came in after her and caught her by the waist. Sinking to his knees, her bent over her, ran his hands up to her breasts and planted tingling kisses along her spine. She arched and he began to unbutton her shirt.

But then his phone, which was always in his jacket pocket, began to ring. It came from outside the tunnel and she realized he had left it by the computer.

"Damn it," he said. He let go of her shirt and looked over his shoulder at the mouth of the tunnel. *"Damn it."*

She sank down and rolled over, groaning her disappointment. But she knew he had to answer it. They'd been silly to imagine they could get this kind of privacy. When you were in the middle of a murder investigation, she'd discovered, your phone rang all the time.

But, though the phone stopped making noises, she didn't hear Tom say anything. It must have been a text message. She was still too shimmery and lazy to climb back out of the tunnel, so she waited for him to return to her.

He came almost immediately. He knelt beside her, his phone in his hand. She rose to a sitting position, disturbed by the expression on his face. It wasn't shimmery anymore.

"What?"

He didn't speak. He just held out the phone. Kelly took it and tilted it so that she could read the display. It wasn't easy in this purple light, which was made for slow, lazy loving, not for tension and fear.

Finally she found the perfect angle and the little black letters became words.

Come to the church at midnight. No police. And don't bring HER.

It was signed merely *Sophie.*

TOM KNEW EXACTLY WHICH CHURCH she meant, of course. The one in which, if he had shown up that day, they would have been married.

The Cathedral Cove Congregational Chapel had always struck him as an odd choice for the Mellons. Though it was large, it was simple to the point of austerity, not ordinarily a Mellon characteristic.

But it did have snob appeal. The brick chapel dated back to pre-railroad days, when Cathedral Cove had been a thriving stop on the Destiny River. By the time trains made river access less crucial, the Cove's quaint charm guaranteed it would survive as one of bustling Atlanta's many getaway destinations. The chapel had never fallen into disrepair and it remained one of the most prestigious houses of worship in the town.

It also prided itself on its long history of unlocked doors. The historical brochure you could pick up just inside the north portal explained that this chapel was always open for prayer.

Tom walked inside slowly, trying not to think about the day Sophie had brought him here and told him this was where she wanted to be married. He hadn't been back since, but every detail was still clear in his mind. It might have been yesterday.

The pews and the elevated pulpit were made of elegantly carved oak, which had been polished as smooth and shiny as glass. The plain columns that lined the nave were simple, undecorated tapers, like large ivory candles. The altar, too, was simple, a rectangle of white marble with gleaming oak trim. The windows were made of clear glass that let the sunlight enter the chapel in wide, clean bands.

It was as un-Mellon-like as you could get. Tom had always assumed that, thwarted here, the Mellons had been forced to play out their preference for drama in the overblown skylarks-and-cherry-blossom reception.

Just inside the nave, he paused and stood at the back of the pews, facing the altar. The same big, clear windows that let in sunlight for the noon service now let in the wavering beams of the full moon. The place was full of shadows that shifted.

The only electric illumination came from a row of small footlights delineating the central aisle and a pair of dimly glowing sconces bracketing the altar. It took a few seconds for his eyes to adjust to the darkness.

But when they did, he saw her. She sat in one of the darker pews, out of the moonlight. She was so small and still his gaze passed over her twice before he noticed her. He wondered how she could manage to remain so motionless. Two days ago, she had twitched like a cornered mouse.

He walked down the center aisle, his footsteps loud in the silence, and, when he reached her pew he slid in beside her.

"I'm here," he said.

She turned her face to him. In this semi-gloom, she looked grayer than ever. Or perhaps the horror of the past two days had drained even more of the life out of her. He wondered how much she had left.

"Thank you for coming," she said softly.

He didn't answer. The irony of this assignation hadn't escaped him. Finally, Sophie had forced him to show up at the church. Now she had five minutes to tell him why.

She gazed at the altar, as if they had all the time in the world.

"It's a lovely church, isn't it? I always felt peaceful here, even as a kid. In fact, it was the only place I ever did." She shook her head slightly. "But not anymore. Even this can't help me now."

"What kind of help do you need, Sophie? Why did you ask me to come?"

She sighed. Her eyes were heavy-lidded and her whole posture seemed dreamy. He wondered whether she had taken something. Maybe a lot of something.

"I just wanted to see you," she said. "I'm leaving Cathedral Cove soon, and I wanted to see you one more time. I probably never will again."

"Where have you been? You must know that everyone's been looking for you. Have you been in Cathedral Cove all this time?"

Her hands were neatly folded in her lap. They appeared to be empty, thank God, although she wore a raincoat, which, like all her clothes, was too big for her and had folds and pockets everywhere.

"I've been at Coeur Volé," she said.

He couldn't help reacting. "But the police have been there repeatedly. They've talked to your mother, and Samantha. They've looked—"

"They don't know where to look. And there's no point asking Mother or Samantha. They didn't know I was there. There's a secret way in, and I'm the only one left who knows it."

He hadn't been truly uncomfortable the whole time he'd been in this chapel, until now. The idea of Sophie methodically shooting her brother, then sneaking into Coeur Volé and prowling silently through its dark rooms while Samantha and Imogene slept, unaware…

It made the skin on the back of his neck prickle.

He wondered where the gun was now.

"Why do you say you'll never see me again?" He tried to sound normal. "Surely someday, when this is all straightened out—"

"Then what? We'll get together and take in a movie? Just the three of us? Me, my fiancé and his girlfriend? Wouldn't that be just darling."

For a minute, in her sarcasm, she sounded almost like herself. But he had no answer. As she had just observed, his comment had been fatuous.

"This isn't ever going to be straightened out, Tom," she said. "And you know it. I want to ask you something. And please, if you can't do anything else, at least respect me enough to be honest."

"All right. I'll try."

She stared at him. "You never loved me, did you?"

He didn't deny it. It wasn't because he was in a church. It was because the look in her eyes, the raw knowledge of unimaginable loss, made even the thought of lying a brutal impossibility.

He shook his head.

"I knew you didn't. You know how I knew?"

God, the possible answers to that one. He shook his head again.

"I knew because, when we made love, you didn't even notice my scars. People like me, we're always careful to cut ourselves where no one will see. But when you're naked with a lover, it's all exposed. All the shameful little white lines, like a history book written in pain."

He narrowed his eyes, ashamed of his self-absorption. He had made love to this woman. He had climaxed inside

her. But her body hadn't been real to him, not in any profound way. He hadn't even really looked at her.

"I wondered what you would say when you saw them,"
she went on. "I almost hoped you would ask, even though
I didn't know how I was going to explain. I thought that
maybe, if I could tell you the truth, it might bring us closer.
And you might know how to make me stop."

He shut his eyes. "God, Sophie." He took a deep breath.
"I failed you in so many ways."

She nodded. "Yes. But I was asking too much. I didn't
love you, either, you know. I just wanted out of my life at
Coeur Volé. I lied to you about everything, about who I
was, about how sick I was, about how sick we *all* were."

But that didn't excuse him. If he'd seen a total stranger
on the street in that kind of pain, he would have stopped
to help. He wouldn't have ignored a suffering dog, much
less a human being. Why hadn't he been able to see how
much she needed him?

"Anyhow, that's all over now. I don't want anything
from you anymore, Tom. I just wanted to say goodbye."

She put one of her hands, with those too-thin, clawlike
fingers, against his cheek. Then she leaned in and kissed
him. She smelled of clothes that needed washing, but under
it he thought he caught the scent of gardenias. He wondered
if, like an unseen ghost, she had slept in her own room last
night.

She stood up and moved past him toward the aisle. She
was so thin he didn't even have to adjust his legs to make
room. He heard her walk away, her footsteps slow and
heavy on the marble floor. He could imagine her shadow
moving along the floor, with all the other shadows.

He didn't want to get up. He wanted to sit there. He felt

a ridiculous urge to drop to his knees and pray to that simple altar. He wanted to ask someone to take this final, painful moment away from him.

But that was melodrama, worthy more of a Mellon than a Beckham. He wasn't a saint or martyr, or even a particularly religious man anymore. To take this problem to God was pure travesty. Tom Beckham was just a stupid schmuck who was finally, ten years too late, doing the hard thing.

The right thing.

He stood and followed Sophie down the aisle. He was only about ten feet behind her when the policemen stepped out of the shadows, blocking her exit through the front portal of the chapel.

She froze in place. And then, slowly, with a face no longer gray but white, she turned and looked at Tom.

"No," she said, her voice cracking under the weight of the betrayal. "Tell me you didn't do this."

"I'm sorry, Sophie," he said. "I did."

BY THE TIME TOM GOT BACK to the police station, just after one in the morning, Kelly was exhausted, worn to shreds from trying to imagine exactly what was happening. Every second had been torment. Had Sophie and Tom met yet? Had Sophie even kept the assignation? What were her intentions? Did she want to hurt Tom? What kind of weapon did she have? Would the police have to rush to the rescue? Would they get there in time?

It was the longest hour of her life. When the police walked in the door, she rose from her seat, praying that Tom would be with them.

Instead, they had a handcuffed woman between them,

and, even though Kelly had been expecting Sophie, for a moment she didn't recognize her. Instead, she saw only a tired, middle-aged woman whose hair needed brushing, who wore clothes that didn't fit. She might have been any bag lady on any urban downtown street.

But those eyes. Those eyes had seen things even bag ladies didn't know. And they were looking at Kelly with an almost inhuman malevolence.

Tom came in just behind her. Kelly had planned to throw herself into his arms the minute she saw him, just for the sheer relief of knowing he was safe. But with Sophie staring at her, impaling her with pure hatred, Kelly found that she couldn't do it.

She sank back onto her chair.

One of the two policemen who stood on either side of Sophie touched her shoulder, letting her know that they had to keep moving. Sophie transferred her gaze to him, and Kelly could tell by the way the young man's jaw tightened that the expression in Sophie's eyes hadn't softened much.

The encounter was that short, that undramatic. And yet, by the time Sophie had been shepherded out of sight, into an interrogation room, Kelly found that her whole body was shaking.

Tom, who looked as exhausted as she felt, came over to her slowly. Standing in front of her, he held out his hands and she took them in her own. They stayed that way a long minute, not saying a word. He seemed unable to speak, and she could find no words that didn't seem merely a waste of air.

The station's front door swung open again and Gwen Mellon, Sebastian's wife, walked in. Kelly corrected herself quickly. *Sebastian's widow.*

"Where is she?" Gwen sounded as if she were teetering on the edge of hysteria. She had her children with her and they seemed to have internalized their mother's raw emotion.

The little boy was in her arms. He looked sleepy and fussy, as if he'd been crying on the way over. Sebastian's daughter, Tessa, stood at her mother's side, wide-eyed and hostile, as if she knew that something terrible had just happened to her life and she wanted to punish whoever was responsible.

"Where is she?" Gwen went up to Tom. "I want to see her. I want to see her."

Tom let go of Kelly's hands and looked at the other woman. "You can't right now. The police need to talk to her first. And they can't do that until her lawyer arrives."

"Her lawyer? Why should she have a lawyer? She killed my husband. She murdered her own brother. She's a *monster.*"

Kelly looked down at Tessa, whose face looked pinched, the skin around her nose and mouth drawn thin and white. She was trying so hard not to cry, but if her mother didn't show some discretion, the little girl was going to collapse.

"Everyone is entitled to a defense, Gwen," Tom said softly.

Kelly had to admire his restraint. He hadn't once even alluded to the terrible truth—that before Sophie had killed anyone, Sebastian had murdered four innocent people.

"A defense? Who defended Sebastian?" She hoisted her son higher and began to cry, dry choking sobs. "I'd like to kill her myself."

Tom put his hand on her shoulder. "Gwen, pull yourself together. The children."

"Yes, the children!" She had tipped, Kelly saw with a sinking heart. The hysteria was in full force. "The children who will never have their father again, thanks to her."

Kelly rose then and went over to Tessa. She knelt beside the little girl. "Would you like me to take you to get a cup of milk? I'll bet there's one around here somewhere."

The girl stared at her. "No," she said. "I hate milk. I want to go home."

An investigator came in then, someone from the Georgia Bureau of Investigation, Kelly thought, though she'd seen so many cops in the past few days it was all becoming a blur. The man spoke to Tom. and then asked Gwen to come with him to answer a few questions.

"Is there someone you can leave the children with, Mrs. Mellon?"

Kelly was going to offer, but as soon as the question was out of the investigator's mouth, the little boy began to kick and scream, unnerved by the very idea. Tessa grabbed her mother's free hand and said in a small but belligerent voice, "I'm not leaving my mommy."

The investigator didn't like it and Kelly was sure he'd find some female officer to tend the children eventually, but for the moment he simply acquiesced. The four of them went down one of the back halls, with Seamus still screaming.

Tom watched them until they were out of sight. And then he turned to Kelly.

"I want you to go home and get some rest. I'm in this up to my ears, so I'll have to stay. But I want you out of here."

She thought of the hotel room they'd rented for another night. Without him in it, it would be too bleak to endure.

"No," she said. "I can rest on the chairs here while you answer their questions, or whatever it is you must do. I don't want to go to the hotel alone."

"Not the hotel," he said. "There's no reason you can't sleep in your own bed tonight. Not now that we've found Sophie."

She thought of her own little bed and she realized to her dismay that, without Tom, that, too, would be bleak and cold.

"I don't want to leave you," she said.

"It's going to take hours. With Bill and Sebastian and now Sophie, they will have a million questions to ask me. It will be easier for me if I know you're away from all this."

She started to protest again, but the station door opened one more time and Brian, her sweet, uncomplaining ex-husband, walked through it. His face was sober and concerned.

She looked at Tom. "Did you call him?"

He nodded. "I want him to take you home. I want him to stay with you tonight."

Brian came up and kissed Kelly's cheek. Then he shook Tom's hand. "I'll get her home safely," he said.

"Thanks." Tom gave him a small smile and then he took Kelly's face between his hands. "Do it for me," he said. "If you can't sleep, work on your glass. It will make me happy, thinking of you getting back to normal."

She didn't have the heart to tell him…she hardly remembered what that was.

CHAPTER TWENTY-TWO

"Go," Kelly told Brian at eight the next morning. She handed him a bagel and a cup of coffee in a travel mug. "I have work to do, and you have a business to run."

"Yeah, but… I know! You come with me." Brian began eating the bagel right there, as he stood in her doorway.

Behind him, the morning was bright blue and cloudless, the kind of day just perfect for starting over. Kelly was so ready for that. She could do it. Maybe the old "normal" was gone, but she was resilient. She could create a new normal, and maybe, in some ways, it would be even better than the old.

But first she had to convince Brian that he didn't have to be her shadow for the rest of her life.

"No. Everything is fine. You just go to work like a good boy."

"I'll go if Tom says it's okay," Brian said, refusing to move out of the way so she could close the door. He took a swig of coffee. "Call him."

"I don't want to bother him."

She didn't admit to Brian that she'd already called Tom twice in the past six hours, just to see how things were going. Both times, he had sounded exhausted, but glad to hear from her. He hadn't been able to talk long, though.

Things were still hectic at the station, and there was always someone needing "to ask him a few more questions."

"Okay, don't bother him. Just come to the store with me. We got in a delivery of basketball jerseys yesterday. I could use an extra pair of hands with the pricing."

Sighing irritably, she pulled out her telephone, as of course he'd known she would. Even when they were married, she had hated pricing new merchandise. Once you'd attached tags to a couple of hundred Shaq jerseys, you'd definitely had your fill of that.

When Tom answered, he sounded harried. "Hey, Kelly," he said, very businesslike, as if to hint that he couldn't indulge in any frivolous chatter. "What's up?"

In the background, she heard a child wailing. God, did that mean that Sebastian's children were still there?

"I'm sorry to bother you," she said, "but I just wanted to let you know that Brian's headed to his store. I'm planning to stay here and work a little. I may go out and buy a couple of new sheets of glass, too. I'm out of purple."

God. She wanted to bite her tongue. He was down there dealing with fratricide and madness, and she was talking about being "out of purple." He probably would have liked to knock her over the head with the telephone.

"Okay," he said. "That sounds good."

"I really wouldn't have bothered you with it," she said, "except Brian would not leave until he had your okay." She shot a dirty look at her ex-husband, who chewed on his bagel happily, ignoring her.

"Good for him," Tom said. "But tell him it should be fine. Sophie has…"

He said something else, but at the same time a woman began to rant loudly in the background and all Kelly could hear was "you son of a bitch, you goddamn son of a bitch."

"Tom? Who is that?"

"It's Sophie," he said wearily. "Her calm last night must have been drug induced, because she's very different this morning."

Kelly heard how tired he was. She wished she could go down there and drag him home, feed him and put him to bed. But she couldn't. She wasn't even sure, in fact, that he would be coming to her house when he finished at the police station. He had never committed to that.

He'd never committed to anything.

"Anyhow," he went on, "the important thing is that Sophie has confessed to shooting Sebastian. She even had the gun in the pocket of her raincoat. It was registered to her father."

"Oh, my God." For herself, Kelly was relieved, of course. It was reassuring to know that the killers had both been apprehended. No one was still out there killing people. But for Sophie, she was devastated. To have been driven to kill your own brother…

"Beckham!" The voices in the background grew louder again. "Where the hell are you? We need you in here."

"Kelly, I have to go."

"I know." She could hear the slight impatience threading through his words. She should just say goodbye and hang up, but it was so hard not to want some crumb of private comfort amid all this public ruin.

She would like to tell him that she loved him.

But he didn't care about that right now. He might not ever care.

"Okay," she said, refusing to bog him down with anything so irrelevant and self-centered right now. "Good luck."

And then he was gone.

Brian had finished his bagel. He tossed the napkin through the open door, over Kelly's shoulder and swished it right into the trash can. Brian had never missed a three-pointer, either at home or during his heyday on the college basketball court.

"I take it I'm dismissed?"

She nodded with a smile. "Dismissed with thanks," she said. She leaned over and kissed him. "And tell Marie I said thanks, too. For the loan of her man."

"That's me," he said jauntily as he headed out toward his truck. "The original Rent-a-Stud. Now for God's sake be careful. If you so much as stub your toe today, your friend Tom will kick my studly ass."

AN HOUR LATER, when Kelly was loading her new sheets of glass into the back of the van, her cell phone rang. She answered it quickly, hoping it was Tom.

To her shock, it was Imogene Mellon.

"Hello," she said uncomfortably. There was something painful about facing people who had experienced this level of disaster. You knew the ordinary phrases of sympathy weren't adequate, but you just didn't have the vocabulary that could handle it.

"I wish I didn't have to call you, Kelly," Imogene said without preamble. "I know I'm the last person in the world you want to hear from right now."

"No, of course not, Mrs. Mellon. I've thought about you and Samantha often during…all this. I wish there were something I could say—something I could do. But I wasn't sure you would be all that eager to hear from me."

There was a pause. Kelly assumed Imogene was trying

make herself deny that, trying to make herself express enthusiasm for talking to Kelly, but simply couldn't.

"Yes, I know we both wish none of this had ever happened," Imogene said. "But it has, and—"

For a minute Kelly thought that the older woman might begin to cry. It would have been the first time ever Kelly had witnessed such a collapse of the Iron Maiden, as she and Sophie used to call Imogene. But surely if anything could break down that Southern will, it was this nightmare scenario. Her losses were beyond comprehension.

"I'm sure you know how uncomfortable it is for me to have to ask a favor from you, Kelly. And after what my son has done, I won't be surprised if you turn me down."

"What is it, Mrs. Mellon?" Kelly prayed that it was something she could do. Something easy, like picking up groceries or medication and dropping them off at Coeur Volé. Or making some calls…

"I'm worried about Samantha," Imogene said. "This has nearly destroyed her. She hasn't come out of her room in twenty-four hours, not since she identified Sebastian's body. She wouldn't even go down to see Sophie this morning. She's a strong young woman, but this—this is more than anyone can bear."

"Yes," Kelly said. "I know. What can I do to help?"

"I'm no good to her. My own sickness is reaching the point that I will have to—" Imogene caught herself. "But this isn't about me. It's about Samantha. I know it's a lot to ask, but could you come to see her this morning? Maybe she'll talk to you, get some of this grief out in the open. Right now it's all bottled up inside. She won't talk to me. She probably believes I can't handle it, and maybe she's right."

Kelly hated herself for the instinctive recoil she felt at

the idea of going into Coeur Volé. But in her imagination the place would stink of madness and death. It had finally, even for her, truly become the House of Usher.

She put the last braces in place around the glass. Then she closed the cargo doors and took a deep breath. Surely she wasn't such a coward. Surely she could put aside her own selfish desire to escape this nightmare.

Her own selfish desire to escape Cathedral Cove.

She realized that she had already been thinking, half-consciously, about moving somewhere else.

Anywhere else. Anywhere clean and wholesome, anywhere she could begin to forget.

Imogene obviously understood Kelly's hesitation. "I know you don't want to come, Kelly," she said. She sounded more tired than insulted. "I even understand it. No one wants to be this close to tragedy. We haven't had a single call from anyone, not one of our friends, since Sebastian's body was discovered."

Kelly squeezed her keys hard. How difficult it must be for this proud woman to admit such a thing. "Mrs. Mellon, I—"

"But you—we opened our home to you, Kelly. When you and Sophie were teenagers, you ate our food and played in our yard. Sophie believed you were her friend. Samantha thought so, too."

"I was," Kelly said honestly. "And I—"

"Samantha hasn't done anything wrong, surely you can see that. She's a good person who is in a lot of pain, and she needs a friend. She thinks she's going to be a pariah. Can't you spare half an hour to show her it isn't true?"

Kelly fought for courage and found it.

"I'll be there in fifteen minutes."

WHEN TOM FINALLY LEFT the station, he drove as fast as he legally could—the last thing he wanted was to see another policeman, even one who was merely writing out a speeding ticket—to Kelly's cottage in the woods.

The closer he got, the more the horror of the past twenty-four hours began to recede. It was as if Kelly's honest simplicity was the only antidote to the snakebite poison of the Mellons.

It had been a harrowing night, hearing Sophie go through the varied moods of madness, complicated by drugs, or lack of drugs—no one was sure, including Sophie, exactly what she had or hadn't taken.

Sometimes Tom had been sequestered in his own interview room, and sometimes he'd watched her through a one-way window. They'd finally gotten the answer to the one piece of the puzzle that hadn't fit: where had Sebastian found the lace to send to Dolly and to put on Lillith's marker?

The answer was strangely sad. Those few extra pounds that Tom had found so appealing, the pounds that had softened Sophie's sharp features, had apparently been a source of shame in the Mellon household. Altering the heirloom dress was unthinkable to Imogene, who'd expected many future generations of slim Mellon brides to wear it. And so a second, secret dress had been made out of extra yardage of the original fabric, which had been packed in tissue for sixty years.

Sophie had said that Sebastian had taken the secret dress, when he'd come home for a visit. One of the cops had gone right to the phone, calling the Raleigh police to get them to add it to their search list.

Finally, though, her lawyer and her psychiatrist had insisted that all questioning stop. By then, not an officer in the room would have argued the issue. Sophie had been led away, muttering to herself.

Watching her, Tom had felt nothing. By then, every nerve in his body had been dead.

But now, as he drove under the yellow-and-dark-red canopy of fall trees, he felt those nerves tingling slightly, coming slowly back to life. He wondered if Kelly was still at the glass store. He hoped not. He needed to sleep, and he wanted her in the bed with him. He wanted to bury his face in her autumn-colored hair and heal himself by breathing in her sweetness.

When he turned the last corner and the little gray stone cottage came into view, he frowned. The minivan was nowhere to be seen. Damn it. He should have asked her where the glass store was. He could have met her there. Though he was heavy-headed from lack of rest, he'd rather watch her pick out glass for hours than sleep one minute alone.

He pulled out his cell phone and dialed hers. It rang, and it rang again. Finally her recorded voice came on. "Hi, this is Kelly. Leave me a message, and I'll call you back as soon as I can."

"It's me," he said. "I'm home. I wish you were here."

After he ended the call, he realized it was ambiguous to say, "I'm home." He should have said, "I'm at your house." But surely she'd understand. Where else in Cathedral Cove could possibly feel like "home" to him?

She'd given him a key last night, so that he could get in without waking her and Brian. He used it.

He knew from the other night he'd spent here that she

ordinarily made up her bed as soon as she got out of it. But this time she'd merely neatened it and left one corner turned down welcomingly. That was for him, he understood.

The sheets and blankets Brian had used were folded and stacked on the sofa. One knife lay in the sink, and it seemed to have butter on it. The remnants of breakfast, no doubt.

He walked over to the workshop, to see if she'd left him a note there. He didn't hurry, enjoying the cold blue morning and the soft rain of colorful leaves on his shoulders.

The workshop was unlocked. When he went in, he noticed that the Band-Aid box was open, and a new wrapper lay crumpled on the countertop. He smiled. She had obviously done some work before she'd left. He hoped this morning's nick was shallow and painless.

He scanned the neat shop, with its many slots full of colored glass and its happy clutter of books and patterns and machines for grinding edges and firing finished pieces.

He realized that he had undoubtedly missed her more, over these past ten years, than she had missed him.

She had found a fulfilling life. She'd nurtured her talent and turned it into a career. She'd found a man to love and marry, and even though the marriage hadn't lasted, the love obviously had. She'd bought a home and decorated it with a hundred joyous pieces of herself.

He, on the other hand, was a complete stranger in his own life. He had nothing to show for the past ten years. Nothing but money and a disjointed, strobe-like sequence of events: cases he didn't believe in, women he didn't really know, friends he didn't really like.

What a waste.

He called her cell phone again. She wouldn't mind being pestered. She would understand. She'd called him several times in the night and he had heard the loneliness in her voice. She'd hear the same thing in his voice now.

If only she would answer.

He tried three more times over the next half hour. Always the same bright, friendly recorded voice. "Hi, this is Kelly…"

The knot in his stomach started once again to tighten. She was free to come and go as she pleased, of course. She didn't have to account to him for anything. But why wasn't she answering the phone?

Finally he called Brian, just because he had to be sure. Undoubtedly Brian would know where the glass store was and Tom could go see for himself.

"Oh, she's finished buying glass," Brian said when he came to the telephone. "She phoned a little while ago and told me she was going over to Coeur Volé. Apparently the old bat called and begged her to go see Samantha, although begged may be an exaggeration. I've never seen that snooty old broad beg anyone for anything."

Tom didn't know why a spear of anxiety shot through his gut. All that was left at Coeur Volé was a pair of shell-shocked women who probably couldn't quite understand what had happened to their family.

He'd seen Imogene in the early hours of the morning. She'd taken a taxi, all alone, to the station, and she had been so weak a policeman had had to help her up the stairs.

When she'd asked to see her daughter, the police had refused. And, just as autocratic as ever, she had slowly made her way back to the waiting taxi, without saying a word to Tom or Gwen, or anyone else in the room.

It was almost impossible to imagine that broken, empty husk of a woman being a threat to anyone. And Sam...

His heart knocked against his ribs, as if it were trying to tell him something.

Then he remembered Samantha's face after they'd identified Sebastian's body. The haunted eyes, the tears dribbling from her full lips. "Beside what's happened to my family," she had said, "your happiness seems almost obscene."

He ran to his car, his legs eating up the leaf-covered ground as fast as they could. He hoped he was being absurd. He hoped he was overreacting. But...

Two of the Mellon siblings were insane.

Two of them were murderers.

What about the third?

Something rotten lay deep within that gene pool. But just as the lovely blue eyes and shining blond hair had been encoded in their DNA, so, perhaps, had the madness.

Was it really possible that, of them all, only Samantha had escaped the Mellon curse?

KELLY SAT IN THE FRONT PARLOR of Coeur Volé, trying not to look as uncomfortable as she felt. Imogene Mellon had handed her a cup of tea as soon as she'd arrived, saying that Sam was getting dressed and would be down in a minute.

It had already been ten.

Imogene wore a long, quilted house robe of dirty blue. She looked exhausted, as if the cancer were really beginning to take a toll.

A picture of her as a young woman stood on the mantel, next to pictures of all three of her children. It was clear that all the Mellon siblings had received their looks from their mother, who had, in her youth, been startlingly beautiful.

Adler Mellon's photograph stood a little aside from the others. His dark intensity was so different, it was as if his genes hadn't been allowed to participate in the creation process at all.

Today, though, Imogene didn't look related to that blonde, vibrant quartet, either. Her gray hair and washed-out eyes seemed to belong to another species.

She was a little incoherent, too, and Kelly wondered whether she was taking too much medication for her pain. Apropos of nothing, Imogene had started telling Kelly a strange story about the large Gainsborough chair, and how Mr. Mellon used to sit in it, eavesdropping on people who had no idea he was in the room.

It was probably just conversational filler, designed to get them through these awkward minutes until Sam came down, but it was creepy. Kelly could almost imagine that Mr. Mellon was somewhere in the room right now. She'd always been afraid of him, partly because she'd sensed that Sophie was.

Imogene paced the room while she talked, touching knickknacks restlessly. Out in the hall, the huge grandfather clock ticked away the seconds in slow-motion time. And still no sound from upstairs.

Maybe it was the way Imogene seemed to be pointing out each item in turn as she fingered them, but Kelly found herself noticing more about the decorations in this parlor than she ever had as a teenager.

And what she noticed was decidedly unsettling. The large central painting was a beautiful but disturbing picture of Leda and the Swan, in which a naked Leda lay back in a sensual daze while the swan spread its huge wings across her body. Other pictures showed gods tossing lightning bolts down from craggy mountaintops or women turning into trees to escape their pursuers.

On the round table by the window were a group of little Japanese carved-ivory figurines, all of men aggressively wielding weapons.

Everything was beautiful, probably priceless. She glanced out toward the huge stained-glass window at the top of the stairs and she realized there was a theme. The theme was domination.

Suddenly, with a hideous flash of intuition, she knew she shouldn't have come.

The Mellon family was in the process of disintegrating. Being this close to them right now was foolish, like standing on the lip of a volcano that had already begun to boil.

She looked at her watch. "Maybe I should come back another time," she said, smiling the best she could. "Samantha seems reluctant to come down, which I absolutely understand. It's probably just too soon. I can come back tomorrow."

Imogene shook her head. "No. The pain gets worse every day. I'll have to increase the morphine, and I don't know how long I'll be able to function on my own. I have to take care of this now."

"Take care of what?"

Imogene just looked at her, without answering.

Kelly shivered. It was cold in these high-ceilinged, poorly lit rooms. The only real light came through the St. George window, and that light was full of colors that lay on the hall like the chips in a kaleidoscope.

"Take care of what, Mrs. Mellon?"

The older woman took a deep breath. "I'm going to die," she said. "And probably very soon. Before I go, I have to set things straight. I have to ensure that Samantha has a chance at a happy life."

Kelly felt strangely relieved. "You want to be sure she has a friend? I can promise you that. I will always be her friend."

"No," Imogene said, shaking her head softly. "It isn't a friend she needs. It's a man. Someone to take care of her, give her a home and children and love, and all the things she deserves."

"But I—" Kelly's throat suddenly felt very tight. "How can I help her do that?"

"You can't," Mrs. Mellon said flatly. "I tried to warn you. I sent you the invitation, but you ignored it."

And then she pulled a gun out of the pocket of her robe.

"Now, I'm afraid, all you can do to help her is *die*."

CHAPTER TWENTY-THREE

TRIG KNEW HE WASN'T VERY SMART, not in the school-smart way. A lot of people teased him. They called him retarded, sometimes, just to be mean.

But he wasn't retarded. Most of the time he was fine. Most of the time, he wasn't this confused.

He stood on the west side of Coeur Volé and looked in the parlor window. He saw Mrs. Mellon in there with Sophie's friend Kelly, and he knew that wasn't good, because Mrs. Mellon hated Kelly.

He went to the window that had a big crack in it, the one where you could hear things. And that's when he got confused.

Sophie, who was the most beautiful and the nicest woman Trig had ever known, had asked him to look after Coeur Volé when she had to go to the mental institution. She'd said she knew he could do it. She knew he watched them all the time anyhow, and she trusted him to make sure everything was safe.

She had specifically told him to take care of Samantha.

So what was he supposed to do now?

Mrs. Mellon had a gun, and Trig knew that she was going to hurt Kelly. That would not be good for the house, which got sicker every time something terrible happened inside its walls. The house was practically bursting now, trying to hold all the crying and screaming and bad things in.

But then he heard Mrs. Mellon say she was only doing it to make Samantha happy. And he knew how much Sophie wanted Samantha to be happy.

So what was he supposed to do? Save the house? Or save Samantha?

He saw Tom Beckham's silver car coming down the driveway, coming fast, getting bigger by the second, like a raven swooping down out of the sky. At first Trig crouched in the rhododendron bushes below the parlor window, hoping Tom wouldn't see him. Tom wasn't one of the bad people, but he might not understand why Trig was listening at the window. He didn't know that Trig was only doing his job.

But then Tom killed his engine and went straight to Kelly's minivan, which was parked in front of the house. Trig could tell that Tom was upset. Trig could read people's emotions. That was one kind of smart he did have.

He saw Tom look over at the house, his face dark, and he knew that Tom was going to try to get in.

He climbed out of the bushes noiselessly and made his way to where Tom stood, holding his cell phone.

"Don't go to the front door," he said in a half whisper, though he knew they couldn't be heard from the house. It just felt wrong to talk out loud about things like this.

Tom jerked around, as if Trig's sudden appearance had startled him. "What?" He glanced at the house again. "Why not?"

"She has a gun," he said. "She won't let you in. She won't want you to stop her."

Tom was rigid, sending off vibes so intense Trig was a little afraid of him. Was he one of the bad people after all?

"Stop her from what?"

"From hurting Kelly. She's going to shoot her, but she feels bad, I think, and she wants Kelly to understand why."

He thought of the two women he'd seen through the window. One old woman, leaning on the table with one hand and holding the gun in the other. One young woman, standing by the door, breathing fast, wondering what to do.

"Kelly doesn't understand, though," he added. "I think she's very scared."

Tom had already opened his cell phone and called 911. Trig watched the house as Tom quietly gave his information to someone on the other end.

"Yes," Trig said when Tom hung up. He had finally decided what Sophie would want him to do. "You'll have to go in the secret way if you're going to help her."

Tom grabbed his shoulder. "Where is it?"

"In the garden," he said. "In the gardener's shed. There's a door in the floor, and a tunnel."

"Show me."

Trig took Tom around to the back, past the dark red roses, past the fallen woman, past the bat-angel and the snake. Lots of people thought the gardener's shed was pretty, like a gazebo with closed sides, but when you knew what Trig knew, it didn't look that pretty anymore.

Tom rushed ahead of him and knelt on the concrete, feeling for the opening.

"Damn it. Where is it?"

"It's at the very back," Trig said.

Tom found it quickly. It wasn't that hard, if you knew where to look. The only one in the Mellon family who didn't know it was there was Samantha. But everyone always hid things from Samantha. They didn't want her to be as strange and sad as the rest of them.

But Trig knew that Mrs. Mellon was wrong this time. If she shot Kelly, Samantha would be very, very sad. And the house—

Tom took off his jacket. As Trig looked at Tom's angry face, he was suddenly sorry he'd shown him the secret door.

He grabbed Tom's arm. "Promise me you won't hurt anyone. The house can't stand any more."

Tom shook his head. "I can't promise that, Trig."

"You have to."

Tom looked as if he might hurt Trig right now, if he didn't let go of his shirt. Frightened by Tom, Trig fell back. "At least promise me you'll try not to."

Tom nodded. "I'll try not to," he said. He pulled the concrete block away and peered into the darkness. "When I reach the house, where will I be?"

"It goes down, and across the garden. Then it goes up again. You come out on the landing, on the stairs. There's a door in the wall beside the dragon."

Tom nodded. "Thank you," he said. And he sounded like he meant it.

Trig wrapped his arms around himself, hoping he was doing right.

"Be careful," he said as the earth opened its mouth and swallowed Tom's body, like a snake swallowing its prey. "Please don't make another bad place."

IT SEEMED LIKE AN ETERNITY, engulfed in blackness, feeling damp, crumbling walls with his hands to make his way.

He hadn't brought a flashlight. On such a bright blue morning, who could have imagined he'd need one?

The air was foul and he wondered how often small creatures had sneaked into this passage alongside their human counterparts and died, unable to get out again.

He wondered if he could hear a gunshot down here. He sent a mental message to Kelly, telling her to hang on. He was coming.

An eternity of darkness and silence so deep he felt as if he'd gone deaf. "Kelly," he said aloud, just to be sure he hadn't.

But finally he encountered stairs and began to climb up again. Six, ten, twelve steps. He stumbled over something that squealed and scurried away in terror. When he stood again, his fingers were slippery with a wetness that smelled disgusting.

Yes, an eternity. But, by the time he reached the top, it had probably been only a minute or two.

He felt around for a handle, a groove, a niche, anything that would open the door. His heart was suddenly pounding so hard it seemed to fill the entire tunnel. He wondered whether they could hear it in the house.

Finally, his fingers caught on something sharp that ripped the skin. It was a small, barbed hook, like a fishhook. He felt again and found a braid of nylon dangling from the hook. Ignoring the flash of pain in the tip of his finger, he wound it through the braid and pulled.

He wished he had a gun. But he had never learned to hunt, though he'd promised himself he would, that night in the glasshouse, while he shot forget-me-not skylarks with his bottle of scotch.

He hated guns. They had never seemed all that important. He didn't represent murderers and thieves. He represented spoiled brats and millionaire egomaniacs. He'd never seen any need to buy a weapon. And now it might be too late.

One more wasted chance in a decade of wasted chances.

But maybe he'd get lucky. Maybe he would be able to sneak up on Samantha from behind. It all depended on where this tunnel really came out, and where the two women were standing.

He hoped that Samantha had continued to talk.

As the door pulled open, the sudden light nearly blinded him, but he fought to keep his eyes open. Even a second's vulnerability might be too much.

He was right. When he emerged, he was only six feet from Kelly. She stood on the landing, directly in front of the dying dragon. She was breathing hard, as if she'd been running. But her eyes were focused on the stairs below her.

Tom looked there, too, and what he saw made him catch his breath. It wasn't Samantha.

It was Imogene.

She was walking slowly up, one stair at a time. Her body was bathed in a green light from the dragon's skin, but her face was red and gray, like St. George. With the floating colors and the intensity of her gaze, she hardly looked human.

In her hand she held a small gun. She could hit Kelly from here, but she'd have to be a good shot. He had no idea what her skill might be.

"Mrs. Mellon," he said. "Put the gun down. The police are on their way."

She glanced at him briefly, but didn't take her eyes from Kelly for long. "No," she said. She took another step.

Kelly turned to him, her eyes wide and wild with fear, but her courage was holding, he saw. She made a small motion with her hand, asking him not to do anything. She clearly felt she might be able to buy time.

"She wouldn't let me answer my cell," she said, as if that were somehow the most important fact at the moment. He knew how awful it must have been for her to know he was trying to find her, but not be able to tell him she needed help.

"It's okay," he said. "I wasn't going to give up until I found you. Brian told me where you were."

Kelly nodded, but her face was still pale and drawn.

"Tom, you should know that she—" She glanced nervously at Imogene, as if she feared she might antagonize her into pulling the trigger. But she forced herself to go on. "She killed Sebastian, Tom. Not Sophie."

Imogene made an annoyed sound. "Do you think I care what you tell him, Kelly? When I'm finished, I'll tell the police myself. I want them to know. Do you think I'd let Sophie go to jail for what I did?"

"But Sophie has already confessed," Tom said. "She even had the gun in her possession."

Imogene shook her head. "She's covering up for me. She knew I was the only one who would have done it. She came into the house, and she took the gun. She may be ill, but she's a good daughter. She doesn't want them to arrest me."

"But Sophie is the one with the motive. Why would you have killed Sebastian?"

"It doesn't matter," she said, her voice exhausted.

Tom sensed that she was almost talked out. He had to get her involved again. He had to make her feel the need to be understood.

He toughened his voice. "I don't believe it. What kind of mother would kill her own son?"

She looked at him. "You know what he was. He was my son, but he was a sociopath. He didn't care about anyone but himself." She took a deep breath. "No, that's not quite true. Maybe he cared about Tessa."

"His daughter? You really believe that?"

"I think I do," she said slowly. "I called him and asked him to meet me at the bank parking lot that night. I let him think I could help him find Sophie. When he saw I had the gun, he began to tell me everything."

Tom saw with relief that she was talking eagerly again.

"He didn't kill Dolly Tammaro, you know. He sent her the lace, just to scare her. He told Sophie he'd done it, just to prove that he could get to the members of the wedding party anytime he wanted to. It was supposed to be a message to Sophie. But then the clumsy fool stumbled out into the street, and Sophie assumed Sebastian had done it. But she still didn't give in to him, so he had to go on. He had to try to force Sophie to come back. He said he did it all to save Tessa."

"That's bullshit. How could killing Kent, and Lillith and Bill possibly help his daughter?"

She looked pained, as if she found it agony to speak of such things. "He needed Sophie. He had urges, like his father. He needed forbidden sex, painful sex, sex with people who cried. He was already starting to fantasize about Tessa. He believed that only Sophie could save him."

Kelly made a small, sobbing sound. Tom felt queasy, as if he had breathed in too much of the slimy, black tunnel air.

"Save him by resuming their sexual relationship?"

Imogene nodded. "And by crying. That's what they really liked. The crying." She took another deep breath. "It was all my fault, really. I should have stopped Adler years ago. But I was afraid of him, and I didn't. I let him turn my son into a monster. And Sebastian would have turned his own son into the same thing. That baby boy, a predator. A beast."

She had started to cry, though the hand that held the gun never wavered. "I had to stop the cycle. Before I die, I had to set things right. You can see that, can't you?"

"No," Tom said flatly. "You may be able to rationalize Sebastian's murder, but how does killing Kelly set anything right? How can that possibly make it any easier for you to die in peace?"

"It's for Sam," Kelly broke in. "She told me she's doing this for Sam."

Tom frowned, incredulous. *"What?"*

"Yes. She says Sam is in love with you, and she thinks that, if I'm out of the way, Sam has a chance to make you love her, too."

Suddenly Tom's blood buzzed with fury. Of all the self-centered, delusional…

She'd sacrifice Kelly to give her daughter whatever plaything she craved at the moment? These people were really too much. For a minute he wanted nothing more than to wrestle Imogene's gun away and turn it on the old woman. But already his blood was cooling, his head clearing. He didn't really mean that. He wasn't a killer….

"It's ironic, isn't it?" Imogene tried to laugh, but the sound couldn't make its way through the tears. "Both my little girls, in love with the same man. But Sophie was too sick. Her father and Sebastian had ruined her. You could never love her after what they did to her. But Samantha…"

She looked at him, her eyes bizarrely pleading. "Samantha is sweet, Tom. She looks like Sophie—all my children look like me. But when you get to know her, you'll see how different she is."

Tom made a guttural sound. The idea was so insane he wasn't sure how to refute it. He was feeling sick from listening to all this insanity.

Surely the police would arrive any minute. Even if they'd thought he was crying wolf, they had to respond to all 911 calls.

"Samantha will end up just like Sophie," he said coldly. "It's in the genes. The sickness will show itself soon enough."

"No, it won't." Imogene shook her head. "She doesn't have the same genes, Tom. She's my child. *My* child. Do you understand what I'm saying? She isn't Adler's daughter."

She clearly saw the shock on both their faces, and it made her smile. "It's true. She's untainted, and she's safe, and we all dedicated our lives to keeping her that way. She's sleeping right now. I gave her something so that she won't have to see this. I don't want any more tragedies to haunt her dreams."

She nodded, and she seemed to be talking to herself. "You will love her, Tom. No one could help loving her."

"You're wrong, Mrs. Mellon. I'll never love Samantha. I'm already in love with Kelly." He looked briefly over at her. He hadn't imagined telling her this way, but it would have to do. "Nothing will ever change that."

Imogene clicked her teeth, dismissing the declaration. "Her death will change it. Right now you think it won't, but it will. You're not in love with her. It's lust. You couldn't sleep with her ten years ago, and it's stuck in your blood. When she's gone, eventually you'll need someone, and Samantha will be there. Her goodness will speak for itself."

"Never," he said. He walked slowly over to the St. George window, careful not to make any sudden movements, and stood close to Kelly. From here, it would be easier to move his body in front of hers if he had to.

Kelly watched him carefully. He was aware that she'd kept her eyes on him every minute, just in case he wanted to send her a signal. In case he had a plan. She was an amazingly courageous woman and he wished to hell he *did* have a plan.

"Mrs. Mellon, I want you to listen to me carefully. If you really care about Samantha, you'll put that gun down. If Kelly dies at your hands, I will never feel anything but hatred for the entire Mellon family."

She looked confused. "You won't hate Samantha. She is good, Tom. Samantha is innocent."

"I will," he said implacably. "I will hate her. I could never have been her lover, but I might have been her friend. If you do this, I will forever be her enemy."

For the first time, he saw the gun waver. Taking advantage of the unguarded nanosecond, he positioned himself directly in front of Kelly.

He put his hand out behind him and Kelly clutched it with cold but determined fingers. He squeezed hard and he tried to let his touch communicate everything he felt.

"You don't want to hurt her, Mrs. Mellon. You killed once, but then you killed a murderer. You killed only to protect innocent people. If you kill Kelly, you will have done an unforgivable thing. An evil thing. That wasn't what you wanted, when you decided to set things right."

Her body seemed to grow smaller. She sank slightly and was clearly leaning hard on the ornately carved banister just to stay erect.

"You know you don't want to do it, Mrs. Mellon," he said again, his voice gentle now. Soothing. "If you had really wanted to kill anyone, you would have used that gun long ago."

For a long minute, the only sounds in the hall were Imogene's labored breathing and the incessant ticking of the grandfather clock below them.

Finally, ignoring Tom completely, Imogene raised her eyes to St. George.

"You were right," she said, as if she were talking to someone she knew quite intimately. "I don't have your strength. The sword is too heavy for me."

And then she moved the gun. She pointed it at her own heart.

"Oh, my God," Kelly breathed.

Tom's muscles tightened. He willed the woman not to do it, but he knew he could never reach her in time.

"Mother, no!"

The voice from above exploded into the silence. They all looked up. Tom knew that the same cold shock coursed through all their veins.

It was Samantha. She looked groggy and tearful, and very frightened.

"Mom?" She leaned over the banister, her long blond hair catching the red light streaming in through the dragon's stolen heart.

"Mom, don't. Please. I know you're tired. I know you're afraid. But we can get through this together."

Imogene's lifted face was lined with agony.

"I killed your brother," she said.

"I know," Samantha said. She began to walk down the staircase slowly, her white nightgown floating in the red light.

"But you can't leave me now, Mom. I need you. We need each other. You are the only one who can tell me about my real father."

Imogene cocked the hammer. The gun was ready to fire. Kelly made a low sound, and her body sagged against Tom's. He turned sideways, just enough to pull her into the safe circle of his arms.

But they were all watching Imogene.

Samantha's voice was gentle, strangely hypnotic. "Tell me, Mom. What was he like?"

The gray-faced, weeping woman began to smile. She looked up at her daughter, the lovely woman who descended the stairs so gracefully, moving through the kaleidoscope of colors. An angel of forgiveness, drifting down to earth, her hands outstretched with love.

"Your father—" Imogene's voice was choked with the tears that were flooding her face. She thumbed the hammer back into place and slowly lowered the gun.

It fell to the stair.

"Your father was a wonderful man."

CHAPTER TWENTY-FOUR

IMOGENE DIED TWO MONTHS LATER, with both her daughters at her side. Any thought of putting her on trial for Sebastian's murder, which had been debated by one lawyer, one court, one psychiatrist after another, died with her.

Sophie continued to improve, although her doctors said she probably would never live full-time outside the clinic.

On the day Imogene was admitted to the hospital, Samantha had put Coeur Volé on the market. She sold it the day after her mother's death, for about half its value—there really wasn't any other way to quickly unload a house with such a gruesome history. She bought a small condo in Raleigh, so that she could be near Sophie's new clinic. And near Sebastian's children.

A family with eight kids moved in to Coeur Volé, unable to believe their luck. A bedroom for everyone! They tossed out all the statues and planted a vegetable garden. They poured concrete into the tunnel so that the teenagers couldn't slip out to meet boyfriends, and donated the St. George window to the local Episcopal church so that the toddlers wouldn't fall against it and get cut. They pulled out the black roses and silver-green grasses and put in a sandbox for the baby.

The entire city of Cathedral Cove seemed to breathe easier.

It was truly over.

A month after Imogene's death, Tom proposed to Kelly, and she accepted. But she insisted on waiting until spring to be married. At least another three months. They wouldn't be ready to put the tragedies behind them, completely behind them, any faster than that. And she wanted their new lives to start off in sunshine.

"Aren't you afraid," Mary Jo had said to Kelly over lunch the next day, "that, if you give him so much time all alone in Atlanta, time to sweat the loss of his freedom, he'll tuck tail and run?"

"Of course not," Kelly had answered firmly.

But it wasn't true, of course. She would always carry the image of Sophie in her heart. Sophie standing in the little room in the north transept of the Congregational Church, standing tall and straight and beautiful, right up until the moment when she'd crumpled into a heap of white lace. Right up until the moment when she'd begun to cry, because she knew her only escape route had just slammed shut.

So how could Kelly not wonder, now and then, if Tom would do the same to her?

Every day, when she talked to him long distance, when he told her how many clients he'd taken in his struggling new private practice, and she told him how the winery tunnel was coming along, then she was sure of him.

But at night, when she was alone in her cottage, which was already sold and technically the property of someone else, then the fears knocked at the door of her heart, and she had to force them away.

Finally spring came, and the day they had chosen arrived.

The idea of a church wedding, with all the trappings, was impossible, of course. Jacob had offered his lovely backyard garden and Kelly had gratefully accepted. Just a justice of the peace to make it legal, Mary Jo and Brian to witness, and a simple gold band to circle her finger.

And Tom by her side.

That was all the "wedding" she wanted.

"Hi, there," Jacob said, poking his head into the guest room, which he'd offered her as a dressing room. He grinned. "You look dynamite."

She smiled back at him. "You, too," she said. It was true. He almost looked like himself again. Now that the truth about Lily's death had come out, he seemed to have found a little peace. He still grieved, of course, but it no longer seemed to be killing him.

He nodded self-consciously and tugged at his tie. "Thanks," he said. "Well. I know you're busy. I guess I'd better get back downstairs and play host."

He blew her a kiss, and then he was gone. Kelly looked at herself in the mirror, a mirror she and Lillith had bought together at a rumble sale in Digger Beach. Her knee-length yellow skirt and white gypsy blouse looked like something she'd wear to an Easter party. She would carry no bouquet, but she had peeked downstairs a few minutes ago and she saw that Jacob had bought daffodils for the table.

The sight of them had brought tears to her eyes. Lillith had loved daffodils.

"I wish you could be here, Lily," she said softly.

Mary Jo, who had been in the guest bath, gathering up Kelly's things and putting them in her suitcase, came up behind her and smiled.

"I think she is," she said.

The sting in Kelly's eyes came back, full force. Mary

Jo, whose own eyes were red, sniffed and cleared her throat. "And if that's true, you'd better watch out. You know how Lily loves a good laugh. She'll probably snap your bra strap while you're trying to say your vows."

Kelly smiled. "I'm going to miss you," she said. "Will you come see me in Atlanta?"

"Hell, yes. If you think I'm going to lose the only baby-sitter who could ever handle my twins, you're sadly mistaken."

Mary Jo glanced out the window for the tenth time in the past ten minutes. Kelly knew what she was thinking. Only five minutes till the wedding. The justice of the peace was there. Brian was there.

But Tom still hadn't arrived.

"Mary Jo, if you don't stop it, I'll strangle you. I'm nervous enough without you pacing around like that."

"Sorry." Mary Jo smiled sheepishly. "I'll just feel better when I…you know…see him."

They fiddled with Kelly's hair a few more minutes, though they hadn't done anything elaborate, just loose curls and a small headband trimmed in baby's breath.

Suddenly, Kelly's cell phone rang. She stared at it. Then she stared at Mary Jo.

Then it stopped ringing. It hadn't been a call. It had been a text message.

Mary Jo swallowed hard. "You'll have to look," she said. "Go ahead. It'll be okay. I'm sure it will. Probably running late. You know the traffic in Atlanta."

Kelly walked over to the bed, where she'd tossed her phone earlier. Whatever happened, she told herself, even if this was from Tom, telling her he'd changed his mind, she would not collapse. That was the difference between her and Sophie. Kelly would not fall apart.

She would survive, no matter what.

Holding her breath, she picked up the phone. She flipped open the face and saw the message written inside.

I'm here, it said, and somehow even the plain black letters held the echo of his teasing smile. *So stop worrying, get your sexy ass down those stairs, and marry me.*

Everything you love about romance...
and more!

Please turn the page for Signature Select™
Bonus Features.

Bonus Features:

BONUS FEATURES

HAPPILY NEVER AFTER

A conversation with
Kathleen O'Brien

What makes for a happily-ever-after?
I actually should be an expert on this one, as I've
found a happily-ever-after myself! I've been married
a long time to a man so wonderful I smile just
thinking about him. But I was young when I married
him, and I have to admit I wasn't thinking all that
clearly. He'd swept me off my feet—that was all I
really knew. Imagine my surprise—and delight—
when I discovered he also had a sense of humor,
brains, loyalty, a strong work ethic, tenderness,
generosity and was fun! In the end, I guess the most
important element of a happily-ever-after is this: you
both have to believe that Forever is the ultimate
romantic fantasy!

**What's the one thing you don't have enough of that
you wish you did have more of?**
Time with my children! I adored motherhood (well,
except for when they had chicken pox, and when
they learned to drive), and they grew up so darn

fast. They're fascinating young adults, and they haven't wandered too far from home, but still I miss those unscheduled, lazy-day chats about nothing and everything. I especially miss their constant music. I can turn on the CD player, but it's not the same as hearing my daughter singing her favorite new Broadway musical or my son working out a new song on his guitar.

Tell us a bit about how you began your writing career.

I came from a family of writers, and I'm simply horrible at math and science...and everything else. So I never really had any other options! When I was a teenager, my mother helped me get a job at the local newspaper, and I loved it so much I thought I'd be there forever. But then an even stronger love entered my life—my husband—and I gave journalism up to follow him to his big new job at a newspaper in another city. It was very difficult at first. He went to the newsroom every day, and I...I was so jealous I nearly went crazy. Then I decided to try writing romances, and I fell in love all over again. It's the perfect job for me!

Do you have a writing routine?

Oh, if only I did! I plan and plot and prepare for ages on each book. And then I have to absolutely force myself to get started. I never feel ready. In fact, facing a blank computer screen is the most terrifying thing I know. Every morning I find myself thinking, "Gosh, I really should polish the silver...or weed the azaleas...or brush the puppy." Anything to avoid writing that first word. When I finally get going, though, I can write for about four hours before my psyche runs dry. Then I can answer reader mail, update my Web site, do research and edit, until it's time for my husband to come home. I try never to write at night unless I'm facing a very tight deadline. It's too much fun to hear what happened for him at the newspaper that day!

When you're not writing, what do you love to do?
I have always been a reader, and I steal time for that whenever I can. I also love movies, puttering around in the yard, going to the beach (Indian Rocks Beach on the Gulf Coast of Florida is my absolute favorite place on earth), walking while I listen to homemade mini-discs of my favorite corny music and swimming.

Do you believe in inspiration or plain old hard work?
Of course I believe in inspiration! I believe, I believe! Clap your hands if you believe! (That was just in case the muse was listening!) Seriously, some of the best lines I've ever written, the best characters I've ever created, seemed to come out of the blue, like magic. But inspiration is not quite reliable enough to count on. I can bubble with great ideas one day and find the well dry as dust the next. On those dusty days, it's good to know how to roll up your sleeves and get serious.

Is there one book that you've read that changed your life somehow?

Rebecca, by Daphne du Maurier. Though I didn't know it at the time, this book made me both a romantic and a writer. It taught me the redemptive power of love, and the transporting power of words. I reread it every few years, and it's magic every time.

What are your top five favorite books?

Rebecca, by Daphne du Maurier

Checkmate, the last in the Lymond Chronicles by Dorothy Dunnett (though of course you must read the first five books in the series first!)

Nine Coaches Waiting, by Mary Stewart

These Old Shades, by Georgette Heyer

The Wishing Star, by Norma Johnston

What matters most in life?

Passion, of course! My parents taught me that the person who loves the most things wins. Never pass up a chance to get a kick out of even the littlest thing. I'm passionate about my husband, my children, my family and my friends, of course. But I'm also passionate about writing, waterfalls, good books, pizza, corny music, Popsicles, rain, color, snowmen, poetry, glass paperweights, robins, puppies, fountains, avocados and naps. All the people in my family laugh at me because they say that every song I hear on the radio is my favorite song in the world. It's true, and I wouldn't have it any other way.

If you weren't a writer what would you be doing?
Probably living in a box under the bridge. As I said earlier, I have no other skills! Or perhaps some bookstore somewhere would hire me, if I promised not to spend *too* much of my time reading the merchandise!

Marsha Zinberg, Executive Editor Signature, spoke with Kathleen O'Brien in the winter of 2005. ✎

TOP TEN
Fictional Weddings
by Kathleen O'Brien

**Top Five Fictional Weddings that
Were Called Off**

1 Elaine Robinson and Carl Smith in *The Graduate*. In this classic coming-of-age film, Dustin Hoffman's Benjamin Braddock symbolizes the struggles we all face trying to grow up. So when Elaine's mother tells her, "It's too late," and she replies, "Not for me," we stand up in our living rooms and cheer. Being young means that there's still time, thank heaven, to marry the cute, confused guy with the good heart.

2 Jane Eyre and Mr. Rochester in *Jane Eyre*. Poor Jane. It wasn't enough that her husband-to-be had a bad temper and a suspicious French "ward." Turns out he also had a crazy wife in the attic. But when the truth pops out, we can't help admiring Jane's courage—or enjoying Mr. Rochester's disappointment—as she declines to stick around and be his mistress. This is one Victorian heroine who refuses to play the victim.

3 Tracy Samantha Lord and George Kittredge in *High Society*. Is there a more delightful movie moment anywhere than the scene in which adorable Bing Crosby coaches the embarrassed Grace Kelly through her apology to the wedding guests? Anyone who chooses that milquetoast George Kittredge over a jazzy crooner with heartbreak eyes would be a fool. And, while Sam Lord may be a little full of herself, she's no dummy.

4 Arthur Bach and Susan Johnson in *Arthur*. Let's be honest—if we'd been in Arthur's shoes, we might not have been able to kiss the 200 million dollars goodbye. But what an inspiring moment to watch the woebegone man-child face down all the manipulative millionaires and claim his real inheritance: love.

5 Miss Havisham and Compeyson from *Great Expectations*. An unforgettable image, the old lady in her tattered wedding dress, holding court amid the ruins of the wedding feast! When Compeyson callously jilted the beautiful Miss Havisham, he clearly didn't realize that he'd end up an obscure footnote in fiction, while the abandoned bride would become a classic character, beloved enough to reappear in novels even today.

Top Five Fictional Weddings that Should Have Been Called Off

1 Maxim de Winter and Rebecca from *Rebecca*. A woman dramatic and sensual enough to dominate a mansion in Cornwall, and one of the greatest romantic novels of all time, even after she's fish-food...well, that's a heck of a woman. You can see why Max married her, but what a disaster!

2 Ilsa and Victor Lazslo from *Casablanca*. The fate of the free world ultimately rested on this marriage, so it seems selfish to wish it hadn't happened. But Rick's heart was broken when Ilsa missed her train, and a hero with this much charisma, intelligence and nobility should end up with his true love, darn it. Couldn't some other nice girl have helped Victor vanquish the Nazis?

3 Daisy and Tom Buchanan from *The Great Gatsby*. Frankly, I don't think Daisy should have been allowed to wed anyone. That's how shallow and dangerous this woman is. But *two* such people in a marriage are a recipe for total disaster. Besides, if she'd married Jay Gatsby instead, he would quickly have seen what a crashing bore she was and ditched her. Come on, Jay. The world's full of beautiful women, and you're *very* rich.

4 Catherine Earnshaw and Edgar Linton from *Wuthering Heights*. Marrying for money is always a bad idea, especially when the stable boy needs only a quick bath and a few good poker hands to become one of the sexiest, richest men on the moors. Cathy should have taken a few lessons in patience from that spunkier Brontë heroine, Jane Eyre.

5 Romeo Montague and Juliet Capulet from *Romeo and Juliet*. Only a couple of highly hormonal teenagers would have been naive enough not to realize their secret marriage might be problematic. With their families warring, and her dad already handpicking another groom, the odds were definitely against them. But selfishly, how can we wish a single word of this classic tragedy to be changed? This is the love story that defines all love stories.

Deleted Scene
Snapshot: The Church After the Jilting
by Kathleen O'Brien

Rich people were crazy.

If Marie Dionne used to have any doubts about that, her temporary, part-time job helping the Mellon wedding planner had removed every last one. She figured the problem basically was that rich people were so used to having everything go their way. When they hit a hitch, they totally lost their cool, squawking and fluttering all over the place.

Look at this chapel, for instance. Because Marie was just temp help, she'd drawn the short straw and the chore of cleaning up the mess everyone had left behind.

Marie had been standing in the back of the chapel—had been standing there for a full hour, in fact, with her feet absolutely killing her—when Mr. Mellon finally came out and apologized to the guests. There had been a change of plans. There would be no wedding today.

It was about time he made the announcement, she'd thought. The guests already knew something was wrong, and they wanted details. They were getting restless, like predators held back too long from feasting on their kill.

They'd already guessed what had happened, of course. Marie had heard the nasty whispers running up and down the pews, well-groomed heads and flowery hats tilting together in the wide swaths of sunshine from the big glass windows.

"The groom's a no-show," they said.

"Guess he sobered up just in time," they laughed.

"Not enough money in the world," they said.

Once or twice, the voices had been kind. "Oh, poor girl," someone moaned softly. "This'll break her, wait and see."

But not often.

Marie knew that, for 200 rich people to sit around elbow to elbow, squeezed into this small, chichi chapel in their too-tight, show-offy clothes and their ridiculous hats, they had to be expecting something exciting to happen.

And finally it did. A high, shrill cry had trembled out of the little room just off the transept. Nothing blood-curdling, nothing very melodramatic, but enough to send a frisson of excitement through the chapel.

The cry was cut off. And then Mr. Mellon, so authoritative in his tuxedo, his handsome face flushed dark, his prominent jaw as hard as the marble of the altar, had stepped out in front of them.

Now, an hour after that, Marie moved through the pews, picking up debris. She carried two bags, one for the pure junk and the other for items to be sent to the lost and found.

The trash bag held about two dozen dirty tissues already, six half-used rolls of breath mints and a cheap ballpoint pen. Apparently rich people couldn't be bothered to locate the rubbish bin on the way out.

Marie knew she sounded bitter, but honestly, she was up to her ears in student loans, and even a tenth of the money that had been wasted on this ridiculous high-society carnival would have paid her tuition for the next two years. Not to mention supplied Ramen noodles and scrambled eggs, the staple of her penny-pinching diet, for the rest of her natural life.

Funny. Just yesterday, while she wrote out the rent check for her crummy efficiency apartment, she'd been thinking maybe she needed to get married. Find somebody to split the bills with.

She picked up the third forgotten umbrella and shoved it into the lost and found bag. Married? For money? Ha! Today had definitely cured her of that idea.

DELETED SCENE BONUS FEATURE

God, did these people have so many things that they didn't have to keep track of any of it? The lost-and-found bag was almost overflowing, and she'd done only about two-thirds of the pews.

She had a compact that looked like real gold, three lipsticks, two pairs of reading glasses, two sunglasses, an asthma inhaler, three loose earrings, unmatched, a guitar pick—she stared at that one a minute, wondering if someone had actually entered this chapel with a guitar hidden under his raincoat.

Then there was the tiny radio with an inconspicuous earbud, hidden inside a season schedule for the Atlanta Falcons. She put the bud up to her own ear, just out of curiosity, and heard a tiny voice telling her the score at halftime. She smiled and stuffed the radio into the lost-and-found bag. Whoever that was, he was her kind of guy. She'd had four brothers, and she'd rather watch a football game than a wedding any day.

Toward the front, she came across one of the wedding invitations, which had been folded into the shape of a paper airplane with *crash* written on one wing and *burn* written on the other. She chuckled, but the sound of her laughter echoing through the empty chapel sounded both heartless and a little eerie. She stopped herself and moved on.

The front pew was empty. The groom had no family, and the bride's mother, the only family member not appearing in the wedding, hadn't ever been brought to her seat. She'd still been waiting in the wings with her daughter.

Marie had a momentary spasm of sympathy. What a terrible hour that must have been. When, she wondered, did Sophie's last hope die? When had it been replaced by...

By what? Marie didn't know the Mellon family. People like her never knew people like them. She had no idea whether the amazingly beautiful Sophie Mellon had really loved the man she intended to marry. Had the hope been replaced by humiliation? By fury?

Or had there been true grief?

Marie thought back to the thin cry they'd all heard from the wings. It had sounded so helpless, almost like the cry of a newborn. And she thought of how Sophie had looked when, just fifteen minutes ago, she'd been led out, still weeping, held up by her tall, handsome brother on one side, and her tall, imposing father on the other. She had looked like a broken puppet, all her limbs limp, as if she couldn't move them on her own.

Grief, Marie decided. Sophie Mellon's heart had definitely been broken.

Marie looked around the church, which was dimmer now, as the sun began to descend the western side of the sky. She'd finished the pews, and the only area left to straighten up was the room where the bridal party had waited.

She made her way there slowly. She wasn't ordinarily the superstitious type, and she didn't believe in all that leftover negative energy garbage. But still...it seemed a little soon to enter that room.

She stood at the doorway, shocked at the mess she saw there. It was even worse than the nave. But of course that was natural, she reminded herself. This was the epicenter of the earthquake. Out there, the people in the pews had felt only slight ripples. In here, lives had tumbled and broken into pieces.

The room smelled sickeningly sweet, and Marie saw that the bouquet, a huge, three-foot spill of gardenias mixed with forget-me-nots, had been left on the sofa, in a hot, bright beam of sunlight that seemed to be squeezing the perfume out of the flowers.

A dozen crystal flutes, half-full still of champagne, stood on every surface, catching the golden light, too, and giving the room a slightly underwater look.

Odd clothes, a tuxedo tie, a garter, a pearl choker, a pair of white gloves, were strewn everywhere.

And, amazingly, three purses had been left behind.

Driven by a morbid but irresistible curiosity, Marie opened the purses. One of them had a speeding ticket, six sticks of Zinger! gum, a bright red lipstick and a picture of a grinning, handsome man Marie had never seen before.

One had a disposable camera with only two frames left unused, a sketch of geometric shapes forming a complicated triple arch, labeled with color names, and, inexplicably, a man's wilting boutonniere.

The third had a bottle of Xanax, a bottle of acne cover-up, a pale pink lipstick, a handkerchief with the initials SM, and a picture of the groom, who clearly didn't know he was being photographed. He was looking away, and the photographer had caught only his profile. It must have been taken in the past few days, but already it had been handled so much the edges were worn and curling.

Shuddering slightly, Marie put them all in the lost-and-found bag and kept going.

Over by the window she found a man's wallet with....Marie counted...more than a thousand dollars in cash. The man's wallet had no ID, but it did have a note that said "Midnight it is, my mystery man. Don't be late or I'll die. Dolly."

Marie slipped that, too, into the bag. She was beginning to wish she hadn't taken this job. The things you found out about people when you got at look at their private things...

As she scanned the floor for additional debris, she saw something sparkling in the nook created by the open door. She squinted, but the light changed, and the sparkle disappeared.

Still...it might be something.

She walked to the corner, and, setting down her two overburdened bags, bent down and picked up the discarded item.

It was a diamond ring. The most beautiful diamond ring Marie had ever seen. The band was platinum, and covered all the way around with fifteen or so small channel-set diamonds. She held it up to the light, and rainbows appeared like magic, filling the room with darting, shimmering flashes of color.

The solitaire in the center was large, oval, and again surrounded with its own border of tiny sparkling diamonds.

Damn. The thing must have cost a small fortune. Marie couldn't help it. She had to know what it felt like to wear a ring like this. She slid it over the third finger of her left hand, and though it caught a little on her knuckle, it fit. She held her breath. Many women would sell their lives, their freedom, their very souls, for a ring like this.

And yet Sophie Mellon had yanked it off and flung it into the corner. Marie closed her eyes, imagining that moment. Had the ring begun to burn, the tiny fires of all these chips of ice turning to agony and pain? Had the intensity threatened to consume her entirely?

"What the hell are you doing with that ring?"

Marie's eyes flew open. The man standing in the doorway was large and, seen like this in the gold sunlight, so gorgeous it made her knees turn to a hot liquid that almost couldn't hold her up.

It was Sebastian, the bride's brother. The best man.

"I just found it," she said as calmly as she could. She removed the ring, though her fingers were shaking so hard she scraped her skin dragging it over her knuckle. Blood rose from the torn spot. She looked at the ring to be sure she hadn't gotten any on it, but Sebastian grabbed it from her.

"That belongs to my sister," he said. He wrapped his large palm around it, and the diamonds disappeared. He closed his eyes briefly. "God knows she paid enough for it."

"I'm sorry," she said, though she knew it was ridiculous. He didn't want her sympathy. He probably didn't even think working girls were actual human beings with feelings anyhow. "It's a beautiful ring. It must have been very—difficult for your sister today."

He opened his amazing blue eyes and looked at her. "What exactly were you doing with it?"

"I—I had just found it. I was cleaning up."

"You were wearing it," he said. He moved closer. He was very large, and he knew how to use that bulk to intimidate. It began to piss Marie off. She didn't like bullies, and her dad and four brothers had taught her enough self-defense moves to make sure she didn't have to put up with any.

"I was looking at it," she said calmly. "It's beautiful. I was just admiring it."

Damned if the son of a bitch didn't put his big, cold paw under her chin. "So you're just a little Cinderella, huh, wishing you could go to the ball? A very pretty Cinderella, too...but not, I'm afraid, a very smart one. Did you really think you could steal it? Did you think we wouldn't find out it had been here? Did you think we wouldn't ask her what she did with it?"

Marie raised her chin. Gorgeous or not, this jerk was way out of line, and if he didn't back off her she was going to shove her knee into his crotch so hard it would come out his nose. That's what her dad had taught her. *Don't kid around about it,* he'd said. *If you have to, make it count.*

"Mr. Mellon," she said coldly, feeling his fingers move as her jaw worked to speak. "I think you're deluding yourself." She decided to use his own snooty syntax. "Do you think for one minute that I would want anything connected to your family or this wedding? Do you think there's anyone in Cathedral Cove who would? Do you think we don't know your whole scary, inbred family is cursed?"

He backed away, clearly shocked.

Good. If no one had ever told him to go to hell before, it was way overdue.

And then she picked up her bags of trash and, pushing past him, left the sickly sweet, godforsaken room.

Yep, she thought. Rich people were just plain crazy.

Behind the Scenes
The House that Most Influenced Me
by Kathleen O'Brien

I used to blame my fascination with houses and their gardens on Manderley, Green Gables, Misselthwaite Manor, Wuthering Heights and all the other marvelous fictional dwellings I'd met in novels through the years.

They played their part, of course. But, though I wasn't aware of it, the obsession actually began much earlier.

It began with the house I grew up in.

The house was not magnificent, although it was built on a magnificent street, a wide, curving boulevard that fronted the bay. The house was clean, white, two stories, built in the Charleston style, perpendicular to the street. Our parents designed it, via an architect who understood that, when they returned from Charleston after World War II, they wanted to bring some of the romance of that city with them.

The house next door was much more impressive, a dark, complicated gray-shingle structure with a labyrinth of gables and porches. It belonged to my father's twin brother, his wife and their children, most of whom were boys who hated me, and who didn't much care that the feeling was heartily reciprocated.

We might have envied them, but we didn't. To my sister and me, our unpretentious white house was magic. It stood for who we were. In many ways it taught us who to be.

Our house was filled with sunlight and air, blending indoors and out, because, we understood, both are vital to happiness. In the living room, ceiling-to-floor windows let the bay breezes in through fluttering Irish lace curtains. The long dining room had two full walls of windows, a panoramic view of the water on one side and an uninterrupted view of the back garden, "the rain forest" my father called it, on the other. A second-story porch ran the length of the house, and a creaking swing invited us to sit there every evening and watch the water shift from blue to topaz to peach in the fading light.

The house taught us that books deserve Respect and Space. Without doubt, the heart of the house was the library. Guarded by French doors whose knobs were gold lion heads, this room felt as sacred as a church. Three walls were covered with built-in bookcases, filled with thousands of books. A small window seat between bookcases looked out over the rain forest, reminding us that books also deserve Time.

In this room, my parents read aloud to us, one chapter a night, from novels like *The Red Pony* and *Treasure Island*. Sometimes I'd climb on furniture to read the titles on the uppermost shelves, the ones that were just for grownups. Wisteria Cottage...my mother said no, it would frighten me. *I Hate Thursdays*...I could imagine what that was. Our housekeeper was off on Thursdays, and my mother, who hated to cook, was always in a temper by the time I got home from school.

Upstairs, each bedroom had its own bookcase, too. Through the years mine held the Bobbsey Twins, *The Sailor Dog*, Nancy Drew, *The Secret Garden*, *A Little Princess*, *I Can Fly*, *The Wishing Star*, *The Velvet Room*. My own magic, at my own fingertips.

26

But the stories didn't exist only on paper. The house taught us how to make up our own. In my parents' bedroom, the fireplace was surrounded by forty-four tiles, each of which was different. One had the alphabet on it. One had a boy driving a pig down a cobbled lane with a stick. Another showed an old-fashioned couple in fancy dress. My sister and I made up stories about those tiles, inventing new rules every day, rules we followed so strictly you'd have thought the punishment was death. Some days you had to use every tile, connecting them however you could to create a tale that made sense. Sometimes you picked your favorite, and told what came after the moment captured there. In the television room, the wallpaper was printed with flowers. My first short story came from those flowers, each of which was given a name and a personality and an adventure. I inherited a four-poster canopy bed from my grandfather, and our stories about the evil lurking under it became so real that my father had to saw off the legs to lower the mattress and allow me to sleep.

In fact, we were so accustomed to making up stories about the house that, years later, I was shocked to learn that the legend of the burglar who turned the handle of our back door, then stopped and decided to rob a neighbor's house instead, was true. I had thought my father made it up.

The lessons learned from our house didn't stop with the bricks and boards. A long front lawn swept down from the house toward the boulevard. By the street, a glossy black wrought-iron fence rose from a low white wall, and behind it day lilies of purest yellow tossed in the wind. Yellow, black, white. Crisp, controlled, clean. Restraint created beauty—that was the lesson of the lilies.

But that wasn't all. On long afternoons, my mother decided what should bloom next in the wide, curving swath of flower bed close to the house. One summer she chose snapdragons. Almost as big as a child, the dozens of stalks bloomed in pink, yellow, white and lavender. My mother showed me how to pinch the blossom so that the flowery dragon mouth would "talk." I heard many secrets from the snapdragons that summer. And from that band of exuberant color I learned the thrill of profusion and surfeit.

Like gods, we divvied up the trees, because we believed their personalities matched our own. The jacaranda, with its spreading canopy of perfumed lavender flowers, belonged to my mother. The magnolia belonged to my softly Southern sister. The pecan trees, the strong, hard-working trees that provided sustenance, were of course my father's. The little purple orchid tree was mine.

When I was sixteen, we had to leave our house. I was young and callous, I'm afraid, and didn't cry. I hadn't learned yet that some losses can't be recouped. It wasn't until ten years later, when I read a poem my mother wrote about the agony of leaving behind the house built from her dreams, that I understood. The magic hadn't really been in the gold lions, the bookcases, the white curtains or the rainbow swath of snapdragons. The magic had been in her, and in my father, and in the pieces of themselves they'd hammered into the house, day after day, year after year.

A hurricane finally destroyed the jacaranda tree. But when my mother died, with the new owner's permission we buried her ashes where once the lavender flowers would have fallen.

I've kept her poem near me ever since, and its lessons have influenced every book I've written. I finally realized that du Maurier, Montgomery, Burnett and Brontë had simply been repeating a truth my heart already knew. A house *is* the family inside it. Our house taught us to become writers, to cherish daily restraint and occasional excess, to give space and time to books, and to talk to the flowers. But it could teach us only because my parents had taught the house.

Whether your lessons are good or bad, the house learns.

And the house remembers.

COLLECTION

From three favorite
Silhouette Books authors...

CorNeReD

Three mystery-filled romantic stories!

Linda Turner

Ingrid Weaver

Julie Miller

Murder, mystery and mayhem are common ground
for three female sleuths in this short-story collection
that will keep you guessing!

On sale September 2005

Where love comes alive™

Bonus Features:

**Author Interviews,
Author's Journal
Sneak Peek**

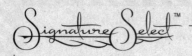

COMING NEXT MONTH

Signature Select Collection
LOVE SO TENDER by Stephanie Bond, Jo Leigh and Joanne Rock
Why settle for Prince Charming when you can have The King?
It's now or never—Gracie Sergeant, Alyssa Reynolds and Ellie
Evans can't help falling in love...Vegas style! Three romantic
novellas that could only happen in Vegas.

Signature Select Saga
SEARCHING FOR CATE by Marie Ferrarella
A widower for three years, Dr. Christian Graywolf's life is his
work. But when he meets FBI special agent Kate Kowalski—a
woman searching for her birth mother—the attraction is
intense, immediate and the truth is something neither Christian
nor Cate expects. That all his life Christian has been searching
for Cate.

Signature Select Miniseries
LAWLESS LOVERS by Dixie Browning
Two complete novels from THE LAWLESS HEIRS SAGA.
Daniel Lyon Lawless and Harrison Lawless are two successful,
sexy and very sought-after bachelors. But their worlds are about
to be rocked by the love of two headstrong, beautiful women!

Signature Select Spotlight
HAPPILY NEVER AFTER by Kathleen O'Brien
Ten years after the society wedding that wasn't, members of
the wedding party are starting to die. At the scene of every
"accident," a piece of a wedding dress is found. It's not long
before Kelly Ralston realizes that she's the sole remaining
bridesmaid left...and the next target!

Signature Showcase
FANTASY by Lori Foster
Brandi Sommers doesn't know quite what to do about her
sister's outrageous birthday gift of a dream vacation to a
lover's retreat—with sexy security consultant Sebastian Sinclair
included as the lover! But she soon discovers that she can do
whatever she wants....